D1323685

GIBRALTAR SUN

(A NOVEL)

BY

MICHAEL MCCOLLUM

5-4-2007

SCI FI - ARIZONA
A Virtual Science Fiction Bookstore and Writer's
Workshop on the INTERNET
www.scifi-az.com

ISBN 1-932657-55-X
314 pages

Michael McCollum
Proprietor
Sci Fi - Arizona
1931 East Libra Drive
Suite 101
Tempe, AZ 85283
mccollum@scifi-az.com

The Rock of Gibraltar

Table of Contents

PROLOGUE

In a fit of exasperation, Germany's Iron Chancellor, Prince Otto von Bismarck, once remarked, "There is a Providence that protects idiots, drunkards, children and the United States of America."

Bismarck's comment has a special relevance for our current situation. For, if not an act of providence, how else to explain that we learned of the Broa before they discovered us? And, having become aware of their existence, what were we to do with that knowledge?

How should we secure our future against a species that enslaves every star system of which they become aware? Do we abandon our own colonies among the stars, retreat back to Earth, and pray the galactic overlords overlook us for a few more generations? Or do we take a more activist approach and risk immediate annihilation?

This conundrum became known as The Great Debate. And if the answer seems obvious in retrospect, consider that it was far from clear at the time. Those who faced the choice lacked our advantage of hindsight. Indeed, the fact that we even had a choice was something of a miracle.

Had a Broan craft stumbled across one of our interstellar colonies, the first we would have known of it was when their war fleet appeared in our skies and demanded our surrender.

Human nature being what it is, our species would never have submitted meekly. Our first impulse, and last, would have been to resist. In so doing, we would now be extinct. The Broa would have turned the Earth into a burned-out, radioactive cinder; and those of us who so loudly hail our recent victories would now be mere dust, blowing on a hot, dry wind.

Therefore, fellow revelers, when you celebrate tonight, consider for a moment what might have been —"

From a Victory Speech by the
Right Honorable Samantha Ries-Morgan
To the World Parliament
12 October 2356

PART ONE:

HOMECOMING

Chapter One

The morning sun was one-third up the vault of the sky as the silver bullet car came into sight of Lake Constance. Racing through a Swiss countryside dotted with picturesque villages scattered among green vineyards, the needle-nosed car jumped from one elevated electromagnetic accelerator ring to another, defying gravity with each effortless leap. At 500 kilometers per hour, the car left a condensation trail in its wake as its passage roiled the humid summer air.

Inside the car, Mark Rykand and Lisabeth Arden cuddled together on one wide seat and watched the world slip by beyond their window. After more than three years in space, the greens, browns, and blues of Earth held a fascination that neither of them could readily have explained.

"Look, Mark, it's the lake!" Lisa said at the first sight of the blue expanse on which could be seen a cluster of white sails. Lisa was a petite blonde with eyes of green and a nose that turned up at the end. Her mouth was a bit too wide for her face, with a tendency to dimple when she smiled. The permanent tan had faded after three years of living in vacuum, bringing forth the naturally fair complexion common to women of the British Isles.

"Won't be long now," he replied as he reached up to caress her cheek. Mark was of average height with a shock of sandy hair and blue eyes, and a smile that turned up more on one side than the other. His muscular physique had atrophied a bit aboard ship, despite his thrice weekly visits to the cramped gym in the engineering spaces. Even so, his torso remained comfortably taut, with no sign of the paunch he worked so hard to keep off.

On the opposite side of the lake, the glass-and-steel pyramid of Stellar Survey Headquarters was briefly visible before the line of pylons topped by accelerator rings dipped behind a low hill. The sight reminded him of the last time he had taken this particular journey.

It was not a pleasant memory.

#

For Mark, the adventure/ordeal had begun four years earlier when he returned home late one night from a party to find an emergency message flashing on his apartment phone. Mark punched for playback and found himself looking into the eyes of a stranger.

The man identified himself as the duty officer at Stellar Survey Headquarters in Germany, and asked that his call be returned as soon as possible. A call from the Stellar Survey could only mean one thing — something had happened to Jani!

Mark had last seen his sister at White Sands Spaceport three months previous when he had seen her off on her latest mission for the Stellar Survey. Jani had joked and laughed the whole time they waited for her shuttle to board. His last sight of her had come as she waved goodbye from the passenger bridge, her wild copper mane blowing in the wind.

It took two tries to punch in the number listed, his hands were shaking so. It took only seconds for his suspicions to be confirmed. "I am sorry, Mr. Rykand," the duty officer intoned. "Your sister was killed in an accident three weeks ago while on a mission in the New Eden System."

Grief washed over Mark like a sea of heavy mud. That grief had turned to suspicion when the officer proved unable to provide details of Jani's death. After a sleepless night, he booked a suborbital flight to Zurich, and from there, rode this very bullet car toward Meersburg and the headquarters of the Stellar Survey.

#

"What's the matter, my love?" Lisa asked, noticing his sudden silence as she snuggled closer. The sweet smell of her blonde hair and the familiar warm softness of her body snapped Mark back to the present.

"I was just remembering the last time I was on this line."

"Oh, sorry," she replied, reaching out to squeeze his hand. After lovemaking, they often spoke in whispered intimacies in their darkened cabin, communicating as couples have done since time immemorial. They sometimes spoke of the tragedy that had brought Mark into her life.

#

Having concluded that the Stellar Survey was lying, Mark searched the information nets for news of *Magellan*. He was not surprised to learn that the starship had returned to the Solar System. After all, how else could the Survey have learned of Jani's death?

What did surprise him, however, was *Magellan*'s location. The ship was not at High Station, the jumping off place for starships of the Survey. Rather, she was docked at PoleStar, the Weather Directorate's orbiting mirror that provided illumination to dark northern climes in winter.

Once the seed of doubt was planted, it quickly grew into a mighty oak of suspicion. Luckily, in his quest for answers, Mark was not without resources. Since his parents' death in an aircar accident, Mark had used his inheritance to pursue a life of leisure. Most nights he could be found at the Cattle Club, depleting their store of liquor. It was during one of these drinking bouts that Mark hatched a plan to discover the truth about his sister's death.

Gunter Perlman was a renowned solar yachtsman for whom Mark had crewed from time to time. By agreeing to pay the freight, he cajoled Gunter into moving his yacht to polar orbit, ostensibly to try out a new solar sail in advance of the Luna Regatta.

Mark chafed with impatience as he and Gunter watched first one icy pole, and then the other, pass repeatedly beneath the yacht's control pod as they constantly fiddled with the orientation of the sail to reshape their circular orbit into a lopsided ellipse.

At long last, the facility appeared in their viewscreen. Not long after, the radio came alive: "Space yacht, this is *Magellan*. You are approaching a restricted area. Advise your intentions, over!"

Gunter replied that he knew of no such restriction. There followed a brief discussion during which he was given the opportunity to declare an emergency. Perlman declined and tilted his sail to begin the long spiral back to low orbit while Mark donned his vacsuit and launched himself out the airlock.

He had barely cleared the yacht when his helmet reverberated with an order to halt. When he didn't respond, the starship ordered three spacers out to intercept him. A deadly game of hide-and-seek followed.

Whether by luck or skill, Mark managed to reach the station habitat before his pursuers. Once there, he grounded on the hull and hid among the maze of heat exchangers, communications antennae, and other protrusions, intending to use the habitat's hull for cover while he made his way to a point directly beneath the nearby starship. From there he would jump for *Magellan*, and once onboard, trade on his status as Jani's only relative to demand answers. Hopefully, he would get them before he was carted off in handcuffs.

He never reached *Magellan*. While working his way around the perimeter of the habitat, he happened on a lighted viewport. As he prepared to skirt the obstruction, he glanced into the compartment within. What he saw took his mind off his goal.

The cabin beyond was occupied by Lisa Arden. With word of an intruder on the hull, station control had roused her from a hot shower and ordered her to opaque her viewport. Dripping wet and sans towel, she launched herself across the compartment in microgravity to comply. She arrived at the port a few seconds late.

Mark's first sight was of a vision; breasts unencumbered by clothing or gravity, wet flanks glistening. The sight should have held him captivated. Instead, his attention faltered when he caught site of Lisa's companion.

The being was approximately a meter-and-a-half tall, covered with brown fur. Its head was round, with two ears that stuck out, giving it a comical appearance.

At first he thought it was a monkey. One look into those large yellow eyes and he knew what it was the Stellar Survey was hiding.

Staring up at him from within the lighted compartment was an alien, one whose gaze reflected intelligence as great as Mark's own.

                                    #

The bullet car plunged abruptly into darkness as it entered the tunnel that would take them under the lake. Mark's ears popped as the hurtling car compressed the column of air in front of it like a cork entering the neck of a bottle.

Thirty seconds later, it popped out on the German side of the lake. The car climbed a low hill carpeted with ordered rows of grapevines. At the crest, the accelerator pylons began a gentle turn toward Meersberg.

                                    #

Captain Landon of *Magellan* had not been happy to discover that a grief-stricken brother had penetrated his security to the point where he had come face-to-face with the biggest secret in the Solar System. They couldn't lock Mark up and keep him incommunicado forever, so they did the next best thing. They told him the whole story and signed him up for the duration.

Magellan had been orbiting New Eden when the granddaddy of all gravity waves had penetrated its hull. Moments later, sensors detected two unidentified craft, one of which was hurling energy bolts at the other. Under attack, and seemingly unable to return fire, the passive member of the pair fled for the refuge of the nearby planet.

At the time, *Magellan*'s Number Three Scout Boat was returning from New Eden's moon. The scout's position placed it thousands of kilometers closer to the battling pair than was *Magellan* herself. Jani Rykand, the scout's pilot, reported that they too had felt the gravity wave and relayed scenes of the battle until it grew close. Then, as the smaller unknown reached minimum distance from Scout Three, it engulfed the scout in an energy beam, instantly vaporizing it and the eight human souls onboard.

Having seen his crewmembers murdered before his eyes, Dan Landon furiously considered how to defend his ship; which, save for a few hunting rifles and light machine guns, was unarmed. In desperation, he launched an interstellar message probe at the aggressor.

Message probes are miniature starships, and like their larger brethren, are not designed to operate deep within a planet's gravity field. The probe disappeared into superlight, then reappeared in normal space as an expanding cloud of debris.

That cloud was moving at 60% the speed of light, directly toward the aggressor. Faster than the human eye could perceive, the smaller of the two unknowns was transformed into a ball of incandescent plasma silhouetted against the blackness of space.

With its tormentor destroyed, the larger unknown ceased its wild gyrations and went ballistic. Captain Landon dispatched one of his surviving scouts to investigate. When the scout's crew boarded the derelict, they found evacuated corridors filled with the corpses of two different types of aliens. They also found a lone survivor representing a third type. The survivor bore a striking resemblance to a terrestrial monkey.

#

Lisa Arden's introduction to the project had come when she was ordered from her duties as a linguistics professor at the Multiversity of London to the PoleStar habitat. Upon arriving in polar orbit, she discovered that she was expected to learn how to speak with the survivor.

The survivor's name was Sar-Say, and though she intended to learn his language, he proved an able student and learned Standard. In pidgin speech, and with many misunderstandings, they began to communicate. Sar-Say explained that he was a member of a race called the "Taff," and that he was a trader, and that he didn't know why his ship had been attacked. Within a few weeks, his proficiency improved to the point where Lisa felt they could proceed beyond the "Me Tarzan, You Jane" stage. She had been getting a lot of pressure from Earth to get their ever growing list of questions answered. Thus it was that Sar-Say and Lisa attended the first of many interrogations.

That was when Sar-Say told them about the Broa.

#

Chapter Two

The bullet car pulled into Survey Headquarters' transport station after passing over the ruins of Meersburg Castle. As the car decelerated smoothly to a halt, Mark and Lisa untangled themselves from one another and gathered their spacebags from the overhead. They were watched with some amusement by Drs. Thompson and Morino, their two scientist companions.

Survey Headquarters was just as Mark remembered it. After an escalator ride from the transport station to the main level, they entered the public foyer. It was an open space large enough to have its own weather had the climate conditioners not intervened. The echoes were drowned out by an anti-echo field. The air around them seemed muffled, like on a lake when the fog rolls in.

"Ah, Mr. Rykand, welcome back!" a feminine voice said from somewhere behind them. Mark turned and discovered Amalthea Palan, the Survey Director's assistant, hurrying across the wide expanse to meet them. It had been Ms. Palan who received him on his previous visit.

He shook her hand before introducing his companions. When the introductions were finished, she said, "If you will all come this way, the Director and his guests are waiting."

She led them past oversize holographic displays of various colony worlds settled in the last century. Interstellar colonization was a hard, dangerous, and expensive business with as many heartaches as triumphs. Each new world had its own benefits and problems. An alien ecology was so complex that it was often years before colonists discovered the deadly disease that would wipe them out, or the environmental factor that made the planet unsuitable for human habitation.

There were a great many people on Earth who had tired of interstellar exploration. Some were opposed to the cost, while others were afraid of the unknown. Still others just didn't see the point.

One such person was Mikhail Vasloff, the founder of *Terra Nostra*, an organization devoted to ending the economic drain of interstellar exploration, and repatriating all colonists back to Earth.

The story Sar-Say told his interrogators made even ardent colonization advocates wonder if Vasloff's position might not be the correct one.

\#

According to Sar-Say, the Broa were a carnivorous race of reptiles that controlled the stargate network and used it to enslave every intelligent species they encountered. Without interstellar capabilities of their own, the other races were helpless against them. Once discovered, an inhabited world was given a simple choice: submit or die.

In this way, the Broa had expanded their domain to more than *one million stars!* After some debate, project researchers settled on the name "Sovereignty" to describe the Broan domain.

Not a few of those privy to Sar-Say's interrogations found the story preposterous, claiming the pseudo-simian was the equivalent of a garrulous shipwrecked sailor, spinning yarns for the gullible natives. The problem, therefore, was how to determine the truth or falsehood of his claims. The obvious solution was to send an expedition to spy out the truth. The difficulty was a simple one. Where among the stars should humanity look for these Galactic Overlords?

Travel via Broan stargate was not like a starship voyage. The gates did not cross the vast gulf between the stars so much as bypass the distance altogether. Like a computer network, the system possessed a topology that was independent of its geography, making astrogation an unnecessary skill among the Broa.

Travelers embarked on a ship in one system and disembarked in another, never caring how many light years separated the two.

Although he had visited more than a hundred worlds, Sar-Say had no idea where his travels had taken him. Besides, without a common coordinate system, there was no way to convert his observations into information humanity could use.

Eventually, frustrated project astronomers hit on a method for testing Sar-Say's assertions. They asked him to describe unusual astronomical phenomena he had seen, in the hope he would describe something they recognized.

Sar-Say had a good memory and was a fair artist once Lisa showed him how to use a drawing tablet. He spent the hours sketching night scenes from worlds he had visited. He rendered several constellations formed from bright blue stars. The astronomers programmed their computers to search out all of the known Spectral Class A and B stars in the hope that they could find a position and viewing angle to match Sar-Say's sketches. They met with no success. The inaccuracies inherent in drawing constellations from memory were just too great.

One of Sar-Say's paintings showed a view of a dark alien sea, over which floated large and small crescent moons. Above the moons hovered a complex ball of gas and dust filled with glowing filaments and dark tendrils. Sar-Say explained that on the world in question, this ghostly nebula was larger than the full moon is on Earth and its diffuse silver glow much brighter. The locals called the glowing apparition, "Sky Flower."

The object was obviously a supernova remnant, and since there had only been a handful of nearby supernovas since the dawn of recorded history, the astronomers reviewed all the possible candidates. They found a good match with a supernova that had exploded around 6000 B.C in the Constellation of Taurus. The light of that particular cataclysm had not reached Earth until the summer of 1054 A.D, when it was observed by Chinese astronomers.

Sky Flower, it seemed, was Messier Object Number One — the Crab Nebula!

#

The party entered a private lift that whisked them silently to the office of the Director of the Stellar Survey. Mark recognized those already seated around the conference table, including one person he was surprised to see. As he entered, Nadine Halstrom, the World Coordinator herself, stood and greeted him. Others included Anton Bartok, Director of the Stellar Survey, and Dieter Pavel, the World Coordinator's representative onboard PoleStar. Pavel was also a one-time rival for Lisa Arden's affections.

"Welcome home, ladies and gentlemen," Bartok boomed out. "We have been waiting a long time for this meeting. We've read your report, or at least the executive summary. However, Coordinator Halstrom wanted to hear of your adventures direct from the source. Who will be the spokesman?"

Mark raised one hand and said, "We drew straws and I lost."

"Then proceed, Mr. Rykand," the Coordinator directed.

"Yes, ma'am. As you know, pursuant to your orders, our fleet set out for the Crab Nebula to see if we could verify Sar-Say's tales of the Broan Sovereignty. We were 375 days in transit outbound, and upon our arrival, we rendezvoused in System 184-2838, which in keeping with the spirit of the mission, we named Hideout…"

#

The expedition to the Crab had actually been to the system of a variable G-Class star some 50 light years distant. Even eight millennia after the cataclysmic explosion, the nebula glowed with an energy equivalent to 75,000 suns. The dynamo that powered it was a spinning neutron star — a pulsar — that was the actual remnant of the supernova. A starship crew unlucky enough to drop sublight anywhere near it would have been struck dead by several kinds of radiation in seconds.

Upon arriving in the Hideout System, a short search revealed a world twice the diameter of Earth orbiting in the temperate zone, which they named "Brinks." Brinks had a moon three times larger than Luna, which they named "Sutton." It was on Sutton that they established their base. Two gas giants in the system were dubbed "Bonnie" and "Clyde."

As soon as the first tunnels were drilled into Sutton's surface and sealed, the team began to sweep the skies for signs of civilization. Several months went by without result before they finally detected a gravity wave emanating from a nearby star, a wave that could only have originated in a stargate.

Having found what they were looking for, Dan Landon approved a mission to reconnoiter the target star. He put himself in command of the contact party and chose Lisa to be their expert on the Broa. Mark joined the roster by the simple expedient of being the only one available who had the necessary temperament and computer skills. Landon surprised everyone by selecting Mikhail Vasloff, the anti-interstellar activist, as the fourth member. He was tapped for the coveted assignment because Landon wanted someone along who would take a skeptical view.

After a preliminary reconnoiter, they made contact with the locals, who identified themselves as the Voldar'ik and their planet as Klys'kra't. The team claimed to be representatives of a race called Vulcans from the planet of Shangri La on the other side of the Sovereignty. To disguise their origin, they traveled in Sar-Say's salvaged transport, a Type Seven Broan freighter, renamed the *Ruptured Whale.*

As a cover story, they had professed interest in various Voldar'ik gadgets. However, their true mission was to acquire astronomical data about the Sovereignty and its network of stargates. That was Mark's job. While the rest of the team distracted their hosts, he plumbed the Klys'kra't planetary database on the pretext of searching for marketable products.

For two weeks, Mark spent every waking moment sitting in front of an alien computer, programming search routines using the peculiar Broan script. He was hampered by the fact that he could not be obvious about what he really wanted, and had to approach queries about the general state of the Sovereignty, the Broa, and all astronomical data as though by accident.

Even if he had been able to compose straightforward queries, the task would have been hopeless. The planetary data base was several times larger than the Library of Congress database on Earth. A lifetime was insufficient to find everything they were looking for.

While Mark labored, Dan Landon broached the subject of purchasing a copy of the database itself, with the cover story that it would help them select trade goods when they returned with a bigger ship. In the meantime, Mark filled the memory of his portable recorder three times with tidbits of interest, if not precisely what he was looking for. Periodically, he returned to the *Ruptured Whale* to upload what he had learned into its computers.

It was on his third such trip that he met Effril, the Taff trader.

#

"What did you do when he told you he was a Taff trader?"

"The truth, Ma'am. I nearly crapped my pants."

"I take it he looked nothing like Sar-Say?"

"No, Ma'am. He was tall, blue and furry. Cautiously, I asked him if there were another species by the same name. He said he wasn't aware of any. Then I explained that I was from a distant world, and being young, had never seen a Broa. I asked Effril to describe one.

"What he described was nothing like the pictures Sar-Say sketched for us of the Galactic Overlords. In fact, Effril's description was a perfect fit for Sar-Say himself, right down to his yellow eyes."

#

Chapter Three

"So Sar-Say is a Broa?" Nadine Halstrom asked.

"Yes, Ma'am," Mark replied.

"There isn't any possibility of a mistake?"

"We confronted him with it. He confessed."

"How did he take the news that he had been outed?"

Lisa laughed. "He's a cheeky little bastard. He promised to make us his personal slaves and let us live out our lives in luxury if we returned to Klys'kra't. We told him to go to hell."

"If he lied about himself, he must have told other lies," the Coordinator mused.

"I don't think so, Ma'am," Lisa replied. "About the Sovereignty itself, he seems to have spoken the literal truth."

"Why would he do that?"

"Because he had no way to ascertain what we knew at first. He couldn't afford to be caught in a lie, else we might have begun wondering if he was who he claimed. Later, it was too late to change his story. So he told us the truth about everything else to keep his identity hidden."

"Why?"

"It was all a plot to get us to take him back to the Sovereignty. He figured that he could get a message to whatever species we contacted. As a master, they would have instantly obeyed any order he gave them. It almost worked."

"So, to sum up," the Coordinator said with a tone of resignation in her voice, "We are facing our worst case scenario. There really is a Broan Sovereignty and it is as big and mean as Sar-Say claims. We were lucky at New Eden. Had things gone differently, it would have been the Broa sending the expedition. We might even now have their boots on our necks. And lastly, there isn't a goddamned thing we can do about it!"

"No, Ma'am," Lisa replied.

"I beg your pardon?"

"There is something we can do about it." Lisa turned to Mark. "Tell her your idea, darling!"

\#

The wardroom aboard the *Ruptured Whale* was a depressing place during that long climb from Klys'kra't. Mark Rykand had been especially dejected, for only he knew how close Sar-Say's scheme had come to succeeding.

However, as Samuel Johnson once remarked, "The prospect of being hanged concentrates the mind wonderfully." In response to an offhand comment from Lisa, he had been struck by an inspiration so bold that it had momentarily stunned him. Even now, a year later, he could think of no reason why his idea wouldn't work... save that the human race lacked the fortitude to attempt it.

In the instant that Lisa turned to him, his confidence drained away, replaced with doubt. *What*, he thought, *if I am wrong?*"

Living with a person for three years gives one sensitivity to their nuances. Sensing Mark's turmoil, Lisa gave his hand a gentle squeeze and smiled. Encouraged, Mark took a deep breath, gazed around at the expectant faces, cleared his throat, and launched into the speech that he had practiced in his head for more than a year.

"Madame Coordinator. Gentlemen. The Broa are probably the biggest threat the human race has ever faced. That is why you sent us seven thousand light years to verify the tall tales of a shipwrecked alien. If even half of what Sar-Say said was true, then we just couldn't ignore the threat.

"We are back to report that the Sovereignty is very real and even more dangerous than we had feared. We are not helpless, however. There is something we can do."

"Then let us hear it!" Nadine Halstrom said, impatiently.

"Yes, ma'am. To make sense, I need to start at the beginning, which in this case, is a trip Lisa and I took while planning the expedition.

#

Planning for the Crab Nebula Expedition had taken place on Earth under stringent security, at a private resort on the North African coast. Mark and Lisa both attended for their particular working groups — Mark for Astronomy and Lisa for Alien Technologies. On the third day of the conference, they found themselves with no commitments. Lisa suggested that they visit the nearby Rock of Gibraltar, explaining that one of her ancestors commanded the British garrison there during the siege of 1782.

"An interesting tale, Mr. Rykand," Nadine Halstrom said, "but what has that to do with *our* situation?"

"During the retreat from Klys'kra't, a bunch of us were sitting around the wardroom, moaning about our troubles, when Lisa said that it was a shame we didn't have an impregnable fortress like The Rock to defend us against the Broa."

"The comment triggered a thought. I suddenly realized that she was wrong. We *do* have such a fortress."

"I'm sorry, but I don't follow you."

"The Broa rule a million suns and so far as we can tell, there has not been a single successful revolt against them in thousands of years."

"I imagine that is precisely what Mikhail Vasloff will tell the public. By the way, where *is* Citizen Vasloff? I expected to see him here."

"In quarantine aboard PoleStar, by your order."

"My order?"

Dieter Pavel cleared his throat. "I sent the order, Madame Coordinator. I figured that we didn't want him rabble rousing until you'd had a chance to hear the report of the expedition."

"He isn't truly ill, is he?"

"His doctor thinks he has a cold. I argued that one couldn't be too careful with E.T. viruses."

"You will go far in politics, my boy," she told her assistant with a smile. "Either that or you will be hanged." Turning back to Mark, "You said we have an impregnable fortress to defend us, Mr. Rykand. What might that be?"

"Why, our anonymity, of course. The Broa don't know where to find us. They don't even know we exist. That, and the stardrive. The stardrive gives us freedom of action."

"Freedom of action to do what? Hide?"

"No, Ma'am. The one thing we cannot do is hide."

"We have remained hidden this long."

"We've been lucky. Evan, care to handle this?"

Dr. Evan Thompson, Alien Technologist, nodded and took over the narrative. "Sooner or later, the Broa are going to discover our little corner of the universe."

"How?"

"Any number of ways. One of their ships may just blunder into one of our systems. In fact, it has already happened at New Eden. Then there is our electromagnetic footprint. We've been spewing radio, television, and holovision in all directions for centuries. What if some Broa picks up one of the early television programs? How long before their war fleet follows?"

"The Broan Sovereignty is 7000 light-years from here. If I understand my Einsteinian physics, that means that our radio waves will not reach them until we begin writing our dates with five digits."

"We don't know that," Thompson replied with a shake of his shaggy mane. "The Crab Nebula is 7000 light-years distant. For all we know, the nebula marks the farthest reach of the Sovereignty. There could be a Broan world just beyond our expanding radio bubble right now."

"Not a very likely scenario, that," Anton Bartok muttered.

"Are you willing to risk the existence of the human race on that assumption?" Mark asked him, taking back control of the conversation.

"If we don't hide, what do we do?" a perplexed Nadine Halstrom asked.

Mark looked at her, his features etched by determination. "Madam Coordinator, we can't hide, not forever. And once they discover us, all will be lost. That leaves us a window of opportunity in which to act."

"Act to do what?"

Mark shrugged. "Simple, really. We attack them before they can attack us!"

#

The subject of the conference sat in his cell aboard PoleStar and contemplated his future.

It had been five cycles since Sar-Say had fallen into the clutches of humans. Having survived the ambush on his transport, he had been shocked when his rescuers did not immediately recognize him. That shock had been compounded when he realized they were not subservients. In fact, they seemed not to know about Civilization at all. The thought that he was the captive of wild aliens frightened him more than had the attempted assassination that led him to this unknown section of space.

Worse, their ship was unlike any he had ever seen, or even heard of. It did not jump from point to point via stargates. Rather, it crossed the black gulf between stars like a water vessel sails an ocean. That alone proved that they were not of Civilization. For he could think of no other invention that would subvert the natural order quite so much as unrestricted access to the stars.

He'd had a great deal of time to think on that first voyage to the humans' home planet. When they tried to speak with him, he pretended not to understand. For when he finally acknowledged their loud words and pantomime gestures, he would have but one chance to get his story right. There was much to consider.

Of necessity, his plan had been a simple one. It was critical that they not recognize him as a master. For if they did, they would likely kill him out of hand. Nor did the prospect of life in a cage appeal to him. He needed to find a way to get them to return him home without realizing that they were doing so. For that, he must gain their trust. He concluded that he would have to tell them the truth about nearly everything.

There was risk in his plan, of course. Not knowing human psychology, he worried that the truth might frighten them into concealment. That would doom him to a lifetime of captivity.

He need not have worried, for the humans reacted with the same primate curiosity that his own people possessed. When they identified Sky Flower, they organized an expedition to seek out Civilization.

They had taken him along on the expedition to advise them and he had been working on the humans to allow him to meet the native subservients, ostensibly to back up their own false story.

His plan had come close to working, but something had gone wrong. The contact group had hurriedly returned to the ship and they had departed Klys'kra't. Later, they confronted him with the fact that they knew his true identity.

If imprisonment taught him anything, it was patience. He'd made good use of the entertainment screen they provided him. As he became more familiar with humans, he came to believe that despite their wildness, Earth might one day make a prime colony, especially with him as its master.

So, despite bitter disappointment, Sar-Say began plotting once more toward the day he would be awarded the Mastership of Earth. So long as they kept him penned in this cell aboard their orbital habitat, he could do nothing. However, should his situation change, he must be ready to take advantage of any opportunities that came his way…

#

Lisa Arden stood on the balcony of the resort hotel on Lake Constance and watched as a full moon lifted its gibbous form over the distant tree-studded horizon. Down below, the surface of the lake reflected back the multicolored lights of the far shore, while in the middle distance, an entertainment ship ablaze with lights made its way toward Friedrichshafen, the soft strains of a string quartet wafting softly to her across the dark waters.

Lisa inhaled deeply, held it for a moment, then exhaled with gusto. It was good to be back on Earth! At least for tonight, all was right with her world. The night breeze was just cool enough to be refreshing. Her man lay sprawled inside on the spacious bed, snoring softly, as men were wont to do following lovemaking. The moon was rising, turning the lights reflected by the lake into a kaleidoscope of colors.

In the sky above, Jupiter was a brilliant white spark and Mars a duller red one, while the stars twinkled as they had for millions of years. On a night like this, it would have been easy to pretend that those stars were the same as they had been for millennia, sparkling diamonds put in the night sky for lovers rather than the home of a comic-looking race of megalomaniacal monkeys.

Her contemplation was interrupted by the sound of a door opening, then by a strong pair of arms enveloping her and warm hands slipping through the opening of her robe to fondle the warm flesh beneath. She leaned back into a bare muscular chest and sighed, content with the world.

"Good evening," a soft voice whispered in her ear as lips nuzzled her disheveled hair.

She twisted her head back to plant a kiss. "Welcome back to the living, darling. I didn't wear you out, did I?"

The soft breath emitted by the ensuing chuckle wafted into her ear as lips nibbled an earlobe. "Want to find out?"

"Not just yet," she replied. "Maybe later. Now I just want to enjoy the night."

"It *is* beautiful, isn't it?"

"More beautiful than just about anything I have ever seen. It's easy to forget how gorgeous the Earth is when you are in space."

"Yes, it is. So, my love, what brings you outside? Did my snoring wake you?"

"No, I am just enjoying the night air... and wondering, I guess, if we did any good today."

"They listened," Mark replied, nuzzling her hair. "That is about the best we could expect."

"But did they believe?"

"I think the Coordinator understood our arguments and probably sympathized with them, not that that will us any good if the political opposition decides to side with Vasloff."

She sighed. "I suppose they can't keep him locked up forever."

"It wouldn't do any good. Lots of people will see the temporary safety of hunkering down and prefer it to the real danger of fighting back. That is the way it has always been, and the way it shall always be."

"But we *have* to fight, Mark. It's what we *do* and who we are."

"You and I have had a chance to think it through," he replied, suddenly serious as he pulled her tighter against him. "Earth's teeming billions are going to take time to sort through the risks. Who knows? Maybe there is a middle ground between digging a hole and pulling it in after us, and going out to conquer the Broan horde."

"You don't believe that."

"No, I don't. Many will."

They fell silent and stared out over the darkened waters for long minutes, enjoying each other's presence and the night. Finally, Lisa said, "We're going to be fighting the Broa for the rest of our lives, aren't we, Mark?"

He nodded into her hair. "You knew that when I first laid out my vision of Gibraltar Earth."

"I guess I did," she replied. "It's just scary to think about all the troubles that lie in front of us."

He laughed. "Name a time when that hasn't been so. At least the Broa don't yet know that we exist. With luck, when they find out, it will be too late."

#

Chapter Four

A brisk breeze swept off the nearby azure sea to penetrate the office high above the largest city on the capital world of the Salefar Sector. The office was at the pinnacle of a golden tower that had no name. It needed none. Even the smallest cub of the planet's indigenous species knew who dwelt in the tower and of the power he exercised over their daily lives. The city's name in the language of the local autochthons was unpronounceable to the occupant of the tower office. He called it simply "Capital." It was one of many cities throughout the galaxy that bore the same appellation. The planet was Sssassalat, a word that had been arbitrarily chosen without regard to the fact that the vocal apparatus of the natives had difficulty forming sibilants.

The wind brought with it a cacophony of alien smells, all of which were picked up by the acute olfactory sense of the small being who perched on the resting frame located behind the desk ornately carved from the expensive black-gold wood that could only be found on the home world. Within the gleaming expanse of desktop were imbedded the instruments the tower dweller used to communicate with his many underlings. Several auxiliary screens were lit at the moment. He paid no attention to any of them.

For the several demi-periods, he had been watching the antics of a multicolored vark as it rode the wind currents tumbling off the lee side of the golden tower. The vark was unaware that it was far from the crags and peaks of its mountain hunting ground. Its attention was focused on searching out a four-winged mardak for a midday repast. As the airborne hunter made micrometric adjustments to its wing shape in order to ride the tricky air currents, its long snakelike neck kept the head rigid in space as it spied what it had been searching for. Then, without warning, the vark folded its wings of taught skin, and dove out of the watcher's view.

As it went into its stoop, the tower occupant felt a moment of wistfulness. The vark's problems were confined to filling its belly each day, and come mating season, of fighting off the other claimants for its brood of females. For one on whose shoulders lay the responsibility for an entire star sector, such a simple life held an atavistic attraction.

Ssor-Fel was not a large being. Most intelligent species would have found his diminutive size unimpressive were it not for the fact that he and his kind were the unchallenged rulers of the known universe. He was a biped, as are most intelligent beings. On the rare occasions when he chose to stand erect, he topped out at a bare meter-and-a-half. His ancestors had been tree dwellers — if the multi-trunk, vine-like growths of home world could be called trees. His arms were long and designed for brachiating, swinging from stalk to branch, and during mating season, for holding his body aloft while he engaged in the ancient ballet of the sexes. When on solid ground, he moved with an alternating gait, first supporting his weight on clenched six-finger fists and then swinging his lower torso forward to ride on club-shaped feet at the end of stubby legs.

His fur was brown, with an intricate pattern of narrow black stripes that extended to his neck. Around his yellow eyes were the white streaks that signified the passage of lifespan. The white specks solidified into a solid mass around two paddle-shaped ears that jutted out at right angles from his head. His snout was likewise streaked with white around the four breathing holes on each side. Below the rows of nostrils, his mouth was open to show the teeth of an omnivore and a long tongue tinged with a healthy pink glow.

Having wasted too much time following the antics of the local fauna, Ssor-Fel reproached himself silently and turned back to the matter at hand. As was normal, there was too much to do and insufficient members of his species to do it. When in a bad mood, he often contemplated this eternal state of affairs. It was as though, having given his race dominion over a vast number of stars, some cosmic force had then decided to play a joke by limiting the number of administrators available to do the work.

His species was less fecund than most intelligent races. That was the consequence of prolonged droughts that had once plagued the home world, causing his people to develop irrigation early. Solved or not, those ancient droughts were still reflected in his genes. When the supply of purple fruit that had once been the staple of life was limited, it made sense for each mating pair to have one or two cubs each twelve-cycle.

With the invention of agriculture and the discovery that insectivoids were tasty, however, that imperative had gone the way of the giant crabs that had once roamed the golden plains. Yet, the birthrate remained low because the memory of drought had been baked into the Race's life matrix.

Despite their habitually low numbers, his species had slowly built a high energy civilization, mastered first a world, then a star system, and finally, the surrounding stellar domains. For the great invention of the Race was the discovery that precisely modulated powers would open pathways to the stars.

It had been this technology that had allowed the Race, though small in number, to conquer every known inhabited star system. Nor were their conquests complete. A large part of Ssor-Fel's duties was to search out intelligent species that had not yet been brought under control, and to remedy that oversight.

Thus, a race who possessed neither sharp tooth nor powerful sinew had taken control of a galaxy, forcing all others to submit to their will. It was how Ssor-Fel's ancestors had built their star-spanning domain, and how they intended to keep it.

#

The Huntmaster of the Salefar Sector shook himself and willed that his mind concentrate on the day's tasks. He recognized his vine gathering for what it was, an attempt to avoid hard decisions to real problems. Having bequeathed him and his fellows dominion over all other intelligent beings, his revered ancestors would not look kindly on this generation were they to do less than their utmost to pass the legacy on to future generations. It would have been easier, he mused, had there not been so many minor and boring details involved in running a Galactic Empire!

Take the report displayed on his primary screen. At first, it seemed mundane. A subject race, the Voldar'ik, were complaining about a shipload of strangers who departed without paying their port fees, and were requesting the sub-sector master levy a judgment against the offending traders' planet.

Ssor-Fel flexed his mobile ears and wondered why such a minor report would wind up on his docket. Economic disputes between subject species were no concern of his. However, as he scanned the dot-and-swirl script on the screen, he quickly discovered something to pique his curiosity.

He reached out and signaled for his assistant.

The door to the office retracted and the assistant entered. Dal-Vas was a young male with a strong work ethic. One day he would be an excellent administrator. He might even aspire to Ssor-Fel's position. Would that there were more like him!

"This report of the economic dispute between the Voldar'ik and these… Vulcans," he said, pronouncing the unfamiliar word carefully. "Have you studied it?"

"Yes, Sector Master."

"Enlighten me."

"As it says, a trading vessel made orbit at Klys'kra't and offered to exchange value. The beings aboard identified their home world as Shangri-La, some 12 jumps distant. They were on an extended trading voyage. Apparently, they had recently visited Vith, for they had a cargo of Vithian goods. Power units, production machinery, some delicacies for the luxury market.

"These Vulcan traders provided their hosts with samples of their wares and the haggling began. Then, with no explanation, the traders departed without paying their port fees. The Voldar'ik confiscated the luggage and samples left behind and filed a claim with Packmaster Daz-Ven on Nesantor."

"Why is this important?"

"Because Daz-Ven could not locate the Vulcans in his Database of Civilization. Per regulation, he forwarded the Voldar'ik request to us."

"Such searches often fail," the Sector Master replied. "No matter how much we try to standardize species identification, subservients often deviate from proper form. Perhaps "Vulcan" is the name of the most prominent tribe or clan on their world."

"That is what the Packmaster thought. He requested full records, including biometric recordings. When he received them, he searched for the Vulcan genotype. Again, they could not be positively identified."

"Do you suppose Daz-Ven has been lax with his database updates?"

"Anything is possible on these third-tier worlds," Dal-Vas replied. "However, our database was updated less than a thousand periods ago, and I could not identify these Vulcans either."

That was the detail that had caught the Sector Master's attention. A sub-sector headquarters database might well be cycles out of date. Civilization was so large and complex that it was easy to fall behind. But a sector capital had a massive staff dedicated to keeping the computers as up-to-date as possible. It was virtually impossible that the Vulcan genotype was missing from Ssor-Fel's record, yet that seemed to be the case.

"What do these beings look like?"

"They are bipeds with orange skin and a thatch of blue fur on their craniums. They have five digits on their hands and are otherwise unremarkable. The arrangement of their internal organs is more or less the same as ours. They obviously evolved on a homelike world circling a yellow star, breathe oxygen, and may once have been tree dwellers."

"Yet, we cannot identify them?"

"No, Sector Master. There is something else, news that I just received from Daz-Ven. I was preparing a written report when you summoned me."

"Enlighten me."

"Along with biometric data, the Voldar'ik forwarded some of the Vulcan commercial samples to Daz-Ven. They thought he might be able to obtain traces of Vulcan organic secretions from their surfaces, the better to aid in identification. He found secretions, all right, but not from these mysterious traders."

"Who then?"

"One of the Vithian power units seems covered in danger pheromone!"

Ssor-Fel blinked. When the Race was still confined to the trees, members of a pack would alert one another to danger by releasing a strong pheromone from glands in their abdomens. It was a signal unique to the Race, one only they would detect and recognize. A power unit soaked in pheromone would go unnoticed by the Voldar'ik. However, Daz-Ven's fur must have stood erect the moment he removed the device from its vacuum packaging.

"The concentration was quite high," Dal-Vas continued. "The contamination was deliberate. It must be a warning, or perhaps a cry for help."

"And did Daz-Ven analyze the genetic signature?"

"He did. He isolated the genetic markers and achieved a positive identification."

"Who is it?"

"A member of the Sar-Dva clan, one Sar-Say by name."

#

Chapter Five

Toronto shimmered golden in the strengthening dawn as the sub-orbital shuttle from Europe flared for a landing at the capital's airport. Lisa Arden and Mark Rykand waited their turn to retrieve their bags and file across the passenger bridge into a glass-and-steel terminal just beginning to stir. They had been summoned before a committee of parliament to report on the expedition to the Crab Nebula and to officially lay out Mark's vision for defeating the Broa. They were not alone. Many of those who had been aboard the *Ruptured Whale* at Klys'kra't had been summoned as well.

It had been two glorious weeks since they set foot on Earth. Most of that time they spent touring the sights and enjoying one another's company. The latter activity resulted in neither of them being particularly rested, especially when one considered that it was seven hours earlier than when they had boarded the shuttle outside of Kiev.

"Well, I guess it is back to work," Mark said as he slung both of their bags over his shoulder and strode toward the long tunnel leading to the main part of the terminal

"It had to happen sometime," Lisa agreed. "Too bad our holiday couldn't have lasted forever."

"Sorry, but I probably wouldn't be up to it… *forever*," he said with a leer.

"I believe the expression is "up *for* it," she responded in the same vein.

Exiting the terminal, they took an auto-taxi to their hotel. The desk clerk gave them a difficult time about checking in so early, but eventually found them a room. After a communal bath that took longer than it should have, they each prepared for a busy day. Mark shaved while watching Lisa dress in the mirror. Both had procured brand new ground outfits for the occasion.

It was just 09:00 hours when Lisa asked, "Ready?"

Mark nodded, slipped into a coat that felt unnatural after so long without wearing one, and ushered her out the door. Ten minutes later, they were on a moving slidewalk, headed for the tower that held the administration offices of the World Parliament.

#

A gray-haired man looked up from his reading when they entered the committee anteroom. "Hello, Mark, Lisa."

"Hello, Mikhail," Lisa replied. "When did you come down?"

"Just this morning. The doctors seemed to suddenly be less concerned with my sniffles. Why do you suppose that is?" he asked in the tone of someone making a rhetorical point.

"I'm sure I don't know."

The reason Vasloff had been stuck in orbit had been obvious to everyone; including him. He was a born agitator and had molded his organization, Terra Nostra, into one of the best lobbying groups in the world. The mere hint of what was waiting out among the stars had caused worldwide rioting three years earlier. When news of the Broan Sovereignty leaked, there would be hell to pay. Terra Nostra's membership was about to balloon, possibly into the billions.

Everyone expected Vasloff and his organization to lead the opposition to Mark Rykand's plan. For one thing, Vasloff had had a year to think up ways to thwart what he called "those idiot expansionists."

Slowly, the anteroom began to fill. Dan Landon walked in a minute behind Mark and Lisa. He nodded to both of them and to Vasloff, but did not speak.

Drs. Thompson and Morino arrived, as did half a dozen others. Several conversations buzzed just below the level where the brain can pick out individual phonemes. From time to time, there were surreptitious glances in the direction of Vasloff. If the Russian noticed, he made no sign; but rather, continued to go over his notes.

At precisely 10:00 hours, a musical tone sounded and the doors to the committee room opened. They filed through the portal to find two long tables with chairs facing a dais on which there was a fancier table with larger and more comfortable chairs. Each witness' place was marked with a nameplate. They spent a minute sorting themselves out. Save for a few staffers busily laying out briefing books, pitchers of ice water, and spare styluses, there was no one else in the room.

When they had been seated for five minutes, a door at the front of the hall opened, and in filed six Members of Parliament. Their leader was Anthony John Hulsey, Member from New South Wales, Australasia. Also present were Thackery Savimbi,

Capetown, Federation of Africa; and Jorge Santa Cruz, of Estados Unidos de Sud America; along with three others that Lisa did not recognize.

As the MPs entered, the witnesses rose and stood respectfully. As the doors closed, a low buzzing sound just below the level of hearing began as the anti-eavesdropping field came alive. The committee members took their seats and gestured for the witnesses to do likewise.

Chairman Hulsey pressed a plate inset into the table surface. As he did so, the amplified sound of a gavel banging wood sounded from hidden speakers. A uniformed functionary intoned ceremoniously, *"Hear ye; Hear ye! The Special Committee of Parliament on the Discoveries Made by the Crab Nebula Expedition is now in session. Citizen Anthony Hulsey, Chairman, presiding. Attend all who have business here!"*

"Sergeant-at-Arms. Are all we have summoned here present?"

"They are, Mr. Chairman."

"This may prove a long session. I suggest we get started. The committee calls Mark Richard Rykand. I understand you have a statement to read?" When Mark nodded, he continued: "Very well, Mr. Rykand, the floor is yours."

#

Mark made essentially the same presentation that he had in the office of the Stellar Survey Director, with the exception that this time he had visuals. He briefly recounted their discovery of one of the home stars of the Sovereignty and of the expedition they mounted there. He told of his surprise and horror when the big blue Taff trader described Sar-Say as a Broa. He spoke of the hurried retreat that had followed.

It had been in a black mood that he, Lisa, and some others sat in the *Ruptured Whale*'s wardroom, commiserating with one another. They had been talking about the overwhelming power of the Sovereignty when Lisa made an offhand comment:

> *"It's too bad we can't defend the solar system against stargates. What we need is a fortress that blocks access to our system, like Gibraltar once guarded the entrance to the Mediterranean."*

"Then it hit me," Mark told the committee. "I realized that the Broa aren't three-meters-tall and covered with fur." He smiled sheepishly. "Well, they *are* covered with fur, but you know what I mean."

"We know," Elizabeth Fletcher, one of the junior MPs on the panel responded. "However, perhaps you should amplify the point."

"The Broa control a million star systems. How can one planet with a dozen interstellar colonies hope to survive a conflict against such a behemoth? The answer, of course, is that we can't. If the Broa knew about Earth, we wouldn't stand a chance in hell. They would overwhelm us before we could get organized.

"But they don't know about us... *yet.* They have no idea that we exist, let alone where in the sky to look for us. So long as that is the case, we have freedom to act against them without fear of reprisal.

"Nor are the Broa all-powerful. They have problems of their own. There is internecine strife among them, as evidenced by the attack on Sar-Say. They have an abnormally low birthrate. The Voldar'ik's master hadn't visited their world in quite some time. The Broa are stretched thin. Much of their domain runs on autopilot most of the time.

"Despite that, of course, is the problem of their inherent power. The Sovereignty has a gigantic population, with a million planetary economies from which to draw resources. If we were to go up against the whole of the Broan domain, we would have no chance at all.

"However, there is no need for us to fight all of them. To secure safety for ourselves and our children, we need not conquer a million worlds. We need to find the Broan home worlds, and defeat only them."

"How do we do that?" the chairman asked.

Mark quickly explained his overall plan, which those aboard the *Ruptured Whale* had come to call "The Gibraltar Earth Strategy."

#

One: Humanity would finish the job they had begun on
         Klys'kra't and obtain a planetary database with its
         astronomical data and maps of the stargate network.

Two: They would use this data to discover the location of the Broan home world and other capitals.

Three: They would build a fleet of starships capable of attacking the Broa in their power centers. The objective would be to destroy the home world stargates and isolate the bulk of the Broa from their possessions.

Four: While the enemy power structure was cut off, humanity would work to foment revolts on as many subject worlds as possible.

Five: They would continue the strategy until the Sovereignty collapsed under the strain. With thousands of former slave species on the rampage throughout their domain, the pseudo-simians would be far too busy to threaten the far-off human race.

#

"Bold, I'll give you that," Thackery Savimbi responded when Mark finished. "But a bit foolhardy, wouldn't you say?"

"Not as foolhardy as waiting for them to discover us," Mark replied. Two places down the table, he noted Mikhail Vasloff stiffen out of the corner of his eye.

"Proceed, Mr. Rykand," the chairman said, glancing at his sleeve chronometer.

Mark laid out the operational details that they had fleshed out over the past year. With interruptions for questions, it was well past lunch time when he finished.

The chairman gazed at the other witnesses. "I know the agenda calls for several of you to present your technical evaluations now. I propose that we hold that for later this afternoon. We will break for lunch, 45 minutes. Committee members and witnesses are requested to be back here at 13:30 hours when we will hear the opposing viewpoint."

The recorded sound of a gavel striking wood punctuated the chairman's remarks.

#

Mikhail Vasloff sat at the witness table with every hair in place and a hint of a smile on his face. He sat with folded hands, waiting for the committee to resume their places after lunch. To look at him, one would have thought that he was here in support of a highway bill or agricultural aid appropriation. None of the mental anguish he had felt in the past few hours showed.

That he could keep his expression passive while seething inside was a testament to his long experience in politics. It had been torture to sit and listen to the stream of heresies spew forth from Mark Rykand.

It wasn't that he disliked Mark personally. He found him a personable young man and an entertaining traveling companion. On the voyage home, the two of them had whiled away the boredom with a chess duel. It had been during those games that Vasloff had tried to win Mark over to his point of view.

He might as well have been talking to Sar-Say.

Vasloff attributed Mark's attitude to the insanity that infects human beings. Having been the lords of creation for so long, the built-in response to any challenge was to attack! In most human beings, the "fight or flight" reflex was permanently stuck on "fight," and while emotionally satisfying, it was a reaction that could well end all life on Earth.

The fact was that the human race lacked the power to challenge the Broa. The overlords had a million worlds; humanity, no more than a dozen, and eleven of those were net drains on resources. Compared to the Broa, humanity was a gnat headed toward a speeding truck.

Mark Rykand was correct about one thing. Humanity's only defense lay in its anonymity. Mikhail Vasloff intended that they do everything in their power to remain anonymous.

When the committee returned, Chairman Hulsey gaveled them to order and introduced Vasloff before turning over the meeting to him.

"Thank you, Mr. Chairman, Members of the Committee," he said in his carefully cultivated speaking voice. "I appreciate the opportunity you have given me this afternoon. I would also like to thank you for springing me from PoleStar, where I was being held in durance vile to keep me from talking.

"Before I begin, I would like it understood that there is nothing personal in my dispute with Mr. Rykand. Our differences are due to the differing ways we view the world. Mr. Rykand is still young. He has the optimism of the young. To him, conquering the rulers of the galaxy is merely a task to be undertaken like any other.

I am older and more experienced in, shall we say, the unpleasant realities of life. There is a reason why the old are more pessimistic than the young. We have been disappointed more often.

"When Mr. Rykand presents his grand scheme for defeating the Broa, I say, 'Bravo!' If such a plan has any possibility of success, I will support it enthusiastically. Unfortunately, the odds are too great against us. His plan has no chance of success. Somewhere, something will go wrong and the Broa will discover the location of Earth. They will send a war fleet to conquer us, we will resist valiantly, and in the end, we will be destroyed.

"The unpleasant facts are facts nonetheless. The Broa *are* the masters of the galaxy. They receive tribute from hundreds of thousands of species. No matter how brave and skilled our warriors, the day will come when the Broa occupy this world, or destroy it. This point is crystal clear in the Klys'kra't data. Mr. Rykand obtained a number of scenes that show the fate of rebel worlds. They are now cinders orbiting their respective stars."

He waited a few seconds for the mental image to sink in, then continued.

"It is not glamorous, I grant you. But the only safety the human race will ever know lies in making ourselves as invisible as possible. Earth has coexisted with the Broa for thousands of years. We just didn't know it. If we keep to our part of space and they keep to theirs, I submit that we can keep coexisting with them indefinitely.

"To this end, I say that we must do everything in our power to keep from coming to their attention. To do this requires some unpleasant actions on our part.

"We must return to Earth and the Solar System. We must reduce the radio noise we broadcast skyward. The earliest TV and radio signals are far away and getting farther, yet they are relatively weak compared to our modern broadcast power. We can do nothing about past sins, but we should not continue them. By shielding our power sources and reducing electromagnetic emissions, we can prevent Earth from becoming a radio beacon in the Broan sky."

"Is that it?" the chairman asked.

"Far from it, sir," Vasloff responded. "Reducing emissions is only the first step. We must also abandon our interstellar colonies. They give us too large a footprint to remain inconspicuous. Even though space is vast, it is exponentially easier to find a civilization spread across a dozen star system than it is to pinpoint a single star."

"What if the colonists refuse to abandon their colonies?"

"Then we must force them. We cannot let a few selfish individuals endanger the human race."

"Anything else?"

Vasloff lifted his hands, palms upward, in a gesture of resignation. "The list is endless. Once the colonies are abandoned, we must erase all traces from those planets' surfaces of our presence. Luckily, our toeholds are so tenuous on most colonies that this will not be difficult. And after the colonists return here and all traces are obliterated, we will have to give up our starships. Not mothball them, mind you; but destroy them completely."

"Why?"

"To prevent what happened in the New Eden System from happening again. If we allow starships to roam this part of space, there is a much higher chance of our encountering a Broan ship than if we do not."

"What you are suggesting," Chairman Hulsey said, "sounds like a totalitarian state of the sort we thought we had outgrown."

"It is no more totalitarian than the militarism that Mr. Rykand is advocating, but it is no less either. I don't like it any better than you do, but the safety of humanity is more important than my personal opinions."

Vasloff continued speaking for another hour, then each of the scientists summoned got their say. Many supported Mark Rykand's Gibraltar Earth plan, but not all. The sun had long since set and stomachs were beginning to growl when the talking finally ran down.

Finally, The Honorable Tony Hulsey gaveled the hearing to a close. It was a confused group of legislators who filed out of the hearing room by one door, and a gloomy group of witnesses who left by another.

Mark commented to Lisa as they strode out of the black tower and onto the street, "No one said this was going to be easy."

#

Chapter Six

Nadine Halstrom stood in front of the glass wall of her office on the 100th floor of the World Secretariat building and stared out across the Toronto skyline. The sun was setting as it often did when she stood here and pondered a problem. She seemed to be doing that more than ever since that damned Sar-Say had come into her life.

"Well," she asked her visitor. "What do you think?"

Anthony Hulsey, Member from New South Wales, and Nadine Halstrom's unofficial troubleshooter in parliament, stretched out in the powered chair and balanced a bourbon-and-branch-water on his oversize paunch. His position of ease belied the inner tension that the coordinator's question had triggered. Finally, after a long minute of silence, he replied, "I don't know what to think, Madame Coordinator."

"That's a hell of an answer, Tony."

"It's the truth, Nadine. The problem would seem to have no good solution."

"How so?"

"Well, let's just state the obvious. The more emotionally satisfying course is the one young Rykand is advocating. We fight as smart and hard as we can. Maybe we win in the end, although that seems farfetched, but maybe we lose. If we lose, the Broa will likely exterminate us.

"Then there is Mikhail Vasloff's plan. We dig a hole, climb in, and pull it in after us. Cowardice is never attractive, but in this case it may be the smart thing to do. After all, we haven't been visited by the Broa in the thousands of years we were blissfully ignorant of their existence. Who is to say that we can't live in peace for several more millennia. All we need do is stop advertising our presence to the universe at large."

"I don't like Vasloff's plan," the coordinator replied. "I've never liked defeatism. We would be trading the last century of human progress for an uncertain safety. "

"I don't care for defeatism either," Hulsey replied. "However, that doesn't mean it isn't the smart play under these circumstances."

"Then how do we choose? Put it to a vote?"

Hulsey made a rude noise. "The people will vote for whichever side lulls them to sleep best. The last thing we need is to turn this into one of our recurring propaganda battles. Vasloff will do that well enough by himself."

"Can't be helped, Tony. This is a secret too big to conceal."

"I had no intention of concealing it," Hulsey said. "However, since we are going to be hammered no matter what we do, we might as well do our jobs."

"Which brings us back to the original question."

After a long pause, Hulsey responded, "I think, Madame Coordinator, that for the moment, we should straddle the divide as best we can."

"Meaning what?"

"We adopt both sides for the time being. We begin planning and preparations for Mark Rykand's Gibraltar Earth program, while at the same time, making preparations to abandon our interstellar colonies. We put whatever resources we need into becoming smarter while keeping both sides working toward their goals. Perhaps in the ongoing process, we will discover a middle way."

"Sounds expensive."

Hulsey shrugged. "You can't take it with you and you can't spend it if you are dead. The advantage of this plan is that we can postpone the crisis until we are much smarter about its dimensions. Take, for instance, the need to build new ships. We will need them whether we attack the Broa or defend the Solar System, so we get started building before we know what they are to be used for.

"No, Madam Coordinator, I see no reason to lock ourselves to a course of action until we have to. Kicking the can down the road has its detractors, but I find it is often the smart play."

"Very well, that is what we will do. I will set up a full net address to announce the bad news."

Hulsey's whistle was barely audible. "I don't envy you at all, Madam Coordinator. But then, I guess this is why we pay you the big credits."

This time it was the Coordinator's turn to make the rude noise.

#

"... and so, my people, that is where we stand. Our intrepid explorers have identified an alien civilization that could be the greatest threat humanity has ever known. This is very bad news, but

far from the worst news. No, the worst news would have been that they found us first.

"*We are currently evaluating two competing proposals for dealing with this threat. One recommends that we prepare carefully, and in secret, and when we are ready, we confront these Broa directly by destroying the stargates in their home systems. This will isolate them and give their subject races the chance to revolt. We will do everything we can to foment and support these revolutions. If we create sufficient chaos in their realm, we will be able to topple them from power and end the threat they pose forever.*

"*The second proposal is that we use our anonymity to keep ourselves safe; that we do nothing to bring ourselves to the attention of the Broa, and everything to minimize the chance we will be discovered. This will require that we abandon our interstellar colonies and pull back to the Solar System.*

"*Each of these proposals has much to offer, as well as many potential drawbacks. I have concluded that we do not yet know enough of the situation to choose between them. I am, therefore, proposing that we initiate a program to study the problem and to determine our best course of action.*

"*Tomorrow, the Honorable Anthony Hulsey will introduce into parliament a bill to establish three research institutes – one devoted to fleshing out the Rykand Plan, another to do the same for the Vasloff Plan, and an independent institute dedicated to the study of the Broa. Since a certain amount of supporting infrastructure will be required regardless of our eventual decision, this bill will also request a major appropriation to begin the design and construction of a fleet. This fleet will be used during offensive operations against the Broa should the Rykand Plan be adopted; or for defensive operations here in the Solar System should we choose the Vasloff Plan. I expect our elected leaders to approve this bill quickly so that we can get about the important business of protecting this planet.*

"*Nor is this a matter only for government. For the risk belongs to each of us equally. In the coming months, we will sponsor town meetings across the globe to obtain your advice. Talk to your neighbors. Dialogue with one another to see if you can come to a consensus. If you think you have a better idea for dealing with the Broa, we want to hear it. Two separate hypernet sites will go up in the morning to give you a place to express yourselves.*

"Finally, I would like to end on an optimistic note. That the Broa are a major threat to our lives and freedom cannot be denied. However, they are not the first such threat. In the Middle Ages, the Black Death nearly exterminated the population of Europe. In the Cold War of the Twentieth Century, children were put to bed each night not knowing whether they would be alive the following morning. Yet, our species got through both of these crises. We have been threatened thousands of times... nay, millions of times...in our history and we have always come through.

"It will be no different this time. Whatever we do, we will be successful. If we choose to confront the Broa, then it will be the best prepared battle ever fought. If we choose to hide from them, then we will hide so well that they will never find us.

"I urge all of you to contemplate what I have told you this evening. Think about the crisis. Think about what you think about the crisis. Consider the pros and cons of both recommended plans, and consider whether there is be a better way. Then, when enough of us have thought this through, we will make a decision via your elected representatives.

"This cannot be the usual political battle that we might have over an appropriations bill, with one party vying for advantage over all of the others. This is something that affects every human being alive, whether here on Earth or in our newest colony out among the stars. Whatever decision we make must be in the service of all humanity.

"As you consider the problem over the coming days, keep this thought always: Consider not what benefits you and yours, but what is good for all of us.

"That is all I have this evening, my fellow citizens. Please remember that we have come through crises before, and we will come through this one in the Lord's good time."

#

"Not what I had hoped for," Mikhail Vasloff said as the Coordinator's image slowly dissolved in the holocube, "but not as bad as it could have been."

He was seated in his office in Terra Nostra Headquarters in the Old Quarter of Amsterdam. He had watched the Coordinator's address in front of a bay window overlooking the Keisersgracht Canal.

"Agreed," Claris Beaufort, his administrative assistant, said. "Although, I think I detected a bit of bias toward the end. The Coordinator described Rykand's plan as 'confronting the Broa' and your plan as 'hiding from them.'"

"Yes," Vasloff replied. "While technically accurate, we will have to find some better way to characterize our position. It will be hard to attract support by telling them we want to 'hide.' No one likes to be thought a coward, not even me. However, sometimes discretion is truly the best part of valor."

"Agreed," Claris responded with a vigorous nod.

"What sort of shape is Terra Nostra in?" he asked.

"We are in surprisingly good shape, Mikhail. We had a surge in membership after the riots three years ago. Tonight's speech should lead to another. Where do we start our campaign?"

"I presume I will be asked to join this peace institute that they are setting up," he replied. "Which gives us our public relations angle. The 'Vasloff Plan,' as the Coordinator called it, isn't about hiding. It's about peace. We are the 'Peace Movement' and our adversaries are the 'War Movement.'"

"Do you suppose that will work?"

Vasloff smiled. "It has worked more times throughout history than I can count."

"How do we begin?"

"Call the bookers of the major news outlets and get me on their morning and evening netcasts. Tell them that I want to share my observations of our expedition."

"Right," Claris responded, penning the order into her datacom. "What else?"

This was far from the first propaganda blitz that Vasloff had organized. In addition to the initial public appearances, he suggested half a dozen things they could do to flood the public with Broa horror stories. Lord knows, there were enough in the Voldar'ik data.

When he finished, she got up from her perch and moved to the narrow stair leading down to the second floor.

After Claris left, Vasloff rotated his powered chair to gaze out on the overcast world below. A canal barge was moving ponderously upstream. As he watched, he reviewed the last few paragraphs of the Coordinator's speech.

True, humanity had faced danger before, but had there ever been a time when the danger was as acute as now? If so, how had his ancestors coped? How had they withstood this oppressive fear and not gone mad?

#

Chapter Seven

To most people's surprise, parliament passed the Coordinator's bill establishing three independent institutes in record time – proving that even legislators can move quickly when sufficiently frightened.

The locations of the three institutes were chosen with an eye toward tradition. The group assigned to flesh out the Gibraltar Earth plan was assigned to the Stellar Survey Academy in Colorado Springs; while the Vasloff Plan Institute would be at the University of Paris. The independent Broa Research Institute was to be co-located with the Harvard Exo-Biology Center.

Two weeks after the hearings in Toronto, Mark Rykand and Lisa Arden found themselves living in a single room in the old section of the Stellar Survey Academy. Their new accommodations were not much larger than their compartment aboard the *Ruptured Whale*. Until recently, it had been the living quarters of four cadets, who had been dispossessed to less "luxurious" quarters.

It took Mark a few days to get used to the academy's quaint architecture, misnamed "modernist." Eventually, he was able to see the beauty inherent in the style, including in the soaring A-frame pile of steel-and-glass that was the Cadet Chapel. Lisa thought the 20th century architecture ugly.

Around their island of quaintness, the rest of the academy soared skyward in a series of modern towers. The academy had been chosen for the nascent institute because most survey members were in favor of the Gibraltar Earth plan.

The Vasloff Plan Institute was to be located in Paris for similar reasons. The French had been culturally opposed to anything new for half a millennium. It was an attitude built into their genes; and one reinforced by the Islamic Crusade of the mid-twenty-first century that had resulted in a nuclear near-miss on the Rock of Gibraltar.

The first month in Colorado Springs was taken up with organizational tasks, including the importation of university professors, scientists from private industry, engineers, and officers from the Earth's small Space Force. Every new arrival had to be assigned housing, office space, and membership on one of a dozen study teams. They also had to be briefed on the expedition to the Voldar'ik sun and given an overview of what humanity knew of the Broa.

The latter tasks fell to Mark and Lisa. Once each week, they presented a four-hour orientation lecture to newly arrived cadre, taking turns to break the monotony. The rest of the time they were available for "consulting," which meant answering a constant barrage of questions from each of the study groups. Many of these were redundant, but referring the questioner to the published answer did not seem to work well. Everyone wanted to hear the information direct from someone who had seen the Sovereignty with their own eyes.

Their weekly lecture was an introduction to the history of the Sovereignty, Broan physiology and psychology – actually Sar-Say physiology and psychology – and what little was known of the physical layout of Broan Space. Unfortunately, the answer to the question: "What do we know about Broan Space?" was "Not much."

The problem, as Mark often told those who asked, was that people who travel via stargate have little interest in the physical positions of the stars in the universe. What they cared about was the sequence of gates needed to jump from System A to System B. Their maps, therefore, were like subway maps. They de-emphasized the astronomy involved and showed sequences of jump points that made no effort to correlate with the actual position of the stars in the sky.

It did not take the Astronomy Working Group long to declare that this lack of astrogation data to be the institute's most pressing problem. Each of the other working groups had other "most pressing problems," and all of them thought either Mark or Lisa could clear up the confusion if they just asked them enough questions.

This barrage of inquiries caused Mark to wonder if they had been smart in abandoning Klys'kra't so quickly after learning the truth about Sar-Say. After all, had they finalized the database deal before they fled, they would now have a full astronomical database to study.

#

"There was another demonstration today," Lisa told Mark after he finished the weekly orientation lecture. The two of them were squeezed side-by-side into their tiny kitchenette, making dinner.

"Oh, where?"

"Toronto, where else? They say a million people showed up to demand 'peace,' but it only looked to be about 200,000 from the pictures I saw."

"Vasloff seems to be doing a good job getting people on his side, doesn't he?"

"No wonder. He is on every news program and talkathon on the net. Doom and gloom sells, I guess."

Mark turned and took her in his arms, planting a kiss on her forehead. Then he just held her. "There is something we should consider, my darling."

"What?"

"He may be right. We could be setting humanity up for a suicide mission here."

"Don't say things like that," she said sternly before returning the kiss, this time on the mouth.

"Why not?"

"Because his way leads to the *illusion* of safety. Our way leads to the *fact* of safety."

"Or to our extermination."

She nodded. "Or to our extermination. Either way is better than what Sar-Say has planned for us."

Mark felt a cold shiver down his spine. When confronted aboard the *Ruptured Whale* about his plans for Earth, Sar-Say had been very straightforward in proclaiming what subservience to the Broa meant. Perhaps he had intended to frighten them into surrendering. If so, he miscalculated. His description of life under the overlords had hardened their resolve rather than weakened it. Still, even though the plan for resisting the Broa was his, Mark sometimes had his private doubts.

"How did your day go?" Lisa asked as she wriggled out of his grip and turned back to the task of chopping celery for the salad.

"Same old, same old. I gave the same talk we have given six times now, got the same questions, gave the same answers."

"It won't be long now. The institute is almost completely staffed. Once we are all in harness, no more 'orientation lectures.'"

"Don't kid yourself. Once the staff is in place, the visiting VIPs will begin to show up. Guess who will have the honor of showing them around?"

Her expression showed mock horror. "Not that! Surely they can get some flunky in the public relations department."

He stirred the spaghetti that was cooking on what in earlier years might have been described as a 'hot plate,' then said, "I have news for you, my dear. Flunkies are us!"

#

Dr. Octavius Brainard was a tall man, heavy-set, and graying. He was a physicist out of Stanhope College and a member of the team studying the application of alien technology to humanity's conquest of the Broan home worlds.

He gazed down at Mark from an elevation of two meters, and boomed, "You were right, young man. Obtaining stargate technology is essential to our attack. Without it, the logistics are just impossible!"

Mark wondered why that fact wasn't obvious to everyone. It certainly was to those who had endured the year-long journey to the Crab Nebula and another year coming back.

The two competing star travel technologies had their pluses and minuses. The stardrive gave humanity the advantage of mobility. They could go anywhere. However, traversing a light year at top speed required a little more than an hour, and crossing 7000 light years required 9000 hours. That was a long way to haul the megatons of supplies required for a successful interstellar war.

Traveling by stargate, on the other hand, eliminated the distance problem. In effect, there was zero distance between gates, which meant that the jump from one system to another required zero time.

Fighting a war at the end of a year-long voyage was too cumbersome to be workable. If Earth was to be successful against the Broa, they would have to establish forward operating bases on the periphery of the Sovereignty and would have to keep them continually supplied. For that, they needed stargates of their own.

Brainard continued: "The problem, of course, is getting our hands on the technology and learning how it works. Any suggestions?"

"Just my original one. That we steal a gate from some out-of-the-way system and then reverse engineer it."

Brainard nodded. "Might work, but it would be risky. For one thing, the Broa are likely to react strongly to the theft of a gate by ships that don't seem to need them."

"There is that," Mark agreed. "The last thing we want is to alert them that they have acquired a competitor."

"There is another scenario, Brainard mused. "Perhaps we can develop the technology on our own without recourse to risky raids on Broan gates."

"Do you think we could?"

"It's conceivable. We know the gate exists. We have the measurements of the jump field that you people made while escaping the Voldar'ik System. We may be able to develop the technology with our current understanding of physics."

"Do you think it possible?"

"I will have to speak to the Director about establishing a separate working group, one composed of the best physicists we can attract. Of course, even if we invent the technology ourselves, we will need to be careful about using it. Gravity waves, you know."

Mark nodded. Gravity waves were something he understood. When a ship entered one end of a stargate pair, it disappeared from normal space. When it exited the other end, it reappeared. In between, it did not exist. The discontinuities caused gravity waves at both ends. One was a "negative wave," produced by the sudden disappearance of mass. The other was a "positive wave," caused by the sudden materialization at the other end of the jump.

Just as Earth was the center of an expanding bubble of radio noise, every stargate was the center of its own expanding bubble of gravity waves. The Sovereignty was filled with stargates and ships jumping hither and yon; which meant it was awash in gravity waves, some thousands of years old and barely detectable, others radiated outward with the strength of youth.

These were the normal waves. There were other, stronger gravity waves. These were generated when a ship entered a stargate at the beginning of its journey, but rematerialized in open space. It had been such a one-way jump, triggered by a wayward energy bolt, that had caused Sar-Say's freighter to be cast into the New Eden system along with its tormentor.

Once humanity learned the secret of the stargate, they would have to be careful not to use their own gates too near Broan stars. That meant that humanity's forward bases would have to be at least 100 light-years outside the Sovereignty. Otherwise, the Broa would detect the human-generated gravity waves and awaken from their ignorance-induced slumber.

#

Chapter Eight

Low lying clouds scudded across the sky as blustery gusts tugged at Professor Alan Fernandez. The storm had caught the trees of Harvard Yard in the process of their annual transformation. Stately Hawthorns and cedars were midway through their annual color change, with half the trees sporting summer green and the other half adorned by yellow and red leaves. The bare limbs of coming winter were foretold by the colorful leaves tumbling across the sere grass, blown by the inconstant wind.

Surrounding the park-like expanse were buildings of red and brown brick with windows filled with darkened glass panes. Some of the buildings dated back half a millennium. Others, outwardly antique, had been erected within the current generation.

As Fernandez hurried along the concrete walkway, he held his left hand clamped firmly over his hat, while a briefcase of red leather dangled from his right.

Fernandez held the Chalmers Chair for the Study of Exo-Biology, a position that had propelled him to the directorship of the Institute for Broan Studies. For more than three years, he had been one of the team that had studied Sar-Say from afar, of necessity. His heart was not up to the rigors of space travel.

To read the reports of others and never have the chance to study humanity's only intelligent alien was not his idea of an optimum situation. Luckily, he had reached a position where he could do something about it.

Rounding a corner where colored leaves swirled in a small whirlpool of wind, he hurried up the steps into the former science building that had been turned into Institute headquarters. The chill wind tugged at his clothes as he passed through the weather barrier into the marble-lined foyer beyond.

Fernandez strode up the spiral stairs to the second floor at a rate prudent for a man of his years and physical condition. His office was at the end of the hall. As he pushed the door open, his secretary looked up from her screen and said, "There you are, Professor. Drs. Knowlan and Hirakawa are in your office."

"Been there long?"

"About five minutes."

"Good, I thought I would be late. Any messages, Marcy?"

"All on your to-do list."

"Thank you," he replied over his shoulder as he pushed through the inner door to the sanctum sanctorum.

As he entered, he found an office around which were scattered boxes and packing crates. Some were half-empty, others had yet to be cracked open. They held the contents of his former office across campus.

"Hello, Hiro. Sebastian. Thanks for coming."

"No problem, Al," Hirakawa said. "What is so important that it couldn't wait for the weekly staff meeting?"

"I am going to make a controversial request. I want you two to back me up."

"What request?"

"I want to have Sar-Say transferred to the Institute."

Sebastian Knowlan chuckled. "I'll say it will be a controversial request. Anton Bartok will squeal like a stuck pig when you present it to him."

"I plan to make the request of the World Coordinator."

"Make that two stuck pigs!"

"Do you think the Coordinator will go along with something like that?" Hirakawa asked.

Fernandez shrugged. "Hard to say. However, nothing ventured, nothing gained."

"What about the safety issue? They have had him in quarantine since *Magellan* brought him back from New Eden."

"A convenient excuse. Sar-Say has been exposed to humans for more than three years. So far, he hasn't caught anything from us, and we haven't caught anything from him. Besides, the biochemists have ruled out the possibility of cross-species contamination in this case."

"Then how is he able to eat our food and survive?"

Fernandez shrugged. "Not my field. Don't we give him supplements?"

"The point, Al, is that his biochemistry is damned close to human, or else he would have starved to death in our care. We need to make sure that it is safe before we let him have contact with Earth's biosphere."

"He's already in contact with the biosphere, Hiro. Every project member who returns to Earth has the potential to carry Sar-Say's diseases. None have. I grant you there may be a risk of contamination–from Broa in general; but this particular Broa doesn't seem to be carrying anything harmful."

"Where are we going to house him?" Knowlan asked.

"Here in this building. We'll turn the third floor into an apartment, with all necessary security measures. Bars on the windows, security beams, multiple manlocks to get in and out. It will be expensive, but not nearly as expensive as sending researchers to orbit."

"I don't know if the World Coordinator will see saving our budget as reason enough."

"There are other benefits."

"Such as?"

"First, he will be available to all of our specialists for close observation, not merely the handful approved for orbit. Instead of interpreting reports written by others, we will be able to do some original research for a change. Second, we will be able to expose Sar-Say to a wider range of controlled stimuli. For instance, how does he act in an unstructured social situation?"

"You mean we throw him a party?"

"Why not?" Fernandez replied, "Strictly in the interest of science, of course. We can make it a faculty social, invite the Mayor, the Governor, the President of the University."

"That the real reason you want him?" Knowlan asked.

"Those are the *official* reasons," Fernandez responded. "There are some unofficial ones as well. Having Sar-Say here will demonstrate the independence of the institute. Are we agreed?"

The two other academics nodded. It was likely that the Survey would decline their request, after which the custody battle would begin. This was as much about turf as it was about science.

#

"They want *what?*" Anton Bartok screamed, his voice rising to a girlish pitch toward the end of the sentence.

Amalthea Palan looked down at the message printout in her hand. "They want us to transfer Sar-Say to Harvard for intensive study,"

"Let a Broa loose on Earth? Are they crazy?"

"It would appear that they are," she agreed. "Either that, or this is a bureaucratic muscle building exercise."

"Tell them 'no!' If they don't like that, I'll take it up with the Coordinator."

"The request was forwarded through the Coordinator's office."

"They can't be serious," he insisted. "Why take the risk of him being injured, or escaping, or worse yet, talking to the press?"

"Professor Fernandez has assured the coordinator that they will provide adequate security."

"Fernandez could build a dozen fences around Harvard, and it still won't be one-tenth as secure as keeping Sar-Say in orbit. Tell him that it is out of the question."

"Yes, sir."

She got up to leave. Bartok considered for a moment, then said, "Be more diplomatic than I just was, Mal."

She smiled at her boss. "I always try, Mr. Director."

With that, she left him alone with his problems.

#

Sar-Say gazed out the viewport at the big blue-and-white world and smiled – or rather, wiggled his big, flexible ears, which for his species, was the same thing.

He had been plotting how to escape his orbital prison, and here he was en route to their planet's surface. He must think about the implications of this gift.

The winged craft was deserted save for the two biologists assigned to accompany him on his journey. He sat in a viewport seat, his body strapped in by the too large human restraints, and pressed his snout against the armor glass as they fell belly first toward the atmosphere. Dr. Samuels was asleep in the opposite viewport seat. His mouth hung open and his arms floated in front of him in the bent position that is the resting position for humans in microgravity. Behind him, Dr. Chandra was working on his datacom.

Outside the viewport, a wisp of glowing gas whipped off the leading edge of the wing as a soft tug pulled Sar-Say forward into the straps. They had reached the tangible limits of atmosphere. It would not be long now.

The light show increased over the next few minutes until the landing craft was bathed in luminescent plasma and a high pitched keening sound echoed through the cabin. The sound was at a frequency too high for human beings to hear, but was well within the range of Sar-Say's ears. Gravity had returned to the boat, causing the passengers to sink into their seats. Dr. Samuels' arms flopped into his lap and he awakened with a snort, looked around, and then leaned his head against the fuselage and drifted off again.

Sar-Say had heard that Dr. Samuels was dating Karen Hansen, one of the psychologists who were always asking him inane questions. If so, he suspected that the biologist had spent the previous sleep cycle fornicating, and therefore, needed his rest. The interplay between male and female humans was one of the things Sar-Say studied most closely. Not only were their entertainment programs filled with the subject, practically to the exclusion of all else, but their sex drive seemed to have considerable bearing on their personalities and outlooks.

Not being of their species, of course; the fascination that humans held for members of the opposite sex was largely lost on him. Conditions had to be perfect to send a Broan female into estrus and only after she exuded a particular pheromone were Sar-Say and his fellows interested in procreation.

Half an hour later – Sar-Say had been among humans long enough to think in their units of time – the landing craft was largely through the incandescent phase of their reentry. Somewhere aft, engines came to life and the ship leveled off from its steep descent just as the shoreline of a large continent came into view.

They flew across an endless green, brown, and tan land for more than an hour before the ship banked hard to the right, then straightened out and dropped its landing gear. A few minutes later, their wheels touched down on tarmac and the ship decelerated rapidly to a halt in the middle of a long runway.

After a minute's wait, the engines came alive again and they began to taxi toward a large steel and glass structure that had the markings of a transportation disembarkation facility.

After five cycles of the home world about its star, Sar-Say had finally made it to Earth!

#

Gustavus Adolfus Heinz had gotten up early on a cold, overcast day to drive to Logan Regional Hub. He had received word that his shipment from Serendipity had arrived and was in bonded storage.

The shipment consisted of a load of Borodin Spice, prized for its aphrodisiac qualities, and was worth more than three million credits for a few hundred kilograms of the alien weed. In that, it was not unusual. All the imports from the interstellar colonies were precious cargo. If they were not, the cost of shipping them back to Earth would have been prohibitive. To be profitable in interstellar trade, a product had to be light and precious. Diamonds from Salaman were in demand. Gold from Marquardt was not. A few pharmaceutical stocks were sufficiently valuable to ship to Earth.

The sun had barely risen, as evidenced by the clouds turning from black to dark gray, when Gus Heinz parked his groundcar at the freight company's impound dock and hiked up the ramp to the office.

"Morning, Gus," the night manager called out after he was buzzed in.

"Good morning, Charlie. I understand my shipment from Serendipity arrived yesterday afternoon."

"Let's check." The manager called up a report on his workscreen, typed in a few symbols, then nodded. "Yep, it's here all right. Duties have been paid. You can pick it up whenever you like."

"Excellent. I have an armored transport arriving in a few minutes. Would you get it out to the loading dock?"

"Sure thing. We'll have it ready in ten minutes."

Unable to stand the interior heat in his heavy coat, Heinz wandered back out onto the loading dock to await the arrival of both his cargo and the transport. While standing out in the wind, he noticed a commotion at the VIP terminal next door.

Several police cruisers were lined up, along with a large truck with some sort of habitat strapped to its long bed. The thing looked like photographs he'd seen of old house trailers in the history books.

A crowd of men and women milled around, obviously waiting for something. From the equipment they carried, a number of them were reporters and cameramen. He could see at least three areas that had been set up for correspondents to make online reports.

"What is going on over there?" Heinz asked the freight supervisor when the latter showed up with his crate.

"They are waiting for the alien," Charlie replied without looking up from the bill-of-lading he was studying.

"What alien?"

"The one the Stellar Survey captured a couple of years ago. They are bringing him down so that he can be transferred to Harvard."

"Harvard? They putting him through college?"

"Some kind of a study center, I believe. It's part of this trouble with aliens you see on the news."

"I'm afraid I haven't been following it very closely," Heinz replied. "Business has kept me pretty busy of late."

"You should," Charlie replied. "They say they've discovered more than a million inhabited worlds out there."

"I'd heard that," Heinz agreed.

"I would think that would interest someone such as yourself," the freight supervisor opined. "That's one hell of a lot of potential customers for someone in the interstellar import-export business."

Gus Heinz took the bill-of-lading, signed it, and continued waiting for his armored truck. While he did so, he contemplated the welcoming committee in front of the VIP terminal.

A million planets peopled by prospective customers was, indeed, something to think about!

#

Chapter Nine

Ssor-Fel perched on the lounging frame behind his work pedestal and contemplated a report concerning the planet Varkanto. It seemed the local master had diverted a river to provide scenic waterfalls for his nearby estate, and as a result, more than 12^5 square *fel* of prime cropland had been allowed to turn fallow. The resulting crop shortage had meant that the shipment of several delicacies much prized in the Zer System, one jump beyond Varkanto, had missed their quota for three periods in a row. The sub-sector master recommended that the miscreant, one Val-Vos by name, be discharged from his position for reasons of incompetence.

As Sector Master, Ssor-Fel was responsible for everything that happened in the region of Civilization under his control. He had to agree with the recommendation. Anyone so egotistical as to ruin an entire river valley so that he could improve his view was not fit to administer a district, let alone an entire planet. For any other malefactor, he would have approved the request without even thinking about it.

But Val-Vos was a name that he recognized. He was the younger cub of Val-Sat, the patriarch of the Val-Za clan. To point out that his loins had produced an idiot would not sit well with Val-Sat, and would likely have a negative impact on his, Ssor-Fel's, future career.

The problem was how to ease the stupid cub out of his position without his sire taking revenge. Perhaps he could promote him to the sector level, make him an assistant with an impressive title, then set him to counting the fish harvest. Eventually, he would grow bored, resign, and go home. The problem was that it would take time, and in the interim, he would be inflicted with the young cub's incompetence.

His sour reverie was interrupted as the soft song of a vath-bird echoed through his office. That was the signal announcing that his assistant wished to speak to him.

Glad to have something else about which to think, he pressed the control on his pedestal to deactivate the security mechanisms.

The door retracted and Dal-Vas knuckle-walked to the resting frame in front of Ssor-Fel's desk.

"I have a report on the Vulcans, Hunt Master," Dal-Vas began without preamble.

"Vulcans?" Ssor-Fel asked, searching his memory for the name. It was in there somewhere. Finally, he remembered. "Ah, yes. The species we have been unable to identify. Have you found them, yet?"

"No, Hunt Master. Their identity remains a mystery. However, I have more information about this Sar-Say who sprayed danger pheromone over their trade goods."

"Yes?"

"Sar-Say is a minor functionary of the Sar-Dva Clan and an ortho-cousin to Sar-Ganth, leader of the Originalists on the Council of Rulers. Sar-Say's task was to tabulate the clan's store of value on subservient worlds."

"An accountant?"

"It would seem so. He was on a tour of clan holdings, traveling onboard a Vithian freighter. Records indicate that the freighter made two jumps en route from Vith to Perselin. Their computer contacted the gate in the Nala System and was preparing for jump. At that point, the records are incomplete."

"Incomplete?"

"The gate suffered an overload and shut down automatically. The repair report indicates an energy weapon strike."

"Weapon? An ambush, perhaps?"

"That is the theory. Security investigated and concluded someone on Vith, possibly a rival clan, tried to prevent Sar-Say from reaching his destination. There is no record that his ship left the Nala system, or arrived at Vith."

"He must be in one system or the other, if only in the form of an expanding cloud of plasma."

"Not necessarily. The gate may have jumped to second-order transport mode when struck, which would have thrown his vessel into unknown space."

"And therefore, caused his irretrievably loss."

"It would seem so."

"This freighter. What class?"

"Type Seven outfitted to be operated by a mixed crew of Vithians and Frels."

"And what sort of vessel were these Vulcans in when they visited Klys'kra't?"

Dal-Vas consulted his record keeper and after a few moments said, "Another Type Seven."

"Coincidence?"

"If so, not a great one, Huntmaster. That is one of the more popular types."

"Did any of the Voldar'ik see the interior of this ship?"

"If they did, it is not in the records."

That was another problem with Civilization. It was too damned big! Even automated recorders and a mania for record keeping couldn't adequately catalog events.

Take these Vulcans, for instance. How could they possibly have misplaced an entire race of subservients? There had to be a record of them somewhere.

After a long pause, Ssor-Fel muttered, "I don't like to float unsolved problems to the Home World, but in this case, I think it prudent. Bundle up everything we know and send it on the next ship. Include all of the biometrics we have concerning these Vulcans and emphasize that we have been unable to identify them.

"Point out that this Sar-Say seems to be in their company, although he was not seen at Klys'kra't. Perhaps he is hiding from his attackers. Also, send a copy of this report to Sar-Ganth. It may be that he will have a personal interest in seeing this mystery solved."

"It will be as you say, Hunt Master."

"Now, please leave me. I have this matter of Master Val-Vos to consider."

#

Captain Dan Landon sat on the bridge of the *Ruptured Whale* and contemplated the news that some idiot had transferred Sar-Say to Earth. Someone, it seemed, was prepared to flirt with disaster. Having lived with the pseudo-simian ever since his crew had rescued him from this very ship, Landon wasn't particularly concerned about alien diseases. If Sar-Say and humans could support the same sort of bugs, they would have discovered that fact long before now.

However, as any imbecile should have known, disease was not the only worry where Sar-Say was concerned. Being the only representative of his species currently in human hands, Sar-Say was uniquely valuable as a study subject. What if someone assassinated the silly looking little monster?

Nor was assassination out of the question. According to news reports, emotions were running high on Earth, with every politician talking about the advisability of confronting the Broa. (Landon was amused in a cynical way about the politico's avoidance of strong, clear verbs such as "attack," "do battle with," "conquer.") Most seemed to be unsure of where to come down on the issue, with not a few of them coming down strongly for both sides.

Then there was the problem of Sar-Say himself. Despite being a prisoner, he had proven himself a skilled manipulator. Somehow he had managed to get them to send thirteen starships to the Crab Nebula and back — a roundtrip of 14,000 light-years! Once in the Klys'kra't system, he had nearly convinced Landon to allow him to join the contact party. The captain still shuddered that he had even contemplated bending mission rules to accede to the alien's request.

The intercom chose that moment to beep for attention.

"What is it?" Landon asked.

"Incoming message for you, Captain,"

"Read it, Mister."

"It's from Admiral Carnes, sir. He is asking you to join him in his quarters at 14:00 hours."

"Does he say why?"

"No, sir. Just the request that you join him and the time."

Landon chuckled. "When an admiral 'requests,' it's an order. Acknowledge the receipt and tell them that I will be there. Then have the Exec break out the landing boat."

"Aye aye, sir."

#

High Station was the headquarters of the Stellar Survey, where starships prepped for their missions and to which they returned from the deep black. It had been unnaturally quiet around the station for the past three years. Now the fleet was back from the Crab.

There was *Magellan*, Landon's previous command, its great globe floating serenely against the limb of the Earth, half in light, half in dark. Beyond it was *City of Tulsa*, one of the great colony ships. And beyond that was *Ponce de Leon*, *Magellan*'s sister ship. The fleet had returned home, leaving only two starships to guard humanity's first outpost in the Sovereignty.

Just before the fleet's departure from Brinks, there had been a great shuffling of crews. Those who would stay behind were culled from the full fleet. They were largely unmarried, male and female, with few ties to Earth. Manning the rear guard meant that they would not likely see home again for five years or more.

High Station lay ahead as his landing boat moved across traffic lanes filled with spacesuited bodies and small intra-orbit craft. There were the local workboats, along with the ungainly ferries that never entered atmosphere. There were even two sleek winged craft whose journeys took them from ground to orbit. These were a rarity since most passengers for High Station passed through Equatorial Station en route, shifting to the extra-atmospheric shuttles. The winged landing craft were docked at the station, their dorsal airlocks hooked to the non-rotating docking sphere like two lampreys on a shark.

The station itself was a long cylinder spinning slowly about its central axis. The cylinder's length was four times its diameter, with a long pole sticking out the end pointed toward Earth. At the other end of the station was the docking sphere. Cylinder and sphere were coupled together by a large bearing and a complex rotational joint, allowing the habitat to rotate while the docking sphere remained stationary.

"We've been cleared straight in to Docking Bay Alpha-Nine, sir," Melissa Trank, the landing boat's pilot reported to Landon, who sat strapped into the copilot's couch."

"Very well, Pilot. Take us in."

The docking procedure was uneventful, with the *Ruptured Whale*'s landing boat floating from sunlight to floodlight as it passed through the oversize rectangular landing port. A few jolts from attitude control jets sent their nose into a waiting docking arm, which took over and positioned their dorsal airlock against one of the numerous station locks. A series of clanking sounds echoed through the boat, followed by the hiss of compressed air.

"How long will you be aboard, sir?" the pilot asked in a tone that carried another question altogether.

Dan Landon smiled. "Want to hit the shops on Level Seven?"

The young spacer smiled back, "You read my mind, sir."

"Go ahead. Keep your comm on and I'll call you if the admiral finishes early."

"Yes, sir!"

#

The admiral's cabin cum office was aft six decks and on the outer station hull, which meant that he could look out. As Dan Landon waited in the one-half gravity of the station's outermost deck, he stood at attention and absently watched the view in the deck while wondering what the old man wanted with him. He had a ship to repair. Two years of voyaging had taken its toll on the *Whale*, a consequence not helped by the fact that the ship was an alien design that had been shot to pieces when they salvaged it.

Admiral Carnes entered the compartment from his living quarters at precisely 14:00 hours.

"Dan, good to see you again," he said, striding across the floor viewport to shake Landon's hand.

"Good to see you, too, sir. It's been a long time."

"It was a long voyage. Come, sit down. Refreshment?"

"Yes, sir. I've been thinking about how good an orange juice would taste for two years."

"Orange juice it is!"

The admiral retrieved a real groundside glass filled with orange liquid and had something brown and alcohol smelling for himself. He handed the glass to Landon, moving with the exaggerated care required to keep liquid in a glass in reduced gravity.

"That was a damn fine job you did out there, Dan. I wouldn't be surprised if there is a star in it for you somewhere in your future."

"Thank you, sir," Landon replied. He wasn't sure he deserved his own flag, not after what had almost happened at Klys'kra't. He had been in the service long enough, however, to keep his opinion to himself.

They both sipped from their glasses. The admiral watched him over the rim of his drink, then set it down on a table. "I imagine you are wondering why I summoned you today."

"Yes, sir. My curiosity has been getting the better of me."

"Tell me your impressions of the masquerade you people pulled off. How successful was it?"

"I beg your pardon, sir?"

"Did these Voldar'ik buy it? Were they even a little suspicious of you?"

"No, sir. They had no reason to believe that we weren't precisely who we said we were, a species called the Vulcans from a planet named Shangri-La. Nor did they have any curiosity about it. There are so many species in the Sovereignty that no one can meet all of them. Having a ship of strangers show up on one's doorstep is fairly common. Besides, the Voldar'ik can best be described as tripods. I imagine every species with two arms, two legs, and a head appears the same to them."

"Do you think we will receive a similar reception elsewhere in the Sovereignty?"

"I don't see why not, so long as we present them with what it is that they expect to see."

"What about your Q-ship?"

"Q-ship, sir?"

"Sorry. Ancient reference. In the days of the First World War, the British built armed merchantmen with hidden gun mounts. Their job was to lure a German U-boat into range and then unmask and sink it before it had a chance to submerge."

"Yes, sir," Landon said. "I see the reference. The *Whale* is a standard Broan Type Seven freighter. That is what Sar-Say said. Outwardly, we looked just like any other ship of the class.

"And inwardly?"

"None of them came aboard, Admiral. We could have had an exhibition of naked dancing on the bridge and they would have been none the wiser."

"What if they *had* gotten onboard?"

"Then they would have seen just what they expected to see. A standard Broan freighter outfitted for Vulcan physiques. Our displays are capable of showing the Broan script. In fact, the crew got so good at reading that crap that they sometimes didn't switch back to default mode on the voyage home."

"So, having no reason to expect that you came from beyond the Sovereignty, it did not occur to the Voldar'ik to ask the question?"

"No, sir. It did not."

"That is good, Captain. What if we build copies of the *Ruptured Whale* from scratch? Is the first *E.T.* who sees one of our homegrown models going to start screaming for his master?"

"I don't see why, Admiral. So long as our ships can communicate on the standard bands, look like the real thing, and jump through stargates, they have no reason at all to suspect that we come from outside the Sovereignty."

"Jumping through stargates is a problem. We've learned all we can studying the operation of your stargate jump generators. To make any more progress, the engineers tell me, they are going to have to disassemble them."

"They're planning on taking the *Whale* apart, sir?"

"I'm afraid we're going to have to. It's the only working model we have."

"Yes, sir," Landon replied. Disassembling the *Whale* didn't sit well with him. A captain becomes very attached to his ship.

If the admiral saw the sudden flash of dismay in his features, he gave no sign. "What about variety, Captain? Won't they get suspicious if we show up solely in Type Seven freighters?"

Landon shook his head. "Sar-Say says the *Whale*'s type is common throughout the Sovereignty. Besides, we can build other types if we wish to. We were able to obtain some quite good holograms of the other ships in orbit at Klys'kra't. We can duplicate their outer looks quite closely. The interiors might give us problems, although if we use the *Whale* as a basis for extrapolation, we ought to be able to pull it off."

The admiral sat back and considered for a moment, then asked, "Have you thought about what you will do with your ship being cut up, Captain?"

"No, sir."

"Surely you have considered the next step, Dan," the Admiral said. "If we decide to take on the Broa, we'll need hundreds of ships, including Q-ships for reconnaissance into the Sovereignty. If nothing else, we are going to have to find another system where we can obtain that database you were negotiating for."

"Yes, sir. I had already figured that out."

"The Coordinator doesn't want to wait. She believes that the time to get started on the fleet is now, and I agree with her. I would like you to lead the effort."

"Me, sir? I'm no engineer."

"You know what it is like to trust your life to a design that has to fool the enemy into thinking it is one of his own. Also, there is no one else with your experience. That makes you the logical man to build the fleet, and frankly, command it once it is completed."

"Command it, sir?"

"Why do you think I invited you here today? Tomorrow, you will receive orders promoting you to Rear Admiral and directing you to take command of the New Mexico shipyards. Your team will immediately begin design on at least three different models of Q-ships. I want to be able to lay keels this time next year."

Landon thought about it for a moment. Flag rank and one of the most important assignments available in the coming fight against the Broa! The prospect was daunting. The learning curve would be ferocious.

"What say you, Captain Landon?" the admiral asked formally.

Landon grinned, stood, and in complete disregard for space station protocol, snapped off a salute. "I guess I will be building Q-ships for you, sir."

#

Chapter Ten

Jennifer Mullins sat at her console in a room hacked from solid rock. The overhead lights were naked glow tubes bolted to the rock ceiling, which still showed the circular marks of the digging machines. A long strand of black electrical cable ran across the ceiling, held there by globs of clear adhesive every meter or so. In between the globs, the cables drooped like the threads of some oversize spider web.

Jennifer was bored. The problem was that it had been two years since they had established Brinks Base, misnamed because it was actually located on Brinks' oversize moon, Sutton. Brinks was twice the diameter of Earth and had been a terrestrial-class world until 8000 years ago, when the star 50 light years distant that would one day become the Crab Nebula went supernova. The resulting radiation storm had sterilized the planet save for some rudimentary sea creatures.

The main dining hall of Brinks Base had a viewport in its overhead – a large periscope device that projected the outside view down into the underground base through at least four sets of transparent safety barriers. Usually, the wide angle surface scope was focused on the Crab Nebula, which was the most impressive sight in Sutton's black sky.

The ball of gas and charged particles looked nothing like the Crab as viewed from Earth. For one thing, they were seeing it from a different angle, and for another, the cloud had been expanding for seven millennia longer than the nebula in Earth's sky.

But even as spectacular a sight as the Crab quickly became routine when there was nothing else to look at. The lack of day-to-day variety was what had triggered Jennifer's boredom.

In the early months on the moon, there had been too much work to be bored. There had been tunnels and chambers to be dug and sealed, power systems to install, environmental control, emergency airlocks in case of blowout, whole instrument clusters to be transferred down from the ships and installed in the base.

Then there had been the hustle and bustle of having the whole fleet in orbit about Brinks. Then the population of the Hideout

System had been 3000 souls, housed in 13 starships. There had been great excitement when the rotating array of the gravity wave observatory had detected the first gravity wave from the Orpheus System, home of the Voldar'ik.

Jennifer remembered how thrilled she had been when *Magellan* and *Columbus* reconnoitered the target system. She had been one of the astrogation officers aboard *Magellan*, and for that entire voyage, her department had worked watch-and-watch — four hours on / four hours off.

Then had come the voyage back to Brinks Base to report their findings, and their subsequent return in the company of the *Ruptured Whale*. *Magellan* and *Columbus* had once again hidden themselves in the comet swarm at the edge of the system, while the *Ruptured Whale* made contact with the Voldar'ik.

Jennifer remembered the feeling of panic when word came that Sar-Say was a Broa and that the *Ruptured Whale* had fled Klys'kra't. The two starships on guard broke orbit for Brinks Base as soon as their charge made good its escape through the Voldar'ik stargate.

As soon as the *Ruptured Whale* returned to Brinks, the expedition commanders convened a series of high level conferences. The decision had been for the bulk of the fleet to return home. Two smaller starships, *Ranger* and *Vaterland*, would stay behind to guard the base. Their orders were to delay departure for four years. If they had not received other orders in that time, they were to destroy the base and return home.

Like everyone else in the fleet, Jennifer had looked forward to going home. Between the Spartan living conditions and the disappointment of discovering that Sar-Say had been telling them the literal truth about the Sovereignty, she often wondered aloud what had attracted her to a life in space. Then had come word that Captain Heinrich wanted to see her. She made sure that her uniform was clean and pressed before reporting to her commanding officer.

"Ah, Lieutenant Mullins, come in," Heinrich had called out in that too hearty manner that often signaled that he had a dirty job to assign. "Strap yourself in."

Jennifer had done as directed, *Magellan* then being in microgravity.

"Lieutenant, we are looking for volunteers to stay behind, guard the base, and operate the gravtenna. As an astrogator, you are qualified. Interested?"

"No, sir!" she had replied, emphatically.

"Are you sure? The extra pay involved is considerable."

"Why me, Captain?"

"It's just not you," he said. "We are canvassing the fleet."

"What about Commander Arlington, or Ensign Boggs?"

"Both married, while you are still…"

"Playing the field?" she asked.

"I was going to say 'single.'"

Somehow, she had come out of that meeting with orders assigning her as chief astrogator aboard *Ranger*, if and when it ever spaced for home. Until that happy day, she was a senior gravitational astronomy specialist, which meant that she sat in a rock room and watched the gravtenna array a thousand kilometers overhead as it performed its never-ending tumbling act.

Brinks Base had seemed crowded when home to the 3000 members of the expedition. With the departure of eleven starships, the population had dropped to barely 200, and half of those were aboard *Ranger* and *Vaterland* at any given time. One thing they did not lack at the moment was living cubic. In fact, Jennifer often felt like she was alone on base as she passed through deserted corridors to and from her duty station. It was depressing.

She had been surprised at how quickly their small group learned one another's quirks. Seeing the same faces day after day contributed to her boredom and despite there being no shortage of male companionship – men outnumbered women four to one – the dreariness of it all had begun to seep in. Most of her Saturday dates ended up in the mess hall, staring up at the nebula through the view periscope.

Twice the dull routine of life had been interrupted when the gravtenna detected a stargate-induced gravity wave. Once the wave had come from the Orpheus System, which reduced the observation to no consequence. The second observation had tentatively added another star to their very small map of the Sovereignty.

Yawning, she stretched her arms wide over her head to relieve the kinks in her muscles, and glanced at the chronometer display on her workscreen. Only three hours to go before Witherspoon showed up to relieve her.

She was in mid-stretch when an alarm sounded and a flashing message replaced the chronometer display:

GRAVITY WAVE DETECTED!

Blinking, she began issuing commands. The screen filled with data displays. One showed a schematic of the rotating observatory and the results of the continuous diagnostic program that monitored its health. Everything was green, which meant the data was likely real and not one of the ghosts that plagued her existence. The waveform displayed in another window showed a strong negative gravity wave. And, best yet, the observation's vector did not point toward either Orpheus or the other system they had discovered

This was a new contact!

Before she could punch her intercom, Brad Wilson, the Duty Officer, was standing behind her.

"What have you got?" he barked.

Normally such abruptness would have irritated her. In her excitement, she didn't even notice.

"Gravity wave, sir."

"The real thing this time?"

"Looks like it. I'll know for sure in a couple of minutes when the computer finishes crunching the data."

"Where does it originate?"

"The vector is still pretty rough, but it looks like it is back toward the Galactic Center."

"Are you sure?"

"Getting there," she replied tersely, wishing he would go away and let her finish her work. Then she realized the reason for his question.

From the vicinity of the Crab Nebula, where she was, G.C. was in the Constellation of Sagittarius. That was a purely arbitrary designation, of course, since the constellations from the Hideout System looked nothing like the constellations back home. However, Sagittarius held more than the center of the galaxy.

It was also the direction where the Solar System was to be found.

The implications were clear. Brinks Base was somewhere inside Broan space. With but three data points and two of those in the same direction, it was impossible to determine just where in the Sovereignty they were.

For all they knew, they might be in its very heart!

#

The wind was cold and blustery, laden with the smell of impending snow. The campus footpaths were all heated and clear, but the lawns of summer had been replaced by cold blankets of white. Winter had come to Colorado Springs and over the past several weeks had decorated the surrounding mountains in deep drifts of glistening white.

Mark Rykand hurried toward the Institute's Headquarters Building, huddled deeply in his electrically heated overcoat. Reaching his destination, he climbed the steps and pushed through the first of two sets of doors. At the second door, a blast of hot air greeted him.

The main auditorium of Institute Headquarters was a large hall that could have been rented out to show commercial holomovies. The floor sloped down from the back, with seats in curved rows. Fewer than a quarter of the seats were filled as Mark hung up his coat before striding down the aisle to the third row. He took a seat as quietly as he could and turned his attention to the stage.

Dr. Hamlin, the institute director, sat at a long table at the right side of the stage. He was flanked by three other senior administrators. A tall Christmas tree that was still in the process of being decorated dominated the left side of the stage. In front of the tree, Dr. Thompson stood behind a lectern and gestured at the holocube suspended above the middle of the stage. A black starfield filled the cube. Dr. Thompson was reporting the results of his Working Group's search for candidate systems in which human advance bases might safely be established when the time came.

The occasion was the Winter Assessment. Although this was the first, similar reviews were scheduled to be held each quarter to judge progress. And, in truth, they had accomplished quite a lot.

There were nineteen working groups in all. Dr. Thompson headed the astronomy group. It was up to them to sketch out the terrain for the coming battle, and eventually, to pinpoint the location of the Broan home star or stars.

There were also groups devoted to strategy, tactics, logistics, force size and structure, weaponry, Broan information technology, enemy physiology and psychology, Solar System defense, politics, personnel requirements, training, and Mark's personal favorite, worst case scenario! That latter group had been nicknamed *The Doomsday Club*. It was their responsibility to consider the possibility that Earth would someday be located by the Broa, and what could be done about it. In the event things went wrong, some portion of the human race must be given a chance to survive in freedom.

One-third of the way around the planet, the institute in Paris was organized quite similarly, or as much so as fit their mandate of fleshing out the Vasloff alternative. Surprisingly, Mikhail Vasloff had no official relationship with the group. To do so would have put a crimp in his rabble rousing.

The unofficial name of the institute in Colorado Springs was *The Gibraltar Institute*, an appellation that was fast becoming official. After initial confusion, the working groups had settled down to their tasks, fleshing out the details of the master plan for taking their undeclared war to the Broa. Slowly, almost imperceptibly, the outlines of the Gibraltar Earth plan were beginning to emerge.

Surprisingly, considering the number of scientists involved, there was universal agreement on the Task One. They needed information! Without it, humankind was blind, deaf, dumb, lame, and just possibly, stupid. A consensus had formed around the need for another scouting party into Broan space. The incursion would take place as far from Klys'kra't as possible.

Once the scouts made contact with a new species, they would negotiate for that species' planetary database. Nor would the "Vulcans" of "Shangri-La" do the negotiating. To confuse the enemy, they would masquerade as a different race from a distant fictional star system.

Once they had a database, they would no longer be dependent on listening for gravity waves. Ships stuffed to their hulls with monitoring equipment would sneak into the cometary halos of numerous systems and eavesdrop on the locals.

Such a scouting expedition would not be underway anytime soon, however. The one ship they could use to pull off a second masquerade was being disassembled for study.

The *Ruptured Whale* currently sat in the same Lunar space dock where it had been repaired after being salvaged from New Eden. This time the yard techs were taking it apart as carefully as a surgeon works on a prenatal infant in the womb. The hope was that once the scientists and engineers examined the Broan equipment, they could reverse engineer it for use in human-built ships.

That was the hope.

Like a six-year-old disassembling an antique mechanical clock, the danger was that they might not be able to reassemble it again.

Following the need for information came the need for a faster way to reach Broan space, the Stargate Option. The team assigned to develop the technology independently was not making much progress. Hopefully, the alien database would give them clues, and possibly detailed information, on how the stargates operated. If not, they would have to obtain the technology the old fashioned way – they would have to steal it.

Beyond that, the plan to defeat the Broa became fuzzy.

There was the need to build a fleet, of course; although they lacked data to estimate its size. The only thing everyone agreed was that it would have to be big. The fleet would include Q-ships, cruisers, blastships, even larger logistics craft, plus numerous types not yet conceived.

The number of things they did not yet know were legion, but of one thing everyone was completely certain. Whether parliament eventually decided to fight or hide, they were going to be busy for the foreseeable future.

#

Chapter Eleven

Sar-Say, if not content, was not unhappy. His transfer from orbit to Cambridge reminded him of the infinite variety and pleasures of a world, even one viewed only through the armor glass window of his prison cell. At the moment, snowflakes were streaming down from an overcast sky. The flakes were large and fluffy, unlike the hard ice pellets of just a few weeks earlier. The photosynthesis collectors on the trees outside had been an explosion of color when he arrived. Now they were gone, leaving bleak branches to reach for the sky like so many frozen tentacles. The black of the branches against the white covering of snow made a surreal effect that he found esthetically pleasing. Save for weeping willows, the trees of Earth were nothing like those of his home world.

Life at the Broan Institute was also easier than it had been aboard PoleStar. In orbit, he had been interrogated daily by researchers working from lists sent up from Earth. Now he had access to the prime questioners themselves. That meant that their sessions trended more toward conversations than interrogations. He found several of his jailors to be surprisingly talkative when given the chance. Sar-Say often listened more than he spoke. In the process, he improved his understanding of these strange bipeds.

There was Dr. Marcia Plessey, who insisted that everyone use her title when addressing her. An older female, with drawn features and a mouth that turned down, she was forever making acerbic comments about "the military." The comments confused Sar-Say at first. His impression from his studies of the Earth's public data network was that the humans had a very small space navy, more constabulary than fighting force. He finally realized that Dr. Plessey's complaints were traditional, a holdover from times when the humans had been quite warlike, and were directed at the uniformed personnel of the Stellar Survey.

Then there was Professor Irving Kostmeier, who could talk for hours if one of Sar-Say's questions triggered an enthusiasm. Despite his tendency for loquaciousness, the Broa detected a sharp intellect hiding beneath the professor's too friendly façade.

One thing the conversations were was never ending. Day after day, his interrogators quizzed him about life in Civilization. As he had before, he told them the truth. With his secret revealed, he had no reason to lie and every reason to keep whatever trust he could with humans. They were a strange species. Individuals not involved in the recent voyage to Sky Flower seemed to treat the expedition as ancient history. Each new acquaintance presented him with a blank screen on which he could write anew.

Despite the long days, the sessions with his interrogators were profitable. For, while they probed his knowledge of Broan Civilization, he learned about Earth and humanity in turn. Nor was his curiosity unfocused. While he interacted with an ever-expanding circle of human academics, he continued to search for those who might prove useful in the future.

Having been discovered before he could make contact with the Voldar'ik, he faced the prospect that remainder of his life would be spent in captivity. The possibility did not frighten Sar-Say. His species was not built to agonize over what might have been. Instead, he put aside his regrets and began to plan anew.

His new plan was elegant, but required the assistance of a few humans to be successful. Homo sapiens, as they rather grandiosely styled themselves, were much more individualistic than were Broa. Given the proper inducements, he was sure he could bribe a few humans to help him. He just had to find them.

"Good morning, Sar-Say," Director Fernandez said as he exited the combination airlock and security barrier leading to Sar-Say's cell.

"Good morning, Director," Sar-Say replied.

Fernandez visited him every morning at precisely 08:00 hours to see how he was doing, sometimes in the company of Dr. Knowlan or Dr. Hirakawa, but most often alone. He seemed solicitous of Sar-Say's welfare.

"I have news this morning," Director Fernandez said.

Sar-Say waited. He had not yet learned to make the automatic responses humans used to signify they were ready to receive information.

"We have gotten permission to expose you to a wider range of people than just us ivory tower types."

The Broa did not understand the reference to towers. That, however, was not the reason he answered, "I don't understand."

"We are going to arrange a faculty reception at which you will be the Guest of Honor. A number of important people will be there. You will meet the elites of our society. Besides, it will be an occasion to show you off."

"Why would you do that?"

Fernandez wrinkled his upper face in an expression that Sar-Say knew meant that he was puzzled.

"A good question," the director responded, realizing that he was talking to an alien. "It will be a chance for you to learn more about us, and we about you. Also, it will enhance the status of our institute. That can't hurt at budget time, you know."

The accumulation of value was one thing that Sar-Say understood. "When will this function take place?"

"At the beginning of next month. There are invitations to send out, schedules to be adjusted, catering to be arranged, all manner of tasks to be completed."

"Will I be caged?" Sar-Say asked, suddenly realizing that this might be the occasion he had been waiting for.

"Of course not. The doors will be guarded, of course; as much for your protection as ours. However, you will be allowed to mingle with the crowd. This will be a learning experience for both of us. If things go well, we may make it a monthly function."

Sar-Say bared his teeth in an imitation of a human smile. On him, it did not look friendly.

"I think I would like that, Director Fernandez."

"If you will excuse me, I have a busy morning."

"I also," the Broan replied. Although he displayed the learned social behavior that humans had taught him, his mind was not focused on that particular interaction. Rather, he was considering his search for a particular human and how this reception might advance his cause.

#

"Want to go to a party?"

"I beg you pardon," Lisa asked.

Mark Rykand gathered her into his arms and repeated, "Would you like to go to a party?"

"A party? Where?"

"Boston."

She tilted her head up to look into his eyes and furrowed her brow in that way he found so attractive.

"Can't we find entertainment closer to home? Say in the Colorado Springs holoplex?"

"This is a special party. It's a coming-out shindig for Sar-Say."

This time the look of confusion was too much for him. He laughed. This caused her skin to flush and her eyes to widen momentarily, as though she was thinking of launching a lightning bolt in his direction. Instead of an explosion, she said softly, "Perhaps you should start at the beginning."

The beginning had come with a summons to Director Hamlin's office. Hamlin had greeted him with the same question: "Do you want to go to a party?"

Mark's reaction had been similar to Lisa's. The director explained: The Broan Institute was planning a controlled social event at which Sar-Say would mingle with regular people. The stated goal was to see how Sar-Say reacted in a crowd situation.

Mark found this explanation suspect. For one thing, en route to the Crab Nebula, Sar-Say had had plenty of practice mingling in groups. For another, the guest list included some decidedly "non-regular" people, including the Governor of Massachusetts, the Mayor of Boston, several media bigwigs, and assorted Harvard notables. The reception seemed more like an apple polishing exercise than a serious experiment in alien psychology.

The invitations had gone out to the directors of both the Gibraltar and Paris Institutes and their wives, more for form's sake than a desire to see them show up. However, the invitation concluded by saying that if the directors were unable to attend, they could send their representatives.

"That's you," Hamlin said, "if you want to go."

Mark considered for a moment. "Lisa and I have a lot of work due next week, but I suppose we could take a day or two off. I know Lisa would like to see Sar-Say again. They were roommates for quite awhile, you know."

"I do. I've seen the surveillance recordings, including the one that isn't supposed to exist."

Mark nodded. All activities in Sar-Say's quarters aboard PoleStar had been recorded for study and security purposes, including Lisa's nude flight across the compartment. "I wouldn't mention that to Lisa, were I you."

That brought a smile to Hamlin's lips. "I would give you the same advice unless you like sleeping on the couch. Do you accept the invitation?"

"Sure," Mark replied. "It might be fun."

Lisa listened as he recounted his meeting with the director, minus the part about security recordings. When he finished, she asked, "Why on Earth would they throw Sar-Say a coming out party?"

"They claim it's a science experiment. If you ask me, I think personal aggrandizement is a more plausible explanation. Professor Fernandez and his band are trying build up credit with the local powers-that-be."

"Why would he do that?"

Mark shrugged. "Prestige, a bigger bite of the budget pie, a desire to be one of the 'beautiful people'? Who knows. They are spending a lot of credits on this thing, so you know it's important to them. I told the director we would go."

"What about my report?"

"Screw the report. Let's play hooky."

She thought about it for a moment, then nodded. "Why not? We deserve some time to ourselves. Besides, I can get in some shopping.

#

"I love Boston!"

The two of them were in an autocab, slowly making their way toward the suspension bridge over the Charles River. The night was overcast and the only illumination came from the lamps of other vehicles and indirect radiance from passing buildings. Ahead of them, the lights of Cambridge and the towers of Harvard were visible through a light haze of fog. The heated roadway glistened with a thin layer of moisture left over from newly fallen and melted snow.

The flight in from Colorado Springs had been uneventful. They arrived at dusk the previous evening and took a water taxi across the harbor to their hotel on the Long Wharf. Their room overlooked the harbor and they left the curtains open so they could be awakened by the dawn.

Mark woke at first light. The previous evening's weather prediction had been for light snow, and a glance out the window showed the clouds already gathering. It had been several decades since the Weather Authority had been caught wrong in a local forecast.

As he stretched, he thought back to the previous night's lovemaking. He and Lisa had settled into a comfortable routine with one another. They were starting to act like an old married couple. Not for the first time, he wondered if he shouldn't do something about that.

Rolling over, he ran his fingertips down the protrusions of her naked spine, reversing the action when he reached the swell of her buttocks. On the third transit, she stirred and asked sleepily, "What time is it?"

"Just after 07:00 hours."

"Let me sleep!"

"No can do. Time and tide wait for no man. Besides, we have shopping to do."

They ate a late breakfast in an alcove overlooking the harbor. They finished just as the shops around Fanuel Hall opened for business. That was their first stop. They shopped until lunch. Rather, Lisa shopped. Mark held her packages. Like most men, he failed to see the fascination shopping holds for women. Was it really necessary to try on everything in the store before making a selection?

After lunch, they took an autocab to Newbury Street, where the serious shopping began. Since Newbury was under the weather dome erected late in the last century, there was no problem with inclement weather. By the time they returned to their hotel, Mark was referring to their afternoon as the "Newbury Death March."

Upon reaching their room, he dropped the packages on the bed and they began their preparations for the evening's festivities. They showered, shaved, powdered, and primped. At precisely 19:00 hours, they called for an autocab and set out for the wilds of Cambridge across the river.

While Lisa studied the city out the cab's bubble window, Mark studied Lisa. Her profile was silhouetted against the passing lights, showing a turned-up nose and lips that had been made for pouting. Her hair was piled high on her head in a formal style that reminded him of a wave breaking on a rocky shore. Her blonde tresses were sprinkled with artificial gemstones, making them sparkle in the passing lights.

Nor were they the only thing that sparkled. Long diamond earrings dangled from each earlobe, and a matching pendant hung around her neck. The pendant was set off by bare shoulders. The shimmering gown she wore was low cut, revealing more than it concealed, and expensive.

"Aren't you cold?" he asked, gesturing toward the fur stole that had slipped down her arms to rest in the crook of her elbow. The fur was expensive, but synthetic, having been purchased that afternoon. A real fur would have cost a year's wages.

She turned to him and smiled, "Some sacrifices must be made for the sake of fashion, you know. You men have it lucky. You should thank Beau Brummel."

"Who?"

"Early 19th century Regency dandy and a countryman of mine. He popularized the style that eventually evolved into the modern man's suit. Things have pretty much been in stasis ever since, meaning you get to bundle up while I have bare skin hanging out all over."

"Hanging out very fetchingly, I might add."

She bobbed her head, making the earrings glitter in the light. "I thank you, gallant sir. Is there any way I can repay the compliment?"

"I'll think of something."

She laughed. "I'm sure you will."

The sound of the cab's wheels on pavement changed as they reached the bridge. The glistening tower of the Science Museum passed on their left. A few minutes later, they were in the quaint streets of Cambridge, and minutes after that, at the entrance to Harvard Yard.

As the door rotated up and away, Lisa lifted her stole around her shoulders. Mark held her hand as she stepped down onto pavement, being careful not to ruin her new shoes by stepping in an errant puddle. The cab's sensors detected that its passengers were clear, and quietly disappeared into the thickening fog. They watched it out of sight before turning for the short hike to the Broan Institute. Lisa was shivering by the time they reached their goal, despite Mark's attempts to fold her into his body to keep her warm.

Once inside, a visit to the cloakroom rid them of the stole and allowed Lisa's full beauty to be revealed. Mark noted more than one appreciative stare as they made their way toward the ballroom where the reception was underway.

He was happy to see full security at the door, and after a minute or so spent passing through various detectors and being scanned by the hard eyes of security men, they entered the chandelier-lit ballroom.

"Showtime!" Mark muttered as they stepped into the light.

Lisa's response was a reassuring squeeze of his hand.

#

Chapter Twelve

"Hello, Lisa. It has been a long time since we have seen one another," Sar-Say said. The Broa bowed in a passable imitation of the sort of courtliness one only sees in holomovies.

Unlike the human guests, Sar-Say did not wear a suit. He did, however, have a red sash draped diagonally across the brown fur of his chest. His only other attire was a pair of shorts cut from some dark, expensive-looking material. It was the first time Lisa had seen him wear any clothing at all other than an equipment belt.

"Hello, Sar-Say. My, aren't you dashing this evening!"

The Broa acknowledged the compliment by saying, "I understand your meaning. Professor Fernandez thought this arrangement had the proper solemnity for the occasion without interfering with my body's cooling system."

"Your command of Standard has improved since last we spoke."

"Yes. My conversations with those here at the institute have given me a great deal of practice. I am still working on my idioms, however. May I say that you look very lovely tonight?"

She smiled. "Thank you for the compliment."

Sar-Say turned his attention to Mark and extended his six-fingered hand. "It is good to see you again, Mark."

"And you," Mark replied, shaking the proffered hand. As he did so, he wondered if Sar-Say was truly glad to see him. After all, he was the one who had discovered the pseudo-simian's true identity and thwarted his scheme for escaping humanity's clutches.

"What are you doing now?" Sar-Say asked.

"We are working in Colorado Springs."

"Ah, the so-called 'Gibraltar Institute.' It is my understanding that you are planning an attack against Civilization... excuse me, the Sovereignty?"

"Where did you hear that?"

"On the news."

"We are evaluating our options," Mark replied cryptically.

"I hope you will not take offense when I tell you that what you are planning is madness."

"No offense taken," Mark lied. "If it's madness, it is a peculiarly human form of the disease."

"Yes, I am beginning to understand that. If I may say so, the psychology of your species is quite fascinating. Your arrogance ... is that the right word, Lisa?"

"It is if you intend to make a negative point."

"Thank you. Your arrogance is a result of your long isolation. For all of your history, you have been masters of this one small world and you project this feeling of mastery out into the larger universe. The truth is that you are not a significant factor in the grand scheme of things. Once you understand the scope of the Sovereignty, you will come to realize this."

"I think we understand the scope already. You told us the Sovereignty controls a million suns."

"Mere words," Sar-Say replied. "The reality behind the words has yet to... is 'sink in' the proper idiom, Lisa?"

She nodded.

"The reality has yet to sink in," Sar-Say continued. "When it does, you will come to understand that your goal is impossible to achieve."

"I seem to remember you offering to let us live out our lives in comfort if we would help you become the master of this planet," Mark said. "Is the offer still open?"

"It is," Sar-Say replied, either not recognizing the sarcasm or choosing to ignore it. "You should be studying how to best integrate your species into Civilization rather than pursue a course which can only end in your extermination."

It was basically the same pitch Sar-Say had made to them as they were fleeing Klys'kra't. It had irritated Mark then and irritated him now. Of course, it had been his stubborn refusal to accept Sar-Say's brazenness that had led to the Gibraltar Earth Plan, so he guessed he should be grateful.

Their exchange with the Broa had gathered a crowd of onlookers. Generally, such weighty matters were not discussed at academic receptions.

"There is always the Vasloff Alternative," Mark said. "If we can't fight, we hide."

Sar-Say signified his disagreement using a Broan gesture rather than the learned human one. "The Paris Institute's studies are merely the other side of the same coin. Your planet radiates too brightly across the communications bands to remain hidden forever. Sooner or later, one of our observatories will detect you. It would be better to voluntarily submit to our rule. I wish I could make you understand that."

"Come a cold day in hell," Mark muttered.

"Yes, that is one of the idioms I have recently learned. An interesting formulation..."

Sar-Say's comment was interrupted by the approach of Director Fernandez, who had noted the crowd gathering and Mark's increasingly heated words. As for Sar-Say, he might as well have been discussing the weather. His matter-of-fact delivery reminded Lisa of how alien Sar-Say truly was.

"Come, come," Fernandez said as he pushed through the surrounding listeners. "You mustn't monopolize our guest of honor. What have you two been talking about, anyway?"

"Just rehashing old times," Lisa replied.

"Well, the mayor would like to meet Sar-Say, so if you will excuse us."

Without waiting for a reply, he ushered the Broa through the crowd toward a clump of faculty clustered around a rotund man with a red face. Mark watched them go. Despite what he was, he still looked like a comical monkey. Perhaps, Mark mused, that was the great danger the little Broa represented.

"Still an arrogant little prick, isn't he?"

Lisa snuggled close and shivered. This time it was not from the cold. "What if he's right, Mark? What if we have set ourselves an impossible task?"

He shrugged. "Then I guess we go down fighting like men. It's not what I would call an optimum solution, but it beats the alternative."

#

"Sar-Say," Director Fernandez said, "I would like to introduce the Honorable Douglas Harrigan, the Mayor of our fair city."

Sar-Say bowed. "Mayor Harrigan, it is a pleasure to meet you."

"And you," the politician boomed out in his best speaking voice, having spotted a guest with a small holocamera a dozen meters from him. The guest was a reporter for one of the worldwide news nets. "I would like to welcome you to our fair city. Have you seen much of it yet?"

Sar-Say shook his head. "Only my quarters at the Institute. I would be interested in a tour."

"Then we must arrange one," the Mayor replied before turning to a second man. "I would also like to introduce Gustavus Adolphus Heinz, one of our leading citizens. He is in the same business you are, Sar-Say: interstellar import/export."

"Good evening, Mr. Heinz," Sar-Say said formally. "You are named after the great Swedish warrior?"

"Very perceptive," the businessman replied. "How did you know that?"

"I have made the study of human history my avocation these last few years… of necessity." His attempt at human humor was met by polite laughter. "Of late, it has become my passion."

"So you were in the import/export business, were you?" Heinz asked.

"In a way. I was what you would call an accountant. It was my task to visit my clan's holdings and ensure that we were receiving proper value from our various enterprises."

"I know how that goes," Heinz replied with gusto. "Your employees will steal you blind if you let them."

"The situation is somewhat different in the Sovereignty, but close enough for the purposes of this conversation."

"I hear this Sovereignty of yours is big."

Sar-Say signaled an affirmative. "We rule five times twelve to the fifth power suns. In human reckoning, that is about a million stars."

Both the mayor and Heinz let out low whistles. "How large a population?" Harrigan asked.

"We prefer a lower population density than here on Earth. On average, there are probably a billion sentients on each world."

Gus Heinz blinked. When he spoke, it was very slowly. "You have a population… of a million-billion people?"

Sar-Say paused to do a calculation in his head. "Yes, that is correct. We have ten to the fifteenth power sentients. They are not, strictly speaking, "people" in the human sense. There are nearly as many species of sentients as there are worlds."

"The prospects for trade must be tremendous!"

"Oh, yes," Sar-Say replied with sudden interest. "There are literally hundreds of millions of starships that transport goods of all kinds to our various worlds. Does this interest you, Mr. Heinz?"

"Of course," Heinz replied. For once his usual poker face slipped and Sar-Say saw a human expression he had not seen before.

"I am interested in all aspects of human life. However, I find that your academics give short shrift... is that the right term?... to the subject of commerce. Perhaps you would have time to teach me your commercial methods?"

"I would like that," Heinz replied, his tone suddenly as guarded as Sar-Say's In that moment, an unspoken agreement passed between human and alien. It was almost as though they could read each other's minds.

In the current situation, there was profit to be made, if only one had the wits to figure out how to make it. Of course, Heinz's definition of 'profit' did not correspond to Sar-Say's.

#

Chapter Thirteen

The plains and forests of Ssasfal, the original world of the Broa, rolled endlessly below the aircar as it made its way toward Valar, the ancient capital of both this world and all of Civilization. Overhead, Faalta, their yellow-white sun, cast its rays down from a purple sky. Yesterday's clouds had dissipated and it was possible to see the glow of the sun off the white beaches of the Larger Ocean far to the right of the aircar's flight path. The golds and reds of the vegetation below were carved into intricate geometric shapes, islands of color in the amber expanse of the great plain that ran east from the capital. The shapes were the work of generations of foresters at the order of the masters over whose domains Sar-Ganth was now flying.

Interspersed among the shrubbery were lakes and rivers, also sculpted to the taste of Those Who Rule. So ancient was the civilization that ruled Ssasfal that barely a square *fel* of planetary surface remained as nature had originally constructed it. Like all of Civilization, the masters molded their domains to suit their individual tastes, letting neither mountain, nor forest, nor desert thwart their desires.

Sar-Ganth, primate of the Sar-Dva Clan, looked down on the scene and considered the effort that had gone into taming this single world. Multiply that effort by several orders of magnitude and one began to comprehend the difficulties involved in running a galaxy-spanning civilization. Those difficulties must be resolved by Sar-Ganth and his compatriots. It was a burden placed on him by his ancestors and one he bore gladly. For, was it not the destiny of the Broa to bend every world to their will as they had Ssasfal? Why else would they have been given domain over so many stars visible in the night sky, and countless others too distant to be seen?

It had not always been thus. There were ancient legends of the days when stargates were new. The legends spoke of fire raining from the sky, turning whole worlds into radioactive wastes. Replacing those killed in such attacks had been the work of generations and the lessons taught had been well learned. Hard experience had shown that there could be but two classes of thinking beings in the universe: masters and subservients.

This led to a solution that was easy in concept, but extremely difficult in practice. Inhabited worlds discovered outside the bounds of Civilization were incorporated into the Broan realm whether they wished it or not. Often, the integration went quickly and with a reasonable expenditure of value. Occasionally, the aborigines resisted. Such stubbornness resulted in significant destruction being visited upon the miscreants before they bowed to the inevitable. Then there were the rare cases when a species proved too expensive to conquer. The only viable option for such cases was total annihilation.

Slowly, over millennia, the Race had worked its will on all within reach, using the stargates as both weapon and reward. Ssasfal had grown rich on the labor and resources of others, as had its people. They had become so rich that they were now utterly dependent on subservients for all but the most important tasks.

As their empire had grown, so too had Ssasfal's population. Not with masters, whose numbers rose slowly, but rather, with their servants and retainers. The last census had counted eight times as many subservients on the home world as masters. This abundance brought the masters a life of ease; which, Sar-Ganth considered, was not an unalloyed benefit.

There was a recent tendency among younger Broa to forsake the life of obligation adopted by Sar-Ganth's generation. He had nothing but disdain for these young drones. They spent their days lying in the sun, and nights in endless rounds of parties, celebrations, and when the females were in estrus, fornication.

True, the number of servants on the home world meant there was no need for a master to perform menial tasks. Those were best left to the unlimited supply of willing hands, claws, and tentacles. But being freed from mundane tasks brought with it a higher duty. There were few enough masters, and the shirkers caused Sar-Ganth additional work.

The power that Sar-Ganth wielded was beyond the imagining of his remote ancestors. He could destroy worlds with a word, although to do so would be a criminal waste of resources. Yet, even his power was not infinite. There were only so many periods in a day or cycles in a lifetime. They must be carefully rationed lest they evaporate before the task was done.

Which was why he was flying to Valar this morning.

His assistant, a Transian named Fos, had been very cryptic over the televisor, merely saying that his presence was required. That his communications were not secure was an article of faith with Sar-Ganth. Very few comm channels were.

"How long?" Sar-Ganth asked as a particularly blue lake passed beneath the aircar. As they banked to make a sweeping right turn, sunlight reflected skyward, turning the lake's surface into golden fire.

"We will be there in eight beats," came the reply from his Danian pilot. Dania's feathered inhabitants possessed the keenest eyesight and quickest reflexes of any species of which Sar-Ganth was familiar. As a result, its denizens were much prized as pilots.

#

The city of Valar appeared on the schedule his pilot predicted. The capital had begun life as a walled city more than twelve-gross cycles past. The walls had protected the inhabitants from the wild clans that roamed the North Plain, one of which had been predecessor to the current Sar-Dva Clan. The old wall was still maintained, having been restored in the previous century. Its usefulness long past, it served as a reminder of how far they had come since some long-forgotten scientific team developed the stargate.

There were rumors that the gates had not been the only means of star travel invented by the ancient Broa. Some legends spoke of ships that could move between stars as easily as their sea-going counterparts moved between harbors.

Sar-Ganth did not know whether he believed the legends. If true, then some leader among his ancestors had been wise to suppress such knowledge. The current social order rested on control of the gates. Any method so disorganized that a ship's captain could voyage wherever he wanted would destroy that order. Why, two subservient worlds might actually trade with one another without the knowledge of their masters!

Surrounding the Old City was a wall of a different kind. For a full *fel*, the ancient battlements were ringed by tall towers. These were built in many different styles, to comply with the individual tastes of the clans that erected them. There were glass and steel constructs; towers where antique wood or stone hid modern iron or titanium endoskeletons; towers of ancient brick erected in the traditional manner. The Inner Ring was where the true power of the Broa resided. It was the base from which Sar-Ganth and his compatriots oversaw the interests of their clans. The Old City within the wall was reserved for ceremonial occasions and for meetings of Those Who Rule.

Surrounding the ring of towers was another concentric wall, this one half the height of the old battlements. Beyond this lay a park-like swath of red and gold vegetation that served both as an esthetic and psychic barrier to what lay beyond the park.

The final concentric ring of Valar was a collection of low structures packed closely together, separated only by twisting footpaths and a few true roads. If there had ever been a plan for this outer ring, it had long since been abandoned to the entropy of urban sprawl.

The buildings in the Outer Ring were as varied in style as the towers of the Inner Ring. Beehive shapes predominated, but there were many twelves of variations. This sprawling outer belt represented Valar's workers' quarters, the part of the city where the subservients lived. No one knew how many of them there were, or from how many star systems they came. Only one thing was certain. Each being residing in the great slum served some Broan master.

Sar-Ganth barely noticed the workers' dwellings as his aircar passed over it. As the car descended like a swooping *avtar* in pursuit of prey, his eyes were fastened on the Sar-Dva Tower. At the last moment, his pilot brought the car to a quick hover, then lowered it to a wide landing stage high up the gold-and-silver structure. The engines barely quieted when the door slid back into its enclosure and Sar-Ganth stepped out into the brisk morning air. He caught a whiff of the city's odor before crossing to a drop shaft into the heart of the building.

                                         #

Fos was waiting for him when he reached his office. The little Transian's exoskeleton was polished to an ebon sheen and inlayed in an intricate pattern with sparkling jewels and colored stones that showed their possessor to be of a high caste. Sar-Ganth had once asked Fos about his decorations, but had long since forgotten the answer. The body decorations of a subservient, even one as useful as Fos, were beneath the ken of a Broa. He had more important matters with which to fill his mind.

It was enough to know that Fos was loyal to him. That was the strength of the Transians, a result of their pack-like social structure. Each member of the pack gave its loyalty to their leader, and if that leader happened to be of another species, the ingrained instinct did not seem to notice.

Sar-Ganth knuckle-walked to his work station and clambered up onto the resting frame. Arranging his arms and legs comfortably on the bars, he leaned forward and asked Fos, "So what is important enough to bring me in on a fine morning like this one?"

"My apologies, Clan Master. The news seemed urgent and confidential. Do you remember the auditor who went missing five cycles ago?"

Sar-Ganth scratched at himself with one long arm as he thought about it. "Vaguely. The Kas-Dor were accused of ambushing him at the Nala stargate, but nothing was ever proven. What have you learned to make this ancient mystery a pressing matter?"

"Apparently, Sar-Say has been located."

"That was the auditor's name?"

"Yes. He was traveling from Vith to Persilin onboard a Vithian ship when lost."

"But he has now been located? Where?"

"Perhaps I should have said that we have discovered he escaped the assassination attempt. He is being held prisoner."

"By whom?"

"A race of bipeds. They call themselves Vulcans. They may be holding Sar-Say on their planet of Shangri La."

A quick search by Sar-Ganth of his memory revealed no species, nor planet, by those names."

"Perhaps you should begin at the beginning," he said. His assistant recognized the sarcasm of his tone, but said nothing. Sarcasm was the least of a master's prerogatives.

Fos recounted his receipt of the information packet from Ssor-Fel, the Hunt Master of the Salefar sector. The packet spoke of an alien ship in the system of a species of tripeds known as the Voldar'ik. He quickly detailed the fact that these strange Vulcan creatures provided their hosts a number of sample Vithian power units, one of which had been heavily doused in danger pheromone.

Sar-Ganth signaled his understanding. "And this pheromone was traced to Sar-Say!"

"Yes, Clan Master," Fos replied, making the gesture of ascent peculiar to his species.

"So our accountant is being held by Vulcans! I assume you ran their biometrics through the Central Records."

"I did," Fos replied. "I could not find a match."

Sar-Ganth 'frowned.' That was impossible. Each subservient race had detailed records of their physiologies, psychologies, and cultures stored in the Ssasfal databases going back two-twelve generations. That Fos had been unable to identify these Vulcans was disturbing in the extreme. There could only be one explanation.

"So someone has discovered a planet and kept it a secret from Central Records?" he asked.

"That is what I surmised," Fos replied.

"You were correct in summoning me. Someone, it seems, has broken one of our most ancient covenants. Until we know who, this news is too sensitive to trust to the communications nets. How are we going to track these Vulcans down if they aren't in the database?"

"They visited this Klys'kra't on a trading mission. There must be other systems where they trade. A search program should uncover some trace of them."

"Excellent. Once we have discovered their trading partners, we can trap these elusive creatures. What makes their world valuable enough to take such a risk? Have the specialists get to work immediately and give me periodic reports as to our progress."

"Your orders will be followed, Clan Master."

#

Chapter Fourteen

Professor Jean-Pierre Landrieu enjoyed the late morning sun as he strolled down the Champs-Elysées toward the Eiffel Tower. A native Parisian, he saw the monument virtually every day of his life. Yet, he had only been to the top of the tower twice... once as a public school student, and again when he was courting his wife. Like a native New Yorker and the Statue of Liberty, the opportunity to visit his nation's most famous symbol just never seemed to arise. Not for the first time, he made a mental note to take his grandchildren up the monument, and having made it, let it slip from his consciousness as it had so many times before.

The trees lining the world's most famous avenue were budding with the first green of spring. That more than anything buoyed Landrieu's spirit. It had been a terrible winter. Paris had been buffeted by both snow and ice storms. Because the city fathers stubbornly refused to put up a weather dome, stating that it would ruin the city's historic skyline, Parisians had been exposed to the full fury of the elements for long, cold months.

There are just so many overcast days that a person can take, or so Pierre Landrieu believed. Of course, the misery of winter was what made the rebirth of spring so delightful.

As he walked, he scanned the famous names that lined the avenue. There was Fouquet's and the Copenhague Nordic restaurant, Charles Jourdan and Guerlain department stores. Some of the businesses on *Les Champs* went back to the 18th Century. Even those that were modern were hiding behind the ancient facades whose original owners had been dust for centuries.

Despite having lived there all is life, Landrieu often thought of Paris as an historical theme park, a city devoted to a past that never existed, whose inhabitants were all just little furry creatures who lived their lives for the benefit of the tourists. God knows, there had been little glory since France lost the contest for world cultural domination. The fact that a majority of French spoke Standard at home was bad enough. The fact that they spoke it with a British accent made Paris's historical pretenses difficult to maintain. He was as patriotic as the next Frenchman, but would it kill the city fathers to put in a few unobtrusive slidewalks?

He was contemplating the dilemma when he· reached his destination, the sidewalk café outside *Léon de Bruxelles'* restaurant. Sidling past a waiter who seemed to pay no attention to him, he spotted his quarry sitting at a table alone, watching the passersby. He threaded his way between tables and extended his hand.

"Mikhail, good to see you again!" he uttered in his own, near-perfect Standard.

"And you, Jean-Pierre," the Russian replied, standing to greet him. The two shook hands and then took their places with a scraping of chairs against cement.

Mikhail Vasloff reached for the wine bottle that decorated his and every other table, and poured red liquid into an empty glass, as well as refilling his own. Landrieu lifted the glass to his lips, made a show of first sniffing and then tasting, and pronounced the wine passable. According to the label, it was a Côtes de Bourg Bordeaux, but an uninspired vintage.

After the initial sip, both men sat back and regarded one another with something more than friendly interest, but less than calculated cunning.

"What brings you to Paris, Mikhail?" Landrieu finally asked. "Are you ready to accept that appointment to the institute which bears your name?"

Vasloff shook his head. "No, that would put me on the government payroll and place too many constraints on my activities."

"Which are?"

Vasloff laughed. "I'm here for a bit of mischief. You would do better not to know. I had some free time, so I thought I would check on progress. How goes the planning?"

"Very well," Landrieu replied. "After a slow start, we are beginning to get real projections and have begun to PERT chart all of the steps required to pull back from the stars. Just this week, we completed our simulation of the resources required to evacuate the colonies."

"What resources?" Vasloff asked. "You send the same colony ships that transported them to their God-forsaken worlds in the first place. You order them aboard, and you bring them home."

"It will not be that easy. For one thing, many of the colonists will refuse the order. That means we will need troops to enforce the evacuation, which will require additional ships. Also, there is the matter of the cleanup."

"Cleanup?"

"Surely you don't think we can just leave these abandoned worlds dotted with empty human cities? *Mon Dieux!* That would give away the game as quickly as if the Broa found a teeming human population. We are going to have to tear down the cities, then reseed the land to erase every trace of our presence."

"How many new ships do you estimate will be required to do the job right?" Vasloff asked.

"Several hundred, including some very large cargo haulers to handle the heavy machinery. The suggestion has been made that we pulverize every single manmade object on each world, including the bricks and mortar, and then dump the dust in the nearest ocean. You can imagine the size of the pulverizers needed."

"Obviously, you have thought it through more clearly than I," Vasloff replied. "Apparently, when the Coordinator staffed the Paris Institute, she knew what she was doing. What news of the Colorado Springs effort?"

"They are also making excellent progress in building a framework and timeline for their Plan of Conquest, or so I am told. Both institutes will be presenting preliminary presentations of our findings in another month or so."

"That fast?" Vasloff asked.

"Yes. We have a fairly detailed plan for making this system invisible to questing Broan probes. In addition to abandoning the interstellar colonies, we will need to develop communications technologies that do not advertise their presence... a return to land-based transmission lines and laser communications in space, for example. Once we have all returned to Earth, we will need to destroy our remaining starships. That will remove the temptation to resume exploration at some future date."

Vasloff frowned. "I had hoped to have more time to get the political situation in hand. We have a good grassroots demonstration effort, but we need more paid media."

"A problem with contributions?"

The Russian nodded. "We are running ten percent below projections. Not that the faithful aren't giving generously. It's just that we have entered the "old news" phase of the struggle. The shock is wearing off and people are returning to their daily concerns. We need something big to refocus attention and get donations up. I'm afraid I can't pull that off in a month. I need at least three."

"I have some small power to delay a decision, I suppose," Landrieu replied. "One of the advantages of being Director-General, you know. A quarter-year delay may be beyond my power, however. Those simpletons at Colorado Springs are pushing very hard for a decision. They have concluded, with some justification, I fear, that the Coordinator leans in their direction."

"Can Alan Fernandez assist in putting on the brakes?"

"I suppose, if he saw such a move to be in his best interest. Will he?"

"He will if I can get messages to the right people."

"I'm not so sure. Fernandez is reveling in his control of Sar-Say. Every time Fernandez issues one of his reports, he frightens people. The pictures the Broa paints continue to be unpleasant. The more he tells us of his species, the bigger monsters they seem."

"That is merely Sar-Say trying to frighten us into submission. I don't think the Broa are monsters," Mikhail Vasloff said, taking another sip of wine. "I think they are more like us than we care to admit."

Jean-Pierre followed Vasloff's example. When he set his wine glass down, he said, "I find that a startling statement."

Vasloff made a gesture of dismissal. "Don't get me wrong. I have spent my life warning against the dangers of star travel, and the Broa are the epitome of what I feared. However, if the situation were reversed, if we controlled a million-star empire and the Broa one lone system, we would probably be hunting them down. At least, my commissar ancestors would have done so, and human beings have not changed very much since their day."

Landrieu nodded. "Considering some of the things we humans have done to our fellows, I suppose they don't look so bad after all."

Vasloff raised his glass and clinked with Jean-Pierre, then said, "And that thought is perhaps the scariest of all!"

#

"Three months delay?" Mark yelped. "What's the matter, isn't Paris keeping up?"

"Apparently not," Dexter Hamlin replied. "It appears some political pressure has been applied to slow down the summer review. You can probably guess where it is coming from."

"Mikhail Vasloff and *Terra Nostra*!"

"Correct on the first guess."

"What are we going to do about it?" Mark asked.

"Do? We are going to do nothing about it. We are going to continue our job and be even more ready when the time comes to go up against Landrieu and his coterie of ass gazers!"

Mark knew Hamlin as the most courteous of human beings. For him to engage in profanity was unheard of. He must really be fuming!

"Give me an update on our progress this week."

Mark's usefulness as a tour director having withered away, he had been appointed Director's Special Assistant. Though impressive, the title basically meant they didn't know what else to do with him.

He knew some astronomy, the result of his hobbies and his service on the astronomy team on the Crab Nebula expedition, but was no expert. His knowledge of the Broan language was good, but did not approach Lisa's level of skill. Besides, most of the Broan data was being translated by computer now. The pseudo-simian tongue was basically a trade language. As such, it was logical, making it easy for a computer to translate the words, if not the nuances.

Being unsuited for anything else, he had been assigned to "assist" Director Hamlin. He did so by keeping track of the wide-ranging studies and once each week, preparing both written and verbal summaries.

Mark began his report with the astronomy team's efforts. They were working off observations of the starfield above Brinks Base and had identified fifty-plus systems within a couple hundred light-years of Brinks that might be inhabited. These were mostly G- and K-class stars of sufficient age and stability to give intelligent life time to evolve.

The Alien Technology Team was deep into reviewing the technology being pulled out of the *Ruptured Whale.* No one had yet found any show stoppers. Broan technology was different from human, but since both obeyed the same laws of physics, it was mostly a matter of learning new ways to do familiar things. A toilet is a toilet, regardless of the physiology of the species using it.

With the *Whale* out of commission, Mark had taken a trip to White Sands Shipyard to see how its replacement was coming. There he and Dan Landon had gone out for a quiet steak and beer together, both to hash over old times and to bring Mark up to speed on progress.

The White Sands engineers were nearly finished with their design of a Type Seven Broan freighter, complete with hidden armaments and with Broan style controls. The only thing they needed to complete the job was the final data from the *Whale*'s dissection. While they waited, they had begun work on a large freighter of a class they had observed in orbit about Klys'kra't.

Mark was surprised when Landon casually remarked that they would be laying the keel of the Type Seven freighter at the end of the week.

"How can you build a ship you haven't finished designing yet?"

Landon took a sip of his beer and said, "We mostly know what we are doing. It's a risk, but one I've judged to be acceptable."

"What if they find something that requires you to start over?"

"Then we go back to the workscreen and start over. Have you ever heard of the Manhattan Project?"

"When they built the weather dome over Manhattan Island and the East River?"

"No, the other one. The first atom bomb."

"I've seen the standard lessons in school."

"They were in a hurry. They started building this huge industrial facility in Oak Ridge, Tennessee before they knew what they were going to put in it. In war you do things you would never do in peacetime."

"I suppose," Mark replied.

"That wasn't the biggest risk they took. When it came time to build the machinery, they couldn't find enough copper for the wiring. So, they requisitioned several billion credits worth of silver from the treasury and used it instead."

Mark reported on his trip to White Sands and then continued his summary for the Director. Obtaining a Broan database continued to be their first priority, of course. Just about everything depended on it. However, the Stargate Acquisition Team had also made progress.

Like exo-biology had been prior to star travel, stargate physics was essentially a hypothetical science. The principle was related to hyperdrive physics, but not exactly the same. Despite the team's progress, they were still predicting that a couple of decades would be required to put theory into practice.

The problem was that humanity might not have a couple of decades.

#

Chapter Fifteen

Sar-Say lounged on the sofa and listened to Gus Heinz go on endlessly about the problems of the interstellar import/export business. The two of them were seated in front of the glass wall in the Harvard Faculty Club, and save for the omnipresent security men at the door, they might have been two businessmen enjoying a drink after a hard day at the office.

Except, of course, one of the businessmen was a pseudo-simian who did not consume alcohol. In front of Sar-Say sat a tall glass of orange juice, for which he had developed a fondness.

"But surely you utilize some form of inventory control to ensure that you don't run short of product," Sar-Say said in response to Heinz's explanation of how he had been shorted in the last shipment from Avalon, one of Earth's interstellar colonies.

"You can place your order, but in an economy of scarcity, which *curaline* is, you don't always get your orders filled. Plus there is the delay between when you order and when you discover the product will be short. Since communications are carried by starships without fixed routes or time tables, it can sometimes take months to discover you won't be able to fulfill customer requirements."

"Why not order twice what you need, then?"

"Can't," Heinz replied, slashing the air with his hands for punctuation. "If they manage to fill my order one hundred percent, it would bankrupt me."

Sar-Say nodded as though the dry technical details of Heinz's business were the most fascinating thing he had ever heard. *Curaline* was some sort of miracle drug refined from an Avalonian plant and sold for enough to make transporting it across light-years economically feasible.

This was one of the private conferences that Sar-Say had suggested the night of his first public reception. They had been meeting sporadically for the past six months and had become comfortable with one another. Ostensibly, the meetings were to increase Sar-Say's understanding of human society. Why humans would want him to learn more about them was counter-intuitive, but they claimed it made it easier for him to answer their questions. In truth, he had gained considerable practical knowledge from the businessman, as well as the half-dozen other outsiders with whom he was allowed to speak.

Sar-Say looked forward to the talks for a number of reasons, not the least of which was that they were held in the lounge of the Faculty Club, and not his prison cell. Director Fernandez said that it was good for him to get out once in a while, and Sar-Say agreed.

Then there was Sar-Say's primary motive. Ever since Klys'kra't, he had been working on a new plan to escape human captivity. The problem was that he required the assistance of a small number of human beings to make the plan work.

Of all his conversation mates, Heinz appeared the best candidate for what he needed done. If all went well, he would be back in Civilization within a couple of years. If it did not, he would likely be dead.

"If communications via starship are so difficult, why not invest in your own starship to regularize traffic to and from Avalon? There would seem to be a need, and therefore, profits to be made."

"Do you know how much it costs to operate a starship?" the businessman asked.

"Surely there are others who have needs similar to yours. You could get rich selling them services made possible by owning your own ship."

Heinz shook his head. "I'm no transportation magnate. Heading out into interstellar space requires resources that are expensive to obtain and maintain. Hell, a trained spacer makes twice the money of a unionized robot truck monitor! The investment has a high fixed cost. One missed shipment, for whatever reason, and you are bankrupt."

"But you *could* hire a starship if you wanted to?" Sar-Say persisted.

"Could and would," Heinz replied, "if I had the need."

"How does one go about such a thing? I know how we do it in Civilization. Surely it cannot be much different here."

Heinz went on to explain how one contracted to charter a starship. About the only people who did so were potential colonists en route to a newly discovered world. In such a case, thousands of families pooled their life savings to cover a cash down payment, then pledged a certain portion of their new colony's revenues over twenty years to pay the remainder of the cost of being transported to their world.

Of course, as Gus explained, the colony ships were the biggest starships ever constructed. They had to be. Once a colony was planted, it could be ten years before they saw another ship. This meant that everything they needed for survival must be delivered in the same trip.

"Yes," Sar-Say agreed. "A colony ship would be much too large for your purposes."

"Damned straight! My cargo is only a couple of meters cubed, and it still takes all of my pull at the bank to get a loan to cover the cost of procurement and shipping. Those robber baron ship captains know when they have you by the short hairs."

Sar-Say had not heard the idiom before, but understood the comment from context.

He asked, "How many private starships are there in human space?"

Heinz responded. "Hundred or so, none of which charge less than an arm-and-a-leg."

With that, Gus Heinz returned to cursing whoever it was that had been unable to fulfill his current order. Sar-Say hid his impatience at the turn of conversation, which was in the direction he definitely did not want it to go. Finally, Heinz's voice cracked and stopped talking to take a sip of beer to restore moisture to his mouth. The beer had gone flat while he was jawing about his troubles.

Finally, Sar-Say glanced at the chronometer on the wall and said, "I'm afraid our time is up. Dr. Fernandez becomes angry with me if I am late for one of his research sessions. Thank you for speaking with me." With that, he extended his arm to shake hands in the human manner.

Heinz extended his own arm, and five-fingers entwined with six. Heinz's expression, which had been sour as a result of his complaints, suddenly turned neutral. Sar-Say felt a moment of panic. However, as they broke their grip, Heinz smoothly slid his right hand into the pocket of his jacket. They exchanged a few more pleasantries, then the business man got up and escorted Sar-Say to the security men waiting to take him back to his cell. He himself continued onward and out into the open air.

At no time did Heinz mention the paper that Sar-Say had passed him during the handshake, a fact the Broa found encouraging.

#

Each of the three institutes studying different aspects of the Broa problem hosted the quarterly progress reviews in turn. The Winter Review had been held in Paris and the Spring Review in Colorado Springs. The Summer Review, originally scheduled for June, but postponed until late August at the request of the World Coordinator, was to be held in Boston. Due to the proximity of Boston to Toronto, there would be several members of parliament in attendance, as well as a larger than normal contingent from the World Coordinator's staff.

Both the Gibraltar Institute and the Vasloff Institute were well along in their studies and the Summer Review would be a preview of the plans to be submitted to parliament in the fall. The final reports would trigger an official inquiry, culminating in a vote in parliament to select the proper course of action. Optimists were predicting a decision before the end of the year. Those with experience in the parliamentary process were predicting a decision the following summer.

As on their last trip to Boston, Mark Rykand and Lisa Arden landed at Logan Regional Transport Hub and took a water taxi across Boston Harbor to their hotel on the Long Wharf. The glass-and-steel structure, the fifth hotel to occupy the site, overflowed the water and extended on pilings out into the harbor.

Mark gazed upward as their boat cruised beneath the structure en route to the loading pier. The hotel floor in this section was transparent in order that the hotel guests could see the water. From beneath, it appeared that the bustling crowd strode on air as they hurried to and fro. It also allowed, Mark noted, boat passengers to get a peek up the dresses of the occasional women who passed directly overhead. Either the women were unaware of this fact, or else it did not concern them.

They were met at the pier by the usual coterie of bellboys and greeters. That the hotel could employ people to perform this function, rather than the usual automated baggage carts, was a hint of their room prices. Mark's personal wealth insulated him from such concerns, but most of the conference attendees were staying farther inland, where prices were more reasonable.

Checking in and getting settled took another twenty minutes. Mark spent half that time lounging on the bed while Lisa busied herself in the bathroom. When she emerged, he asked, "Well, we've arrived. What would you like to do now?"

The two word response did not surprise him.

"Go shopping!"

#

The Summer Conference was held in Harvard's extensive conference center. In addition to banquet halls and a commercial-size auditorium, there were numerous smaller rooms where the conferees could break into groups and argue with one another.

As soon as they reached the center, Lisa made a beeline to the Alien Assessment Group, dedicated to the study of Broan culture and mores, with an eye for cataloging their weaknesses. Based on what Sar-Say had told them and what they had observed on the Crab Nebula expedition, the group had made considerable progress.

It would have been natural to assume that any species capable of achieving dominance over a million star systems possessed godlike powers. Yet, if the Broa were godlike, they were gods with feet of clay. The AAG had catalogued dozens of weaknesses which might prove advantageous in the coming conflict.

Prime among these was their birth rate, which was barely breakeven. For thousands of years their population had been static, or at best, growing slowly. In fact, their empire had grown faster than their population, stretching their span of control nearly to the breaking point. As a result, thousands of worlds did not see the overlords for decades at a time, and largely conducted their affairs autonomously.

In addition to being spread too thinly, the Broa had a tendency toward internecine warfare. Some researchers maintained that this was not surprising. After all, the Broa held total power within the Sovereignty, which made the acquisition of territory a zero sum game. To gain influence and property, a Broa must necessarily do so at the expense of some other Broa.

The Broa had dozens of other quirks that might prove useful to humanity. Their small numbers made them inattentive to much of their far flung empire. Nor did the birth rate seem to be solely to blame for this problem. Careful analysis of what little data they possessed suggested that not every Broa was involved in the administration of their empire.

Indeed, some statisticians maintained that only small subset of the Broan population, a civil service of sorts, actually ruled their subject worlds. This seriously exacerbated their span of control problems and led to some favorable conditions from the viewpoint of humanity.

One of the most positive aspects of Broan inattentiveness was the fact that news traveled slowly and unreliably between the million subservient star systems. This gave everyone hope that they could slip into some out-of-the-way system, bargain for that system's planetary database, and slip out again undetected.

While Lisa went off to her group meeting, Mark popped in to sessions at random to see how things were going. He spent the morning visiting small rooms where teams of academics argued with one another over minutia that might prove important one day.

That evening, Director Fernandez hosted a banquet for the conference attendees. This was the official kickoff event to the Summer Review. After giving a speech of welcome, Fernandez announced that the first plenary session would begin the following morning, with Director Jean-Pierre Landreu giving his institute's report. He would be followed by Mark's boss, with the Colorado Springs report, followed by someone Fernandez described as a "surprise guest speaker."

There was considerable murmuring among the tables of diners at that last point, but Fernandez refused to say more. His only response was, "No more business tonight. Please eat as much as you want, but drink responsibly. We want everyone sharp tomorrow. The time is fast approaching when decisions will have to be made, and we need everyone at their best in supporting those decisions. It would be a shame to doom the Earth to perpetual slavery just because someone was hung over at a critical moment!".

The admonition sobered the crowd considerably, reminding them of the weighty responsibility they carried. It was also a reminder that though their approaches to the problem of the Broan Sovereignty were different, their goal was the same: the long-term survival of the human race.

#

Chapter Sixteen

The large theater-like lecture hall was half-full when Mark arrived for the opening session of the Winter Review. He scanned the crowd slowly, looking for Lisa's distinctive blonde curls. When he spotted them, he moved down the nearest aisle toward where she was sitting.

Beside her was a familiar figure.

"Mark!" Lisa exclaimed as he sidled his way to the empty seat to her right. "Look who's here."

"Hello, Dieter," he said, holding out his hand.

Dieter Pavel rose to his feet and shook Mark's hand. He had first met Pavel aboard PoleStar. Pavel had been the Coordinator's representative.

"Hello, Mark," Pavel replied.

"How are things in Toronto?"

"Getting interesting. There is a lot of lobbying going on behind the scenes. You would think we were having a general election, or something."

"What's the consensus?" Lisa asked.

"There isn't one," Pavel answered. "Opinion seems to be tracking ideology. The conservatives want to go kill them all as soon as we can gather enough ships. The progressives are for making it didn't happen. The moderates are of both minds, as usual. I expect whatever comes out of this conference, plus the debate in the fall, to solidify support in all three camps... support for what they already believe, that is."

"Typical," Mark snorted.

Pavel shrugged. "Human beings are human beings, Mark. They've responded this way since long before Caesar's critics had a few sharp things to say to him on the Ides of March. They will probably respond this way in One Million, A.D., if we get that far."

Mark nodded. "I love mankind, but can't stand people!" he quoted.

"Exactly," Pavel said, recognizing the literary allusion.

As they spoke, the principals for the conference filed out onto the stage. The arrangements were standard for this sort of event: A long table to one side for the participants to sit, an ornate wooden lectern for the presenters, and an oversize holocube that was already flickering with interior static.

Mark and Dieter took their seats to Lisa's right and left. It seemed almost like old times.

Dr. Fernandez stepped to the lectern and after twiddling with the controls of the hidden holo projector, he pressed a switch.

Instead of the sound of a gavel banging wood coming from the overhead speakers, a short refrain of the Harvard fight song wafted over the audience. Slowly, over a period of seconds, a myriad of individual conversations ceased and the audience turned their attention to the stage.

"Good morning," Fernandez said, his amplified words issuing from the same speakers. "I hereby call the Winter Plenipotentiary Session of the Broan Institutes to order. I hope all of you are seated comfortably and have taken care of necessities before sitting down. It is going to be a long day. We will break for half-an-hour at 12:00 for a quick lunch, and will then get back to it."

He paused for dramatic effect and then got to the meat of his remarks.

"Ladies and gentlemen, we are here on a vital mission. Out among the stars is a threat greater than any we have previously faced. The facts are these: We know about the Broa, but they are unaware of our existence. What do we do? As assigned by the World Coordinator, we have two teams fleshing out two competing plans. The Colorado Springs team has been assigned the task of figuring out an offensive strategy. The Paris team is working on a defensive strategy. My own team is studying a single specimen of the enemy to obtain insights in support of both plans.

"Over the next two days, we will hear reports from both groups. Keep in mind that these are constructive suggestions that those reporting have been ordered to evaluate. Whether you agree or disagree, it is your duty to give these speakers your undivided and polite attention. If you find that you must have a conversation with the people around you, then I request that you take it out into the foyer.

"Since Colorado Springs led off the Spring Review, our first speaker this morning will be Jean-Pierre Landrieu, Director-General of the Institute in Paris. Director Landrieu will give you a rundown on what his team has accomplished since last we met.

"Director Landrieu!"

\#

A tall silver-haired man with an indefinable quality that labeled him "French" strode to the lectern and spent a few seconds adjusting the controls. Suddenly, a picture formed in the holocube. It showed the logo of the Paris Institute, a stylized white dove with an olive branch dangling from one closed claw.

"Bonjour," he said. "I would like to thank Director Fernandez for hosting this meeting. I think all of us will learn a great deal as this is to be our penultimate act before we submit our respective plans to parliament. Later, each working group will set up shop in the breakout rooms and invited guests will be able to ask detailed questions of the experts. My intention this morning is not to get into every specific of our plan to make humanity safe, but rather to give you an overview. As Director Fernandez said, it is our mission at the Paris Institute to come up with a method to avoid a direct confrontation with the Broa.

"I have heard some refer to the mission of the Paris Institute as 'figuring out how to hide from the monsters.' The implication is that a defensive strategy is somehow dishonorable, even cowardly, too effeminate to be considered by the more macho among us.

"Such a reaction is normal human behavior. For all of our history, at the sound of trouble, the women have grabbed up the children and run away, while the men have grabbed their spears and charged toward the sound of battle. It is our species' natural fight or flight reflex, and it has served us well.

"But giving in to an unthinking reflex can also get you killed. If the sound of battle consists of the chatter of machine guns, or the whine of an electromagnetic dart thrower, the men would do better to grab up their spears and follow the women and children. For there are situations when one finds himself hopelessly outmatched. Better to fight another day than to make a useless charge at an enemy you have no hope of defeating.

"The first thing we at the Paris Institute considered was whether we have any hope of defeating the Broa. Here is what we found:

"According to Sar-Say, and confirmed by the Crab Nebula expedition, the Broan Sovereignty consists of approximately one million stars spread across the Orion Arm of the Milky Way. Like all really large statistics, one million is a number that is difficult to comprehend. Oh, we speak blithely of millions and billions, but how many of us can truly visualize such a large number? In truth, we count much as our ancestors did: *one, two, three, many.*

"Let us take some time to understand what it means that the Broa have conquered a million star systems. Sar-Say has told us that they prefer their worlds less populated than Earth, so assuming each subject world supports one billion beings – Sar-Say's estimate – we face *one thousand trillion* sentient beings! To put that in perspective, ladies and gentlemen, that is a population *one hundred thousand* times our own!

"Consider, the military power inherent in such a population. Even if each of our ships destroys one hundred Broan ships in battle, their fleet will still be a thousand times larger than ours. If they invade the Solar System, they could easily devote an entire battle fleet to each of our ships, and still have hundreds of other fleets available for the assault on Earth.

"If that doesn't frighten you, consider some additional statistics. Assuming that their worlds average the same surface area as Earth, their trillions of people live on 1.5×10^{14} square kilometers of land. They sail 3.6×10^{14} square kilometers of ocean. What of their industrial power? They mine enough iron in a century to construct a full scale model of the Earth. They generate enough power in the same period to vaporize our world. I am not speaking of merely scorching the surface as we once feared we would do ourselves during the nuclear era. I am speaking of boiling the whole thing down until there is not so much as a pebble remaining.

"I hope these examples have given you some idea as to the size of our challenge, ladies and gentlemen. Speaking of going to war against the Broa is like declaring war on an earthquake. It is as though the people of Pompeii assembled their legions to march on Vesuvius.

"In our arrogance, we human beings do not like to admit there are forces in this universe against which we are powerless. Unfortunately, such forces do exist. Sometimes the only defense is to get out of the way. This, ladies and gentlemen, is one of those times!"

Director Landrieu paused for dramatic effect and to sip from a glass of water. He put the water down and looked out over the audience, judging the effect his words were having, before he continued:

"We cannot hope to defeat the Broa. Our only hope of survival is to get out of their way. It is the mission of the Paris Institute to figure out how to do that.

"I am here today to tell you that we have succeeded in our mission!"

#

A low murmur flowed across the audience like a wave hitting a beach. Landrieu pressed a control on the lectern and a three dimensional flowchart appeared in the cube.

"This, ladies and gentlemen, is our plan. To avoid the attention of the Broa, we must lower our profile in the universe. To do that, we will have to abandon our interstellar colonies and substantially reduce the electromagnetic noise we broadcast into space."

Fernandez went on to explain that each time humanity planted a colony in another star system, the probability that they would be discovered by the pseudo-simians doubled. Not only did multiple human occupied star systems increase the likelihood of a Broan ship or probe stumbling across them, but the colonies broadcast electronic noise to the heavens. He asked the audience to visualize human space as a white spot glowing in the blackness of space, a spot that had been expanding and brightening over the last couple of generations.

Landrieu highlighted a different section of the flow chart.

"We also must reduce our own electromagnetic signature here in the Solar System. This planet is the focus of a radio bubble that has now expanded to a thousand light-years in diameter, and which now encompasses several thousand stars. The bubble sweeps past more stars each year. Sooner or later, one of those stars will be ruled by the Broa.

"Unfortunately, barring the invention of a time machine, we can do nothing about past sins. Somewhere out there, episodes of *I Love Lucy, The Honeymooners,* and *The Howdy Doody Show* are sweeping starward, ready to be picked up by a Broan eavesdropping station." Landrieu halted and smiled at the audience. "I presume you North Americans know those names. Being French, I would have chosen different examples.

"However, the original broadcasts were relatively low power and the strength of these signals is very weak after so many years. As you can see from the diagram…" The holocube flashed to reveal a different colored chart. "The power level of much of what was broadcast by our ancestors has dropped below the level of the cosmic background radiation or has been absorbed by interstellar gas and dust.

"However, the radio noise we ourselves pump skyward is a different matter. We broadcast much more powerful beams at the stars and at frequencies that penetrate gas and dust. These signals are dangerous to us. While we cannot call back our own signals any more than we can call back those of our ancestors, we must strive to limit future emissions to the lowest level reasonably attainable. Therefore, our institute will propose a complete overhaul of our planet's electromagnetic infrastructure to eliminate such emissions."

Landrieu reviewed the steps to reduce humankind's footprint in the universe. They involved a return to the days when electronic signals traveled via copper wire and fiber optic cable. No signal exceeding 100 milliwatts would be allowed at any frequency able to penetrate the ionosphere. For space communications, only comm lasers would be used, and those carefully regulated to prevent beam dispersal.

The timeline for completing the pullback from the stars would be set at twenty years, and when the evacuation ended, each of the 250 ships needed to accomplish the task would be destroyed.

"So long as we are able to travel to other stars, some percentage of humankind will do just that. To prevent a foolish individual from striking out for the Deep Black, we will have to eliminate their capability to do so. That means we must forego starships."

There was much more to Director Landrieu's talk. He spoke of new laws to be passed and basic rights to be sacrificed in the pursuit of safety. It was 12:15 hours when his presentation finally wound down.

"That is what we of the Paris Institute will present to parliament in the fall," Landrieu said in closing. Thank you for listening. I believe it is now time for lunch."

#

Chapter Seventeen

Mark's boss was next on the agenda. As is usual at such meetings, the moderator's plea to limit the meal to half an hour meant that it took 45 minutes to reassemble a quorum. By the time the principals returned to the stage, three-eighths of the auditorium seats were filled.

Noticeable among those missing was Dieter Pavel.

"Where's your friend?" Mark asked Lisa as the two of them resumed their seats. Lunch had been a hurried affair at the university's main dining hall.

"He had work to do," she replied, "since you wouldn't take him up on his offer."

At the break, Pavel had offered to host the two of them at one of Boston's better restaurants. Mark refused, citing time constraints. He suggested that Pavel accompany them, but Dieter begged off.

"Sorry, but it would have taken too long. I need to be here when my boss speaks."

"That's okay," Lisa replied. "I accepted his invitation to dinner. You're invited, too, of course."

"I wonder," Mark mused, reflecting on his past rivalry with Pavel.

Mark unclipped the datacom from his belt while Lisa rooted around in the oversize handbag she carried. She extracted her com unit after a few seconds. Both of them keyed for the briefing books the Gibraltar Institute had prepared for the conference. The classic view of the Rock of Gibraltar from the land side was instantly displayed on their screens. The identical logo shimmered in the holocube on the stage.

After the audience settled down, Director Fernandez stepped to the lectern and introduced his colleague from Colorado Springs. Director Hamlin strode to the center of the stage.

"Ladies and Gentlemen, I would like to thank Alan Fernandez for his hospitality this week. He has kept us occupied and fed us well. I would also like to welcome the Members of Parliament and the representatives of the Coordinator. And I would be remiss if I failed to acknowledge the hard work put forth by the members of my own team to get ready for this meeting.

"Friends, I am here today to share with you the progress we have made in plotting a proactive strategy for ending the Broan threat. Jean-Pierre did me a favor this morning when he outlined the size of the Sovereignty for you. That means I do not have to plow the same ground.

"Jean-Pierre was correct in his main point. We cannot fight them head on. If we had every army there ever was at our disposal, they would be woefully inadequate to launch a frontal assault against the Broa.

"Therefore, let us stipulate that the Broan behemoth is so large that we are like the mouse who accidentally finds himself in the elephant's cage. He is frightened to be there and spends all of his time trying to keep from being crushed by the elephant's careless steps. However, being alert to danger is not the same as being so frightened that one loses one's ability to think.

"Thinking, ladies and gentlemen, is what we have been doing these many months in Colorado Springs. I am here today to brief you on some of our conclusions.

"As Director Landrieu has stated, the most important thing we must safeguard is our anonymity. Should the Broa ever discover the location of Sol, we will lose the war before it has barely begun. Thus, safeguarding the location of Earth must be our first and overriding priority. All of our plans have taken this point into account. We have designed multiple layers of safeguards into our plans to prevent the Broa from discovering where we are to be found in the galaxy. In fact, we have established an entire section that does nothing else.

"It is important that we treat the Broa with respect, but that we not let that respect grow into unreasoning fear. No matter how great their power, the pseudo-simians are not gods sitting atop Mt. Olympus, ready to launch lightning bolts down on any mortal who displeases them. They may be the elephant, and we the hapless mouse, but we are not helpless against them. In studying them, we have noted a number of frailties — weaknesses we can exploit, if only we choose to do so.

"I can hear the questions going through your heads even now. 'What weaknesses?' you ask. 'They are lords and masters of more than a million suns!'

"That very fact points to the first of their frailties. The Broa have built an empire that is impressive in its scope and duration. At first glance, their conquests make them appear so powerful that the only sensible thing for us to do is lie down and let someone throw dirt over us. However, first impressions are not necessarily accurate.

Hamlin smiled. "I am put in mind of something one of my old professors once told me. 'Dex, lad,' he said. 'When faced with an insurmountable problem, sometimes it helps to expand the scope until the solution becomes obvious.'

"*Think*, ladies and gentlemen. We view the Broa as gigantic because we are seeing them from the vantage point of the mouse as we stare upward at the great gray mass towering above us. But size is relative. If one looks at the Broa from a different vantage point, say that of the galaxy as a whole, they do not seem very large at all. In fact, they become merely a bigger mouse.

"Astronomers long argued over whether the probability of life among the stars was high or low, and whether or not the development of intelligence is routine. Our own early explorations answered the first part of that question when we discovered so many terrestrial-class worlds suitable for colonization.

"We have Sar-Say to thank for answering the second part of the ancient SETI debate. Judging from the size of the Sovereignty, we now estimate the likelihood of an intelligent species arising on any world possessing an oxygen atmosphere to be approximately 10 percent.

"When one considers the 100 billion stars in this galaxy alone, and 100 billion galaxies beyond our own, the number of intelligent races in the universe must be truly astronomical! In fact, some of my specialists have argued that intelligent life *must* arise on a terrestrial world, given sufficient time.

"The fact that the Broa have conquered a million species is impressive, but think of all the races they *have not conquered!* Given the target rich environment in which they find themselves, one must question why they stopped at a mere million stars? Why leave a billion or so other races in the galaxy unmolested?

"The answer is obvious, is it not? They have conquered as much territory as they can hold. Having gorged themselves on a feast of stars, they now lie bloated, moaning from the resulting bellyache. What then, are the factors that are holding them back?

"I submit the primary limit to their power is their population. According to Sar-Say, and from data we obtained at Klys'kra't, the number of Broa is likely less than the total population of Earth. They have a million planets to colonize, yet they cannot reproduce sufficiently to fill even their home world!"

The director reached for a hidden glass of water and slowly sipped while watching the implications sink in. There was a general muttering in the audience. When the murmur died away, Dexter Hamlin continued:

"The Broa are conquerors with a low fertility rate and they are prone to infighting, which to judge by the circumstances of our first contact with them, must depress their population even further. I submit they have long since reached their comfortable span-of-control, and in their avarice, have gone well beyond. What is our evidence for this conclusion? The Voldar'ik had not seen their planetary master in several years, nor did they consider that in the least remarkable.

"Yet, with fewer Broa than humans, how is it that they are able to hold so many other races in bondage? What makes them such potent conquerors? Why do a thousand-trillion sophonts meekly pay homage to these infertile little monkeys?"

"The stargates!" someone yelled from the front row.

"Precisely," Hamlin answered back. "The stargates!"

"The Broa are a one-trick elephant. It is a very good trick, but still just a trick. They are able to keep their subject species in line by essentially imprisoning them in their home star systems. If you are a good slave, if you meet your production quotas, if you do not make trouble, then perhaps you will be allowed to trade with your neighbors. Assert your independence or cross the masters in any way, and suddenly your stargate doesn't work and your sky fills with Broan warships.

"The stargates are the lever the Broa use to multiply their power a million-fold. Having identified the source of their power, we can design a strategy to use against them. That strategy includes military action within the Sovereignty to be sure, but is not primarily military in nature.

"I tell you here and now that we do not plan a general attack on the Sovereignty. My colleague from Paris was correct when he said to do so would be suicidal. Nor do we propose to launch a direct assault on the Broa themselves. Some have suggested that we bombard their home worlds from space with the biggest bombs which we are capable of manufacturing. I submit to you that were we to do so, we would not only be guilty of immorality, but we would be making a dreadful mistake.

"Their control of the stargates is what holds their subjects in thrall, and that is where we must strike at them. We propose to bring down the Broa by breaking their monopoly on star travel within the Sovereignty. We will do this by giving their captive species the secret of the stardrive!"

#

Flannigan's had started life a century earlier as a typical Irish pub. Over the decades, its owners had taken it upscale, until it eventually relocated to the two hundredth floor of one of Boston's tallest buildings. It was *the* most expensive restaurant in a town of expensive restaurants.

"My, Lisa, you look lovely this evening," Dieter Pavel said as Lisa and Mark left the elevator and strode to where he waited in front of the entrance. He leaned over and kissed her hand.

"Thank you, Dieter. You are very handsome yourself."

"Good evening, Mark."

"Evening, Dieter."

"Shall we go in?" he asked, gesturing to the intricately carved crystal door leading into the restaurant.

The Maitre d' led them to a window table with a spectacular view of the city and the bay. It was spectacular, that is, when not obscured by evening mist, which was the case this evening. All that was apparent through the glass was a multicolored haze backlit by a few nearby towers, dimly glimpsed.

A steady stream of waiters and stewards visited their table to clear away the extra plates, deliver hot bread, then to offer them the wine list. Dieter performed the ceremonies of sniffing the cork and sampling the vintage. When he professed himself satisfied, the steward poured each of them a glass.

"So," Pavel said. "To what should we toast?"

"Long life," Lisa said.

"Safety," Mark replied.

"To long life and safety it is."

After clinking their glasses, all three of them drank.

"So, Dieter," Mark said, "where did you go during the afternoon session?"

"I had to talk to some people," Pavel replied unhelpfully. "I understand I missed quite a show."

"Director Hamlin did seem to get his point across," Lisa agreed. "It took ten minutes to quiet the crowd after he sprang his surprise on them."

"Give the slaves starships? I must say, I would never have thought of that. Instead of trying to conquer the Sovereignty, we sow dissension and let it come apart on its own. I wish I had been there to hear the details."

"It's simple, really," Lisa said. "We spread our stardrive technology to as many systems as possible, then sever the stargate links to the Broan home world and centers of power, bottling up their fleet. In the ensuing confusion, revolutions break out all across the Sovereignty, complicating the Broan problem to the point where they won't have any resources left to bother us."

"Do you really think the slaves will revolt?"

Mark said, "Why not? They are intelligent beings. Let's say you lived at the bottom of a well and your neighbor kept you in line by threatening to drop rocks on your head. What would you do if someone suddenly dropped you a ladder?"

"Delivering the ladder could be a problem," Dieter mused. "How do we flood the Sovereignty with tens of thousands of *agents provocateurs* and expect to keep our secret? Some of them will inevitably be captured. Or do you expect the cyanide pill strategy to be one hundred percent effective?"

"No," Lisa said. Her expression revealed how she felt about the prospect of suicide upon capture.

"Then how do you get the information into the hands of the slaves without risking Earth?"

"Trojan horses," she replied.

"I beg your pardon?"

"Derelicts," Mark said as he bit into a warm breadstick. He savored the taste for a moment. The quality of the food made the prices on the menu seem reasonable. "It is doubtful we would get very far if we tried to deliver the specifications in person. For one thing, 'Beware Greeks bearing gifts' is probably a universal sentiment. So we do it all by remote control.

"We build hundreds or even thousands of small scout-size starships, complete with working generators and the plans to make more in their computers. Nothing obvious, mind you, just the sort of thing you would find in a repair manual. The ships will be designed for a fictional species, complete with photographs of loved ones on the bulkheads.

"Once we obtain a planetary database and figure out who is what in the Sovereignty, we transport these Trojan horses to carefully selected stars and release them. We aim them to pass through the heart of the target system at a velocity guaranteed to get them noticed. When the locals intercept and board, they discover a ship of non-Broan origin that appears to have lost a battle, one with an interstellar capability that doesn't rely on stargates."

"Won't their Broan masters be notified the moment our derelicts appear on sensors, thereby giving away the game?"

Lisa shook her head, causing her blonde curls to cover her face momentarily in a gesture that both men found intriguing. "Not if we send the scouts into systems with absentee masters, like Klys'kra't. If their sort of intelligence is anything like ours, they will start plotting revolution as soon as they realize what they have salvaged."

Pavel turned pensive. He didn't speak for long seconds, and when he did, it was with skepticism. "Have you considered the long term consequences of your plan?"

"Which are?" Mark asked.

"Let's say you are successful and you spark so many rebellions inside the Sovereignty that the Broa lose control. Aren't you solving one problem by creating a bigger one?"

"What do you mean?"

"We currently face the threat of a single alien species. You propose to multiply that threat by a million."

"Not really," Mark replied. "As Director Hamlin said this afternoon, there are a lot more intelligent species out there than the Broa and their slaves. If every race of thinkers in the universe is a danger, what difference if we add a million more to the billion that are already out there, but that we don't yet know about?"

"A scientist's viewpoint, not a politician's," Dieter said with a laugh. "If we explain it to the public that way, we are liable to be lynched."

"Facts are facts," Mark said stubbornly.

"You make it sound easy."

"It won't be easy at all. We will have to build our own network of stargates and establish forward operating bases where we can marshal our forces. We'll have to scout out the Broan home worlds and power centers. Then we'll have to select the systems into which we introduce our Trojan horses, all the while massing for strategic strikes against their gate network to bollix up their communications at the right moment.

"Still, if we judge it right, if we can sow confusion just as our various schemes come to fruition, it ought to work..."

"And if it doesn't?"

Mark shrugged. "Then we'll try something different..."

"A cavalier attitude,' Dieter said, his voice rising in tone and volume.

"Any idea what is on for the morning session tomorrow?" Lisa interrupted, changing the subject to short circuit the growing testosterone confrontation. "The program just says 'special guest speaker.'"

"No idea," Dieter replied, visibly regaining control.

"It's not the Coordinator, is it?"

He shook his head. "She's in Europe all this week. I guess we will find out in the morning. Are you both ready to order?"

They nodded and Pavel signaled the waiter who had been skulking just outside of range of their conversation.

To Mark's surprise, he found the remainder of the dinner enjoyable. Pavel, it turned out, was a skilled raconteur when he wasn't being an obnoxious bureaucrat.

#

Chapter Eighteen

The auditorium was nearly filled the next morning as everyone awaited Director Fernandez's "special guest speaker." The extra attendees included members of working groups who had spent the previous day in breakout sessions. Interestingly, a number of the newcomers were from the media.

"Who invited them?" Mark asked, hooking his thumb in the direction of the men and women with small tripod mounted cameras and microphones clustered in the back.

"Three guesses," Lisa replied as the two of them took their seats.

Mark laughed. "Alan Fernandez is a bit of a publicity hound, isn't he?"

As before, the dignitaries filed onto the stage and took their places behind the long table. The holocube was nowhere to be seen and the lectern stood alone beneath bright floodlights. There followed several minutes in which datacoms were synchronized and papers shuffled. Finally, Alan Fernandez rose and strode to the lectern.

"Good morning," he said. "I hope all of you have sufficiently recovered from yesterday's marathon session. I know I slept soundly last night.

"Yesterday we heard first from the Paris Institute and Director-General Jean-Pierre Landrieu, who outlined the plan to make this planet as unobtrusive as possible in order to avoid coming to the attention of the Broa. I must say that the Paris plan was well thought out and left us with much to consider. I do not think any here will disagree when I say that it is the more 'conventional' of the two approaches presented.

"Director Landrieu was followed by Director Dexter Hamlin of the Colorado Springs Institute, whose task it is to flesh out the 'Gibraltar Earth' plan. I must say that Director Hamlin's talk was especially stimulating and gave all of us something to think about. I would categorize the work of our Colorado Springs group as being the more 'proactive.' Of course, that is what we assigned them to do and I think we can all agree that they have given us a rather large helping of food for thought."

Fernandez paused, smiled and looked up at the audience, as though enjoying some private joke.

"There is, however, a third opinion that we should consider before finalizing our plans for parliament. It is an opinion that we have not heard before, and for good reason. However, I felt it important that we at least listen to what our next speaker has to say.

"Ladies and gentlemen, I would like to present the one being on this world who knows most about the Sovereignty, and whose opinion is germane to our discussions. It is my honor to present Sar-Say of the Sar-Dva Clan, and a member of the ruling species of the Broan Sovereignty. Sar-Say, the floor is yours!"

The audience erupted into pandemonium and the news crews began to speak excitedly into their headsets. Director Fernandez retreated as two stage hands carried a low platform out and set it behind the lectern.

Sar-Say stepped out from behind a curtain. He wore the 'formal' outfit that he had the night of the reception and walked upright rather than on his knuckles. He approached the lectern and awkwardly mounted the low platform, bringing his head to human height. He gazed around the crowd while he waited for silence to be restored.

After two entreaties from Alan Fernandez, the noise trailed off and an expectant hush fell over the auditorium. Sar-Say scanned the crowd in a very human gesture, then began to speak in a tone that indicated he had studied the principles of oration. He did not appear to be reading from the holographic teleprompter.

"Ladies and gentlemen, Members of Parliament, Executive Office Officials, Members of the Press. I would like to thank you for inviting me to speak this morning. As you may know, I have an entertainment screen in my quarters and I have been avidly following your debate. Seeing your political institutions at work gives me a much better understanding of your species, and I must say that I am impressed by what I see.

"However, one thing that I find lacking from your studies is a certain amount of sophistication regarding my species. You appear to be framing your arguments strictly in human terms.

"Of course, it is possible that I misjudge you. Not being human myself, there may well be nuance to your arguments that I miss. But I have also seen people on my holovision concocting fantastic schemes to go forth and slay the 'ugly little monkey gods,' as one commentator put it. Surely I have not misunderstood the meaning of that statement.

"Despite being one of the 'enemy,' my purpose here is to aid your debate. Hopefully, I can improve your understanding of what you face, and therefore, allow you to come to a better decision than you would without my input. I do not expect you to believe everything I say, but I assure you that every word I speak is the truth."

Sar-Say emitted the sound that substitutes for a laughter among the Broa. He raised his arms in an unrecognizable gesture, before dropping them again. "I imagine many of you are thinking, 'Wouldn't he say that if he were lying to us?' True, but you need not believe what I say. It is enough that you listen to me."

Lisa leaned over to Mark and whispered into his ear. "What do you think of my star pupil now?"

Mark responded, "I would say that he has learned Standard about as well as someone can. Congratulations, I think."

"Thank you… I think."

They both settled back to listen once more.

Sar-Say continued. "Ladies and gentlemen, what I have to say involves your future. Let me describe what awaits should you voluntarily choose to join the Broan Sovereignty, which my people simply call 'Civilization.'

"We are not the monsters we have been portrayed in your media. We do not eat children, or rather, the small offspring of our subservients. Mostly, we eat fruits and vegetables, with only an occasional helping of meat, derived from non-sentient beasts we raise for the purpose—just as you do.

"If we bring you into our Sovereignty, we will not insist that you change your diets to match ours. Each species must follow its own nature. There are beings who hunt their food and swallow it while still alive. That is their nature. We do not waste time attempting to change things that are inherent in a species' makeup. To do so would be both costly and futile. To use an Earth expression of which I am quite fond: 'My mother did not raise any stupid cubs.'

"I can hear the unspoken objection before it forms in your throat. 'But you Broa rule a million stars!' This is a misconception. We are not human, and do not conform to the human mold.

"We do not 'rule' our subservients as you define the term. Civilization is too broad and diverse to allow us the luxury of emulating some ancient human king or emperor. We do not rule other species for the simple reason that we cannot rule them. There are too few of us to control every aspect of life in Civilization.

"The method by which we control our domain does not translate well into Standard. I want to say that we 'guide' our subservients, but that word is a pale substitute for the reality I am attempting to communicate. For the good of all, we establish common-sense rules, and enforce them when they are violated. One of our rules is that no subservient species may make war on any other. We enforce this edict by controlling traffic through the stargates.

"Think of it. Let us say that you are the leader of a warlike species and you wish to conquer one of your neighbors. To this end, you build a vast armada of warships and are now ready to launch your invasion. Only, when you reach the stargate, it will not pass any of your ships. All of your efforts have been for naught. You have bankrupted yourself preparing for a war that you cannot wage.

"Is that really so bad? Would you of Sol Three not like similar protection for your own world? There are, after all, many races among the stars that neither of us have yet met. One of these may well be ruled by such a warlord. Are you safer alone, or as a member of a Civilization composed of a million suns?"

Sar-Say continued at length in that vein, stressing the benefits of joining the Broan Sovereignty. After several minutes of this, Mark had to admit that he was being damned persuasive. He made the Sovereignty seem more a collection of equals than an oligarchy run by and for the benefit of the Broa. Mark knew otherwise, but wondered how many members of the general public did. Would they hear Sar-Say's siren song and see the truth, or would they be taken in by a string of smooth lies? Considering some of the political arguments he had observed, he wasn't sure.

One thing was certain. The pseudo-simian had learned his human psychology lessons well.

Eventually, Sar-Say ran out of benefits to extol and turned to the negatives: first the carrot, then the stick.

"You face a choice in the near future," Sar-Say said in a deeper, and somehow more threatening, tone. "It is not the choice you have been debating these past few days. You believe it possible to maintain your independence, and are arguing over the best way to do so. This argument misses the point. Since it is inevitable that we will find you, the choice is whether to submit willingly, or be overcome by force.

"Your leaders tell you that we Broa do not allow other species to compete for the leadership of Civilization. This is true. Letting each species go its own way leads to warfare and endangers everyone. If you choose to join us, the transition to Civilization will go quite smoothly. If, however, you resist, we will bring you under control by force.

"Let me describe to you what that entails. When you are inevitably discovered and refuse our offers of membership in Civilization, we will assemble a war fleet and send them through stargates on single-ended jumps into your Solar System. One moment, you will be secure in your isolation, knowing that you are safe from the terrible Broa. The next, you will find yourself surrounded by thousands of warcraft more powerful than you can possibly imagine.

"What happens next depends on the strength of your resistance. If you prove no stronger than most species, you will lose a few cities to bombardment from space. If, however, you put up a strong fight, your world will be destroyed."

He paused and let that point sink in. When he continued, it was in the same confident tone with which he had begun.

"Ladies and gentlemen, I urge you not to close your minds to joining us voluntarily. It is literally the only choice you have if you are to survive. We are coming. Your fate rests in your hands alone." He paused and consulted the antique timepiece he wore on one arm just above a six-fingered hand.

"I see that it I have been speaking for about as long as an audience will tolerate. I therefore will conclude my remarks.

"Thank you for listening to me."

#

At first his remarks were met with a sullen silence. Then isolated shouts and jeers broke out. These soon turned into a crescendo. People rose to their feet and shouted at the stage. Some actually shook their fists. Others, however, sat in their seats and looked pensive, as though they were trying to process a wholly new thought. Alan Fernandez beamed as he strode to the lectern to help the pseudo-simian down. From backstage, four large men appeared. They were Sar-Say's 'bodyguards,' here to escort him back to his cell.

The guards waited patiently while Sar-Say spoke privately with Fernandez. Then they surrounded him and escorted him from the stage.

Alan Fernandez returned to the microphone and announced a twenty minute recess, following which they would begin the reports of the working groups.

Twenty minutes later, about half the crowd was back in their seats, awaiting the resumption of the program. These were the members of the various institutes who were doing the actual work. Members of Parliament and the Coordinator's representatives had largely departed.

The twenty minute time limit came and went without anyone reappearing on stage. Five minutes went by, and then ten, and still the conference did not reconvene. Mark looked at Lisa questioningly, and she shrugged her shoulders. Out of the corner of his eye, he caught sight of a familiar figure striding down the aisle from the back of the auditorium.

Dieter Pavel made his way to where they were sitting and spoke in a stage whisper. "Lisa, you are wanted upstairs. Mark can come too if he wants."

"Upstairs?" she asked. "What's wrong?"

"Not here," Pavel replied, jerking his thumb toward the wide door leading from the auditorium. "Out in the foyer."

The three of them walked up the long slope to the door, and turned right toward the lift. When they were alone in a brightly lit corridor, Lisa asked, "What is going on?"

"Sar-Say has been kidnapped!"

#

Chapter Nineteen

"Upstairs" proved to be the office of the Harvard Convention Center manager. When Dieter Pavel ushered Lisa and Mark inside, they found all three Directors clustered around a visibly shaken security guard. The guard wore the epaulets of a Lieutenant and had a white bandage running diagonally across his left temple.

There was one other in the office, Tony Hulsey, leader of the Coordinator's faction in parliament. The Guard Lieutenant wasn't the only one visibly shaken. Alan Fernandez's complexion was the color of dirty snow.

Dexter Hamlin glanced up as Mark and Lisa entered. His dark eyes were focused on Lisa. "Good, you're here. We are in need of your insights."

"What happened?" she asked.

"Four guards were escorting Sar-Say back to his cell when they were jumped by an unknown number of assailants. They were all simultaneously stunned by illegal tasers. The jolts knocked them out for a few seconds, and when they came to, Sar-Say was gone. Lieutenant Forster got a pretty good knock on the head and one of his men has a broken arm."

"Any idea who these assailants were?

"None. We only know they were damned well organized."

"How could they have known the route in advance?" Mark asked on impulse.

The Lieutenant looked at him and said, "My fault. We went straight up the pedestrian mall by the most direct route. We wanted to get Sar-Say back under lock and key as quickly as possible."

"Surely we must have some suspicions as to their identity," Lisa said.

Hamlin turned back to her. "They could have been from any number of factions. There are the Religionists, who think Sar-Say is one of Satan's minions; the Earth Firsters, who wish we had never invented electricity, let alone space travel; the Radical Conservatives, who think we're going to spend too much tax money regardless of what we decide. Hell, it might just be a local gang who think they can make a healthy credit by holding him for ransom. Personally, I wouldn't put it past members of Terra Nostra."

"Why them?" Mark asked. "True, Vasloff is in favor of pulling back from the stars, but kidnapping Sar-Say won't advance his cause any."

"It may be someone else," Lisa said, her face frozen in a pensive frown.

"Who?"

"It could be Sar-Say himself."

"Go ahead," Hamlin said.

"I'm just speculating, you understand," she replied, hesitantly.

"Speculate away. That is why we asked you here."

"I spent a lot of time living with Sar-Say," she replied. "He is quite intelligent, possibly more intelligent than we are. I doubt he would give up on the idea of escape just because his first attempt didn't work."

"Are you suggesting that this was a jail break?" Alan Fernandez demanded, his voice turning into a squeak as he completed the sentence.

"Precisely," Lisa replied.

"To what purpose?"

"Why, to get off this planet and back to the Sovereignty, of course."

The director of the Broa Institute shook his head. "That's crazy. No human would betray Earth that way."

"Are you sure? He can offer those who help him riches beyond imagining."

There followed a long silence, after which Dexter Hamlin mused, "That puts a different slant on things."

"How so?" Hulsey asked.

"Think of it," Mark's boss continued. "Sar-Say may have been kidnapped by someone who means him harm; in which case, we will probably be pulling his body out of the bay this afternoon. Then again, perhaps he was kidnapped for money.

"In the first case, his death will be a major loss to our research, but it also guarantees the Broa will not learn of our existence from him. In the second case, we pay the ransom, get him back, and hunt down the perpetrators. The result is that he returns to our custody with no lasting harm done. But what if Lisa is right? What if this is a jailbreak organized by Sar-Say himself?"

"Then Earth is in grave danger."

"What are we to do about it?" Jean-Pierre Landrieu asked. Like Fernandez, he looked sick to his stomach.

"The police have already been notified. We had best get the army involved, as well," Hamlin replied. "There is a division of Peace Enforcers at Fort Monmouth. They can be here this evening."

"No need for that," Fernandez objected.

"I disagree. We are going to have to shut down the entire Boston Metro Area. That means we will need troops to throw a cordon around the entire city. Nothing in or out until we find Sar-Say, dead or alive."

"The kidnappers have probably already left the city."

Director Hamlin nodded. "I would have, were I them. However, we can't overlook the possibility they are hiding locally. They must know we would set up mandatory traffic checkpoints as soon as we learned of the kidnapping. In fact, the police are doing that right now. It isn't like they can slap a blonde wig on him for a disguise."

"What if he has escaped Boston?"

"The traffic monitors can give us the registration of every vehicle that has left the city since the kidnapping and where they are now. We will have to track them down and cross-reference their drivers and passengers to everyone who has had contact with Sar-Say since he has been here at the Institute.

"People with contact?" Hulsey asked.

"Think about it. If this is a jailbreak, then Sar-Say had to arrange it with someone. We get a list of those who have come in contact with him and see if any of them have the resources to arrange his escape. Then, of course, there are the starships."

"What about them?"

"We need to secure them… right now! If Sar-Say has escaped, he needs a starship to complete his getaway. Again, he can offer any and all accomplices anything they want. But to reap their reward, they have to get him home first. Who is to say there isn't a starship captain out there just waiting for the shuttle that is bringing him to orbit?"

"That means that we will have to shut down the shuttles," Hulsey said.

"Not just them. All launches ground-to-orbit. For all we know, he is heading for one of the electromagnetic launchers and planning on leaving Earth marked as a cylinder of oxygen or something."

"Surely he couldn't have arranged all of that while he has been here. We record his every movement and utterance for exhaustive study," Alan Ferguson said.

"It doesn't make much sense to escape otherwise," Hamlin replied. "Why trade his small comfortable prison for the larger, much more dangerous one known as Planet Earth?"

"Then in addition to grounding everything headed for orbit, we should move the starships to where he can't get at them," Tony Hulsey replied. Unlike the academics, he seemed completely at ease dealing with a crisis of this magnitude. "How many are there in the Solar System at the moment?"

"There can't be more than a couple of dozen."

"All right. We get guards aboard each and every ship, and then we dispatch them out to the vicinity of Jupiter. Somewhere that a ground-to-orbit shuttle can't reach, anyway."

"High station?" Mark suggested.

Hulsey nodded. "That should be far enough. Nothing from Earth is going to reach that orbit without transferring at Equatorial Station first. We'll have to monitor that, too; although there shouldn't be any comings or goings. Not with our blockade in effect."

"These are needlessly drastic measures," Alan Fernandez said sourly.

"Perhaps so," Mark's boss replied. "But if Sar-say gets aboard a starship and somehow gains control, our fate will be sealed. With the safety of humanity in the balance, drastic measures are called for."

#

Sar-Say had not left the Boston Metro Area. In fact, he was in the basement of an older home in Cambridge, not four blocks from the university.

"All right," Gus Heinz said, sitting on the sofa facing the small alien. "I've held up my end of the bargain. Now where is my money?"

"You will receive what I promised and more as soon as I reach my home," Sar-Say said. As he did so, he dipped his tongue into a glass of cold water, formed a tube, and sucked up the refreshing liquid. His adventures over the past few hours had left him parched.

"Your note didn't say anything about that," Heinz replied menacingly. "It said that you would give me one billion credits if I helped you escape. I've helped you. Now, where is my money?"

"Surely you didn't expect me to have it on my person?" Sar-Say asked, spreading his arms wide in a human gesture. Unlike at his speech earlier in the day, he was now clothed normally... that is, in his fur alone. His gesture made it clear that he lacked pockets in which to sequester a billion credits.

"I expected you to be able to get it," Heinz said.

"How? Do you suppose they were paying me for my services?"

"Why not?" asked the interstellar importer/exporter. "You give them information about alien technology and they pay you what the information is worth."

At that moment, Sar-Say began to worry about the success of his plan. This human was not very intelligent. Or rather, his intelligence was focused in his business and making money. He seemed to have few other interests in life, save the Boston Beans flyball team.

"I am sorry, Gus, but I was their prisoner. They paid me nothing for the valuable information I provided, even though I spoke honestly and at length."

"So you lied in the note?"

Sar-Say noted the human's voice had dropped an octave, making his manner seem more menacing. As an alien, Sar-Say was actually more aware of the significance of these unconscious changes in voice and face than were their owners. His years of captivity had taught him the skill of reading human expressions.

"Not at all," Sar-Say replied. "I pledge to you the sum of one billion credits or their equivalent as soon as we reach any Broan world."

Heinz stood angrily, his fists two white-knuckled balls at his sides. "Then I've taken this risk for nothing. So have the people I hired to break you out."

"That is not true. Please, sit down and let me tell you my plan to get home and to pay you. In fact, I will make you my prime human contact when I am made administrator of this world, which will make you far richer than a mere billion credits."

At the mention of additional riches, Sar-Say noted the muscles in Heinz's face relax and his breathing begin a return to normal.

#

After he had gotten the big, rotund human quieted down, Sar-Say recounted the plan he had worked out over the long months of captivity.

The easiest thing to do would have been for Heinz to hire a starship to return to Klys'kra't, the coordinates of which Sar-Say had memorized. Presumably there was a ship's captain and crew amenable to promises of future reward.

Nor would such promises be empty ones. When Sar-Say was awarded the mastership of Earth, he would have near infinite resources with which to reward those who helped him. If Gus Heinz desired the Governor-Generalship of Australia, then that would be his reward. If he also wished to house himself in a mansion, supplied with a steady stream of nubile females, Sar-Say would arrange that too. In truth, once he assumed his rightful place as Master of Earth, there was no limit on his ability to reward supporters, and good reasons for others to see that cooperation paid in cold, hard credits.

All of this was for the future. Today's problem was that promises of future wealth would not hire a starship. It seemed to him that Heinz was particularly ill suited for the task. As an interstellar merchant, Heinz dealt with shipping agents and other intermediaries, never directly with starship captains or crews.

Sar-Say proposed that Gus take out as large a loan as he could manage, even mortgaging his business if need be. Having obtained funding that he had no intention of repaying, Heinz would contract with a starship captain to transport machine tools and luxury foodstuffs to whatever colony the captain was scheduled to visit on his next voyage.

The cargo would consist of several vacuum-proof shipping containers, one of which Heinz would modify to smuggle Sar-Say aboard the starship. This container would require both breathing equipment and a cooling system that would operate for several days with little possibility of failure.

Heinz would book passage aboard the starship, along with a number of accomplices. Once the starship was in superlight, Heinz would make an excuse to visit the cargo hold, release Sar-Say, and break out the weaponry they would smuggle in the other cases. Once they were armed, taking control of the ship should not be difficult.

Commercial starships were highly automated, which meant that they could extend their foodstuffs for the year-long voyage by disposing of the other passengers and crew.

Sar-Say did not bother to mention this last point to Heinz.

When he finished his explanation, Heinz scratched the stubble on his face and said, "It's going to take a lot more than I can arrange with a bank to swing this deal."

"What is your suggestion?" Sar-Say asked.

"I know a guy who handles large sums of money quietly. He's expensive, though."

"Would this man also like to make a billion credits for aiding my escape?"

"Sure," the businessman said. "Who doesn't like money?"

Sar-Say made the gesture of assent. "Get the money and we will speak again of the number of men we need."

#

Chapter Twenty

The blockade was clamped down on Boston at nightfall, even while the battalion of Peace Enforcers were moving into position around the city. In previous centuries, such a cordon would have been virtually impossible because of suburban sprawl.

The information revolution had changed the face of the city and of the world. People like their elbow room. Most cities were now commercial islands in a sea of open space, with the populace spread as thinly as possible around them. Entire towns had disappeared during the century-long Diaspora, returning the surrounding countryside to its natural condition, or to farmland.

Though decried by some, like the exodus from the family farms throughout the twentieth century, the emptying of the suburbs had benefited just about everyone. Now, when the need to seal off a major port like Boston arose, at least it was possible to draw a line around the city that encompassed the whole of the city's population.

Other technologies assisted in the search for Sar-Say as well. Civil disturbances over the years — riots, strikes, terrorist attacks — had caused every city on Earth to be continuously surveyed by overlapping security cameras. These had caught the attack on the mall from three different angles.

Four men were recorded loitering for an hour prior to the assault. When the tight group of guards and alien moved into view, they each drew concealed electric stunners from their jackets and fired in unison. The jolts sent the four guards down. Lieutenant Forster fell into a flower bed, causing the gash on his forehead. Another guard collapsed into a pedestrian bench and lay on the ground with his arm sticking out at an unnatural angle.

Sar-Say showed no evidence of distress during the attack. He shifted into a fast lope using all his limbs, while his four rescuers struggled to keep up. The five entered an underground passage to the metro station.

A few minutes before the attack, a woman whose face was covered by a flowered hat had placed a plastic drinking cup over the lens of the passageway security camera, blocking its view. As a result, the party disappeared into the non-surveillance section of the subway. Nor had any other camera caught their emergence from the underground.

"Well, we have their pictures," Lisa told Mark as they ate a hurried dinner. "That's something."

"Not much," he replied. They wore sun goggles, droopy hats, and seem to have all worn their hair unstylishly long, with full beards concealing most of their faces."

"Disguises?"

"Either that or a renegade group of Hasidic Jews!"

Lisa giggled. "Any chance of identifying them from the camera images?"

"My boss says that the police are trying to program the computers to watch for individuals with similar body sizes and walks. That means a lot of innocent people are going to be hassled by the police over the next few hours, but we might get lucky and catch one of them."

"What else?" she asked.

"They are questioning the researchers with access to Sar-Say and checking their email accounts. One of them may have gotten sloppy."

"What's the chance of that?"

"Pretty damned close to zero. What do they have you doing?"

She sighed. "I just sit around and answer questions about Sar-Say. I know it is silly, but I'm worried about him."

Mark frowned. "Why, for God's sake?"

"I guess I like him. He isn't a bad person, you know. He's just dedicated to escaping custody and going home."

"Not to mention taking over the Earth for his own profit."

She sighed again. "That, too, I guess. I certainly don't want him to escape, but I don't want him killed either."

"It was a possibility earlier, but there isn't much chance of that since we discovered he arranged this."

She shook her head. "Not much chance of that until his accomplices realize that whatever they have planned isn't going to work. What do they do then? They certainly aren't going to deliver him back to the Institute here at Harvard. Most likely they will kill him to protect themselves."

"At the moment, I would be very relieved if we found him floating face down in the bay."

"Don't get me wrong," she said. "I would, too, rather than see him escape. But I hope we get him back alive, if for no other reason than that I have too much time invested in teaching him Standard to see all of my work go for naught."

He nodded. "That speech of his was something of a spellbinder, wasn't it?"

She agreed. "He nearly convinced me, and I know better!"

They sat in silence, each consumed by private thoughts for the rest of the hurried meal. Twenty minutes later, they kissed in front of the convention center, and Lisa disappeared inside once more. With nothing to do, Mark turned and strode up the mall toward where the abduction occurred.

He couldn't have explained his motivation. He just wanted to see the spot.

#

The man Gus Heinz brought to see Sar-Say reminded him of a race known as the Kaylar. They were short, broad, had no necks and bullet-shaped heads. Their shoulders were broad and their hips narrow, giving their torsos a triangular look. Those characteristics also described this new human.

"Sar-Say, I would like to introduce Benny Ludnick. Benny's the man I told you could help us."

Sar-Say held out his six-fingered hand. "Welcome, Mr. Ludnick. Gus has told me a great deal about you."

"Did he tell you that I can get a million credits just by reporting where you are?"

"A reward?" Gus Heinz asked with what Sar-Say considered too keen an interest.

"Announced as I was coming over here," Ludnick said, nodding.

"You can do that, of course," Sar-Say replied. "Or, you can make one billion credits if you help me return home."

"Why would any of us help an alien? It would be like betraying our own family."

"More like saving your family, Mr. Ludnick. Did you see the reports of my speech to the institutes?"

"I saw excerpts on the news."

"Then you know this resistance your government is planning is useless. We will find you anyway... if not tomorrow, then next year, or certainly within a decade or two. We are very good at detecting signals emanating from star systems outside Civilization. When we detect such a signal, it is our policy to protect ourselves and our member species by bringing those systems into Civilization, by force if necessary. Many of you will die in the process, possibly all of you."

"You don't paint a very good picture."

Sar-Say lifted his shoulders in a convincing imitation of a shrug. "I speak the truth. If you turn me in, you will likely die during the conquest. If, on the other hand, you assist me, then your species will be saved much death and destruction, and you personally will become rich beyond your wildest dreams. Are you interested?"

"Damned, straight," the bullet-headed man replied. "The first rule of life is to look out for Number One. But can you deliver? Where would you get your hands on a billion credits?"

"By taxing the people of Earth after we bring you into Civilization, of course," Sar-Say said, finishing with, "Save for those who aid me, who will have a lifetime exemption from all such taxes."

"What do I have to do to earn this money?"

Sar-Say told him of the plan to take over a starship once it was underway, emphasizing that they would need four or five good men to make the plan work. "Each will receive a voucher for one billion credits for their services the moment I reach my home. When we return to Earth at the head of the fleet, you will be equally rewarded for your help."

"And how long will this take?"

"I estimate 18 months to two years. Most of that time we will be superlight, crossing the interstellar gulf between here and Civilization. Then I will need some time to organize a fleet and return here via single-ended stargate jump. The return voyage will take no time at all."

"What if I am caught after you make your escape?"

"I suspect they will execute you," Sar-Say replied. He had learned that humans respected an admission against one's own interest. He watched Ludnick carefully to see if he had exceeded his knowledge of human psychology.

That caused Ludnick to pause for long seconds, before answering, "Then I'd best not be caught. What about money to arrange your deal?"

"That will be your responsibility. At the moment, I have none. We will need quite a lot of money, I fear. Do you have the wealth needed to charter a ship outright?"

"Not bloody likely! You have to be a small country to have your own starship."

"A pity," Sar-Say replied. "Then we have to go with the hijacking plan."

"That isn't as easy as you make it sound," Ludnick replied. "They are very careful to inspect outgoing cargo before it is loaded onto an orbital ferry."

"Then you will have to figure out how to prevent that."

Ludnick nodded. "There are ways. They are expensive, but it can be done."

"Then do it. How soon can you be ready?"

"I haven't said that I am in yet."

"Come now, Mr. Ludnick," Sar-Say said. "If you weren't interested, you would not be here. Must I increase my offer?"

"To what?"

"How would you like to own Manhattan Island when I return?"

The broad-shouldered man's eyes momentarily grew wide.

"I ask again. How long will it take to complete preparations?" Sar-Say asked, confident that he had recruited another, and probably more capable, ally than Gus Heinz.

"Couple of weeks. What about the blockade?"

"We will have to wait it out," Sar-say replied "They can't keep this city locked up forever. It will probably be canceled before this week is out."

"I'll need guarantees if I join you," Ludnick said truculently to cover the slip he had made when Sar-Say increased his offer.

"What guarantees?"

"That no harm will come to my family when you return."

"You have my word," Sar-Say replied. "Select the coordinates of some out-of-the-way area where you and your family will go once you hear that the Broan fleet has appeared in the Solar System. I will make sure that the fleet commanders know that this place is not to be harmed… not that your planet will be harmed at all if your people show some common sense when we arrive."

"Then we have a deal," Ludnick said, standing to offer his hand.

Sar-Say reached out and shook again. He had learned this clasping-of-hands ritual early in his captivity. Even so, it always gave him chills to touch palms with a human. Perhaps, he thought, it was the difference in their body temperatures. Certainly, he was no longer afraid of being contaminated by human germs.

Perhaps, he decided, he was just being too fastidious.

#

Five days following Sar-Say's escape, the major players in the hunt for him gathered at the Broan Institute at Harvard. All three institute directors were there, having delayed their departures from Boston until the crisis passed. So was the Boston Mayor and Chief of Police, along with a Peace Enforcer general named Parsons and his aide, and the directors' various assistants. It was in his capacity as assistant to Dexter Hamlin that Mark attended the meeting. Lisa was there because of her specialized knowledge of Sar-Say. Dieter Pavel was also present, having been assigned to follow the investigation by the World Coordinator.

The meeting was held in the conference room just down the hall from Sar-Say's quarters. Normally, institute researchers used the room to plan their interrogation sessions. Now its walls were covered with maps that detailed progress of the search.

"What do we know?" the P.E. general asked of the police chief.

"We think we have found where they emerged from the subway," Chief Martin Darlen, a gruff, white-haired man in a blue uniform replied. "We found cameras disabled at the subway exit at Beacon and Sacramento Streets. The tunnel camera was unplugged and someone threw a towel over the street camera. There was a blind spot that would have allowed them to park a vehicle long enough to hide the alien after they came up from the subway."

"What about other cameras in the vicinity?" Jean-Pierre Landrieu asked. "They would have seen the vehicle leaving the scene shortly after the kidnapping."

"They probably did," the police chief replied. "However, there's a hell of a lot of traffic on Beacon at that time of day. There are literally thousands of possibilities. Also, if they were smart, they waited awhile before leaving the dead zone. The longer they waited, the harder it will be for us to track them down."

"All right," Mark's boss said. "That is probably a dead end. How are things going with your people, General?"

"Nothing to report, sir," Parsons said. "My men are inspecting every vehicle that leaves Boston on the surface. We have air transportation grounded. The maglevs are being halted at the cordon line and inspected before being allowed to proceed."

"Inspected how?" Dexter Hamlin asked. "Surely there are all kinds of hiding places on a train."

"We're using sniffers calibrated to detect Sar-Say's peculiar body odor," the general replied. "If he were aboard the train or hidden in one of the cars or trucks we inspect, we would 'smell' him."

"Could we track him that way?"

The general shook his head. "Too much time has passed, not to mention the recent rain washing every trace away."

"What about the researchers? Have they all checked out clean?"

"Director Fernandez?" General Parsons asked. "That is your bailiwick."

Alan Fernandez had not fared well during the last week. He had pronounced bags under his eyes and deep creases at the ends of his mouth from frowning all of the time. He also looked like he hadn't slept much. Mark Rykand almost felt sorry for him, until he remembered that Fernandez was the reason Sar-Say was on Earth.

"We have interviewed all of the researchers," he replied in a monotone that emphasized his fatigue. "They all deny having anything to do with Sar-Say's escape. We've checked their network files and email accounts. Nothing out of the ordinary has yet been found."

"Have you checked *everyone* who has had contact with Sar-Say?"

"All of the institute staff," Fernandez replied.

"Do you mean there were more?" the general asked.

"We had a few social functions that Sar-Say attended. He met a number of people, including the mayor. However, he hardly had time to strike up a conspiracy with them."

"Are those all? The researchers and the party goers?"

"Yes, except for his discussion companions."

"His what?" General Parsons asked in a deceptively quiet voice.

Fernandez went on to explain that they had a small contingent of private citizens who came in periodically to hold discussions with Sar-Say, finishing up with, "The interaction helps us study him. In fact, the Mayor suggested the program."

"I did?" Mayor Harrigan yelped.

"Certainly," Fernandez replied. "You suggested it at Sar-Say's first reception, when you introduced me to Gus Heinz. Remember, they were talking about business, and you whispered to me that Heinz was an important contributor to the party and that I should treat him with courtesy."

"I did no such thing!"

"You did so!"

"*Gentlemen!*" General Parsons said in his best command voice. The exclamation caused both men to remember where they were and to regain their dignity. "Who is this Gus Heinz person?"

"A local businessman," the Mayor replied. "He is in the import/export business."

"What sort of import/export?"

"Some pharmaceutical. Very rare. Can only be produced on Borodin."

"Borodin, the colony in the Dagon System?"

"Yes."

"This Heinz is in the interstellar import/export business?"

Fernandez nodded.

"And he has access to starships?"

"I suppose so."

With each question, the general's complexion grew redder. It was now almost purple.

"*And you forgot to mention this?*"

Alan Fernandez melted under the General's gaze. "I didn't think of it."

"How many others does Sar-Say meet with regularly that you have forgotten to tell us about?"

"Half a dozen. I can get you the list, if you like."

"Please, do."

Fernandez was gone for a few minutes, returning with a new printout on which there were seven names. Gustavus Adolphus

Heinz was number four on the list. Parsons nearly tore the list out of Fernandez's hands and gave it to Chief Darlen.

"Would you please check these people out, starting with this Gus Heinz?"

"Yes, sir," the Chief of Police replied, reacting like a P.E. private under the General's withering gaze.

#

Chapter Twenty One

Sar-Say was worried. It had been nearly 20 hours since he'd met with Benny Ludnick and he had not heard anything since. He was aware that anxiety tended to make time pass slowly, but the day just past had been excruciating in its pace. Not only was he worried that his plan would fail, but he was becoming very tired of Gus Heinz's basement.

It had seemed a good idea to hide out relatively near the site of his break for freedom. For one thing, he had been on the open streets for only a few minutes. His rescuers led him along an underground tunnel into a nearby service tunnel and then up to street level where an enclosed vehicle waited.

All of his rescuers but one departed the scene hastily at that point, after removing the fake fur they had worn over their faces and changing their clothing. The ringleader also changed clothes and removed his disguise. The clothes he put on were those of a service technician for one of the local utilities. The back of the vehicle in which Sar-Say huddled was cluttered with tools. The vehicle itself bore the stylized representation of a bell inscribed on its outside panels.

Sar-Say and the ringleader waited in the parked vehicle for more than an hour. Then, after an interminable time, the driver placed the vehicle in motion and pulled out into a street with dense clumps of traffic moving in both directions. The delay had been intended to make the authorities' surveillance devices useless by giving them too many vehicles to inspect.

The drive to Gus Heinz's house had taken less than five minutes. It was literally one right turn and two lefts from where they emerged. The garage door opened as they neared the house. The driver pulled into the garage, offloaded Sar-Say, then backed out quickly and disappeared into traffic once again.

"Jaime will get rid of the truck," Heinz said as he led Sar-Say down into the basement. "He'll ditch it across the river in Southie."

That had been two days ago. In Sar-Say's estimation, that was as long as he should stay in one place. Being this close to the scene of his rescue, the humans might institute a house-to-house search.

He needed to move to a more distant district of the city, or better yet, leave Cambridge altogether.

It was with relief that he heard voices near sundown. Sar-Say's hearing was sharper than that of a human, and he quickly recognized both Heinz and Ludnick's voices. A minute later, there were loud footsteps on the stairs and Benny Ludnick entered the room where Sar-Say was staying.

After performing the palm clasping ceremony again, Ludnick began to speak.

"You sure as hell have messed up this burg."

"Burg?"

"City. The P.E.s have us locked down tighter than the membrane on a snare drum."

Sar-Say, who was proud of his mastery of Standard, suddenly realized that his education had not been as complete as he thought.

"You are saying that there are difficulties?"

"Damned straight. The Peace Enforcers won't let anything fly, they are inspecting ground cars leaving the city, and the Coast Guard has a couple of ships making sure that no one gets out of the bay."

"So it is impossible to leave the city?"

"Pretty much."

"How easy would it be to move me to another location within the city?"

"No problem. They aren't interfering with traffic inside the cordon. Where do you want to go?"

"Somewhere other than here. I think it wise to gain some distance between me and the university. Can you make arrangements to move me?"

"Sure."

"When would you be ready?"

"I suppose we could do it tomorrow night. Let me check with some guys."

"Where would I go?"

"South Boston, I think. It's pretty far from the university, both in terms of culture and distance. I have a house there that I rent out. It's empty at the moment. I'll set you up with food and water. If you keep the blinds closed and the lights off, no one will know you are there. You should be safe long enough for them to give up this blockade."

"Excellent. It would be better if Gus Heinz does not know where I have gone. He and I have a public history. You and I do not."

"Sounds smart."

"What of the starship? Have you managed to find one leaving for the colonies within a few weeks?"

"That is a problem, too. There's an orbital blockade as well. All of the ships have been moved to High Station. There isn't a single one we can reach at the moment, and none of them are going anywhere until the blockade is lifted anyway."

"High station? That is the Stellar Survey research station, is it not?"

"It is."

"And you cannot get me there?"

"Not a chance. They are watching all of the launch facilities, and probably have guards aboard Equatorial Station, where you have to change from shuttle to inter-orbit ferry."

"How long can they maintain this blockade?"

"They can't keep the city shut down for more than a week, I would think. As for this starship thing, if it goes on for a month, the owners are going to start bitching. I've had some dealings with government bureaucrats. I would say you will be on your way within the next 30 days. Besides, it will take us about that long to get ready."

"Then I must hide out for the full month while you make preparations for our escape. Do you have an entertainment device in this house you rent?"

"A holovision set? Sure, everybody has them."

"Good, then I can keep track of the news while you prepare and possibly avoid dying of boredom."

"Shit happens," Ludnick replied, obviously not interested in the least in either Sar-Say's comfort or boredom.

"Have you found the men you need?"

"I have three. I haven't told them what they will be doing, yet. I just told them that there is a shit pot full of money to be made. They are definitely interested. I have two more to feel out. I just haven't had the time."

"It is good that you have not told them about me. That one million credit reward might entice them to betray us."

"My thought, exactly," Ludnick replied. "Now let me tell you about the shipping containers and what we will do to modify them…"

#

"So this Heinz lives in Cambridge?" General Parsons asked his aide. The two of them were in their command vehicle.

"Yes, sir. On Crescent, East of Oxford, in the middle of the block on the North Side. About half-a-kilometer from where the attack took place."

"Ballsy," Parsons replied. "You would think Fernandez would have mentioned that before we sealed up the whole damned city."

"Yes, sir."

"What assets do we have in the area?"

"We have an infiltration squad ready to go. They are currently here in the university. They are waiting for full dark to use their active night camouflage."

"Who is in charge?"

"Sergeant Chen."

"Good man. I worked with him down in Nicaragua when that nut of a scientist thought he could distill botulinum without us finding out about it. Have they got sniffers?"

"Yes, sir. We had the cordon team deliver two of them to the squad. They have plans of the Heinz domicile. With luck, we'll be able to penetrate it without being discovered and take a discreet air sample. If Sar-Say has been there, we should know it immediately."

"Good. If he hasn't, Heinz will think he has termites. Keep me apprised."

"Yes, sir."

#

Peace Enforcer Sergeant Jacob Liu Chen lay in someone's flowerbed and used his combat goggles to scan the subject house. It was a clapboard frame, two-story affair that must have been easily three hundred years old. This was one of those Cambridge neighborhoods where the owners were either fifth generation, or else snobbish newcomers paying for the ambience. The lawns were well groomed, with a lot of shrubbery and flowers in evidence. Chen liked that. It gave him and his men something to work with.

The Heinz house was flanked on both sides by two others, with a narrow passageway on each side. There was a large, fenced backyard. The fence was constructed of 12-centimeter-wide planks nailed to a pair of horizontal beams and about 2 meters tall. It had once been painted white, but was in need of a touchup. He suspected Heinz had received more than one visit from the local neighborhood association.

In his goggles, he could see two of his troopers crouching in the shadows next to the backyard fence, one on each side of the house.

"Zwicky?" he whispered into his headset microphone.

"Yeah, Sarge?" came the whispered response.

"Any sign of a dog?"

"No dog."

"All right. You and Spears are cleared for entry into the back yard."

No sooner had the order been given than both figures moved forward and over the fence.

"Sniffer Team One, advance to Point Able!"

Two troopers carrying one of the sniffers advanced to the right front corner of the house. They crouched in the bushes and began the careful job of drilling a small hole in the clapboard. House plans on file with the city indicated that the kitchen was inside where they were drilling, and the drill would break through inside a kitchen cabinet, where it would be unobserved — assuming the plans on file were correct. Even if they were not, the hollow drill they were using was small enough that it would probably not be observed by the inhabitants.

"Sniffer Team Two, advance to Point Baker!"

The second team moved to the opposite side of the house and began drilling through the red bricks that formed the walls of the basement and the foundation for the frame building above. The tiny drill bit was quietly chewing through the mortar between bricks. The basement windows had been painted white, but the one nearest the second sniffer team showed the lights off in what plans called the laundry room.

There followed five minutes in which the only sound was the chirping of crickets. A boom microphone team reported muffled voices inside the house, possibly in the basement, and a single occupant in the upper part of the house. They could hear the latter moving around the kitchen. Whoever was in the basement, their conversation was too muffled to pick out individual words.

"We're through," Sniffer Team One reported. "All we can smell are various cleaning solutions and soaps. Apparently, we're in the cabinet beneath the sink where they store such things. It's overpowering our sensor."

"Okay, pull back and go to your secondary target."

"Moving now," the whispered response came.

"Team Two?"

"We're through the bricks. Stand by."

There followed another long period of silence. Then the leader of Sniffer Team Two reported in an excited whisper.

"We have a positive hit, Sarge! Definite match with the alien's body chemicals."

"All team members, move in. Entry Plan Delta. Get into position and prepare for my order. Move!"

#

"So we figure that we can give you three weeks of oxygen in the shipping crate with this regenerator, but it is going to be cramped," Ludnick told Sar-Say as he sketched out the modifications they were making to smuggle him into space once the blockade ended.

"What about waste disposal?"

"You'll have to use bags. It is going to get stinky in there, I'm afraid."

"That is not a problem," Sar-Say replied. "Our olfactory senses are different from those of you humans. We do not have the same distaste for some odors that you do. How airtight are these cases?"

"Very," Ludnick replied. "This particular model is used to ship items that would be ruined by exposure to vacuum. The manufacturer guarantees it to be leak proof, or your money back."

"That will not do me any good if it leaks," Sar-Say replied.

"True," Ludnick replied. "Sort of like a guarantee from a parachute packer."

The reference escaped Sar-Say. He decided to ignore it. "What about an interior release mechanism for the crate seal? I do not like the idea of being locked in a box with no means of escape, especially if my air is running low."

"We can put one in, but you will have to be careful about using it. The crate will be in vacuum for a long period once in orbit. They only pressurize the cargo holds after they've finished loading.

Pop the release at the wrong time, and you will be breathing vacuum."

"A pressure sensor will eliminate that possibility. We can conceal the sensor inside one of the side braces where it won't be seen."

They had been going over the plans for twenty minutes, with Sar-Say making changes and Ludnick writing them down on the back of an envelope he had pulled from his pocket. The sketches of the cargo container were laid out on a low table. The scene might have been that of two graduate students working together on their thesis.

They were interrupted as Gus Heinz arrived with refreshments... beers for him and Ludnick, orange juice for Sar-Say. He was just pouring the orange juice out of a refrigerated bulb when a loud crash echoed through the house.

"What the hell...!" Ludnick exclaimed, looking up where dust was slowly drifting down from the basement rafters.

There was the clatter of many feet overhead, the crash of doors being kicked in, and before any of the three could react, the sound of heavy boots on stairs.

The next thing they saw were two big Peace Enforcer troopers as they burst into the basement with their needle rifles at the ready.

"Freeze!" came the order. Both Heinz and Ludnick turned to face the soldiers, then with nearly identical curses, raised their hands over their heads. Sar-Say just stood there, looking from one trooper to the other, dismay apparent in his posture to anyone familiar with Broan body language. All of his plans had turned out for naught, again!

"We've got him!" one of the troopers said into his intercom. His call caused numerous other soldiers to come stomping down the stairs. Within seconds, both men and Sar-Say had their arms restrained behind them in handcuffs.

A sergeant looked the three of them over and said, "Call the General. Tell him everything is secure. We've captured the alien!"

#

Chapter Twenty Two

The meeting was held in the big conference room one level down from the World Coordinator's office in Government Tower in Toronto. It was a week since Sar-Say's capture and three days since he had been returned to PoleStar. He would never again be allowed on Earth.

The interrogations of both Gus Heinz and Benjamin Ludnick had been swift and effective. When informed as to the maximum penalty for their crime, they told investigators everything they wanted to know. In the case of Heinz, it was difficult to shut him up.

Both men said that they had been seduced by the size of the bribe Sar-Say offered, as well as his claim that the Broa would eventually find Earth with or without their help. The investigators' official report pointed out that Sar-Say could have offered a great deal more – the entire planet, if necessary. Sar-Say's ability to offer huge rewards, they argued, put him in a different class than other prisoners, a much more dangerous class.

To ensure that he did not escape again, an entire platoon of Peace Enforcers were assigned to guard him. Individual P.E.s would operate only in pairs, and would be rotated periodically to other duties to ensure they didn't also fall victim to the blandishments that had snared Heinz and Ludnick.

When Mark heard of the arrangement, he was put in mind of an old saying: *Quis custodiet ipsos custodes?—Who will guard the guardians?* It was a problem as ancient as its Latin roots.

Those invited to the emergency meeting included the three institute directors, their personal staffs, several members of the coordinator's staff, and members of parliament. Mark Rykand was there supporting his boss. Lisa had again been invited for her specialized expertise. Dieter Pavel was there. So was Dan Landon, resplendent in his dress Admiral's uniform. General Parsons of the Peace Enforcers was also present.

Upon entering the conference room, Mark walked over to where Dan Landon was standing and shook his hand.

"Good to see you again, Admiral."

Landon smiled. "And you, Mark. Lisa is as lovely as ever, I see."

"More lovely."

"Just like old times. One more and we could have a Klys'kra't reunion!"

The two of them were facing the floor-to-ceiling window, overlooking Toronto. Both were startled when a voice behind them said, "I'm up for it. Where's the party?"

Mark pivoted to discover Mikhail Vasloff standing behind him. His surprise was such that he didn't remember shaking hands and he stammered a greeting.

"So, anyone know why we are here?" Vasloff asked in that hail-fellow-well-met tone that he had learned to perfection.

"Not a clue," Mark replied. Only later did he remember that Dan Landon remained mute.

"It must be important. The Coordinator sent her personal aircraft for me. I must say, I could get used to traveling that way."

"I wish I had," Mark mumbled. "Lisa and I were sandwiched into tourist for the jump to Toronto."

At hearing her name, Lisa turned her head. She had been talking to one of Jean-Pierre's minions. At the sight of Vasloff, she wore the same startled look that Mark suspected was on his own face.

Vasloff made a few more comments, then excused himself and went over to shake hands with Alan Fernandez. Fernandez had had a bad time since Sar-Say's escape. He was taking most of the blame in the news media, blame that he richly deserved, in Mark's opinion.

Before Mark could ponder further, Nadine Halstrom swept into the room, trailed by Anton Bartok and Tony Hulsey. At the Coordinator's gesture, the principals sat at the long, mahogany table, while their aides took seats around the periphery.

Mark moved to his seat in front of the glass wall through which sunlight poured. He luxuriated in the heat on his back for a few seconds before the window darkened and the overhead lights came on. Behind him, the glass began to emit the low frequency white noise indicative of an anti-eavesdropping field.

"Thank you for coming," the Coordinator said after everyone was settled "The recent scare regarding Sar-Say has caused a strategy review by my administration. Since you are all involved, we thought it best to tell you our decision before we go public.

"Tony, will you do the honors?"

"Yes, Madam Coordinator," Hulsey replied, getting ponderously to his feet. He turned to the crowd and said, "I don't have to tell you that Sar-Say's recent escape unnerved everyone here in Toronto, as I am sure it did all of you. I haven't had a full night's sleep since the news broke. I keep having visions of alien hordes invading my bedroom.

"Nor am I the only one. The cabinet has been in marathon session for much of the past three days. I can't remember when we've had a more difficult decision to make, or as much acrimony making it..."

"Get on with it, Tony," Nadine Halstrom said, her voice betraying her fatigue.

"Very well, Madame Coordinator." He turned to survey the expectant faces around the table. "After a great deal of debate, we have made a decision. As much as many of us would like another option, we have decided to support the Colorado Springs plan.

"As of this moment, we are activating Operation Gibraltar Earth!"

#

Hulsey's statement momentarily stunned the listeners. Mark, who was seated directly behind his boss, could tell that Hamlin was smiling by the way his ears shifted position. Lisa reached over and gave his hand a quick squeeze. A couple of other attendees were exultant.

They, however, were in a minority. The announcement elicited gasps from several people, and an audible snarl from Mikhail Vasloff. Alan Fernandez looked crestfallen. Mark caught the eye of Dan Landon, who seemed unsurprised. Possibly, he had gotten a preview.

Nadine Halstrom waited for the news to sink in before continuing. When she spoke, her tone was deceptively mild.

"I take it there are some objections to this decision. Mikhail, why don't you start?"

Vasloff struggled to regain control. When his purplish complexion had begun to fade and he could once again speak coherently, he asked simply, "Madam Coordinator, how could you?"

"How could I not?" she replied coldly. "Sar-Say's near escape proved that hiding from the Broa is just not a viable option."

"I fail to see how you came to that conclusion."

"I'll give you two reasons: Heinz and Ludnick."

"I beg your pardon?"

"Don't you understand? Two human beings were willing to betray the species for a billion credits each, and without much thought on the matter, I might add. *A billion credits!* Why do you suppose Sar-Say chose that number? Because it is probably the biggest number any normal person can comprehend."

"The Paris plan has taken that into account, Madame Coordinator. We can prevent such things from happening in the future."

"How, *Gospodin* Vasloff? Sar-Say was able to find two willing accomplices just by passing one of them a note. How many others would have been willing to take his bribe? If a billion had proven insufficient, what number would not have been? No, this incident proves that any thought we had of hiding out forever among the stars was just so much utopianism. It's a plan that puts all of us at the mercy of the most feckless and greedy among us."

"We could just kill him, Madame Coordinator," General Parsons suggested. The matter-of-fact nature of his tone caused a chill to run down Lisa's spine.

"We considered it, General. Believe me, we considered it seriously! Unfortunately, killing Sar-Say won't solve our problem. Once word gets out of what the Broa can offer, some idiot is liable to go looking for them on his own.

"No, ladies and gentlemen. We have been betrayed by our own avaricious natures. There are too damned many nuts on this planet to make hiding out a viable option. To be really sure that no one betrays us, we would have to give up space travel altogether – pull everyone out of the colonies, return them to Earth, and then destroy both our starships and our interplanetary vessels."

Director Landrieu nodded. "Similar to our recommendation, Madame Coordinator."

"I know it is, Jean-Pierre. But the technology is too well known to put the genie back into this particular bottle! We would have to be constantly on our guard against some clandestine starship project; and not just for a little while – for centuries! It just won't work.

"The fact is that we can't trust a goodly percentage of our populace. Some would betray us for money. Others are just plain crazy. We can't guarantee what our policy will be after the next election, let alone for the next thousand years. The only long term solution is to deal with the foe now, while our minds are concentrated on the prospect of being hanged."

Nadine Halstrom looked around the table, determination in her eyes. "'*Broa delenda est,*' it would seem, ladies and gentlemen. The Sovereignty must be killed if we are ever to be safe.

#

"Well, Mark, are we going to sign up?" Lisa asked. It was night outside their hotel room and they had the curtains open. The lights were off because they were lying in bed, naked. Not that anyone could have seen them on the 120th floor, or that they would have minded if someone did, but the city was much more beautiful when viewed from the dark.

They were cuddled in the spoon position. Mark had his arms around Lisa. His left hand roamed lightly and lovingly, eliciting giggles and an occasional moan of pleasure. His right arm was trapped beneath her, causing him to slowly lose feeling in his fingers. He had considered asking her to shift position, but decided that the moment was too delicious to disturb.

"Well, are we?" Lisa asked again.

"Sorry," he replied. "I was distracted by your beauty. Are we what?"

"Going to join the expedition to relieve Brinks Base?"

"Of course. We started this whole mess. It's only fitting that we see it through to the end."

"What if they split us up?"

"They can't. Policy is that married couples in the Survey serve together. I don't see it being any different in the new Space Navy."

His left hand happened to be resting lightly where he could feel her pulse. He noted the sudden increase in her heart rhythm.

"Married couples?" she asked, her voice suddenly whispery, as though she was not getting enough air. "Is that a proposal?"

"It is if you will have me," he replied.

She didn't answer directly. Instead, she went into the contortion necessary to turn to face him, getting tangled up in the sheets as she did so. The brief struggle with the bedding elicited several un-ladylike expressions. When she was free, she pressed her body the length of his and asked, "Would you repeat that, please?"

"Lisa, will you marry me?" Now it was his turn to be breathless.

Green eyes searched brown for long seconds, as if to judge whether he was joking. Then, in one slow motion, she lifted her mouth to his and kissed him. Chaste at first, the kiss quickly turned carnal. It was several minutes before the two of them broke to steady their breathing.

When he could speak again, Mark asked, "Was that a 'yes?'"

"That was definitely a 'yes,'" she replied. Neither of them spoke for quite a while. They had other things on their minds.

#

PART TWO:

INTO THE DEEP BLACK

Chapter Twenty Three

As Sar-Ganth sunned himself on the patio of his sprawling domicile on the shores of the Talan Sea, he reached out to occasionally pull a *varith* fruit from the branch of one of his prize trees. Pulling the stem from the purple-red fruit, he inspected it closely before popping it into his mouth. His teeth bit through the thick outer skin to be rewarded with a sudden gush of deliciously tart pulp and juice.

He contemplated the fact that the simple pleasures of life were the most memorable. The taste of *varith* fruit, the attentions of a female in estrus, the thought of dismembering his rival Kas-Ta. The first two pleasures were within his grasp. Unfortunately, the final one was currently beyond his reach.

Still, one could hope…

"Administrator Fos is here to see you, Clan Master," one of his numerous servants announced.

"Send him in."

The black beetle of a being scurried into his presence on all twelve legs before hiking himself up on the last four.

"Good morning, Clan Master."

"Good morning, Fos. Is it time for your periodic status report already?"

"Yes, master."

"I hadn't noticed. I have been too busy with my daughter's new pup. Very well, what have you got for me?"

"The clan accounts are in good shape," Fos said, beginning where he knew his master had the keenest interest. "Our overall store of value has increased by nearly one-eighth in the latest cycle, and even Davinan has turned in a surplus for a change."

Davinan was a planet in the Fasdol sector, one where the Sar-Dva Clan's investments had been largely wasted. The previous cycle, Sar-Ganth had appointed a new ruler for the planet, and the new regime seemed to be doing better in extracting the ore that was stinking mud hole's primary export.

"Excellent. Send my congratulations to my ortho-nephew and tell him that I am pleased with his progress."

"Yes, Master."

"What of our other enterprises?"

Fos went down the list of clan activities that were turning in comfortable, and sometimes spectacular, excess value. If this trend continued for another cycle, Sar-Ganth would have a sufficient holdings to purchase another world. The clan currently ruling a planet in the Vorash Sector had made a botch of exploiting the place, and Sar-Ganth had an idea how to make it profitable.

Fos continued the recitation of their accounts. The news was good. He would have no difficulty dispensing to each clan member their share of excess value. Such payments were important. Without them, Sar-Ganth would quickly lose his stature, his position, and potentially, his life.

The Greater Sun was high in the sky when Fos finished his recitation of the accounts and hesitantly mentioned that there was one more item to discuss.

"Make it brief," his master said. "The midday meal is nearly upon us."

"Yes, master. There remains the ongoing problem of Sar-Say and the Vulcans."

Sar-Ganth signaled his confusion. "Sorry, but that name escapes me."

"If you will remember two cycles ago, Clan Master. We received a report that our missing auditor was being held prisoner on an unregistered planet."

"Oh, yes. Now that you mention it, I do remember. We established a surveillance routine.

"That we did," his assistant agreed. "We have been paying a significant amount to maintain the search. To date, we have discovered nothing of these Vulcans. Whoever erased their file was an expert."

"No trace at all?" Sar-Ganth asked incredulously.

"None, Master. It is as though they disappeared into vacuum."

"They have to be out there," Sar-Ganth replied. "A ship of Vulcans implies a planet of Vulcans. They were on an extended trading mission. They must have stopped at other worlds."

"I agree," Fos said. "Someone is hiding them, or else we would have found something in two cycles of searching."

"How much value has the search consumed to date?"

Fos told him.

Sar-Ganth signaled his surprise. "You were correct to bring the matter to my attention. I suppose I will have to take the matter up with Those Who Rule."

"Is that wise, Master? Had you violated custom to such an extent, wouldn't you do whatever was necessary to conceal the evidence. I fear the destruction of the Vulcan world before we can identify the miscreants who have hidden them."

"It is a risk," Sar-Ganth agreed. However, we lack the resources to make a proper search. Our missing auditor will have to take his chances. Shut down our surveillance routines. I will take the matter up with the council."

"It shall be so, Clan Master."

#

Mr. and Mrs. Mark Rykand jockeyed for position in front of their cabin's tiny mirror as they prepared to meet the coming day. Their compartment aboard *New Hope II* had but a single sink inset into the bulkhead, with insufficient space in front for two people to simultaneously perform their morning ablutions. However, during the twelve months they had been en route to Brinks Base, they had developed a routine.

First, Mark would use one of their two small wash cloths to wash away the previous day's grime. This was made necessary by the ship's two-minute-shower-once-every-two-weeks rule. Then he would relinquish his place to Lisa to do the same. While she washed, he would sit on the bed, smear depilatory cream over his face and let it sit for a minute. When she finished, he would use his cloth to wipe the cream away, taking the day's beard with it. He would then brush his teeth and comb his hair quickly, before once again relinquishing the mirror, where Lisa would begin her much more extensive morning preparations.

While she washed her face, brushed her teeth, and applied her makeup, he made the bed and then retracted it into its recess. That allowed him room to extend the two cabin chairs from their cubbyholes, and gave him a place to sit as he dressed.

The work uniform of the new Space Navy was royal blue, with gold stripes. Mark's uniform bore the insignia of a Fleet Lieutenant, as did Lisa's. His assignment was in Astrogation, while she remained in Alien Assessment. Because of his experience with the astronomy team on the previous expedition, he was Prime Astrogator aboard *New Hope.*

With the ship moving superlight, there wasn't much for an astrogator to do, save for the hour each week when they dropped sub-light and took sightings of their position. There were also the numerous weapons drills the captain insisted on. In his copious spare time, Mark assisted in delving into the data he had retrieved at Klys'kra't.

Lisa's job kept her busy. Several scientists aboard *New Hope* were refining humanity's understanding of Broan psychology and she was much in demand for her observations and insights regarding Sar-Say.

It had taken two years for Dan Landon's shipyard and others to pump out the vessels needed to support a return to Brinks Base. There had been eleven starships in the last expedition. This time, there were eighty vessels of all types carrying the machinery and equipment that would turn Brinks Base into humanity's secret bastion within the Sovereignty.

Before they could begin operations against the Broa, of course, the fleet must cross the 7000 light-year gulf between Earth and Hideout. Once again, it would take them more than a year to reach their destination... or as Lisa often remarked, "It only *seems* like a century."

"Are you about ready?" Mark asked his wife as she poured herself into her coverall. He watched appreciatively as she sealed herself in and quickly combed out her blonde curls.

"Ready," she replied.

"Then let's go to breakfast," he said, sliding his toes into his ship slippers as he did so. Just as they had done every morning for the past 368 days, they unsealed the hatch and stepped out into the corridor, turning left toward the mess hall.

A new day aboard *New Hope II* had begun.

#

Jennifer Mullins was bored. But then, who wasn't? As she sat in the astronomy control room, the strains of Williams' *Star Wars, Opus 3,* reverberated from the rock walls. Jennifer loved the Old Master composers and, being alone, had the volume turned up to where the music was just below the threshold of pain. She tapped her foot in time to the beat while she worked on her weekly status report.

Status: Nothing to report!

At least, that is what she would like to have written, but of course, it just wasn't done. Dr. Powell insisted on at least two pages of text each week to basically say, "Nothing to report."

It had been more than a month since their last gravity wave observation. Triangulation put that particular wave in a system nearly 200 light-years away, almost due galactic north from Brinks. It had been thrilling to realize that the stargate that had originated the wave had done so at a time when human beings were still struggling to get into space. Of course, that had been the last thrill she'd had.

Even her Saturday night dates were beginning to pall. For one thing, Henry Sortees was very debonair, but he was beginning to repeat his jokes, and his performance in bed was little better than adequate. It was a shame there wasn't any new blood on the base. After four years of exile, even the talk of how many credits they were amassing back home had ended.

The problem was that no one knew how long it would be before they were relieved. Hell, she told herself, the Broa might have followed the expedition home and conquered Earth while they were stuck on this godforsaken airless rock of a moon. Perhaps no one would ever come to tell them that they could go home. Perhaps they had no home to return to!

In the meantime, the slow, unglamorous work of watching the sky continued. The contact the previous month had added a fifth confirmed Broan world to their list. Five worlds in four years. At this rate, Brinks would have a population the size of Earth's by the time they finished their survey of the Sovereignty. That is, if the air plant and hydroponic gardens held out.

Life went on, to be sure. Approximately 40% of the original expedition's rear guard had either married or taken up housekeeping in the interim, and two dozen children had been born. That, at least, was the bright side of life. Whenever Jennifer felt blue, she would walk to where the nursery-kindergarten had been set up.

There was something about the high pitched squeal of children's voices that perked her up. She would watch the little darlings/barbarians chase each other around, oblivious to the fact that they were cut off from the rest of humanity, and smile. Often she became wistful, wishing for a child of her own. If only Henry were more skilled at the oldest of humanity's sports, perhaps she would have considered a long term commitment and motherhood.

The opus ended in its usual crash of symbols and horns. She keyed her display and scanned the list of available music. Even that was getting old. How many times could one listen to the same symphony without becoming jaded to even the classics?

She glanced at the chronometer. Only 45 minutes left in this watch, after which she would adjourn to the commons and spend another evening watching holos she had seen five times before, or else join in one of the interminable bridge tournaments that never seemed to end.

She reached out to key her selection into the music list when a different sound enveloped her. From all around, the sound of alarms blared in her ears.

She blinked, and turned back to her main screen. On it was a bright red text box with the blinking words, LASER DETECTED, inside. There was also a coordinate indicating that the monochromatic light was coming from the sky in the direction of Earth. Her boredom suddenly forgotten, Jennifer keyed for analysis. The machine was still calculating when her comm unit buzzed.

"Observatory," she snapped out, not taking her eyes from the screen.

"Powell," came the reply. "What have you got?"

"A comm laser, sir," she replied. "Definitely human."

Her words were cut off by the resumption of the alarms. Absentmindedly, she keyed them to silence.

"A second comm laser, sir. And a third!"

Within a minute there were a dozen of them.

"Any messages yet?"

"Not yet. Just carrier waves. However, I think it safe to say that the fleet has arrived to relieve us."

"Sounds like the only explanation," her boss replied. "However, let's not get anyone's hope up until we know for sure. Study the situation and when you have an official message, make the announcement."

"Yes, sir."

"Powell, out."

"Observatory out," Jennifer replied. She turned back to her work. The comm lasers remained strangely silent, although she remembered that no message would be started until the ships on the other end were sure their beams had fallen on Brinks Base.

Then, as she was beginning to suspect something was wrong, the screens began to display messages. The first was the time of transmission and the name of the ship – virtually all of them strange to her – then the standard fleet greetings announcing arrival. Finally, there were several personal messages appended to the transmissions, mostly to the captains of the two vessels that had stayed behind.

Discovering that she had been holding her breath, Jennifer exhaled loudly and keyed Brinks' response to the flood of incoming messages. The response was impersonal, giving the arriving ships approach information and a synopsis of what had happened in their absence.

Her duty done, Jennifer sat back and marveled as the number of comm lasers announcing ship arrivals continued to climb. "My God," she thought, "they've brought everything, including the kitchen sink."

Her mood was considerably buoyed half an hour later when she was relieved by Eric Powell, who was himself amazed at the number of ships breaking out of superlight.

"It's an invasion!" he muttered as he scanned all of the identifications.

"If so, it's a happy one," Jennifer responded.

"Do you know what this means?" Powell asked, straightening up from where he had been hunched over the monitors.

"I do indeed," Jennifer said, jumping up and hugging him. "It means we get to go home. In a little over a year from now, I will be frolicking in the surf at Waikiki!"

#

Chapter Twenty Four

Dan Landon smiled to himself as he sat in the command chair of Starship *Abraham Lincoln* and contemplated the fact that he never wanted to be anywhere else. Two years in command of a shipyard had taught him that he much preferred flying starships to building them. Despite his distaste for the construction end of the business, he had done a sufficiently good job that he had been inducted into the Space Navy, promoted to Fleet Admiral, and given command of the second expedition to Broan Space.

"Honest Abe" was not itself a faux Broan design. While the New Mexico shipyard had been popping out fake Type Seven freighters, Type Two Transports, and Bulk Carriers, the Sahara shipyard had been building humanity's first true interstellar warships.

The *Lincoln* was a blastship of the *Luis Ramirez* class, the second out of the cradle. Her armament consisted of lasers and particle beams powerful enough to melt another vessel at a thousand kilometers. Her magazines were stuffed with enough superlight missiles and warheads that she could raze a planet if need be.

There was nothing subtle about Dan Landon's new command. *Lincoln* had been designed to take on the largest Broan ship of which humanity was aware. Hopefully, it would not come to that. The *Lincoln*'s current task was to remain out of sight and guard the Q-ships that would probe Broan worlds as the *Ruptured Whale* had probed Klys'kra't. If everything went as planned, she would not show herself to the enemy for several years, and then only in the company of a hundred other vessels of equal or greater striking power.

"Honest Abe" had been constructed on the simple principle: that bigger is better. As such, she represented a calculated risk. Each behemoth in her class was three times larger than their Broan adversaries, making them much too large to fit through a stargate. When humanity finally acquired stargate technology, they hoped to build them large enough for blastships. Otherwise, the main human striking force would have to cross the vastness of intra-galactic space the hard way.

Landon's elevation to Fleet Admiral had put him in command of eighty ships of all types. Most were Q-ships. The fleet had formed up in Earth orbit over two hectic weeks while final touches were put on the new constructs. They had launched en masse. When the fleet was well past the orbit of Neptune, they had disappeared into the blackness of superlight.

It is the nature of superlight travel that each ship must make the voyage essentially alone. Vessels moving faster than light had no way to detect or communicate with one another. The only chance for outside contact came when the ships dropped sublight once each week to take their bearings.

Routes and breakout times were rigidly controlled in the hope that the fleet could maintain some semblance of order. However, space is so large that it was rare to catch sight of even one other vessel during the hour spent observing the universe before returning to superlight flight.

Even during the final breakout, when some eighty ships entered the Hideout System in practically the same microsecond, no two vessels were close enough to see one another. After 7000 light-years in transit, the fleet was scattered over half of Hideout's northern celestial hemisphere.

While they made their slow way from the outer Hideout system toward Brinks, Landon had one particularly nagging worry. It had been more than a year since he had been able to tally his flock. How many had made it the full distance?

Fleet protocol called for Landon to wait 30 days before searching for stragglers. If any ships failed to appear by the deadline, he would launch a pair of Type Seven freighters to backtrack their route. Starships that experienced engine problems had orders to make for one of a dozen designated star systems in which to seek refuge. The Type Sevens would stop for three days in each of these refuges to scan for laser and radio emissions. Any ship that made it to a refuge sun had a slightly better than even chance of being detected and rescued, assuming they retained the ability to communicate. However, if they broke down in interstellar space and were unable to make the designated systems, they were irretrievably lost. There would be no way to find them in the vastness that lay between Sol and Hideout.

To Dan Landon's immense relief, when everyone checked in, he discovered that his whole flock had successfully made the voyage.

#

"Admiral, welcome to Brinks Base," Captain Hans Heinrich, base commander, said as he saluted. "Are we glad to see you!"

"I'll bet you are," Landon replied.

"Yes, sir. We were beginning to worry that you had forgotten us."

"Not for a minute, Captain. We just had a lot to do before we could come back."

"I see that, sir. I've never seen so many starships in my life. And there doesn't seem to be a familiar name in the bunch."

"No, they were all constructed over the past two years. We've got the shipyards programmed and the pipeline flowing. There will be a lot more where they came from. I suspect you will get command of something bigger when you get home. We owe you and your people a great deal for sticking it out here."

"I hope you will have time to tell them yourself, Admiral."

"I'll make a point of it. How long do you think will be required to brief my people on what you have learned?"

"About ten minutes, sir. We will talk very, very quickly!"

Landon laughed. "I take it you are anxious to space for home."

"Yes, sir."

"I'm afraid we are going to have to keep you a bit longer, Hans. However, we won't make it longer than we have to."

"If you will come this way, Admiral, I'll introduce you to my staff and give you a rundown on what we have been doing."

"Lead on, Captain."

As the two officers shuffled their way through Brinks Base, the only way to move quickly in the moon's one-quarter gee, they passed a woman with a toddler in tow and a baby on her hip. She wore the uniform of a ship's botanist. Landon smiled and nodded.

"Well, I can see one thing you have been doing!"

Heinrich nodded. "There is that, sir. We have had quite a little population explosion here on base."

#

A dozen officers awaited them in what Landon remembered to be the base commissary. In his absence, it had taken on the ambience of someone's oversize living room. As they entered, the officers drawn up in double file snapped to attention. Captain Heinrich began the introductions.

"Admiral, my second in command. Captain Gareth Cardozo, of *Vaterland.*"

"Captain Cardozo."

"Commander Marcos Severance, my executive officer. And Commander Jonas Barksdale, Captain Cardozo's exec."

"Commanders."

"Lieutenant Jennifer Mullins, Astrogation and one of our base astronomers."

"Lieutenant Mullins," Landon said, nodding. "We are going to want to talk to later."

"Yes, sir. I'm ready."

Heinrich continued down the line, introducing each officer in turn. Landon nodded and shook their hands. Having finished the introductions, Landon stood back and looked at each of them in turn before speaking. "Ladies and gentlemen, I want to thank all of you for your service. It has been long, lonely, and difficult. However, let me assure you that it has been worth it.

"My fleet and I have arrived to perform various reconnaissance missions within the Sovereignty and to obtain information vital to our war effort. We will perform these missions based on the information you have obtained in our absence. Rest assured that you have all of humanity behind you, and that you will receive a hero's welcome when you return home.

"Please let your people know that it is my wish to get you into space within the week. That should give you enough time to pack your belongings, say your goodbyes, and to attend the blowout bash I am throwing for you.

"Also, let them know we have brought news recordings and summaries so that you can catch up on events Earthside... the important things — who is sleeping with who in Hollywood and what the latest fashions are like."

The small joke received a polite laugh.

"Very well, don't let me detain you. You are dismissed back to your duties or to your quarters. Lieutenant Mullins, please stay for a moment."

The assembled officers filed out and disappeared in both directions along the corridor.

"Relax, Jennifer," Landon said as he turned toward the lieutenant.

Her posture dissolved into a relaxed stand. "Good of you to remember me, sir."

"How could I forget? You were one of my best astrogator trainees aboard *Magellan*."

"I'm glad to hear that, sir."

"I want to hear of your observations of the Sovereignty. How many additional star systems have you located?"

"Five, sir. One just a month ago."

"Five? How does that equate with our initial projections?"

"Lower than projected sir; but considering how big space is, a respectable number."

Landon nodded. "Any hard data on these systems?"

"A couple of them seem to have quite a lot of stargate traffic, judging by the number of gravity waves emanating from them. Also, there is one thing you should know."

"What is that, Jennifer?"

"Four of the five are located back the way you just came. If these are representative of how Broan space is laid out, you may have just flown through the heart of the Broan Sovereignty."

Landon frowned. "Now that is a sobering thought, isn't it?"

"Yes, sir."

#

The party was laid on for the fifth day after the fleet began transporting supplies and equipment down to Sutton's surface. With so many newcomers in the base, the party would essentially take place just about everywhere.

Mark and Lisa had come down from *New Hope II* the day before to organize the transfer of scientific information. They were sleeping on the floor in the library since every other bed in the base was occupied, many by more than one person. After four years of the same old faces, the original inhabitants of the base were anxious to make the acquaintance of their replacements. Several temporary relationships were consummated in that 120 hours.

When they arrived at the mess compartment, where the party was centered, they encountered an interesting dichotomy. The space had been divided into two separate social functions. On the starboard side sat various single crewmembers of the departing ships, invariably surrounded by newly arrived spacers. Surrounding the male departees were mixed male and female groups, usually talking shop. Around the female crewmembers were clustered all male galleries.

"I don't think I've seen that many horny females in one place in my entire life," Mark whispered as he scanned the crowd.

"What about the men?" she whispered back.

"Not even close to a record for the men," he responded. The jibe earned him an elbow to the ribs.

On the port side of the compartment, a completely different party was in progress. Here could be found the married couples from the two fleets. They were seated on chairs, cushions, or the bare floor A number of women from the relief fleet were holding the babies of departing fleet members, cooing to them and trying to get them to laugh. The older children seemed shy, understandable since they had just been descended upon by five times the population they had been born into. The sight of so many unfamiliar faces must have been frightening to a three-year-old.

"Which side do you want to join?" Lisa asked.

Mark, having been married just over two years, nonetheless knew the response required of him. "Let's join the married folks."

"Are you sure you wouldn't want to hang on every word of that blonde bombshell in the corner?"

"Not me," he replied, only half insincerely. "I've caught my limit and I'm happy."

"Good answer," she replied.

They joined the couples and soon Lisa was cooing to a baby not six months old.

"Steve Simms," the baby's father said, holding out his hand.

"Mark Rykand," Mark replied.

"I know who you are, Lieutenant. I remember you from the first expedition. You're the one who got everyone stirred up."

"I did at that," Mark agreed. He gestured widely with his hand, taking in the bacchanal in front of him. "Who would have thought of this scene that day we returned from Klys'kra't with our tails between our legs?"

"It's hard to believe, all right," the other sighed. "At times I thought this day would never come. Can't say I'm looking forward to the voyage home, I'll tell you that. Another year in vacuum and I may lose it."

"It's hard," Mark agreed. "This is the third time I've made the transit. It seems as though I've spent half my life between Earth and Brinks Base. It will be better when we figure out the stargates."

"I've been thinking about that," Simms said. "In fact, I've been thinking about it for most of four years. Are we still planning on stealing a gate from the Broa?"

"We'll have to," Mark replied. "They are trying to develop stargates on our own back on Earth, but with us a year from Earth, even if they succeed, we won't know it."

"It's liable to rile the Broa up when we do."

"I know it. Unfortunately, we don't have much choice. Without stargates, the logistics just don't work."

Simms nodded. "Have you considered that there may still be gates in abandoned star systems?"

"I beg your pardon?"

"Look, Lieutenant, my job was to catalog that shit pot full of data you brought back. Captain Heinrich thought it would give us a clue as to where to point our telescopes to see if we could detect the emissions of a Broan world."

"A good plan. Did you detect any worlds?"

"A couple of probables, but without gravity waves we really can't be sure. Still, I've spent a lot of time with the Voldar'ik data, and found several references to worlds that have been destroyed by the Broa. Do you suppose they went to the trouble of dismantling the gates after destroying those systems, Lieutenant?"

"I don't know," Mark replied, suddenly intrigued. A system with a dead planet and a stargate was something he had never considered. It might make sense for the Broa to leave a gate in such systems. There would be salvage and mining operations, possibly survivors to enslave and cart off. Besides, how did one get the *last* stargate out of a system anyway? You could jump in without a stargate, but you couldn't jump out.

If such a gate disappeared, the Broa might never notice the loss. Even if they did, they would be faced with nothing more than a mystery. A little careful preparation might even convince them that the gate had fallen victim to a natural disaster – a wayward asteroid, for instance.

"An intriguing thought, Mr. Simms," Mark replied. "I will report it to the admiral and make sure he knows who thought up the idea."

"Thank you, Lieutenant."

#

Chapter Twenty Five

Hideout, the star, was just peeking over the horizon as Construction Specialist Grant Papadelous aimed his big cutting laser at a gray outcropping of lava and switched on the power. His goggles instantly darkened as the bright, violet laser spot formed on the surface and immediately began vaporizing the rock. A heavy incandescent plume fountained skyward as the spot disappeared into a glowing, 5-cm diameter hole.

Despite the fact that his tractor cabin was pressurized, Papadelous worked from inside a heavy, armored vacsuit. Safety was paramount when the job took place on an airless, primitive moon some seven thousand light-years from Earth.

As the spot disappeared down the incandescent hole, Papadelous scanned his instruments with the boredom of someone who has performed the same task a thousand times. The work order called this a 200-meter long communications channel from the surface into the new gallery they had hollowed out of Sutton's interior. Cables would be strung through the channel and then the whole thing would be filled with vacuum setting epoxy to seal it up again. After that, the gallery could be pressurized and interiors installed to make the new volume livable.

What the cables would be used for, he had no idea. That wasn't his problem. Boring the hole was his task, after which he would bore another, and another, and another, ad infinitum. As a boy in Greece, his mother had told him the tale of Sisyphus, condemned by the gods to ceaselessly roll a rock to the top of a mountain each day, only to have it fall back of its own weight every night. Somehow, his current job put him in mind of that myth, except that he had been condemned to dig endlessly until he carved away the whole of this ugly moon.

Nor was he the only vacuum jack at work on the surface while others busily carved new tunnels and living galleries below. With eighty ships in orbit about the airless moon, Brinks Base had just suffered the largest population explosion in its brief history and an expansion of living and working quarters was the first order of business.

The sudden appearance of the system primary above the jagged horizon put the sun directly into Papadelous's eyes, which in turn caused his head to throb. The star wasn't the culprit in producing his headache. Rather, the send off they had given the crews of *Ranger* and *Vaterland* the previous evening was the primary cause. The party had been a raucous one, a bash that Grant had enjoyed immensely, especially the latter part.

He smiled at the memory of the bacchanal. He had found himself conversing with a female lieutenant for the first couple of hours. Him and about half the men in his construction battalion... at least those who had been shuttled down from the heavy equipment carrier. It had been just past midnight when he finally managed to talk her into accompanying him back to her soon-to-be-vacated compartment. What had followed made the interminable voyage from Earth almost seem worth it. His new found, and very transient, friend had made love with an urgency that spoke of her excitement at having someone new in her life. His memory of the night had been marred only by the realization that he hadn't gotten her name the next morning. All he remembered was that she said she was an astrogator aboard *Ranger*.

The laser drill cut off automatically when the sensors detected a slight weakening of the incandescent plume, indicating that the drill beam had penetrated a cavity in the rock... presumably Gallery A-17 in the new annex if Grant's three dimensional diagram was correct. The computer shut down the laser quickly enough that there would be little more than a scorch mark on the opposite wall where the drill beam had focused momentarily after breakthrough.

With his current hole drilled and another one facing him in a few minutes, actually a series of holes into which would be anchored the foundation of a communications tower, Grant paused to scan the horizon and sky.

In the distance was the sharp, black outline of a mountain. It must be a tall one, he thought, since its lower slopes were hidden somewhere over the horizon. It had been the mountain that had kept Hideout's rays out of his eyes as long as it did. Nearer to him, he could see two other yellow construction tractors hauling equipment to various spots around the rugged black plain.

The amount of equipment they had hauled out from Earth was staggering. Of course, it had to be. Brinks Base would become the headquarters for humanity's war against the Broa at least until they got the human stargate network up and running. Even then, Brinks might not be graced by a stargate. It all depended on how distant the nearest Broan world was.

If only a few light years separated the base from an enemy world, then it would be too risky for ships to jump directly to the Hideout System. Their secret base would remain a secret only until the first gravity waves reached Broan controlled space. After that, someone would wonder why an uninhabited system possessed an unregistered stargate, they would send a ship to investigate, and the jig would be up.

Overhead, several bright stars strung out in a single line crossed the sky with visible motion. These were humanity's ships in orbit. One need gaze skyward only a few minutes to see dimmer lights detach from the brighter ones. These were the landing boats that were shuttling supplies down from the freighters. In addition to all of the Q-Ship holds stuffed to their hull plates with necessary equipment, six large colony ships had accompanied the fleet. It would take more than a month to unload these behemoths of their treasure.

Beyond the moving ships was Brinks itself, an oversize Earth. The blue-white world was currently in half phase, with a very indistinct terminator line marking the transition from light to dark.

The black line of the horizon with its mountains beyond, the ships overhead, the blue-white ball as a backdrop... all should have combined into an awe-inspiring view. Perhaps it would have had not Papadelous's head been throbbing so.

Giving in to the inevitable, he muttered the command that would cause a small white pellet to appear on the shelf of his helmet in front of his chin. Leaning forward, he tongued the pellet into his mouth and grimaced at the tart taste before rotating his head to get at the drinking nipple. He washed the pain reliever down with a mouthful of tepid water and began counting the seconds until it began to work.

Having done the only thing he could at the moment for his headache, he checked his workscreen for the next job and put the tractor in gear. As it bounced over the uneven ground en route to where the communications mast lay prone on the surface, Grant Papadelous contemplated the fact that the jouncing wasn't doing his headache any good.

#

"Everyone have a good time last night?" Dan Landon asked his staff. The dozen officers gathered around the long table constructed of locally quarried nickel-iron all looked as though they wished they were somewhere else. Most were listless, while a few glanced nervously at the open doorway, as though visualizing the quickest route to the local head. Their condition answered his question more eloquently than words ever could. It was with a certain malicious mischief that he boomed out, "All right, enough fun. Let's get down to business. Commander Aster. What did you learn yesterday?"

Aster, a small intense man with an unruly shock of blond hair, leaned forward and planted his elbows on the table while keying his datacom to life. After a second, he responded to Landon's question.

"Just what you heard, sir. The caretaker staff discovered five possible Broan systems during our absence. Four of them are back in the direction of Earth, one is due galactic north."

"Analysis results?"

"Two of these contacts have issued a single gravity wave apiece. Two others have issued three waves, and one has issued more than a dozen."

"So we can assume that particular contact is a primary Broan world?" Landon asked.

"It's a good assumption to start," Aster replied. "The last discovery is more than 200 light-years from here, so the fact that there has only been a single wave may be misleading. Presumably traffic in that system could have increased considerably in two centuries."

"What of the radio and optical observations?"

Lieutenant Gretchen Stephens, Astronomy Section, spoke up. "I've reviewed their records. They have recorded definite radio signals from three nearby star systems, as well as two confirmed instances of monochromatic radiation."

"Comm lasers?"

"Yes, sir. Obviously these systems are inhabited, but there is no evidence as of yet that they have stargates in operation."

"No gravity waves in five years?"

"No, sir."

Landon frowned. "What are you implying?"

"Sir?"

"Are you suggesting that these systems lack stargates, and therefore, are *not* subjects of the Broan Sovereignty?" Landon asked.

"No, sir. What we know of them is that they would never do that."

"What we know of them comes primarily from Sar-Say and I have reason to distrust him," Landon replied coldly.

There were several brief nods. The Broa's near escape on Earth had sent a shiver through the officer ranks of the Stellar Survey... most of whom had since transferred to the Space Navy.

"Just because we have not yet detected a gravity wave from these other systems doesn't mean the Broa are not present, Admiral."

"No ship traffic in five years? That's a long time between visits, don't you agree?"

"Yes, sir."

Landon turned to a small mouse of a man who looked especially miserable this morning. Funny, Landon thought, he wouldn't have thought Dr. Luigi Penda to be the partying type. Penda wore the uniform of the Space Navy, with the rank of Senior Scientist. However, he did not wear it well. Some people looked disheveled, regardless of their wardrobe.

"Dr. Penda. Is it possible that these systems are emitting gravity waves and we aren't detecting them?"

"How far away are these systems?" the scientist asked.

"All within a dozen light-years," Gretchen Stephens replied.

"Not according to our theory about how gravity waves work, Admiral. The discontinuity of a mass materializing within the gate is what produces gravity waves. Theory says that these waves should be omni-directional."

"Could the Broa have overlooked these systems, even though they are emanating radio waves and comm laser beams?"

"No, sir. If we detected them, the Broa would have as well."

"Then, assuming for a moment that these systems aren't radiating gravity waves because they lack stargates, it is logical to assume that the Broa have chosen not to occupy them on purpose."

Penda shook his head vigorously, then appeared to regret it. "I agree with Lieutenant Stephens. That does not comport with what we think we know of their behavior."

"Yet, the systems have not been visited by starships via Broan stargate in five years," Landon persisted. "If the Broa bypassed these worlds on purpose, what does that tell us about their situation?"

Penda shrugged. "Perhaps the beings that inhabit these systems are just too different. They couldn't very well establish a colony on a gas giant like Bonnie or Clyde, even if an intelligent species were discovered to inhabit those giants. Likewise, an intelligent species found on a planet close to their star, say at the range of Mercury, would be difficult to conquer, just because of the difference in physiology. How would the Broa force an intelligent molten rock being to do anything?"

"Or they may be too technologically primitive for the Broa to worry about," another officer suggested.

"Unlikely," the scientist responded. "They need farmland to grow crops, mines to produce metals, raw materials of all kinds. We know they mine otherwise inhospitable and uninhabitable worlds. A planet with a population of potential slaves would be especially valuable as a raw material source."

Landon frowned. Everyone seemed especially obtuse this morning. He continued: "Okay, they have no reason to bypass an inhabited world, at least of oxygen breathers. So if they are actually doing it, what are the implications?"

"I suppose it could be proof of what we suspect, namely that their conquests have reached the point of diminishing returns," Dr. Penda replied. "If they lack the manpower or resources to conquer without limit, as we suspect, they would begin to cherry pick their victims. Especially valuable worlds would be conquered, while less favored ones would be left alone."

"Would that be feasible?" Commander Connors asked from down the table from Penda. Antoinette Connors was a statuesque brunette, with an aggressive personality. She was also Landon's most capable strategic planner. "Wouldn't they have to conquer any planet with a technologically advanced race? Otherwise, they risk being challenged by some competitor, essentially the same as we are planning to do."

Penda shook his head. "Without the stardrive or stargates, these unconquered species are trapped in their home systems. In effect, they have been frozen in place until such time as the overlords are better able to absorb them. Think of them as oil reserves that have yet to be extracted from the ground."

"Assume that the hypothesis is correct," Landon said. "How does that change our strategic and tactical situation?"

"How would it, sir?"

"Because, Doctor, unconquered systems within the Sovereignty could prove a source of allies. Presumably the bypassed star systems are aware of their situation and the fate that eventually awaits them."

"Yes, sir."

"Put some of your people to studying the implications. This may change our strategy. In the meantime, we know of five systems that are Broan fiefdoms. What do we do about them?"

The conversation quickly turned to operations planning.

Their orders were very clear regarding positively identified Broan star systems. Barring compelling reasons not to, such systems would be visited by a two-ship reconnaissance force. Initial reconnaissance would be conducted from the edge of each star system, with the recon ships hidden in the proto-comets and floating icebergs of the Oort Cloud.

#

"We've got orders," Mark told his wife as they ate dinner in the commissary. Like everywhere else on the base, the compartment was a mass of packing crates and equipment stacked haphazardly among the iron tables and benches.

"Who is 'we?'" Lisa asked. "The two of us or our ship?"

"Ship," he replied. "*New Hope* has been assigned to a scouting mission."

"To where?"

"It's called Target Gamma. It's the system with the heavy stargate traffic."

"Oh, goody! We get to sneak up on a star that is probably the home base of the entire fucking Broan Space Navy!"

"Not very ladylike," Mark admonished.

His jocular response was answered with a comment even less suitable for ladylike lips.

"Actually, we should only be so lucky," Mark responded. "Pinpointing the enemy's primary naval base this early would be something to tell the grandchildren."

"If we live to have any," Lisa replied. "When do we leave?"

"That's up to Captain Harris. I understand our second ship will be *Galloping Ghost*. She hasn't even begun unloading. That will take at least a week."

"Good," Lisa replied. "It will give me time to brush up my colloquial Broa."

#

Chapter Twenty Six

"Stand by for breakout," Mark Rykand announced. His words echoed in his ears as they were carried via annunciator throughout Starship *New Hope II.* Their voyage was coming to an end in the outskirts of a star system known to be in the hands of the Broa. The war against the pseudo-simians was about to begin in earnest.

"Status check, Astrogator!" Captain Jonah Harris ordered. Harris had been executive officer on a Survey starship before being transferred to the Space Navy and given his own command. He was still new enough at his job to betray traces of emotion in times of stress. This was one of those times.

"Everything is nominal, Captain," Mark responded in what he hoped was his best competent-but-bored-astrogator tone. He, too, was feeling the tension as the computer counted down the seconds to breakout.

The plan was for them to drop sublight well out from the target star, which everyone was calling Gamma, after its arbitrary target designation. After checking more than a hundred stars, the astronomers had come up with general rules for virtually every feature to be found in any system. Among these were the minimum and maximum distances for the leftover remnants of star formation that made up the Oort Cloud.

New Hope was more than a week out of Brinks Base. She had dropped sublight four hours earlier to take position readings and coordinate with *Galloping Ghost.* The final position fix had required them to measure the angular bearings to more than a dozen marker stars in order to pinpoint their precise position. Once they had that, they searched for their consort in a sea of black. *Ghost* had dropped out just far enough away to make rendezvous inconvenient, but not impossible. With both ships maneuvering toward one another at maximum acceleration, it took just over one hour for them to match orbits.

Once they had *Ghost* in visual range, Mark Rykand's astrogation department spent another twenty minutes making sure that their jump data was synchronized with that of the other vessel, another "Type Seven" Q-Ship. By departing the same point in space and by following a rigid course-and-time plot to their target, both ought to drop out relatively near one another on the outskirts of the Gamma System. Indeed, the only difference in their course plots was a slight variation in timing to guarantee they wouldn't collide with each other post-breakout. There was nothing they could do about the possibility of colliding with debris in the Oort Cloud.

That was the reason Mark's heart rate, and that of just about everyone else's, was increasing with each second that brought them closer to Gamma. The Oort Cloud of any star is the home of the massive frozen snowballs which might one day fall into the inner system to become comets.

The cloud was huge, extending nearly a quarter-light-year out from the system primary. Its mass was greater than the mass of the star and all of its planets combined. Still, since the Oort Cloud covered billions of cubic kilometers, some regions contained no more matter than the void between stars.

"The chances of hitting an iceberg are infinitesimal, Captain Smith!"

The quip echoed through Mark's brain even as he told himself that there was no danger. "Captain Smith" was the fabled Edward John Smith, captain of history's nearly mystical ocean liner, the ill-fated *Titanic*. No doubt Smith's navigation officer had given him the same assurances that Mark had given *New Hope*'s commander.

"Nothing to worry about, Captain," he'd said when queried about it. Of course, he had then proceeded to worry.

"Ten seconds to breakout!" Mark announced over the ship's annunciator. "Stand by."

The seconds ticked down until, suddenly, the viewscreen was no longer black. Or rather, it was no longer completely black. One moment they were moving at superlight velocity, listening to the hum of the stardrive, and the next moment they popped back into the real universe. They all rebounded into their restraining harnesses as the ship returned to microgravity. Mark's stomach reacted to the sudden falling sensation as it normally did. Luckily, he'd had a light breakfast.

It took a few seconds for the computer to find the local star. When it did, it pointed one of the hull cameras in that direction.

It wasn't much of a star, not when seen from a point well beyond this system's outermost planet. It was, in fact, only slightly brighter than the other stars on the viewscreen, a dimensionless diamond shining steadily against the ebon firmament.

Gamma looked an orphan. Yet, somewhere in the volume of space framed by the hull camera lay one inhabited world, at least a couple of stargates, and just possibly, the whole fucking Broan Space Navy!

"Breakout complete. All systems are nominal," Mark reported.

"Very well, Mr. Rykand," Captain Harris replied. "Log our arrival. Mr. Campano! Begin deceleration. Ms. Sopwell! Start your infrared sweep of the vicinity. Find me an ice ball large enough to hide behind."

The normal space navigator and the sensor operator acknowledged their orders. Normal space engines came online and the ship began to slow its headlong rush toward the star as weight returned.

"Communications!"

"Yes, Captain?" came the reply from the ship's comm center.

"Start your sweep with the comm laser. Make sure that you don't point it within 30 degrees of the star. Let me know when you get a response."

"Aye aye, sir."

The general tension began to ebb away as it was overcome by the routine bustle of a ship in space. The next few hours (or days) would be filled with looking for a point from which they could surreptitiously observe this system. The scanning laser beam was intended to find *Galloping Ghost*. Not wanting to alert the locals, they were using the narrow beam of a comm laser as though it were radar, hoping to alert *Ghost* to their location.

Ghost, of course, was doing the same thing.

When they caught sight of one another, the two ships would tie themselves together with the same comm lasers they were using for the search. They would then take up their individual observation stations. The stations would be far enough apart that should one ship be discovered and attacked by the enemy — unlikely at this distance from the star — the other could make good their escape, but close enough to provide mutual support, should that become necessary.

Most people had no concept of just how large a star system was. Gazing at the tiny blazing dot in the middle of the viewscreen, Mark was beginning to get a good idea.

#

New Hope did not find a single snowball behind which to hide. They found a dozen of them. The dimly glowing conglomerations of nitrogen, helium, oxygen, and water ice orbited one another in a loose gravitationally bound group, their blue surfaces dimly illuminated by the distant star.

The collection of snowballs was the perfect place in which to hide a ship. *New Hope* had insinuated itself into the heart of the complex formation, being careful not to let the drive field touch any of the surrounding snowballs. As far out as they were, it was nearly inconceivable that anyone would spot them even if they took no such precautions. However, "nearly inconceivable" is not the same as "inconceivable."

The one way the inhabitants might spot *New Hope* was by her infrared radiation signature. So far as the surrounding universe was concerned, *New Hope*'s skin was a blistering 300 degrees Kelvin. To a sufficiently sensitive infrared telescope, the ship would stand out against the black background like a small star.

By positioning themselves among the floating snowballs of the Oort Cloud, their ship's radiation was largely masked by the cold masses around it, whose temperature hovered just above absolute zero. With *New Hope* hidden by one particularly large proto-comet, they had spent a busy two days arraying their spy gear where it could see the whole of the inner Gamma system.

The first thing they unshipped was the astronomical telescope, a compact 3-meter diameter instrument with enough light-gathering power to spot a candle from across a solar system. They had anchored it on the far side of the biggest snowball and then run a cable to the back side, where a short range antenna beamed the telescope's images back to the ship. The second group of observation instruments to emerge were two different dish antennas to scan the electromagnetic spectrum for communications. Finally, they had unloaded two small gravity telescopes. These last were hauled by landing boat several thousand kilometers to each side of *New Hope*'s lair. Otherwise, the mass of the snowballs would mask or distort gravity waves from the local stargates.

"Big ears online!" the voice of a vacsuited spacer reported when the last of the big radio telescopes had been planted on the surface of one of the nearby ice mountains, its feet insulated against the absolute cold.

Lisa Rykand scanned her instruments and noted that they were already picking up radio hash from Gamma. She hurriedly activated the software program that would filter that, along with other naturally occurring radio noises. The hiss emanating from the speaker died away, to be replaced with the slightly musical rasping of artificially generated signals.

"Lock onto that," she told the communicator assisting her. As part of the Alien Assessment group aboard ship, she had no particular technical expertise concerning the instruments they were using. On the other hand, the comm techs had no expertise in interpreting what they were hearing. It was, she had long since decided, a case of the deaf leading the blind.

"I wonder why every technologically advanced species uses radio waves," she mused.

"Beg your pardon, Ma'am," Comm Specialist Leonard Wolfling, the tech on duty, said. "Did you say something to me?"

"No, just musing."

"About what, Ma'am?"

"About what we are doing here. We are watching them in the visible and invisible light spectra, we are listening to them on all of the electromagnetic frequencies, and we are waiting to detect the gravity waves their gates produce. But what if a species develops something other than radio to communicate with? They could be ordering their fleet to attack us at this very moment and we would be deaf as a post."

"Not possible, Ma'am. Everyone uses radio."

"I don't think you give them enough credit, Specialist."

"I don't mean they aren't smart enough to invent something else, Ma'am. I mean it's physically impossible."

"Why is that?"

"Because there are only four kinds of energy in the universe. At least, that is what they teach us in comm school. There are gravity, electromagnetic radiation, the strong nuclear force and the weak nuclear force. That's all there is, nothing more. So, if you want to communicate over long distances, which one do you choose? I suppose if you could generate gravity waves at will, they might make a pretty good comm device, but we can detect those, too. Since generating a gravity wave takes either a small black hole or a stargate, everyone chooses electromagnetic radiation for their comm gear. It's really the only thing they can do."

"I hadn't thought of that," Lisa replied. "Makes sense."

"Anything else I can help you with?" Wolfling asked as his eyes constantly scanned his control screen.

"No. I was just curious."

Then had begun the long vigil. That there were plenty of radio waves on which to eavesdrop had been apparent in the first seconds after locking in on the small radio star that was the system's single inhabited planet. Making sense of those signals was the work of many days.

The indigenous race did not speak Broan among themselves. Thus, most of their communications were in their native language or languages. This made the intercepts so much gibberish to Lisa and her two other Broan translators. They recorded it anyway, especially the video feeds, for later analysis by the linguistics computer. Once the comm technicians figured out how they were encoding the pictures, or rather holograms, they watched video feeds.

The beings were humanoid to the extent that they possessed two arms, two legs, and a head. They were also armored, with each individual looking somewhat like a knight in non-shining armor. Their faces were immobile in that they seemed to be covered in overlapping scales or plates, but their features were arranged more or less in the human pattern. Two small black eyes were positioned above breathing slits… six vertical holes with a ridge projecting above to keep rain out. The mouth was in the familiar place, but when opened, revealed a double row of teeth and several cilia. These latter performed the same function as a tongue.

Most people thought they looked like they had a mouthful of worms and did not find the resulting mental image esthetically pleasing. Lisa disagreed. Whatever environment had produced these creatures, evolution had once again followed its ironclad law: "form follows function." If they were well suited to their environment, then they were beautiful, by definition.

It wasn't until the second week of monitoring that they picked up a broadcast in the Broan language. The accompanying visuals answered one of the most important of their mission objectives. Were there any Broa in the system?

On the screen, Sar-Say's twin looked out at them. He seemed agitated, haranguing some poor unseen subordinate about a late report on local production of some product whose name was gibberish. The Broa was screaming that the report must be on a ship leaving for the sector capital the following day, and why hadn't it been transmitted yet?

Sure enough, the following morning, their visual light telescope watched a vessel depart planetary orbit and accelerate toward one of three stargates located well out from Gamma. A few days later, that ship jumped through the stargate to somewhere else. *New Hope*'s gravity wave detectors reported the departure simultaneously with the ship's infrared image merging with that of the stargate, and then disappearing.

#

"So, Lieutenant, what have we learned?"

"Not as much as I would like, Captain," Lisa replied to Captain Harris a month after their arrival in the Gamma System. "Apparently, the star or planet are called "Harlasanthenar" in the native tongue, and the species refers to themselves as "Dastanthanen," which is our transliteration of the true name. What they really call themselves has a couple of sounds in it the human voice box is not equipped to duplicate.

"The fact that 99% of all intercepted broadcasts are in the local patois has severely handicapped our ability to understand their communications. The linguistic computer has been crunching the pictures and soundtracks and has come up with the meaning of barely two hundred sound groups, and most of them are very tentative. It would take one of the big computers on Earth a year or more to make sense of everything we have recorded, and even then, we might not understand the language."

"All right," Captain Harris responded. "We aren't likely to understand their language any time soon. What *do* we understand?"

"Our important finding is that this world is ruled directly by the Broa. There are at least a dozen in residence, possibly more. Their presence makes this a poor system for first contact and precludes our releasing a Trojan Horse here." Trojan Horse was the colloquial name for the small starships that humanity would eventually set loose in selected systems to spread knowledge of the star drive.

Mission rules on Trojan Horses had not yet been finalized. However, none of the 'wrecked' ships would be introduced into systems with Broa known to be in residence. Otherwise, when the locals discover an unknown blip inbound at high speed, they would immediately report the sighting to the local master. The whole subterfuge would depend on keeping the Broa ignorant of the star drive sufficiently long for their servant species to recognize what it was they had found in the small derelict scouts.

"That's why they sent us here, Lieutenant. We can't very well begin our campaign to sow dissension throughout the Sovereignty until we know the lay of the land."

"Yes, sir. It means quite a workload for us, I'm afraid."

Harris shrugged. "We all knew it wouldn't be easy. If you wanted a life of leisure, you wouldn't have joined the Space Navy. What else do we know about the Dastanthanen?"

"We've got good recordings of their non-communications emissions, sir. That allows us to estimate their industrial output. Pretty much the same as we found at Klys'kra't. I can tell you that their yearly output of goods is about the same as that of Earth, despite their population being one-fifth our own."

"How can you know that?" Captain Harris asked.

"By the intensity and distribution of their energy emissions, Captain. We're pretty far out, but we have some fuzzy scans of their planet's surface at night. We can estimate their population by the number of lumens they emit from the various landmasses."

"And there are a million of these worlds, most of which are equivalent to the one we are watching?"

"Yes, sir."

"That is a pretty sobering thought."

"We knew about the size of the Sovereignty before we came on this expedition."

"Knowing something intellectually is one thing, Lieutenant. Seeing it with one's own eyes is something else again."

"Amen to that, sir."

#

Chapter Twenty Seven

Sar-Ganth stood at the window in his office in the Sar-Dva Tower and gazed out over the greenbelt separating the inner city of Valar from the subservients' quarters that surrounded it. Normally this view soothed him. Not today. For nearly two cycles, he had been attempting to bring the matter of the Vulcans of Shangri La to the attention of Those Who Rule, and for two cycles, other priorities had frustrated his efforts.

One of the problems, of course, was the need for secrecy. If another clan had indeed found their own private world, the last thing he wanted was for news of his concerns to reach their ears. If they realized that their perfidy had been discovered, there might well be one more dead world circling its star before they could be brought to justice.

Keeping the secret until evidence had been gathered meant that Sar-Ganth could not just walk into the meeting chamber of the Ruling Council and lay out his suspicions in open forum. No, he needed support from the highest level of the council without the knowledge of the rest of the council members.

After careful thought, he decided to approach Cal-Tar of the Cal-Zoree, Dar-Tel of the Dar-Lant, and Zel-Sen of the Zel-Sun-Do, the three most senior council members. In addition to their seniority, they each represented one of the Founding Clans; and therefore, would never contemplate violating custom to the extent of failing to notify Central Records of a new discovery.

Indeed, such a development threatened their power more than it threatened the Sar-Dva. Thus, the three ranking councilors would likely be even more anxious to discover the perpetrators of this monstrous hoax than was Sar-Ganth, and would keep his secret.

Since it took a triumvirate to issue the order he needed, his initial plan had been to approach the three privately at their estates, asking that they issue a Civilization-wide watch for these orange-skinned, blue-furred bipeds. Such an order would involve official dispatches to every sector or subsector master, ordering them to establish an active watch for these aliens. These masters would distribute the warning to their subservient worlds.

The Vulcans should not be difficult to spot. He knew of several species whose skins shaded toward orange: everything from a reddish light tan to the florid color of a *grava* fruit. However, he knew of no pigmentation that resulted in fur that was electric blue in color. That, therefore, would be the characteristic they would watch for.

The more scientific approach would be to identify them by their bio scans. Unfortunately, not every backwater planet took bio scans of visitors, and those that did often did not forward them to central records for several cycles. Bio scan matching would be used, but the blue fur would be the initial key characteristic used in identifying them... at least on worlds where the inhabitants possessed color vision.

Optimally, Sar-Ganth should have been able to gain the support he needed within a single twelve-day. Nothing lately had gone optimally. His plan had been thwarted when Zel-Sen left on an extended tour of inspection of his clan's holdings. Since the Zel-Sun-Do were the oldest and most powerful of the Founding Clans, Sar-Ganth decided to wait for the clan master's return before seeking support from the others.

Unfortunately, when Zel-Sen finally returned to his estate, Sar-Ganth had been off world, busy with his own clan's business. When he again had time to think of the mystery of the Vulcans, Fal-Tar came down with *als* fever. He nearly died, and it took many rotations of the planet before he was well again.

By the time Sar-Ganth was again ready, it was nearly time for Those Who Rule to reconvene in their Old City council chambers for their thrice-each-cycle meeting. In one respect, this simplified Sar-Ganth's problem. Since the council was soon to be in session, he could arrange an audience with all three senior councilors at the same time, citing Sar-Dva proprietary business as the excuse.

Now the day had arrived and all that was required was for him to wait quietly, betraying no sign of inner turmoil, as the chronometer flowed toward the sun-zenith mark. Despite his years, he felt like a cub on his first off-world visit. Finally, it was time for his appointment with the councilors.

He ordered his aircar to be brought up, then walked slowly from his office, down the ornate corridor beyond, and out to the landing stage. The car touched down just as he emerged into the light. The door opened and he arranged himself in the rear, feeling better than he had in some time as he did so.

The long wait was over. The time for action was at hand.

#

Old City had been constructed entirely out of red granite blocks, giving it a rosy glow when Faalta set behind the distant peaks of the Vedans Mountains. The pinkish color softened the lines of what had once been a fortress city on the banks of a river that had long since been diverted to other uses.

As the aircar put down on a landing stage atop what once had been a battlement, Sar-Ganth gazed at the squat council building with its castellated roofline and its soaring guard towers. The windows were of stained glass, showing scenes of famous battles.

When the car touched granite, Sar-Ganth stepped out and began knuckle-walking toward the stone ramp that led down into the main square. No powered vehicles were allowed inside Old City, and the guards flanking the council building entrance were decked out in archaic battle armor. However, their blast weapons were both up-to-date and obviously well maintained.

They brought their arms up in salute as he proceeded through the high doors into the interior. While the exterior of the old building was as it had been for centuries, the interior was filled with modern conveniences. Sar-Ganth moved to a sliding ramp and was whisked to the third floor.

The third floor of the council building was reserved for Ssasfal's reigning aristocracy, the city-dwelling clans that had originally joined an alliance to conquer the barbarian hordes that surrounded them. The Sar-Dva Clan had been part of those barbarian hordes. Sar-Ganth had no problem with the fact that his ancestors had been brought into Civilization by force. As bad as it had been for those who lost the Great Conquest, civilization had proved an unalloyed good for all subsequent generations. What he objected to was that this ancient historical fact relegated him and his to second rank status in perpetuity.

As he entered the Realm of the Founders, he felt the familiar irritation rising within. No matter how successful he and his fellows were, no matter how much value and status they accumulated, they could never aspire to this hallowed place. He stifled the emotion with difficulty by concentrating on the issue at hand. After a momentary halt to regain his equilibrium, he proceeded to the over-decorated section of the building that housed the spacious offices of the Zel-Sun-Do.

Sar-Dva arrived at precisely the moment of his appointment and used the small metal spear held upright by an iron bracket beside the door to announce himself. He did so by lifting the spear and using it to pound the heavy wood of the door. He carefully avoided the antique iron inlays in the wood, lest he damage the butt of the antique door knocker.

The requisite time elapsed and the door opened. An obsequious subservient made the posture of obedience and inquired as to his business. He gave it and was admitted.

The whole performance was unnecessary, since Sar-Ganth's appointment had been confirmed electronically. However, as in everything having to do with the Council of Rulers, ancient ritual was rigorously adhered to, lest the majesty of these precincts be diminished.

The three senior councilors awaited him in a plush inner chamber that Sar-Ganth noted was equipped with anti-eavesdropping equipment. Zel-Sen gestured for him to take his place on the visitor's resting frame while Cal-Tar and Dar-Tel watched him with impassive eyes and said nothing.

"You asked for this audience, Clan Master. How can we serve you and the Sar-Dva?" Zel-Sen asked, bypassing the usual ceremonials. His abruptness signaled that his time was short, and in any event, more precious than that of the leader of a "younger" clan.

Sar-Ganth once again swallowed his irritation, and said, "I thank the Senior Clan Masters for seeing me. What I have come to say is highly confidential."

"You made that clear in your communication," Dar-Tel replied. "We have all agreed to keep your secrets."

"Not my secret, Dar-Tel. The secret of the Council and of The Race."

"Get on with it," Cal-Tar ordered. Advanced age had turned the fur around his muzzle white and caused his spine to curve. The latter made it difficult to walk. It also did not improve his temper.

"Very well," Sar-Dva replied. "I have reason to believe that some clan or faction has discovered a new world and has not shared that fact with the rest of us."

The flat statement took the others aback. Sar-Dva watched impassively as they processed his words in silence.

Finally, Zel-Sen spoke. "That is a serious charge, Clan Master. Can you substantiate it?"

Sar-Ganth launched into his story of Sar-Say and how he had been waylaid en route from Vith to Persilin. He spoke of the Vulcans' visit to Klys'kra't, and of the Voldar'iks' subsequent complaint. He told them about the discovery of Sar-Say's pheromone on one of the samples the Vulcans had offered their hosts.

"Upon learning this, Ssor-Fel of the Salefar Sector queried Central Records to see who these Vulcans were. He reported finding no record of them. I, too, searched Central Records. I also found nothing."

"And you surmise that these failures to identify them are proof that someone is running their own private world?" Zel-Sen asked.

"Why else would Central Records have no knowledge of them? We have an excellent bio scan from their time with the Voldar'ik, yet those scans match nothing on record."

"Bio scan records are notoriously unreliable," Cal-Tor reminded him.

"For individuals, yes. But for a whole species? Up until Ssor-Fel made me aware of this incident, I believed that the genotypes of all the species within Civilization were kept in Central Records."

"That has been my belief as well," Dar-Tel said.

"Then we will adopt as our working hypothesis that Sar-Dva's suspicions are well founded," Zel-Sen responded. "Apparently, *someone* has violated ancient custom. The question is, who and why? The gravity of the offense would appear to outweigh any possible benefit. What would a clan gain from such a risky enterprise?"

"Value and position," Sar-Dva replied. "They may be a landless clan attempting to claim a place on the Council."

"Possible," Zel-Sen agreed.

"Or," Sar-Dva continued, "They may be an existing council member seeking to gain advantage over the rest of us. If someone has access to a world the rest of us do not, they could enrich themselves to our detriment."

"If true, this must be stopped immediately," Cal-Tar demanded.

"How do we stop it?" Zel-Sen asked.

"These Vulcans are traders," Sar-Dva replied. "The ones at Klys'kra't claimed that they were many jumps from their home world. If we can track the planets they visited while trading, perhaps we can get an idea of where their star is located."

"That might work," Zel-Sen agreed. "They must have left records on the worlds they visited. We will send a Priority Inquiry as soon as the council has adjourned this session. What else?"

Sar-Dva made the hand gesture that signified his dismay at having to point out the obvious to his betters. "An Inquiry is just a start. We must also send orders for all planets in Civilization to be on the watch for them. With their blue fur, they are distinctive. If we can but capture one of these elusive Vulcans, we can learn a great deal."

"Very well. We will order all port masters and administrators to enter the Vulcan descriptions into their automatic surveillance devices. We will also distribute their bio scans to every part of Civilization, and order any being who matches those scans held until we can be notified. Will that be sufficient to ease your fears?"

"It will," Sar-Ganth replied. "Surely they cannot evade a Civilization-wide search for long."

#

"Well, that was a waste of time," Lisa said, snuggling closer to Mark. The two of them were in the ship's mess, having just finished the evening meal. Through the bulkheads they could hear the thrum of the star drive as they left Gamma behind, en route to Brinks Base.

"We got a lot of data," he reminded her. "Anything that adds to our knowledge of the Broa isn't a waste."

"I know," she replied. "Still, it's disappointing to have to write off a potential target."

"Hopefully, some of the other expeditions had better luck."

They had spent two months observing the Dastanthanen of Harlasanthenar, and had discovered nothing but bad news. In addition to the Broan presence, the frequency of ship traffic in the system wrote it off as a potential place to visit in order to trade for a planetary database.

While they watched, more than a dozen ships had come and gone through the system stargates. Some emerged from one of the three gates (Babylon, Nineveh, or Tyre) and made orbit for Harlasanthenar. Most, however, ignored the planet and made directly for one of the other gates in the system. These latter vessels were obviously in transit, making the Gamma System a crossroads of sorts for traffic en route to other worlds. The presence of Broa on the planet and the amount of ship traffic through the system combined to make Gamma useless for their purposes.

What they were looking for was a backwater world visited by the Broa once every decade or so, a world where a Q-Ship could slip in quietly, trade for a planetary database, and then slip out while leaving as thin a trail as possible.

While watching the comings and goings, however, they noticed something odd. Each jump through Babylon and Nineveh caused the gravity wave telescopes to ring like a bell. However, jumps through the Tyre stargate barely registered. At first the physicists thought their equipment was malfunctioning. After running diagnostics, they had to admit that the gravity waves from Tyre were just a lot weaker than the other two.

Based on observations of the New Eden incursion, gravity waves had always been assumed to be omni-directional. Their observations of the Gamma gates seemed to prove that idea false. Rather, the expedition physicists maintained, each stargate emitted a funnel-shaped gravity disturbance aligned along its longitudinal axis.

The observation, if true, had all sorts of implications. It explained the relative paucity of gravity wave detection by Brinks Base. It also called into question whether there were indeed inhabited stars within the Sovereignty that lacked stargates. It was possible that some species had escaped conquest by the Broa. It was also possible that they were slaves whose gates were pointed in the wrong direction for detection by the Brinks gravitational observatory.

Lisa had observed the heavy space traffic and come up with an idea of how they might spy more effectively on the Broa. She broached the subject with Captain Harris at their next briefing, the last before they were scheduled to return to Brinks Base.

"Sir, I've been wondering if we aren't going about this the wrong way."

"I beg your pardon?" Harris's distracted response came while he scanned a fuzzy photograph before him. They had been going over the data on a ship caught in transit between stargates. The contact was intriguing because the ship's emissions indicated it was a large Broan warcraft. The glimpse of a potential adversary held the captain's full attention.

"When we abandoned Klys'kra't, we took the *Ruptured Whale* through the local stargate to escape without arousing suspicion."

"Your point?" came the irritated reply.

"Well, sir, watching the local traffic, I wondered why we can't just sneak in and jump through one of the stargates. After that, we would just be one more ship en route for somewhere else while we photograph and scan the hell out of everything in sight. We could catalog a dozen star systems in the time we took doing just this one."

Harris looked up from the fuzzy picture of an oversize globe he had been studying. "Write it up and we'll submit it for consideration when we get back to Brinks Base. I would have thought someone would have evaluated such an approach before now. Possibly they considered it and ruled it out as too dangerous."

"I suspect we spent so much time trying to figure out how not to be noticed that we overlooked the obvious, sir."

"Possibly so. Anyway, it won't hurt to send it in for evaluation on our return," he replied. "Now, let's get back to the business at hand, shall we?"

"Yes, sir."

#

Chapter Twenty Eight

Brinks Base had grown enormously in the months *New Hope* had been gone. When they left on their mission to Gamma, the base had been one big construction zone. Now, a mere ten weeks later, it was a veritable fortress deep in the heart of enemy space.

Most notable were the big sensor arrays surrounding the underground living quarters. There were infrared telescopes to sweep the sky for anything hotter than the cold of deep space, radio telescopes to pick up electromagnetic emanations — to be turned into high powered radar transmitters, as needed — and every kind of passive sensor invented by man. There were even neutrino detectors to detect ships by the emanations of their power plants. They had no difficulty picking up the myriad of human craft in a string-of-beads orbit around the moon.

Nor were the sensors there merely to provide warning. During its caretaker phase, the plan for defending Brinks Base had been to evacuate at the first sign of the enemy and blow the place up. To that end, a massive nuclear charge had been buried in the heart of the base, ready to erase all evidence of the species that had constructed it.

The strategy had changed. Should the Broa suddenly appear in the Hideout System, the first response would be an attempt to blow them out of the sky. One or more blastships were on station near the moon at all times for just that purpose. The other ships of the fleet were also available for defense. The cargo hold of every Q-ship was stuffed with offensive and defensive weaponry. Even the massive colony ships had been given the means to defend themselves.

The primary offensive weapon of the fleet was the Superlight Missile: *SM*, for short. Superlight missiles were modifications of the *ftl* message probes, one of which Dan Landon had destroyed the Broan Avenger at New Eden.

SMs were militarized and miniaturized versions, designed to accelerate to superlight, then overload on command, they returned to normal space just short of their target, spraying a billion pieces of shrapnel into the enemy vessel's path.

Interspersed among the many sensor arrays were shallow hemispherical depressions carved into the rocky ground of Sutton. Each depression cradled its own SM, ready to fly.

There was one other means of defense with which every ship had been equipped, one that no one talked about much. Bolted to each vessel's thrust frame was a nuclear charge. Should a captain find his vessel in danger of imminent capture, he had orders to self destruct.

Starship captain was the most sought after job in the new Space Navy, and the one with the most rigorous psychological screening. Command skill was important, but having the courage to use the self destruct as a last resort was essential.

It was just one of the reasons most captains had gray hair.

#

"Wow, things have grown around here since we left, haven't they?" Lisa asked Mark as the ship's boat arrowed toward the circular pattern of sensor arrays and missile batteries that had sprouted from the black and brown plain above Brinks Base.

The two of them were strapped into a single bench seat at the front of *New Hope*'s landing boat, with Mark's knees almost in the pilot's kidneys. The pilot's head filled their field of view, but it was possible to see their destination by looking past his ears and through the forward viewport. The dozen other passengers were packed side-by-side into the long fuselage, with only fist-size viewports of their own through which to catch occasional glimpses of the airless moon.

"They've had enough people working," Mark said. "I'm surprised we didn't come back to find a bubble city, complete with hanging gardens."

"That would be nice," his wife said wistfully. Military construction had three priorities: function, function, and function. They wouldn't so much as paint a flower on a bulkhead unless that flower aided them in target acquisition.

The pilot pitched the boat up at an angle that robbed them of their view, and cut in the underjets. They grounded in a cloud of dust that was slow to dissipate in the low gravity. Heretofore, a landing on Sutton required one to seal up his or her vacsuit, and then walk-bounce to the nearest surface airlock. Not this time.

As soon as they grounded, an oversize arm reached out and hooked onto their boat just behind the cockpit. Silently, it hoisted them like a mother cat picking up her kitten, swung it over an open rectangular pit lit by flood lamps, and then lowered it inside.

The pit was barely larger than the boat. There was a gentle shock when they were deposited on the floor. The arm detached and withdrew. The sky then disappeared as a heavy roof section moved into place, sealing off the pit.

The boat was buffeted by an external rush of air and quickly enveloped in expansion fog. After a few seconds study of his instruments, the pilot announced, "All ashore who are going ashore! Last one out, close the airlock."

Lisa and Mark undid their single lap belt and waited for the others to clear the narrow aisle before gathering their own kit bags and following. As instructed, Mark palmed the control that would close the airlock. As he did so, an amplified voice told them to hurry, as the pumps were about to once again suck the air out of the chamber.

Both of them hurried to a small airlock inset into the rock wall. There was just enough room for both of them to squeeze inside. The outer door closed, leaving them sealed inside a steel box little bigger than a coffin.

"Cozy," Mark said, enjoying the feel of warm softness pressed against him as he wrapped Lisa in his embrace.

His wife wriggled suggestively in response. Just as she did so, the inner door made a series of clicking noises and withdrew into its recess to reveal a grinning crew of vacuum jacks lining the rock hewn tunnel within. There were several whistles as the couple disentangled themselves.

"Home, sweet home!" Mark said as he let Lisa exit the lock first. He followed, carrying both kit bags.

Lisa crinkled up her nose and turned toward him. "What's that smell?"

He breathed in the base air. "Drying paint and body odor, I would guess," he replied. One thing was certain. Of all the improvements that had been made to Brinks Base, the atmosphere scrubbers had not been one of them.

#

"I think you're right," Alfred Bastion, senior scientist said while reading the summary of *New Hope*'s mission to Gamma.

"About what, sir?" Mark asked.

"The damned gravity waves are focused along the axis of the gate. No wonder we've been seeing fewer of them than we predicted."

"But the wave they detected in the New Eden system was uniform. They've since checked that by dropping sublight just beyond the expanding wavefront and mapping it in a dozen places."

"The wave at New Eden was very powerful, and from a single-ended jump. No stargate at the destination to focus the wave. I fear we have extrapolated our strategy from a single data point. These observations you brought back are going to force us to reevaluate."

"Reevaluate what?"

"Everything," the physicist replied. "Most of all, you've just proven that we can't be sure how far Earth is from the edge of the Sovereignty."

"I don't follow."

Bastion looked as though he had bitten into a spoiled lemon. "When we first discovered stargates and gravity waves, we did a calculation. We concluded that since gravity waves move at the speed of light, the Sovereignty can be no closer to Sol than the number of years since the Broa developed their gate technology, which puts them quite a distance off.

"This new data tells us that there may be Broa-occupied star system almost next door to Sol, but with its gate oriented in the wrong direction for us to see them."

"That's a cheery thought," Mark mused.

"Indeed," Bastion replied absentmindedly. He was already considering what other bad things might flow from the fact that stargates focused gravity waves.

#

"Congratulations on your work at Gamma." Dan Landon said. Lisa was perched on the spindly arrangement of wires that the engineers laughingly referred to as a 'visitor's chair.' Even her dainty weight would have crushed it had they been in Earth's greater gravity field.

"Thank you, sir. I'm just sorry we didn't find you a candidate system for our next contact."

The admiral shrugged. "Negative data is data, too. At least, we know what system to avoid."

"Yes, sir. Harlasanthenar appears to be a major Broan hub, possibly even a regional capital. We'll want to steer well clear of it."

"And we will. Luckily, the other expeditions had better luck. I think we have two worlds that ought to be safe to contact. How would you and Mark like to tackle one of them?"

"Sir?"

"You have the experience from our visit to Klys'kra't. More importantly, you are probably our most knowledgeable expert on the Broa and their language. We need that planetary data base badly. Would you like to try again?"

"Yes, sir. We would *love* to try again."

"It might be dangerous."

"Dropping out of superlight into an Oort Cloud is dangerous, Admiral. Compared to that, this should be easy. We pop in, haggle awhile for show, give them whatever they want for the database. Then we pop out again."

"You'll be getting orders in about a week. Along with *New Hope*, we'll send one of the blast ships and a couple of Q-ships to guard you. If you get in trouble, they will try to get you out again."

"At the risk of blowing our cover, Admiral?"

He nodded. "Better that than to risk your capture and dissection."

Lisa shivered at the word 'dissection.' Unfortunately, if the Broa ever began wondering about their origin, that was probably the least she could expect. For that reason, in addition to a self destruct for the ship, every member of a ground party would be carrying suicide pills on their person at all times. In fiction, the spy always has a false tooth filled with cyanide. Not only was such a thing susceptible to accidental breakage, it would show up on bio scanners and start the host race to wondering at its purpose.

If Landon noticed the reaction, he didn't acknowledge it. "Anything else we need to talk about, Lieutenant?"

"Yes, sir. I had an idea while I was away that might greatly aid our explorations."

"Let's hear it."

She explained her idea that a ship might sneak into a Broan system and then jump through the local stargate. After that first jump, they would just be another ship in transit for somewhere else.

They could jump from gate to gate until they plotted the positions of dozens of stars. They could also use their transit time through normal space between gates to spy on the locals.

Landon leaned back in his chair, a twin to the one in which she perched. "Sounds interesting. Write it up and get it to Strategy and Intentions. Have them look it over. If they pass on it, then we'll give it a try."

"Yes, sir."

#

Chapter Twenty Nine

New Hope was again in the absolute blackness of superlight velocity, en route to an alien star system in the hands of the enemy. The star was called Etnarii in the language of the dominant people. The planet was Pasol, and the people were the Ranta. Rough translations of the three terms were: "sun," "world," and "the people."

The Etnarii System was home to a single inhabited world, which appeared to be predominately agricultural. The world's energy signature was one-tenth that of Harlasanthenar and its lack of importance in the Broan scheme of things was emphasized by the fact that the system possessed a single stargate.

Throughout the Broan realm, important planets had half a dozen or more stargates (or so Sar-Say and the Strategies and Intentions Group maintained). These were the hub worlds of the Sovereignty, the crossroads. As in the Gamma System, which itself was a minor regional hub, ships arrived via stargate and then made a beeline for some other gate that sent them to the next star in the chain, never halting or interacting with the species whose system they had just traversed.

This made for a busy sky, with ships constantly moving from gate to gate. In the Gamma System, the span between ship arrivals was shorter than the time it took to transit between the Babylon, Nineveh, and Tyre gates. Thus, there were usually multiple starships in the system at any given time, each on its own business.

In the Etnarii System, there was only the one entrance and exit. Etnarii was a cul-de-sac. In the whole time the Delta Expedition had watched the place, they detected no arrivals or departures. In fact, for more than a month they had wondered if the system had stargates at all, despite the evidence that a gravity wave had been detected emanating from it. Eventually, a careful infrared scan of the sky located the gate hovering at about the orbital distance of Jupiter on the far side of Etnarii.

The Ranta were a humanoid species and bore a closer resemblance to humanity than most. They were either descended from avians or else the pseudo-mammals of their world had evolved a fluffy form of feathers. Estimates of their heights (never reliable when all one had to go on was a video picture) placed them at three meters tall. Their bodies were spindly by human standards, with long, stork-like legs and elongated torsos from which hung two long, triply articulated arms.

Their heads were encased in a skullcap of feathers, as were the visible portions of their arms. (They wore poncho-like garments that concealed much of their torsos.) Their faces, showed no sign of birdlike features. They had two eyes placed high on a round head, spread wide for good stereoptic vision. Their nostrils were a two vertical slits that widened and narrowed in time with their breathing. Their mouths were also oriented vertically and placed between the slits, giving their faces a long look. Their ears were scalloped at the edges, as though modeled on a spike-leaved plant, but the convolutions within seemed to mimic the shape of the human ear.

The covering feathers came in several colors, confirming that the Ranta had color vision. Some of the color variations were sufficiently extreme that the alien sociologists were arguing that they were a mating display... much as in terrestrial peacocks.

A Ranta's voice issued forth from its food intake aperture, just as did human voices. Whatever means they used to generate sound appeared no more versatile than a human voice box, which meant that communicating with them should not be a problem. Their language was not complex, but with only two months' study by the previous expedition, the specialists and computers had been unable to translate more than a few words.

The Delta expedition's most exciting discovery was the complete lack of communications in the system in the Broan tongue. They took the lack to mean that there was no Broan master in residence. There might be other explanations, of course: perhaps the master had been on a long vacation, or communicated only by hand-delivered proclamations on parchment, or just wasn't very loquacious.

However, such speculations were meaningless until they actually made contact. For the moment, they took the lack of Broan speech to mean a lack of Broa in the system.

All in all, the system seemed perfect for a low key visit by a group of "traders" from a distant world on the other side of the Sovereignty.

At Klys'kra't, they had been Vulcans – orange skinned, blue haired bipeds from the planet Shangri-la. At Pasol, they would be Trojans from the trading world of Troje.

Once again they would go in disguise. Whether such elementary precautions were really necessary had been the subject of spirited debate after the crew discovered what Trojans were supposed to look like.

"Hairless?" Lisa demanded when Mark told her. "They want me to shave off the beautiful head of hair that I have spent all my life getting just the way I want it?"

"Not just the hair on your head. They want us to depilate our eyebrows, the hair on our arms and legs, even our 'you-know-what' hair."

"I suppose they want us to dye ourselves blue this time!"

"Tiger stripes," he replied. "We'll each carry an individualized pattern of black and yellow stripes over a base of tan. Our lips will be dyed black and our earflaps red. It isn't much, but it just may confuse them enough to keep them from identifying us as the visitors to Klys'kra't."

She was silent for a long time, then smiled impishly. "I suppose we can make tiger stripes chic, and checking to make sure we've gotten rid of all of our body hair might be fun."

He leered at her, "I may just have to check you over several times."

"Ditto," she replied.

#

The bridge of *New Hope* was once again a tense place as they prepared for breakout on the edge of the Etnarii System. It had been six hours since the expedition's four ships rendezvoused well beyond the target system. In addition to *New Hope*, there were the Q-ships *Revenger* and *Allison*, one a Type Seven Freighter, the other a Bulk Transport, and the blastship *Chicago*. The three other vessels would remain hidden in the Oort Cloud unless needed. Then, depending on circumstances, either one of the Q-ships would mysteriously appear in the system and voyage to Pasol to aid their brethren, or else *Chicago* would break from hiding and rush to the rescue.

Of course, 'rescue' might involve bombarding the planet from space to ensure that any captured human agents were not left alive to be questioned about their origins.

The entire bridge crew was decked out in their disguises, each with a distinctive black and yellow stripe pattern that covered their bald pates, faces, necks, and hands, the only parts of their bodies that stuck out of their skin-tight, yellow shipsuits. Had one cared to investigate further, they would find the stripes traversed every part of their skin save for the palms of their hands and the soles of their feet. In fact, a couple of the crewmen – one male and one female – had become masters at body painting before preparations for the masquerade were complete.

The shipsuits were of standard human design, but the individual names embroidered in Broan script above the right pockets were aliases. Captain Harris was Hass Vith, Mark Rykand was Markel Sinth, and each of the rest were other nonsense syllables that could not be found in any Earth dictionary. This close to the target world, all of the displays in the ship had been switched over to the Broan dot-and-swirl script to get the crew used to using them. Nowhere in the public areas of the ship (those not given over to hidden weaponry and additional engines unknown to the Broa) was there any indication of the ship's true origin. Even the astronomical data onboard had been converted to correspond to a Sol-like star system a thousand light-years from Etnarii, and in the opposite direction from their true home.

Back on Earth, some of the most creative minds had spent years thinking about the masquerades needed during the initial contact missions. Many of those minds were now headquartered at Brinks Base, where they continued their quest to ensure that no telltale detail betrayed the fact that Earth existed, or where it was to be found.

It wasn't that they were trying to masquerade as another species. That would have been impossible. Even if they had used prosthetics to improve their disguises, the bio scanners that checked them for infectious diseases would clearly show the extra features to be fakes, leading to unwanted curiosity. Some body modifications could have been explained away as mere fashion, but questions would have formed in alien brains that they did not want asked.

So, other than the lack of body hair and the different coloring, they were still human beings. The disguise was intended to confuse the enemy, but not to the point where anyone would wonder why their visitors were obviously in disguise.

The other expedition that had been dispatched from Brinks Base would also be in disguise, but not the same one. Having Trojans show up in two different systems simultaneously might also generate interest at some future date. The plan was to slip in like ghosts, transact their business, and then slip out again.

Unfortunately, there was one risk they hadn't figured out how to abate. Every vessel entering the Etnarii System via stargate generated a gravity wave. Their arrival via stardrive would not. In fact, the only way to actually generate an arrival wave would be to discover the system the Etnarii gate connected to, travel superlight to that system, and then jump through to Etnarii as though they were regular Broan traffic.

At Klys'kra't, they had waited for a Broan ship to jump outbound through the gate before pretending to be a new arrival. The thought had been that anyone monitoring the gravity waves might not notice that one wave seemingly had spawned two ships.

If they discovered any starships in the Etnarii System, they would pull the same scam, assuming they could get themselves into position in time. If the system were empty, then they would have to go in and brazen it out.

#

"All Hands, Breakout Complete!" Mark announced over the ship's annunciator. His words echoed back at him, making him sound as though he were at the bottom of a well.

"Where are we, Astrogator?" Captain Harris demanded.

"Midpoint of the Oort Cloud, sir. Right where we want to be."

"Any debris close enough to be a danger?"

"Checking now, sir," Emily Sopwell, the sensor operator answered. She was sweeping circumambient space with the comm laser, making sure that it did not point anywhere near the planet or star.

This time they had popped out of superlight moving tangential to Etnarii so that they could safely sweep the volume of space in front of them, secure in the knowledge that their presence would not be detected.

Half an hour after breakout, Ensign Sopwell announced, "I have a laser beacon, Captain. It's *Chicago*."

"How far?" the Captain asked.

"I make it six million kilometers, sir."

"Not bad, considering how far we've come since rendezvous," Harris announced to no one in particular. "Astrogator, plot us a course for rendezvous."

"Aye aye, sir."

In this case, they would be making all of the course corrections to join up with the big blastship. Fleet orders were to home on *Chicago* immediately after breakout, and that was what they were doing.

Two days later, they pulled alongside of the oversize cylinder. It was festooned with gun mounts, laser mounts, and particle beam accelerators. Around the waist of the ship was a string of hemispherical shapes that were its superlight missiles, ready for launch.

A hundred thousand kilometers or so beyond *Chicago* were two other laser beacons. *Revenger* and *Allison* were also making their approaches to rendezvous.

"Captain Styles has sent a message to you, Captain," the communicator on duty announced. Styles was *Chicago*'s commanding officer.

"Read it."

"His compliments, sir. You and the ground party are to join him inboard the blastship for dinner and a pre-mission briefing."

"Time?"

"19:00 Hours, sir."

"Signal him that we will be there."

#

Chapter Thirty

New Hope's landing boat was partially filled as they made their way across the void to *Chicago*. This time Captain Harris and Commander Vanavong, *Hope*'s executive officer, were ensconced on the forward acceleration bench. Mark and Lisa were relegated to the second row, where the view was not nearly as good. Behind them were Bernard Sampson, Alien Linguist, and Seiichi Takamatsu, Alien Technologist, the other members of the expedition ground party. Takamatsu was a specialist in Broan computer technology, having spent the last five years studying the *Ruptured Whale*'s computers. It would be his job to validate the Pasol database when they obtained it.

Their approach to *Chicago* was uneventful, even dull, for those in the rear seats. They could see little beyond the backs of the captain and exec's heads. What little of the view the two officers did not obscure was taken up by the pilot. As they made their approach to the blastship, they made out an occasional dull lump on a hull painted to match the blackness of space. Unlike the Q-ships, the human designs on the expedition incorporated full stealth capability, including a surface finish designed to make them difficult to see, even at close range.

There was an increase in the cabin lighting as the big ship's hangar bay doors swung open to admit the small landing craft. After that, it was a series of bumps and grinding noises as the landing boat was secured to the deck, followed by the inevitable hissing roar as the blastship's hangar bay was repressurized.

A light on the forward bulkhead turned green, followed by the pilot's voice announcing that it was safe to disembark.

The blast ship's rotation had been halted to bring the boat aboard. Thus, they were in microgravity. Mark and Lisa unsnapped their seat-belt-for-two and waited for Sampson and Takamatsu to lever themselves to the boat's aft airlock. Sampson palmed the control that opened both doors simultaneously, something impossible to do had the sensors detected a pressure differential between the inside and outside. He then disappeared head first through the open lock, followed by Takamatsu.

Mark let Lisa go first. She deftly levered herself out of her seat with her arms, pivoted in place, then pulled herself hand over hand, using the seat backs as grips. He followed her, conscious that he wasn't nearly as graceful – a fact he put down to both larger size and the presence of a Y-chromosome. When he reached the airlock, he jackknifed through it like a diver entering a sunken wreck, to find an oversize steel compartment beyond. *Chicago*'s landing bay was brightly lit by overhead flood lamps. Scattered around the bay were the blastship's attack boats. A double line of Marines stood at attention, blast rifles at 'present arms' and boots hooked into the hexagonal deck grating, giving the illusion of gravity. An orange cord had been strung from a hook above the boat's airlock to a similar hook over a nearby hatch. A clump of blastship officers awaited them just inside the hatch.

Mark followed the others along the guide line, halting to hover at its end where *Chicago*'s welcoming party waited. No one said anything until they were joined by the captain and the exec.

"Captain Harris?" a pert middle-aged woman in the uniform of a commander inquired.

"Yes."

"Commander Butterfield, sir. *Chicago*'s exec. Captain Symes asked me to meet you."

"Good of you to come, Commander. I fear we would have become lost in this big old beehive of yours."

"It does take some getting used to, sir. If you will follow me, I'll take you to the Officer's Mess where the captain will join us. Oh, and we should have spin back on the ship in another ten minutes."

"Thank you, Commander. Lead the way."

With that, Commander Butterfield pulled herself along the guide rope until she reached the hatch. There she transferred to the ubiquitous guide rail attached to the overhead that ran the length of every corridor in the ship. The rail was used for locomotion when the ship was in microgravity, and the party from *New Hope* was soon strung out behind her like beads on a string as she swiftly moved through a seemingly endless sequence of corridors. Several of the blastship crewmen observed their passage, many attempting unsuccessfully to hide smirks as their visitors passed.

The expressions baffled Mark the first time he saw them. Then he realized what they were smirking about. Everyone aboard *New

Hope was already in disguise. Trailing the blastship's executive officer were six completely hairless, monkey-like figures covered in black-and-yellow tiger stripes.

They must have looked damned incongruous against the blastship's gray bulkheads as they imitated the monkeys they resembled, pulling themselves hand over hand along the guide rail.

#

"Captain̂ Harris, ladies and gentlemen, may I introduce Captain Wellington Symes, commanding officer of *TSN Chicago*."

They each shook hands in turn with *Chicago*'s commanding officer. By the time they had reached the mess hall, sufficient spin had been placed on the ship that they did not float off the deck. Mark Rykand estimated the pull at about one-tenth gee. It would be raised shortly to one-third gravity, the shipboard standard.

Symes was a bear of a man with a hulking look and a grim expression. Unlike most of the expedition's officers, he had been a member of the Space Navy even before its recent massive expansion. His seniority and record had given him command of one of the half-dozen most powerful ships in the fleet. Prior to this command, he had skippered nothing larger than a frigate for the simple reason that prior to Sar-Say, the space navy had possessed nothing larger.

"Mrs. Rykand," he said after being introduced to Lisa. He surprised everyone by leaning over and kissing her hand. The custom had seen a revival in the previous generation, although it was again dying out.

"Captain Symes, thank you for your kind welcome aboard this magnificent ship."

"Think nothing of it. We didn't get a chance for a pre-mission briefing back at Brinks Base. I thought it an excellent time to mix business with pleasure. Besides, I don't think I have ever seen a more beautiful bald and striped woman in my entire life."

Despite herself, Lisa blushed under the body paint.

Symes bounced a couple of times on the balls of his feet. "We seem to have enough gravity to begin. Ladies and gentlemen, please take your seats. You will find nameplates on the table. Several of my officers will be joining us shortly.

As predicted, a number of black-and-silver figures showed up while stewards poured wine into tall, low-gravity glasses. Each new arrival was introduced, which in turn slowed conversation as the six visitors introduced themselves. Mark noted several officers, male and female, glancing surreptitiously in his direction. One small blonde wearing the bars of a Lieutenant seemed especially intrigued. He asked her if she liked his paint job.

"It's... striking. Does it wash off?"

"Hopefully not," he said. "After all, we might get rained on."

"Do you mean that you are that color forever?"

"For a few months, anyway. About the time our hair starts growing out again, the dye will fade and we'll get our old complexions back. At least, I hope we will."

"Is it really worth it?" she asked, mirroring the conversation they'd had aboard *New Hope* when it had been announced they would have to shave off all of their hair. "I mean, do you think the aliens will be fooled?"

He shrugged. "Since we don't know the Broan capability for gathering information about us, the powers-that-be decided to make it as difficult for them as possible. We were orange skinned with blue hair at the last system we visited. Now we have stripes and are hairless. We're not trying to look like some other species. We just don't want to look like ourselves.

"In this form of camouflage, we use rather outlandish color schemes in the hope that these will be what stick in the minds of any aliens we meet. Hopefully, when they describe us to their masters, they will tell them that we are bipeds, as are some 80% of the races in the Sovereignty, and that we have a very striking skin tones and no hair. What is important is that they not link us with the visit to Klys'kra't. That way, they won't be able to see the pattern to our actions."

"What if they send along pictures with your descriptions?"

He shrugged. "Then someone is likely to notice that beneath the outlandish skin colors, we and the Vulcan traders have the same features."

"Vulcan traders?"

"That was our last masquerade," Mark replied.

The blonde lieutenant looked puzzled. After a moment's hesitation, she asked, "And if one of the aliens asks you why you have painted yourself when their scans clearly indicate that you aren't striped and that your skin is covered with hair follicles?"

"That's easy. We'll blame it all on fashion. After all, you ladies have been painting yourselves for thousands of years. Why can't we men do the same?"

Dinner was served while the various officers divided into separate conversations with their neighbors. Mark noticed Lisa laughing at the joke of a handsome, and too young, Ensign. Once he caught her eye as she looked across the table at him, and a nonverbal message passed between them. Lisa's look said, "Serves you right for talking to that blonde!" She then went back to laughing at the ensign's jokes.

Eventually, dinner was done and the stewards had refilled their wine glasses. Captain Symes rose at the head of the table, raised his glass carefully so the wine would not slosh out, and said, "Ladies and gentlemen, a toast."

They each raised their glasses as carefully.

"To a successful mission!"

There followed a chorus of agreement and everyone drank before returning the glasses to the table clips that secured them. By common understanding, the toast marked the end of the social portion of the evening. From here on out, it would be all business.

#

As if on cue, a holocube dropped from the overhead and lit up to show a long-range view of Pastol.

Captain Symes stood and strode to stand beside the cube. "Let us begin the mission briefing. Captain Harris, do you have any preliminary words for us?"

"I'll save them," Harris replied. "Proceed."

"Very well. *Chicago* deployed her long range sensors as soon as we came to a rest with respect to this system's Oort Cloud. We have been monitoring the planet for a full day now and have largely confirmed what the Delta expedition discovered. Pastol appears to be a largely agricultural world, with relatively small cities and a lot of ocean traffic. However, we have one bit of new information to impart. We seem to be in luck. There is a starship in orbit."

"Broan?" Harris asked, suddenly concerned.

"Everything in the Sovereignty must be presumed to be Broan, Captain. However, if you are asking whether it is a warship, we think not. It appears to be a bulk hauler. We surmise that it is here to take on a load of whatever it is they grow down there."

"Amazing," Seiichi Takamatsu muttered under his breath from two seats to Mark's right. His words had been meant to be sotto voce, but they attracted Symes's attention anyway.

"You have a comment, Specialist?"

Takamatsu shifted uncomfortably in his seat. The silence stretched until Seiichi cleared his throat. "Sorry, Captain. I was just remarking on what an amazing transportation system the stargate network is."

"How so?"

"Well, sir, they're cheap! So cheap, in fact, that the Broa can actually ship food across interstellar distances economically. They allow commerce between stars as easily as between continents."

"If one doesn't mind being ruled by the Broa."

"True, there is that. However, stargates are machines. They don't care how they are used. The fact that the Broa rule a million star systems is just another measure of the stargate's efficiency. They could never have grown that large if they relied on the stardrive."

"An interesting philosophical point, Specialist. However, this is neither the time nor the place," Captain Symes said, obviously impatient with the interruption. "Shall we return to our mission briefing?"

"Sorry, sir."

Symes turned to the image in the holocube. "This ship in orbit is a godsend. We will be able to introduce *New Hope* simultaneous with its departure, much reducing the chance they will note that you didn't come through the stargate."

"Any idea when it will depart orbit?" Captain Harris asked, obviously thinking about the difficulties of approaching the gate without being observed by another ship in the vicinity.

"No indication, I'm afraid. We know they have arrived within the last month. The economics of shipping here should be the same as they are at home. That bulk carrier is expensive to operate. Surely it won't stay in orbit any longer than is required to load cargo."

"And if it does stay in orbit?"

"If it is still there next week, we will go in as planned and pray no one is monitoring the gravity waves too carefully."

The rest of the briefing was taken up with the minutia required for a successful mission. Upon reaching the planet, *New Hope* would stay in orbit. The four assigned to the ground party would take the ship's boat down to the surface. In addition to being a Broan linguist, Bernie Sampson was a trained pilot.

Once on the ground, Mark would be team leader, essentially reprising Admiral Landon's role during the mission to Klys'kra't. He would be a trader from a far-distant world, out on a mission to open up new markets. Lisa would be his assistant. Sampson would be their personal pilot. Seiichi Takamari would play a visiting scholar, along on the expedition, but not part of it. He would express an interest in learning what knowledge the Ranta possessed that his own distant world did not.

Mark would make a show of sampling the local agricultural products and choose those he thought might be in high demand on the fictional world of Troje. He would then bargain aggressively for his chosen delicacies. *New Hope* carried several of the Vithian power units and other devices they had salvaged from Sar-Say's wrecked ship. They would use these samples as trade goods, along with several human gadgets that had been designed to betray no hint of their origin. Eventually, when a deal was nearly concluded, the "scholar" would express interest in purchasing the local planetary database, stating that it would be too much trouble to extract only the parts that were different from the Trojans' own database.

Master Trader Markel would publicly object to the expense, but then give in reluctantly and ask their hosts for a quote on what the scholar was asking. Whatever the price, he would scream that he was being robbed, haggle a bit, and then give in.

Following Mark's recounting of the basic mission plan, Captain Symes requested a review of contingency planning. What would they do if the landing boat broke down when the ground party was on the surface? What if *New Hope* were unable to leave orbit? What if either the ground party or the ship were captured?

Under what circumstances would either *Revenger* or *Allison* come to rescue them? The crews of both were decked out in the same masquerade scheme as was *New Hope*'s crew. It would look funny to have creatures with different paint schemes, but identical bioscans, suddenly appear, claiming to be unrelated to the Vulcans.

After nearly two hours of going over contingencies, Captain Symes called a halt. "I think we've discussed everything that has occurred to us. The question is 'what hasn't occurred to us?' Captain Harris, any final thoughts?"

"No, sir. We all seem to be just about talked out."

"Very well. You have my permission to proceed on your mission. I recommend an early departure. You'll want to be relatively close to the gate when that big bulk carrier jumps outbound."

"Aye aye, sir."

#

Chapter Thirty One

Pastol was large on the viewscreen as *New Hope* sat in a close parking orbit and waited for clearance from the Ranta to allow them to disembark. Like most terrestrial worlds, Pastol was a "big blue marble." Its seas were more extensive than Earth's and its continents correspondingly smaller. At 10,000 kilometers diameter, it was slightly smaller than Earth and a bit farther from its G5 primary, Etnarii. As a result, the local gravity was about 90% standard and the temperature distinctly colder. In addition to its sparkling blue seas, the planet possessed two oversize polar ice caps, one distinctly larger than the other, the result of a 30-degree axial tilt as it orbited its star.

The approach everyone worried about had been without incident, almost boring. They crept to within ten thousand kilometers of the stargate before powering down everything but essential life support, imitating a hole in space. Then they waited. As predicted, the bulk hauler departed Pastol orbit a few days later.

They watched the alien climb toward them for a week. When it reached the stargate, it disappeared. As close as they were, the resulting gravity wave rattled every dish and stowage compartment door in the ship. What had been a theoretical subject for most people became very real.

"Did you feel that?" dozens of crewmen asked simultaneously.

"Sure did," came the myriad awed responses.

They had wasted no time. Powering up the normal space engines, they swept close to the gate before sending the standard Broan arrival notice. The response came promptly once the radio signals were given time to cross the intervening gulf of vacuum.

"What ship and where from?" the terse message asked in Broan trade talk.

"Trading vessel *New Hope* out of Troje, Hass Vith, commanding. Owner, Master Trader Markel Sinth, aboard."

Half an hour later, had come the demand, "What is your purpose here?"

"We are on a trade mission to open up new markets. We have heard of your delicacies and have come to taste them for ourselves. Request permission to approach the planet."

Again the long wait, followed by, "Approach approved. Take up equatorial parking orbit at 12^3 *kel* and wait to be inspected."

The voyage to Pastol had taken five days and had been utterly uneventful. At the end, they took up a parking orbit as directed and now waited for inspection.

"Ship coming up from the planet," Emily Sopwell reported.

"Armed?" Captain Harris asked.

"Not obviously so. Small ship. About twice the size of our landing boat."

"Probably local health inspection," Bernie Sampson said over the intercom.

"All right. Communicator, announce that we are about to receive visitors. No speech other than Broan trade talk from here on out. All hidden spaces are to be locked down. All false doors to be closed as of now!"

"Yes, sir."

The communicator made the announcement. Within a few minutes, various symbols began to appear on the main viewscreen in Broan script. They signified that all ingress and egress to the classified parts of the ship had been sealed. To the casual observer, the holds would appear stuffed with merchandise. In fact, the actual trade goods were only stacked two layers deep. What appeared to be additional goods behind them was actually a cleverly camouflaged bulkhead hiding the part of the ship where weapons and the stardrive generators were housed.

The ferry craft matched orbits efficiently, and was taken aboard through the hangar bay hatch. The hatch was sealed and the bay pressurized with air containing a touch of ozone. At the same time, a similar mixture was pumped throughout the ship.

The ozone was part of the masquerade. It would hopefully convince the visitors that they were from a hotter star than Sol, one with sufficient ultraviolet output that it would drive the ozone layer all the way to the ground. Personally, Mark thought the masquerade planners had gone a little far with that touch, since it caused his eyes to water. Still, one never knew what clues to Earth's location might turn out to be important, and therefore, misinformation was the order of the day.

Two Ranta emerged from their ship, to be met by Lisa in her yellow jumpsuit. Virtually every viewscreen in the ship was tuned to the hangar bay cameras for the meeting. Sure enough, the Ranta were easily three meters tall, dwarfing his diminutive wife. One was covered in fluorescent green feathers while the second visitor's covering was more blue-green.

This was one world where their gaudy yellow-black striping scheme would not stand out, Mark thought upon seeing them.

Lisa spoke with them for several minutes before gesturing for them to follow her. The ship being in zero gravity, they were forced to pull themselves hand over hand along a guide line.

When they arrived at the spacious, palatial cabin of Master Trader Markel Sinth, Mark was ready for them.

"Master, it is my pleasure to introduce ValikSanMor and SerBis(Dek)Fos, of the Ranta Organization for Out System Trade. Gentlebeings, may I present Master Trader Markel Sinth, leader of our expedition and owner of this vessel."

"Greetings Markel Sinth," the green one said. "We are here to inspect your ship and make sure that it is safe for you to enter our biosphere."

"We are ready to be inspected," Mark replied, not adding a name because he wasn't sure which was which. "What do you require of us?"

"We need two specimens of your crew to be scanned for microorganisms. I am afraid that you are not in our standard database, and therefore, the scans will have to be full spectrum."

"Very well. Will I and my assistant be sufficient?"

"You appear to have different physiologies. Why is that?" the blue-green inspector asked.

"We are of different sexes. I am male and my assistant is female. I hope this is not a delicate subject with your race."

"Why would it be? Are there more variants?"

"More sexes? No, only the two. I'm afraid that you are not in our standard database either. Is it the same with you?"

"We have three sexes," Green said. "I and SerBis(Dek)Fos are of the genetic material donor sex. When you go down to the planet, you will meet members of the fertilizer and receiver sexes."

"Are they outwardly different from you two?"

"To no great degree. Many aliens cannot distinguish one sex from another. We, of course, have no difficulty in discerning the differences."

Mark made the Broan gesture for mirth, something these creatures should be familiar with. "Yes, we also have an instinctual understanding of such things. There are species, I understand, that cannot... tell the difference, that is."

"It must make for a confusing mating season," the blue-green Ranta, the one named Ser, replied.

Mark wondered if he was making a joke, then decided not to test out the theory. Instead of laughing, he asked, "What do you require of us?"

The resulting examination was thorough. Both Mark and Lisa were prodded, asked to display the various orifices of their bodies (from which swabbed specimens were taken), then scanned with a couple of devices that were different from the Voldar'ik bio scanners, but which served the same purpose.

When they were done, the two inspectors conferred briefly in their own language, then announced themselves satisfied. "You do not appear to have any organisms that can feed on our kind. Your bio-chemistry is sufficiently different that none of our organisms are likely to find you edible. While different, your chemistry is close enough that you should be able to eat our food, although supplements are advised."

Mark nodded. "That is good to know. We had heard that your foodstuffs are edible by our kind, but having your verification of the fact puts to rest many concerns. If your food turned out to be poison to us, this trip would have been a waste of time and value."

"You are approved to enter our biosphere," ValikSanMor said. "We must now inspect your ship."

"Of course," Mark replied, gesturing for them to follow him.

Captain Harris led the tour through the Potemkin Village portion of the ship. Outwardly, their vessel bore a resemblance to Sar-Say's wrecked transport, save for the human-style controls.

Once again, the two appeared not to be particularly interested in what they were seeing, as though they had done this a thousand times before. However, local rules called for ship inspection upon arrival, and inspect they did.

When they were done, they gave *New Hope* a clean bill of health.

"Will you be bringing this vessel down to the planet?" ValikSanMor asked.

"No," Harris replied. "It would be too difficult to decontaminate after such a visit. Our own world's health regulations are as stringent as your own. We will send down our auxiliary craft with Master Markel Sith and three others, if that is acceptable."

"Your business is your business."

"A very proper attitude," Mark replied. "One of our party will be a scholar of our people. He is along to learn about other cultures… a requirement before he will be allowed to practice his profession. Is it possible for him to be given access to your planetary database?"

"Something can be arranged in exchange for value."

"Of course," Mark replied. "It is good to meet a race whose outlook is so much like our own. Where should we land our auxiliary craft?"

"We must make our report first. We will provide you coordinates and communications bands within one planetary rotation. You need only orient your instruments to the westernmost point of the largest continent to follow our instructions."

"Thank you. May we present the two of you with tokens of our appreciation? Is that the local custom?"

"It is."

"I will have my assistant retrieve the items."

With bribes in hand, the two inspectors returned to their own boat and departed. As soon as the hangar bay door closed, Captain Harris ordered the ship spun up and the ozone purged from the atmosphere.

So far, the masquerade appeared to be working perfectly. Of course, with aliens, one could not always tell.

#

Ship Commander Second Grade Pas-Tek of the Avenger-class warship *Blood Oath* was irked. He and his ship had been on patrol for half a Greater Cycle and had been looking forward to going home. Instead, they had received orders to divert from their planned route in order to deliver special orders to half the minor planets in the sector.

The order was for all Sector, Sub-sector, and Planetary Masters to be on the lookout for a group of orange-skin, blue-fur-bearing bipeds who had incurred docking fees at some backwater planet and then skipped out without paying what they owed. Along with descriptions and stereo images, there were complete bioscans on the miscreants for the benefit of those races that did not see in color.

The stated offense hardly seemed to merit even the briefest flicker of attention from Those-Who-Rule. Yet, the dispatch he carried was coded at the highest priority, meaning that it was important enough to dispatch warships to deliver it to out-of-the-way systems that might otherwise not receive word in the lifetime of currently living beings.

The problem was that Civilization was just too large for messages to be distributed efficiently by starship. There were too many worlds and too few ships to do the work. Even if they had the ships, they would lack the Masters to man them. Aboard his own vessel, Pas-Tek was the only Broa. The rest of the crew were Ventans, with a couple of Basiks thrown in for diversity, and his personal guard force of Banlath warriors. It was becoming harder and harder each cycle to entice good young Masters to join the Navy.

Pas-Tek had often wondered why the gates that were his portals to distant worlds could not also carry messages. It would be a simple matter to establish transmitters and receivers on each gate in a star system, and to transmit messages between gates in a single system. The problem was getting messages between gates in different systems.

Surely an automated vessel could be developed that would shuttle between pairs of gates and transmit the messages to the intra-system transmitters. In this way, messages could cross Civilization in one-eighth the time they were now taking. Such an invention would relieve his own ship of the tedious task of jumping from system to system and transmitting high priority directives to the local Masters and subservient governments.

Already on this voyage, he had touched at Versal, Dratf, Meginianalod, Strmpf, and Pepcal. He had yet to visit Modat, Sserrtal, Bestafal, Etnarii, Sasta, and Desh. Only after this dreary litany of little visited outposts of Civilization was complete would he and his ship be free to return home for a well needed rest.

As he contemplated the unfairness of it all, his cabin communicator squawked.

"Yes?"

"You asked to be notified when we reached the gate, Master," Saton, his Ventan sailing master announced.

"Any traffic?"

"Two ore freighters preparing to jump. I sent our identification and they are now clearing the way for us."

"They should have made way when their long-range scanners first picked us up. We may have to teach these freighter shipmasters a lesson one of these cycles."

"Yes, Master," Saton replied without emotion. His commander often made such threats, but had yet to carry one out. Whether his inactivity came from moral scruples, or merely a lack of initiative, the sailing master could not say. The business of Masters was the sole province of Masters. Lesser beings wisely steered clear. As the shamans often said, 'When Darvan Beasts mate, it is easy for those of lesser races to be accidentally crushed in the throes of passion.'

"Very well, Saton. You may jump when we are in position. Next stop, the ever lovely, sulfurous mud pools of Modat.

"I look forward to it," the sailing master said with no hint of irony. To his race, what the Ship Commander described was very like home.

#

Chapter Thirty Two

The landing boat keened from the high speed wind beyond the hull as it dropped toward Pastol's verdant main continent. Bernie Sampson was concentrating on his flying, aiming for a small spot one hundred kilometers to the east of the westernmost point on the continent, a small peninsula from which a space beacon radiated skyward. The rest of the ground party, Mark, Lisa, and Seiichi Takamatsu, gawked at the scenery ahead.

Pastol's oceans were a deeper blue than those of Earth, the result of Etnarii's G5 spectral class, which made it a bit cooler than Sol, with more yellow in its spectrum. Below them, huge ships plied the waters, leaving V-shaped wakes of whitecaps behind them. Ahead, the large continent was just beginning to appear on the horizon, the outlines softened by atmospheric haze.

To port, large cumulonimbus clouds were forming below them, a portent of an active weather cycle. For a planet devoted mostly to farming, plenty of rain would seem to be a blessing, although that assumption was grounded in their experience with terrestrial ecology. On an alien world, water falling from the sky might be considered a problem, especially if the locals were the equivalent of cactus farmers.

"Look at those mountains!" Lisa exclaimed as more of the continent climbed above the distant horizon. The eastern end of the continent was protected by a snow-capped range of peaks that rivaled Mount Everest on Earth. Directly in front of them were more than a dozen cloud defying peaks.

"Lower gravity," Takamatsu responded. "It allows a larger mass of rock to be supported by the planetary crust."

"I just hope the electric heating circuits in our jumpsuits don't short out," Mark replied. "It looks cold down there."

"Which is probably why the locals developed feathers," the technologist replied. "They need the insulation."

"Is everything a scientific fact to you?" Lisa asked. "Can't you just enjoy the beauty?"

"Sorry," he said, grinning. "Just practicing for my role as the misunderstood scholar on this expedition."

"Keep it up," Mark said. "We all need to stay in character from this moment until we are safely aboard ship again. No telling what kind of slip will give the show away down there."

"Yes, Captain Bligh," his wife replied in Broan trade talk, mangling the final name the way Sar-Say had when she first met him.

"Would you people please be quiet? I am trying to fly up here," Bernie Sampson said over his shoulder from the pilot's seat.

The rest of them shut up, concentrating instead on the scenery as they passed over the mountain range and encountered the vista of a vast plain stretching before them. One thing became immediately evident. The plain was covered with farms for as far as the eye could see.

#

The landing boat grounded in a flurry of exhaust from the underjets, coming to rest on a hard surface that shimmered in the sunlight.

Around them were towering buildings on the periphery of the combination airport/spaceport. Several sleek aircraft were parked at what could only be passenger terminals, connected to the buildings by long, spindly tubes. As on Earth, form followed function.

As soon as the whine of their engines faded into inaudibility, two Ranta emerged from the nearby structure and made their loping way toward the boat. A human being would have had difficulty keeping up with them at the speed they walked, a natural consequence of their long legs.

"Showtime!" Mark muttered as he unstrapped. "Everyone sit tight until I give you the signal to come out. I'll go put my toe in the water and hope that the local crocodiles don't bite it off."

He made his way to the midships airlock. Checking the telltales that showed the quality of air beyond, he palmed the control that opened both airlock doors simultaneously. His ears popped as pressure equalized in the boat. He stepped through the open lock as soon as the pressure doors retracted, and immediately shivered in the cold wind.

He made the Broan gesture of welcome and said, "Greetings! Thank you for allowing us to visit your beautiful world." That at least, was the sentiment. What he actually said was, *"Hello. Appreciation permission us here planet esthetic good."*

Despite the jangled syntax of the common tongue of the Sovereignty, the two Ranta seemed to have no problem following the gist of his greeting.

"Greetings. I am BasTorNok, Senior Inspector of this Place of Arrival. This is CanVisTal, representative of our Out-System Trade Council. Welcome."

"I am Mårkel Sinth, Master Trader and leader of our team."

"And your purpose here?" CanVisTal asked.

"We are on a mission of trade exploration for our Master, the exalted Sar-Tal of the Sar-Ganth Clan. He bade us to seek value beyond our normal sphere of commerce in the hope that we might enhance his standing with Those Who Rule."

"He sounds very like our Master."

"Who is?"

"Zer-Fal."

"Is he here on this world? It is our custom to pay our respects to the local Master and to present him with gifts."

"No, he is at the Subsector Capital on Gasak, which you passed through on your way here."

"Yes, of course. We visited the system but found little there that could not be obtained much closer to our own star. Perhaps we can leave our offering with you, to be presented to your master the next time he favors you with a visit."

"That would be proper," BasTorNok replied.

"My apologies, Trader," CanVisTal said, "but we do not know of your star. Why is that?"

"Our star is Tanith and our planet, Troje. Our species identifies itself as Trojan. We are a small world in a system with but a single stargate. We do not get many visitors and thus, must seek our fortunes by visiting other systems where value may be found."

"Where are you located?"

"On the other side of Civilization, obviously, or else we would know of one another. Our world is 1.2×12^1 jumps from your system."

"That is very far. It must be difficult to earn value at such a range." CanVisTal replied.

"It is very difficult. Which is why we came here looking for delicacies that we might sell at home as a luxury item, perhaps a food product that can be concentrated prior to shipment to keep the bulk down."

"We will show you all of our flora. Perhaps there is something you will find both tasty and suitable."

"Perhaps," Mark agreed.

"It is uncommon for a species not to be in our planetary database. It makes it much easier to accommodate visitors," BasTorNok said, refusing to be diverted by talk of lucrative trade deals.

"Yes, someone has been lax in their duties," Mark responded, then quickly added, "Not the Masters, of course. Their servants."

"Yes, of course," BasTorNok replied. It is impossible to read the emotions of aliens, Mark knew, but he suspected that the response was more a formality than a heartfelt defense of the Broa.

Mark made the Broan gesture that translates into a shrug and continued. "Civilization is large. Frankly, we have found much about our own database which needs correction. We have brought a scholar along for just that task."

"What have you discovered?"

"For example, we did not know of your beautiful world until we reached Gasak, save for a symbol in our chart of the stargate network. It was there that we heard of your agricultural products, and so we came here to see for ourselves.

"Your vessel in orbit is not very large. Not only do you have a long journey ahead of you, the quantity of cargo you carry is limited. How do you expect to make a profit?"

"We do not, at least, not on this trip. We are exploring. *New Hope* is my personal vessel. As you note, we can only transport samples of what we find in our travels. If we come to an agreement on an exchange of value, we will send a bulk transport such as the one that exited the Gasak gate as we were preparing to jump here. My world has three such vessels it can devote to the long voyage, and we can arrange for more if your products prove the delicacies we have been told."

"Do you expect there to be much demand for our foods?" CanVisTal asked.

Mark 'shrugged' again. "Who can say until we have seen what you have? I can tell you that my people will pay well for a new delicacy. We have specialists called *cordon' bleus* who are experts in preparing sustenance from many worlds. Indeed, in our history, before the coming of the Masters, there were ships that sailed around our world for spices and rare delicacies. Many such ships were lost on the voyage, but those that made it back earned their owners large stocks of value."

"Yes, it was the same with us," CanVisTal replied. "As you can imagine, a world such as ours does relatively little manufacturing. The Masters have assigned us a different role. Therefore, those are the goods that we value. What do you have to offer?"

"Much. We have Vithian power supplies, Gorthan verifiers, even a few Laca reformers. We also have specialty merchandise from Troje that may interest you."

"Vith is very far from your home," BasTorNok responded. "I am surprised that you trade with them."

"Our master has a relationship with their master. We do not question his reasons for sending us there. We but go at his behest."

"Of course. Masters have their own reasons for doing the things they do. Welcome, Trader Markel Sinth. We are pleased that you have come. The rest of your crew may debark now."

"Excellent," Mark replied. It would be good to get the introductions over with and get in out of the cold. Despite his electric heating, he could still feel the chill wind tugging at him through the fabric of his suit.

#

Two weeks later, Lisa Rykand was royally sick of touring farms and tasting alien foods. So far, she hadn't poisoned herself, but the tastes had not been to her liking. She was also tired of being perpetually cold, despite the parka she wore over her yellow jumpsuit. Even though Pastol's gravity was lower than Earth's, the atmospheric pressure was actually higher than standard by seventeen percent, the result of less planetary boil-off during Pastol's formative period. This gave the wind a force and a bite that was beyond her experience. It also sucked the heat out of a person.

The purpose of the Ranta's covering of feathers became immediately obvious the first time they took her on a tour of one of their farms. The wind that day would have put Chicago to shame, although the locals assured her that the velocity was nothing unusual. As she bundled in her cold weather gear, her guides wore little more than the garments she had come to think of as "Greek tunics," yet they seemed perfectly comfortable. That was when she noticed that their feathers were fluffed up, and not only from the wind. Like the birds at home, the Ranta were able to vary their insulation by ruffling their feathers.

The Ranta farms they visited were all models of agricultural efficiency. Automated machinery tilled the rows and harvested the various species of plants. Harvested foodstuffs were stored in giant silos that were veritable skyscrapers.

Rather than merely bringing them the various products and letting them sample them, the Ranta insisted that they see the source of the products for themselves, which meant touring numerous working farms, each replete with some sort of museum for visitors. Lisa doubted that every farm on Pastol was so equipped, and so recognized a formal sales campaign when she saw one. Her linguistic skills were reduced to praising the farmers' products, even when she didn't particularly like what she tasted or smelled.

There was one plant that looked like hay, but smelled like cinnamon, which the Ranta used to feed a domesticated animal that looked like a cow with six legs. Lisa sampled the hay and explained that her species did not possess the proper micro-organisms in their intestines to assimilate the cellulose content. Her particular guide that day had expressed his disappointment, but signaled his understanding. Like his six-legged cow, the farmer was a vegetarian.

She asked him why he was raising the animal if he did not intend to eat it. His explanation made little sense to her. Unfortunately, that was true of a great deal of the explanations the Ranta gave her. It had quickly become obvious that the two species lacked common referents for many of the things they tried to discuss.

One thing that was very clear, however, was that the Ranta seemed squeamish at the thought of eating an animal's flesh. Their reaction was similar to a human being who has encountered cannibals. The ground party discovered that on their first day when mealtime came around, and they had opened an array of self-heating ration packs for dinner. Three of these contained meat. As cooking aromas filled their assigned quarters, their guides promptly abandoned them, explaining that the smell was making them ill. Since then, they had subsisted on cold rations heavy in fruits and vegetables.

As their tours of the hinterlands continued, Lisa became worried about their mission. They needed to find at least one foodstuff on this world that they could plausibly claim would be a sensation on the fictional Troje. Unfortunately, the Ranta knew enough about their biochemistry that they couldn't just stuff their mouth full of the local cinnamon hay and pronounce it good.

Finally, when touring a farm that was devoted to the raising of purple cabbage-like growths studded with red berries, she found something that was not only palatable, but which might actually sell in the better restaurants on Earth if they had truly been interested in the interstellar import business.

"What is this?" she asked, holding up the red berry that she had just bitten into. She was surprised to discover that the berry had an intriguing sweet-sour taste.

The farmer who was her guide for the day responded, "We call it *vasa*. It is the reproductive structure of this *setei* plant."

"We call this sort of thing a fruit. I don't see any seeds."

"What are seeds?" the farmer asked.

"The parts of the fruit that bear the plant's genetic code. The outer part is just to attract animals, who then eat the fruit, and spread the seeds far and wide in their excrement."

The farmer seemed puzzled by the explanation. "The plants on your world actually attract animals to eat them?"

"Certainly. Is it not the same on your world?"

"No. In time, the *vasa* dries out and spreads its spores to the winds."

"If you squeeze *vasa*, does it produce a red liquid with the same taste?"

"Yes, although I fail to see why you would do this."

"We have a process which we call *winemaking*," she said, using the Standard word, of necessity. "If you squeezed these *vasa* berries into a pulp and drew off the liquid, placing it in containers, I believe that it would be worthwhile to transport it to our home world, where we could sell it for excess value."

"It seems a great deal of trouble," the farmer answered.

"Perhaps, but it concentrates the essence which my species finds palatable. I must speak to the Master trader of this."

It was thus that the ground party decided that they would go into the *vasa* wine business, especially after the puzzled Ranta squeezed out a bottle of juice as a sample of the concentrated product.

#

"It will be expensive to build the necessary machinery to squeeze the quantities of *vasa* you request into this juice you prize," CanVisTal protested.

Mark Rykand smiled inwardly. If there was one universal constant, it was the art of the deal. Serious negotiations had begun two days previous and they had been at it from Etnarii-rise to Etnarii-set.

To his surprise, Mark found the negotiating exciting. It was the thrill of the hunt, the chase after the elusive animal that would put food on the family table. Even the fact that the whole negotiation was a sham did little to dampen his enthusiasm. To disguise his true interests, Mark had spent as much time plugging his ersatz alien merchandise as in negotiating for the fruit juice. In exchange for lodging and technical assistance, he had already presented CanVisTal with a Vithian power unit. Like the Voldar'ik of Klys'kra't, that particular device seemed the most attractive. It was a shame Sar-Say's ship hadn't carried more of them.

"I am sure that you will build the price of the machinery into the cost of the wine," he responded to CanVisTal's objection. "Also, strictly speaking, what we have in these containers is merely the juice of the *vasa* berry. We will have to try fermenting it into true wine. We will also do distillation experiments on the journey home, to see if we can make a more concentrated liquor from it."

"Distillation? I know the word, but I do not understand the context with respect to *vasa*."

"It is a way to concentrate the juice and to give it a stimulative effect on my species. While the juice will sell well on Troje, if the concentrated form is the same as our other wines, my people will pay a great deal more for it. You will also earn more value. It makes more sense to distill the *vasa* juice here than to ship it to Troje to concentrate it."

"Anything that adds value is to be pursued," CanVisTal replied.

"Yes, our masters will be pleased," Mark agreed.

All of this talk of processing, pressing, encapsulating, and distilling *vasa* juice was so much camouflage for the real task of the expedition, which was the acquisition of a planetary database and its maps of the stargate network. The penultimate act of that particular play was about to begin. Mark pretended surprise when Seiichi Takamatsu burst in and interrupted the negotiation.

"What may I do for you, Scholar?" he said in his most stern tone. The nuance was lost on the alien, but it was necessary that he stay in character.

"I need to speak to you, Trader," Takamatsu said, also playing his part.

"Can't you see that we are in the middle of negotiations here?"

"Sorry, but it can't wait."

"What can't wait?"

"The task you have assigned me, Trader, is impossible. I need more access to the Pastol database if you expect me to bring our own data up to date."

Mark shook his head vigorously. "The access we have bought you is already more expensive than we had budgeted. Perhaps you can wait until our next star system to complete your work."

"It isn't likely to be any less expensive on our next stop. Besides, I have finally learned to find information in the Pastol data. In another system, I would just have to start all over again."

CanVisTal listened impassively to this byplay, which had taken place in Trade Talk for his benefit. When both Trojans seemed unwilling to carry on the conversation, he made the gesture of obeisance and asked, "What is the problem? May I help solve it?"

Mark turned to the Ranta with an exasperated look. "We are a trading planet and we have specialists in the ways of other species in order that we may better anticipate their needs."

"That is wise," CanVisTal replied.

"Scholar Tama here is learning the art," he said. "That is the reason he is along on this voyage. When he returns home, he will be allowed to join the Guild of Scholars and to begin his profession.

"We have had him looking up matters in your planetary database that seem to be missing in ours, both to fill the gaps and to judge how badly we need an update."

"We could give him increased access," the Ranta trade representative said.

"There isn't enough time. Now that we have discovered your wonderful *vasa* juice, we must proceed to the next world on our list so that we may speedily complete our voyage and return home. The sooner we bring this to the attention of our Master, the sooner we will come back so that you can begin full scale production."

"I understand."

"Current plans are to depart as soon as you have filled our first order."

"That will take three more days, as I have told you. The equipment we require for squeezing out the juice is being modified."

"I remember," Mark replied. "That doesn't leave us with sufficient time for the scholar to complete his work."

"We could purchase a copy of their database," Tanamara said, right on cue. "I could work on it during the voyage home without delaying your damned schedule!"

"WHAT?" Mark screamed, overacting for the alien's sake. "Do you have any idea how much that would cost?"

The two of them glowered at one another until CanVisTal stepped in. "Is it my understanding that the scholar would like to copy our planetary database and study it at his leisure?"

"It's out of the question," Mark said stubbornly.

"Perhaps the cost would not be as great as you think," the Ranta trade representative said. "Since we are going to be in the *vasa* winemaking business together, I may be able to talk to our Keeper of the Data and discuss a special price... say three parts out of twelve less in exchange for the data, to be compensated by a one part in twelve increase in the price you will pay for *vasa*."

The hook having been neatly set, Mark made a show of considering the offer, then reluctantly said, "It would help us update our own pitiful excuse for a database. All we would need are the standard public files. I see no need to pay for your lists of annual crop totals and other useless information."

"Of course," CanVisTal said. "However, it may be more difficult to extract the data you do not need than it will be to include them, but adjust the price as though they were not there."

"Very well," Mark said. "If you will give me your estimate, I will make a decision before we leave. Scholar, you may have your way this time, but don't ever ask me for this sort of thing again."

"I will ask the Keeper of the Data for his price tonight, and you shall have it in the morning."

"That will be acceptable," Mark replied grudgingly, while inside, his heart began to pound. Hopefully, the Ranta did not have a bio sensor focused on him at the moment, or else they would wonder at his excitement at getting back to the haggling over the price of red berry juice.

#

Chapter Thirty Three

As Broan Avenger *Blood Oath* accelerated away from Holsto in the Bestafal System, Ship Commander Pas-Tek flapped his ears to show his exasperation. He had thought Modat was bad, with its boiling mud baths and atmosphere that stank of sulfur. Holsto was worse. The sandstorms were unending, the result of the planet lying on its side as it orbited its star.

His arrival there had corresponded with the height of summer in the northern hemisphere, when Holsto had its north pole pointed directly at the system primary. The scorching of the polar region caused all of the ice there to melt. Conversely, the southern polar ice cap now covered one-third of the planet. In half a revolution of Holsto about its star, the situation would be reversed.

This alternating imbalance drove ferocious storms and a continuous strong wind that picked up sand and dust in the Great Northern Desert and dumped its load on the strip cities huddled on both sides of the equator.

None of this would have mattered had his superiors allowed him to communicate with the locals from space. However, the policy of Those Who Rule was that a ship commander on messenger duty must assume orbit and travel to the surface where he could deliver the council's message to the local rulers in person. The rule was an ancient one first promulgated in response to a planetary rebellion that had been laid at the snout of an absentee Master.

Those who served the council must never miss an opportunity to demonstrate the power of the Race to their subservients.

This meant that Pas-Tek's fur had been burned, frozen, and sand blasted on the various planets this mission required him to visit. Yet, despite his desire to return home to his mate and cubs, he still had Etnarii, Sasta, and Desh to visit before he could warp orbit for home.

Luckily, Etnarii was a much more pleasant world than the one he had just come from. It was a bit cold for his kind, but he would take that over sulfur smell or blowing sand any time.

As he draped himself over the resting rack in his cabin, his private hatch alarm sounded. Grumbling, he ordered the unwelcome visitor to enter.

As expected, Saton, his sailing master, passed through the hatch and made the sign of obeisance.

"Yes?" he asked the Ventan. "Can't you see that I am resting after the ordeal of washing all the sand from my fur?"

"Apologies, Commander, but I have a maintenance item for you."

"What has broken now?"

The jump generator timing circuit is a few twelfths of a micro-octave out of calibration."

"Will it get us through the next jump?"

"It will, but possibly not through the one after that."

"We are scheduled to put in at Pastol when we get to the Etnarii system. You and the engineers can recalibrate while I am down on the planet."

"Yes, Master."

"Let me know when we approach the Etnarii gate. With the timing circuits questionable, I want to be in the control center when we jump."

"I will, Master," the Ventan said before withdrawing from his cabin.

Now then, where was he? It seemed to Pas-Tek that he had been about to fall asleep. Despite his active mind, he was sufficiently tired that it shouldn't take long to surrender the cares of command for a few hours.

As he closed his eyes, he listened to the thrum of *Blood Oath*'s engines. Everything sounded normal. However, timing circuit problems were best not left for the next scheduled maintenance. His race had excellent hearing, but long before a timing problem became audible, it would cause the engines to explode as soon as the generators began building energy in the jump field.

"Now *that* would be the perfect ending for this mission," he thought to himself. Of course, having one's ship explode in a stargate was the single excuse Those Who Rule would accept for failing to complete his mission.

But only if he died in the explosion.

#

Mark Rykand was agitated. It had been two days since CanVisTal had promised to get him a quote on a copy of the Pastol Planetary Database. The trade representative, who had previously hovered over them like a mother hen with her newly hatched brood, had been strangely absent. Mark's sense of anticipation built to the point where his mind was racing through the possible "what might have gone wrong" scenarios.

The problem was that he could not show any overt interest in the database. To the Ranta, he must appear unconcerned, even a little hostile to the idea of spending hard earned value on a scholar's enthusiasms. Outwardly, his only interest must be the procurement of a sufficient sample of *vasa* juice to take home to Troje.

That process, too, was going slowly. It seemed that the average *vasa* berry only produced a few milliliters of fruit juice, and therefore, the process required a lot of berries.

One would think that the Ranta would have an efficient method for harvesting the berries, but one would be wrong. The Ranta ate the cabbage part of the *setei* plant and usually discarded the berries.

Mark sympathized. He had once been in Arizona, where he pulled the ripe fruit off a prickly pear cactus and popped it into his mouth. That was when he discovered the small spines that dot the skin of the red, bottle-shaped fruit. He made his discovery when one lodged in the roof of his mouth. His guide, recognizing what had happened, broke down laughing. Later he explained that it was necessary to remove the spines before consuming the succulent fruit.

Compounding the raw material problem was the fact that most *setei* plants had not yet reached the reproductive stage, and therefore, lacked *vasa* berries. It would be several months, CanVisTal explained, before they would reach the prime harvest season.

It seemed to Mark that even the gods were attempting to thwart him. Feigning great interest in the red liquid, he had consumed a sizeable quantity of the juice over the last several days. *Vasa* juice was tasty enough that it might actually be saleable on Earth; that is, if he were really interested in it as a product, and if there weren't a year-long voyage between Pastol and home.

If they couldn't sell it as a wine, they could certainly use it as a laxative. That, at least, was the effect it had on him. Despite this, Lisa's discovery of the red berries had been a stroke of luck. Their cover story would have worn thin had they not found a product they could convincingly claim to be tasty.

His foul musings were interrupted when his wife stuck her head around the corner of the partitioned cubicle and said, "CanVisTal is here to see you."

"About damned time," he muttered, making sure to do so in Standard rather than trade talk. It would not have done to have the locals how much exasperation these delays were causing him.

"Greetings, Markel Sinth," CanVisTal boomed as Lisa led him into Mark's humble office.

"What news of my *vasa* juice?"

"We nearly have the quantity of berries that we require, and will deliver them in three days."

"Excellent. We are running late, so if you will have them delivered to my landing boat, we will take our departure as soon as they are onboard."

"There is the matter of payment," the trade representative replied.

"Yes, there is always that. We agreed that for this lot of juice, we will pay you two Vithian power units, one Gorthian reformer, and a dozen of those small zinc statues from my home world. I will have my pilot return to the ship to obtain payment."

"That would be good," CanVisTal replied. "There is also the matter of the planetary database."

"Oh, yes," Mark replied, feeling his throat constrict around the words from tension. "I had almost forgotten. How much?"

"Sixty four power units, twelve reformers, and six verifiers."

Mark didn't have to feign anger as he exploded in protest. The price was ridiculous, not the least because *New Hope* didn't carry that many power units in its fake cargo hold. He told CanVisTal that, explaining that in their long voyage, they had stopped many places and exchanged what he sought for other commodities.

"Credit can be arranged," the trade representative said.

Mark smiled inwardly, and the negotiations began. It took more than an hour, but eventually a price was agreed upon. They would provide the Ranta with a dozen power units in addition to the ones they owed for the *vasa* juice, plus all of the reformers they had aboard *New Hope* (not that he admitted as much to CanVisTal). For the remainder of the debt, he agreed to have what he owed aboard the first bulk carrier that came to Pastol for concentrated *vasa* juice. No power units, no *vasa*.

"Can the database be ready when you deliver the juice?" Mark asked.

"Most certainly," CanVisTal said.

"Then I will send my pilot to orbit to pick up the goods."

"We will have the juice at this facility three sunrises from now."

Mark rose and stuck out his hand. "A custom of my people." He showed the Rasta how to shake hands, finishing with, "This is the way we seal a bargain."

CanVisTal turned to leave. Just as he did so, Mark's communicator beeped. Surprised, he plucked it from his belt and pressed the message button.

"Mark?" Captain Harris's voice issued from the hidden speaker.

"Yes."

"Are you alone?" Harris asked. With a start, Mark realized that he was speaking Standard.

"Not quite. I have the Ranta trade representative with me."

The captain was curt. "Get rid of him and call me back."

"Why?"

"We've got trouble. Harris out."

#

Pas-Tek lounged at his control station aboard *Blood Oath* and watched his mostly Gorthian crew go about their business. The Gorthians were competent spacers, having had interplanetary travel long before the Race discovered them on a small world circling a blue-white giant of a star. As a result, their bullet-shaped heads had eyes half the diameter of Pas-Tek's own. Their vision extended to shorter wavelengths than did his, which made much of their artwork unintelligible to him. He just couldn't see in the ultraviolet shades of color.

"Gate just coming into range now, Ship Commander," his sensor operator announced.

"Very well. How are the timing circuits?" he asked into his intercom.

"Holding steady, Ship Commander," his chief engineer's unseen voice responded. "There should be no difficulty this jump."

"Are you certain, Engineer? We don't want to spread pieces of our ship all over the gate."

"We are within safe parameters, Commander, if barely."

"Very well. We can't stay here." In truth, of course, he would have preferred to stay in the Gasak system, the local Subsector capital. There was a large population of the Race here, diversions, comfortable quarters in which to lounge and breathe fresh air.

Instead they were about to jump through one of Gasak's half dozen gates to the cul-de-sac system of Etnarii, with its boring farmers and endless talk about the weather and crops. He had never been to the backwater farm planet before, but he had talked with ship commanders who had. None of them spoke well of the place, although he reminded himself, it was still better than the last few planets he had visited.

"You may approach the gate, Sailing Master!"

Saton acknowledged the order from the astrogator's station and began programming their approach. It was possible to transit a stargate at high speed, but such maneuvers were not done save for combat situations.

The gate was a small target in a big universe, and nothing would ruin a mission quite like colliding with one. In addition to destroying his ship, a collision would put the gate out of commission. In a big system like Gasak, that would not be a problem. The accident would be noted immediately and steps taken to repair or replace the gate. In a backwater like Etnarii, it would be a catastrophe. The place had so little traffic that it might be cycles before anyone knew that the link was down.

For these and many other reasons, *Blood Oath* slowed to groundcar speed as it approached the gate. For one thing, the gate was oriented at nearly right angles to their orbit. Saton was decelerating at a rate that would bring them to a halt just in front of silver ring. He would then rotate the ship a quarter-turn and use maneuvering thrusters to slowly nudge the ship into position at the exact center of the gate. Only when the ship was at rest to the limit of detection would he divert power to the jump generators and begin the buildup of energy that would throw them to a distant star.

"We have passed the outer boundary," the sailing master announced some time later.

"Are the timing circuits still holding?" Pas-Tek asked.

"Still holding," the engineer replied from his station at the heart of *Blood Oath*.

"Very well. Sailing master, take us through."

There passed a hundred heartbeats in which nothing happened. Then there was an indescribable sensation, followed by a change in the starlight falling on the ship's hull.

"Jump successfully completed, Ship Commander."

"Very well. Plot an orbit for Pastol. Chief Engineer, you may begin making preparations for the recalibration."

Both crewmen acknowledged his order.

When Pas-Tek was convinced that everything was in order, he left his station to return to his cabin. This being a new system to him, he needed to study up on the local customs. Not that a member of the Race had anything to fear from trampling on local customs. In any dispute between subservient and master, the masters always won. However, knowing how a particular race of subservients thought made completing his mission easier.

Just three more planets and he could go home!

#

Chapter Thirty Four

Mark Rykand casually walked CanVisTal to the door of their assigned quarters and bade him goodbye. The trade representative halted for a moment and asked, "Is something wrong with our deal?"

"Wrong?" Mark asked.

"The call from your ship. It was not bad news, was it?"

"No. Captain Harris merely wanted to confirm that the cargo was ready for transfer as soon as the landing boat can get back to orbit. We should have your payment here tomorrow."

"Then I must depart to see that our portion of the bargain is upheld," the Ranta replied.

"That would be best. We are very behind schedule and I would like to depart as soon as the *vasa* juice is ready. The sooner we leave, the sooner we return to Troje, and the sooner we can get the bulk carrier here with the rest of your payment."

"Then we both have a reason to hurry," CanVisTal replied before turning on his heel and striding out the door at the disconcertingly fast pace that was the normal Ranta walking speed.

Mark's hands trembled as he reached for his communicator and signaled the ship.

"Harris, here," came the immediate reply.

"What's the matter?" Mark asked. Both men were speaking Standard to make sure that their signal could not be intercepted and understood.

"A ship just popped out of the stargate."

"What ship?"

"A Broan Avenger."

Mark gulped. "Bad news" didn't seem to cover it. The mission to obtain a planetary database had so far gone off flawlessly, and now this worst of all possible scenarios.

"Are you sure it's an Avenger?"

"The emissions spectrum matches the recordings from the Battle of New Eden."

It hadn't been a battle, of course. More of a slaughter. When *Magellan* had first spotted Sar-Say's ship, it had been under attack by a craft Sar-Say identified as a powerful warcraft. He had named the type "Avenger" and apparently, another was en route to Pastol. They were so damned close! Why couldn't the Broa have waited another week to schedule a visit?

"Any idea whether they are looking for us?" Mark asked.

"They don't appear to be in a hurry to get here. At the moment, they are just accelerating away from the stargate at a leisurely pace."

"What are your orders, Captain?"

"For you and your people to get your asses on that boat and get back up here. We need to break orbit as soon as you are onboard."

Mark's stomach tightened into a tension knot. At the same time, his mind raced. To have come so far and then fall short was a crushing blow. Worse, it was not the first time this had happened to him.

"I think that would be a mistake, Captain."

"How so, Mr. Rykand?" the tone of command was evident in Harris's voice.

"We had this problem at Klys'kra't. We were close to obtaining a planetary database then, and we let it slip through our fingers."

"From what I heard, Lieutenant, it was the right decision," Captain Harris replied.

"You're probably right, sir. If Sar-Say had managed to get word to the locals, no telling what would have happened. We just couldn't risk Earth that way. Still, I lie awake at night and wonder if we shouldn't have brazened it out."

"Is that your recommendation now?"

"Yes, sir. I think it is. This system has but one stargate. If we run for it, we have to run right past that inbound Avenger. What if the Broan captain orders us to halt for inspection? Or the Ranta might note that as soon as the Broan ship appeared, we abandoned our goods and ran. It would be better to stay and carry on as though nothing is wrong. After all, we aren't supposed to know that a Broan warship is in this system."

"You're risking the lives of your ground party and of everyone on this ship, Mister."

"Yes, sir, but I think the benefit is worth the risk. The Ranta claim they will have the database in three days. If the Avenger isn't in a hurry to get here, it will make orbit in four or five days. That gives us a minimum of 24 hours to wrap things up, return to the ship, and be ready to space as soon as the Avenger assumes a parking orbit.

"They slip in and we slip out. That way, we won't have to confront him en route and it won't look to the Ranta like we're running away."

"What if something goes wrong, Lieutenant?"

"If something goes wrong, we fight our way to safety. Also, there is always *Chicago* to rectify any mess we make while trying to get clear."

There came a long pause in which Captain Harris considered his recommendation. Finally, the voice that issued from the communicator bore a trace of resignation along with fatigue. "We'll follow your recommendation. I hope you know what you are doing."

"That makes two of us, Captain."

#

Three days later, CanVisTal made good on his promise. Five large hundred-liter tanks were loaded aboard the landing boat with great ceremony, and the trade representative handed him a record cube containing the standard planetary database of Pastol.

"There, Master Trader, we have met our part of the bargain."

"Thank you, CanVisTal. And we are ready with our portion," he said, pointing to the alien goods piled up just beyond the landing boat airlock.

At the Ranta's signal, his work crew began moving tanks into the boat, where they were strapped to the aft passenger benches. To clear the airlock door required them to bend nearly double. The Ranta then began loading the pile of power units, reformers, verifiers, and statuary onto a small self-propelled cart.

When the goods were safely inside a nearby warehouse, CanVisTal made a speech about how trade was good and how he hoped their *vasa* winemaking venture would add a store of value to both species. He managed to take half an hour to express a sentiment that should have gone a minute or two. To the four shivering members of the ground party lined up outside the boat, it seemed interminable.

Eventually the trade representative ran down and Mark responded with his own speech. He thanked CanVisTal for his courtesy and praised the business acumen and fairness of the Ranta.

Finally the speeches were done, CanVisTal shook the hands of each of them as Mark had taught him to do, and the time came to enter the boat.

Mark was the last one to board. It was with a sigh that he pressed the control that sealed both airlock doors. He took off his heavy coat, stuffed it into a small storage compartment, then squirmed his way forward past shining containers of *vasa* juice. He slid onto the first bench where his wife was holding the lap belt ready for use.

He took one final look around. Seeing nothing amiss, he turned to Bernie Sampson, and in a loud official voice, said, "Pilot!"

"Yes, Lieutenant?"

"Would you please get us the hell out of here?"

"Gladly, Lieutenant. Hang on to your butt because this is going to be one of the fastest transits you've ever seen."

Seconds later, they were aloft and climbing for altitude. As soon as they cleared the continent, Sampson accelerated through the sound barrier — sound propagated more slowly on Pastol than Earth because of the lower temperature — and began to climb for the deep black.

#

Mark never realized how much he had missed *New Hope* until he was safely back onboard. No sooner had the hangar bay been pressurized than he was out through the airlock. The temperature seemed colder than Pastol. His breath made smoke as he breathed. He was followed by three excited members of the ground party.

It was good to be home again.

Captain Harris met them at the hatch. "Did you get it?"

Mark held up the glittering jewel of the record cube between thumb and forefinger.

"Is it authentic?"

"I don't know yet. I doubt the Ranta would cheat us. They're too anxious to sell us their juice. Still, you can never tell about aliens, so we'll make some copies and have Suichi check it out."

"You called, boss?" the ersatz Trojan scholar asked from behind Mark.

Mark turned to him and handed over the cube.

"The first thing I want is for you to make a dozen copies. After that, check to see if it's really the database. Look for maps of the stargate system."

"Yes, sir."

"Don't look before you've made the copies. We've come too far to screw things up now."

Takamatsu grinned. "Not to worry. I know how to do my job."

"Good, then do it." The intensity of Mark's response was an indication of the strain he'd been under the last few weeks.

Both he and Harris watched Takamatsu disappear through the hatch before Mark turned to the captain and asked, "What is that Avenger doing?"

"Just boring in as though he hasn't a care in the world. He'll make orbit tomorrow afternoon."

"Do you think he suspects us? Has he made any hostile moves?"

"None," Harris replied. "And he'd better not. I have both of our superlight missiles tracking him as we speak. If he twitches in our direction, I'll blast him out of space."

#

"Pastol Space Control, this is Trojan Trade Ship *New Hope*. We are ready to depart orbit."

"You will have to wait," a Rantan voice replied. "There is a Warship of the Masters that has priority."

"Understood. Our sensors indicate that he will reach orbit on the other side of the planet. When he does, we would like to depart for the stargate."

"Your request is noted. Stand by."

"Just like our Navy," Harris muttered under his breath. "Hurry up and wait!"

Half an hour later, the Broan Avenger slid behind the disk of Pastol and was presumably taking up the same parking orbit that *New Hope* was in. Moments later, a voice emanated from the communicator, announcing that they were free to depart.

Harris acknowledged the order and gave the same command Mark had when leaving the planet.

"Astrogator, get us the hell out of here, but don't make it look as though we are in any particular hurry."

"Yes, sir."

"When you are clear of the local orbital junk, boost speed to something that makes it look like we are anxious to make up for lost time, but don't show them any performance better than they expect to see."

"Already plotted, Captain."

There followed four tense hours while they watched to see if anyone was pursuing them. In fact, there were only two ships in the system… their own and the Avenger. That fact did not put anyone's mind at ease, however."

At the end of first watch, Captain Harris called his staff together in the wardroom. In addition to Mark, who was his astrogator, he included the rest of the ground party.

They debriefed him as to what had taken place on the surface while he and the crew had waited in orbit. If the ground party despaired of ever obtaining the database, those aboard *New Hope* had the worst of it. There is a certain calming effect that action has on the human psyche. Those aboard the ship did not have the benefit of that calming. All they could do was sit and wait and imagine the worst.

At the end of the debriefing, Seiichi Takamatsu reported on his initial search of the data in the record cube.

"It's a planetary database, all right. It must have 50 terabytes of information stuffed in there. Most of it is Ranta junk, but I did manage to locate the map of the stargate network. Care to see it?"

He didn't wait for a response as one was not needed. Instead, he punched a series of commands into his datacom and the large holoscreen at one end of the compartment lit up.

A series of rainbow colors swirled for a moment, and then a diagram based on Broan symbols came up. The screen was filled with glowing gold stargate symbols connected by dim red lines. There were so many of them that Mark had difficulty making out the shape of the map.

"This isn't a star map, per se," Takamatsu said. "It's more like one of those maps of the tube in London. The interconnecting lines show the topology of the system rather than location in space. The scale is expanded for important systems, diminished for minor ones."

"Can you tell us where to find the Broan home world?" Harris asked.

The scientist held up his hands in a gesture of exasperation. "Captain, give me a break. I just barely managed to find this diagram before the briefing."

"It's huge!" Lisa exclaimed, looking at the screen.

She was right. It looked as though some giant spider had gone insane while spinning his web. Red lines went everywhere on the screen, jumping from stargate to stargate in seemingly random order.

"I wonder if we have bitten off more than we can chew?" one of Captain Harris's staff officers mused.

Looking at the interconnections between a million star systems, Mark Rykand wondered the same thing.

Only, he wondered to himself while he studied the face of the enemy. Lisa was right. There were a lot of stargates in the Sovereignty and finding the most important gate or gates, the ones leading to the Broan home world, would be quite literally like looking for a needle in a haystack.

Still, they now had a diagram of the haystack and that would make the hunt a great deal easier.

#

ᐧᐧChapter Thirty Five

The mountains on this world are impressive," said Gastan Nor. The squat Banlath was *Blood Oath*'s guard commander and leader of Pas-Tek's personal bodyguard detachment. He and six of his fellows had accompanied the captain on each of the "courtesy calls" they had made on his mission. It had been a century or more since a Master had been harmed by subservients, making Pas-Tek's retinue more of a luxury than a necessity. Still, the Banlath were renowned for both their loyalty and ferocity, and their presence around Pas-Tek had the desired effect on the local leaders whenever he delivered his dispatches.

Besides, he would have felt vulnerable without them, and that might cause Those Who Serve to get the wrong idea about Those Who Rule and their representative.

"Must be the gravity," Pas-Tek replied absentmindedly, not bothering to look up at the display that showed the icy mountain range below. His attention was focused on a small display on which the standard database entry for Pastol was displayed. The world seemed a simple place with little interaction with the rest of Civilization, save for their food exports. Pas-Tek liked that. It meant that his stay here would be of minimum duration and that he would soon be en route to the next-to-last system on his list. That is, if the engineers could get the drive recalibrated in time.

"We have landing clearance," his pilot announced.

"Then let us not delay," Pas-Tak replied.

A short time later, his boat set down at a small spaceport at which a large number of Ranta were gathered. These were the senior leaders of the planetary government. Protocol required such a welcoming committee for any master who visited this world, especially for one engaged in the official business of Those Who Rule. Barring sickness or death, any government official who chose not to greet him would be looked upon as being unworthy of his or her post.

As he rose to exit the boat, Gastan Nor produced a body cape. "You will want this, Commander. It is quite cold outside."

Pas-Tek allowed the garment to be fastened around him before proceeding to the airlock. He waited until Nor and his six guards had positioned themselves in a defensive perimeter around the boat, then stepped out into the weak sunlight.

"Who represents Pastol?" he asked in a soft voice that nevertheless carried across the cold wind.

A tall being with purple-green feathers stepped forward and said, "I am LasTiVar. I represent the council that rules in your absence, Master."

"I am Ship Commander Pas-Tek of the Avenger *Blood Oath*. I am here to deliver dispatches from Those Who Rule. I require a place where we can talk."

"We have prepared transport to take you and your party into the city, Master."

"Is your council here?" Pas-Tek asked.

"They are, Master."

"Then we will meet here at this landing site," the commander said. "I have two more systems to visit after this one. I have no time for ceremonials."

"I understand, LasTiVar replied. "I will summon the council members to that building there."

He gestured toward a low building that looked like a warehouse. Not very impressive, but functional. That was all Pas-Tek required. The sooner he was back aboard ship, the sooner he would be on his way.

He and his entourage followed the Rantan leader to the warehouse and out of the cold wind. There was a delay while one of his guards set up the portable projection equipment. While they waited, several very tall Rantans arrived to array themselves in a respectful semicircle about him.

When LasTiVar signified that all were present, Pas-Tek slipped out of his cloak and climbed up onto a handy packing crate. Even then, his head did not reach the level of the Rantans'. Even so, there was no doubt as to where the power lay in this gathering.

"Loyal subjects of Pastol. Greetings from Those Who Rule. I am Pas-Tek, Ship Commander of the Second Grade. I bring instructions from the Ruling Council. They require that you do all in your power to hunt down a gang of criminals."

At his signal, the guard running the projection device brought up the hologram containing the council edict. The edict was read by

Zel-Sen, Senior of the Council. Behind him lay the majesty of the council chambers, a reminder to all within Civilization of the power that controlled their lives.

"Greetings, Loyal Subjects and Beings," Zel-Sen's image began. "I bring the tidings of the Ruling Council. May peace and prosperity rule your lives! The Council has need of your assistance. A gang of thieves is operating within the bounds of Civilization, preying on the unwary among us. They must be brought to justice.

"These thieves call themselves 'Vulcans'..." Zel-Sen went on to describe the miscreants. While he spoke, various views of them appeared in the lighted cube above the projector. There were views of each of the Vulcans who had visited Klys'kra't. Many showed them engaged in various activities. Some of the views were still shots and close-ups. The orange-skinned, blue-haired aliens had been caught from numerous angles. Finally, Zel-Sen gave a reference for where the medical scans could be found in the record cube.

He finished with, "All beings are ordered to be aware of these criminals and to report any news of them. If you have any information, you will notify the nearest Sub-Sector or Sector Capital. They are to be detained if you encounter them."

The recording ended with Zel-Sen assuming the posture of command to emphasize that the matter was of great importance, as though the fact that the edict had been delivered via warship was insufficient prod to action.

While the recording played, Pas-Tek watched the Ranta. They stood immobile as the old Master gave them their orders. Since reading the emotions of a species he had never before met was not one of Pas-Tek's skills, he did not know what to make of their manner. Outwardly, they appeared respectful, but who could say what thoughts were going on inside those feather covered skulls?

"Have you seen these beings?" he asked when the recording ended, just as he had done at every previous planet. The question was pro forma. He had already heard it answered in the negative a dozen times.

There was a long silence before LasTiVar responded, "We do not get many visitors here."

"Yes, but have you seen them?"

"We have seen no species with orange skins and blue fur. I will, of course, check with those in the external affairs group to be sure, but I do not believe that they have been here. However…"

Pas-Tek's ears pricked up at the momentary hesitation. "Yes?"

LasTiVar continued. "Although the colors are not right and they do not have fur, the overall shape of limbs and features appear similar to that of the Trojans. Perhaps they are related to these Vulcans."

"Who are these Trojans of whom you speak?"

They are traders. We have just concluded an arrangement to produce a liquid form of our *vasa* berry."

"'*Just?*' When did they visit you?"

"A few days ago."

Pas-Tek blinked in surprise. "Please repeat."

"We first met them less than two twelve-days ago."

"And where are they now?"

"The departed just as your ship made orbit. They are en route to the stargate."

Pas-Tek blinked in surprise. He couldn't be this lucky! The very criminals, or possibly their close relatives, were actually in this system! All he need do was to chase them down and his career was assured. Even if they jumped to Gasak before he caught them, he would continue the chase until he ran them down.

Then he remembered. The engineers had his star drive disassembled, trying to fix the generator calibration! That meant that he would have to catch them *before* they reached the stargate. Luckily, there were few ships that could outrun *Blood Oath*.

"Quick, tell me everything you know about these Trojans! Better yet, I want to see the records you made of them."

"Yes, Master."

#

It took the Rantans an obscenely long time to retrieve the records Pas-Tek wanted, or at least that was the way Pas-Tek perceived it. In truth, a scurrying young alien arrived with a record cube in less time than it would have taken to be seated in one of the fancier restaurants on Vil, Pas-Tek's home. The tension coursing through his body as he waited just made it seem like forever.

The record cube went immediately into the portable projector and he was soon looking at some not-very-good photography that the Ranta had made of their Trojan guests. By his departed ancestors, they did look like the recordings of the Vulcans! Not the superficial features, of course. These beings were hairless, with intricate yellow and black shading all over their bodies.

But the essentials were identical. Like most intelligent species, they were axially bisymmetric bipeds with two arms and a globular head in which all of the sense organs were located. The eyes had the shape of a *vandan* fruit, and the nose was doubly slit under an overhang of flesh. The mouth had a distinctly fleshy look to it, at least in the outer part. Inside, the teeth were white and standard omnivore in shape. The tongue was short, broad and pink, showing no sign of being split.

In fact, they not only looked like the Vulcans, two of the Trojans bore a striking resemblance to two of the individual Vulcans of Klys'kra't!

"Guard, depress the color on those two views," Pas-Tek ordered. The two views in question were of the female Vulcan and female Trojan. Suddenly, the garish orange skin and blue hair of one picture faded to gray as did the black and yellow stripes in the other.

Pas-Tek peered at the result closely. He was not an expert at judging alien facial features, but it looked to him like the same being, save that in one of the pictures, she was bald.

"What say you, Gaston Nor?" he asked his guard leader.

"Either this species does not have much genetic variation, or that is the same individual," Nor replied. "Fos, do a comparison analysis! Quickly."

The guard operating the projector made a few adjustments to his controls and a program used to categorize individual species took over. For most beings, the program would have announced their species, home world, and the name of their master within the span of a single heartbeat. For this unknown female, however, the two pictures were compared and various difficult-to-change characteristics – such as the distance between the eyes – were evaluated.

In less time than it would have taken Pas-Tek to give an order, the projector announced that the two images were of the same individual.

"It appears that Pastol has been visited by thieves," he said to no one in particular. To LasTiVar, he asked, "Who had the most contact with these visitors?"

"CanVisTal spent the most time with them."

"Where is this CanVisTal?"

"Why, at his station, encoding reports on the Trojans."

"Where is his station?"

"On the other side of the landing field," the leader of the Ranta replied. "He is cataloging the trade goods in an attempt to evaluate their worth."

"What trade goods?"

"Why the goods the Vulcans left behind in exchange for our *vasa* juice."

Bring this CanVisTal here," Pas-Tek ordered. "Also, I want to see these trade goods. Have them fetched immediately."

Throughout he tried to remain calm, but this news triggered his battle reflexes. It was difficult not to order his guards back to the landing boat and to launch himself in full pursuit of these brigands.

However, as an old teacher had once told him, a wise commander obtains all the information he can about an enemy before launching a battle. So, Pas-Tek willed himself to be patient.

Eventually, a tall Rantan was brought before him. The being seemed agitated.

"You dealt with these Trojans during their visit here?" Pas-Tek asked in a tone of command.

"Yes, Master," the Rantan replied. "I am in charge of making trade agreements with all who visit our world. Did I do wrong?"

"No one is questioning the propriety of your actions," Pas-Tek replied, willing himself to calm down. "Please tell me all that they did here."

"They were seeking trade opportunities and were looking for new foodstuffs that they could introduce to their far-off world. They found the *vasa* berry and negotiated with us to squeeze the berries into liquid form. We expect to gain much value from the arrangement."

"I doubt it," the ship commander replied. "You have been dealing with known thieves."

"Thieves? The Trojans? It hardly seems likely. They paid well for the juice, more in fact than I expected to get."

"Is that all they purchased? Juice?"

"No, Master. They had a scholar with them. At his request, they bought a copy of our planetary database. They paid more than it was worth as well."

"Your planetary database? What would they want with that?"

"They claimed their own database was corrupt and incomplete."

"And what did they pay you with?"

"Vithian power units, converters, and some of their folk art."

"Vithian power units are what they left behind at Klys'kra't. Where are these units?"

"As you ordered, I have sent my helper to retrieve them from the warehouse where they are stored."

An interminable number of heartbeats later, another feathered Ranta rushed in from the cold with an armful of goods. He spread them at Pas-Tek's feet.

The ship commander had just bent over to examine them more carefully when he took a breath. The hair all over his body stiffened. Everyone in civilization knew that when a Master did that, someone was in trouble.

"What is it, Master?"

"Can't you smell it?"

"Smell what, Master?"

"That stink. These power units reek of danger pheromone. So did those at Klys'kra't. This is proof, if any is needed, that the Trojans and the Vulcans are the same people!"

#

Chapter Thirty Six

Mark had mid-watch duty, the "night shift" aboard ships in space. As head of the Astrogation Department he could assign himself to any watch he wanted. He'd chosen the unpopular mid-watch because it was quiet, and to give his two bleary-eyed assistants a break. They had been standing watch-and-watch the whole time he was on the planet. Upon hearing his decision, Lisa pointed out a drawback to the arrangement, namely that he would be sleeping alone for the rest of their time in the Etnarii System.

It had been a full day since *New Hope* departed Pastol. They had two more days to go before they rendezvoused with the stargate, where they would fake a jump to the Gasak System before returning to Brinks Base. They could have made the transit faster, of course; but to do so would reveal their ship to be no ordinary Type Seven freighter, and the masquerade must be maintained. So they plodded outbound, accelerating at 0.8 standard gees.

Of course, modern-day starships had redefined what it meant to "plod." Unlike the primitive rockets of the early space age, *New Hope*'s normal space generators were capable of thousands of hours of continuous acceleration. This meant that starships avoided the long coasts that had been the normal mode of spaceflight in earlier centuries. Instead, they accelerated under continuous power until they reached speeds approaching one percent of the speed of light. And having spent the first half of their voyage gaining velocity, they spent the second half shedding it.

Accelerating at eight-tenths gee, *New Hope* had traveled in a single day essentially the same distance that Earth moves in its yearly circuit around the sun. Even so, they had covered barely one-tenth the distance to the stargate. However, continuous acceleration is like compound interest. It adds up in a hurry. Their velocity was such that they would reach the midpoint of their voyage in only twelve more hours, and would rotate the ship to begin decelerating to keep from overshooting the stargate.

For much of the time since leaving the planet, they had focused a comm laser on *Chicago* in the Oort Cloud. The Pastol planetary database was much too large for them to transmit the whole thing to their distant guardian, but those parts researchers found interesting went on the beam.

In addition, the members of the ground party spent the day recording their impressions of Pastol. Alien Assessment Team researchers peppered them with questions designed to elicit ever greater detail from their recollections. They were so persistent that when the interrogations ceased so the victims could resume normal shipboard duties, it seemed like a respite.

Mark found the mid-watch as quiet as he had hoped it would be. After the hectic events surrounding their departure, it was pleasant to sit under the blue "night light" and feel the cool breeze of the air system wafting against the back of his neck. Things were quiet, that is, until Mark finished logging the required hourly position check. It was at that instant that a computer alarm sounded in his ear.

"What's the problem, Mr. Rykand?" Ensign Malkovich demanded in a voice that nearly cracked from adolescent tension. Malkovich was the most junior of *New Hope*'s officers.

"Checking now," Mark replied as he punched up various displays. The cause of the alarm was not difficult to discern. Throughout the climb toward the stargate, they had kept a full sensor suite focused on Pastol.

"Oh, shit!" Mark muttered under his breath.

"What is it?" the Ensign asked. This time his voice did crack.

"That Avenger just left orbit, Mr. Malkovich. It's hauling ass after us. You'd better roust the captain."

"The captain is rousted," a weary voice called from the entry hatch. Glancing over his shoulder, Mark saw Captain Harris, still sealing the closure on his ship coveralls as he entered the bridge. Ensign Malkovich immediately relinquished the command chair to the captain.

"Report!"

"The Broan Avenger just broke orbit, sir. He is accelerating this way, pulling 1.4 gee. I would say that our cover is blown."

"How long before he overtakes us?" Harris asked.

"Forty four hours if he intends to follow us through the gate. If he accelerates continuously, he'll close to weapons range in..." Mark punched a few numbers into his workstation. "... I make it 34 hours."

"Time to the gate on our current flight plan?"

"Another 48 hours, Captain."

"So they catch us before we get there in either event. How long to the summit?"

'The Summit' was the point in a voyage where velocity reached maximum and they turned the ship.

"Deceleration in 12 hours, Captain."

Harris quickly programmed his command board. Various velocity and acceleration curves filled the main viewscreen. He studied them for long seconds before shaking his head.

"Negative, astrogator. We'll delay turnover for four hours and let our velocity build. That should keep us ahead of him. Then we'll turn up the wick and decelerate at emergency max for a Type Seven. That should get us to the gate first without blowing our cover."

Mark did some work of his own and confirmed the captain's figures. "First by a hair, assuming he doesn't adjust his own velocity profile to match our maneuver."

Harris shook his head. "If he is truly after us, then he shouldn't have much performance margin to spare. Hopefully, we'll get outside his pursuit envelope."

"And if we don't?"

"We'll face that when it happens."

"Yes, sir."

"Communicator!"

"Yes, sir," Vivian Domedan responded. She was the third member of the mid-watch bridge crew, and if anything, younger than Ensign Malkovich.

"Put a report on the laser beam to *Chicago*. I want Captain Symes to know our situation."

"Yes, sir."

"Shall I order the ship to battle stations, Captain?" Malkovich asked.

"Not just yet, Ensign. Worst case, he can't overtake us for another day and a half. If we're going into battle, we need the crew rested."

Slowly, the talking died away and they all watched the blip on the screen. Accompanying the display was a range-to-target indicator. Mark became hypnotized as the Broan warship gained on them. Finally, after an hour of silence, Harris spoke up. "Ms. Domedan!"

"Yes, Captain."

"Put notes in the computer files of the battle staff. We will have a strategy session in the wardroom at 09:00 hours this morning. We need to figure out how to lose this shadow without giving away our secret."

"Aye aye, sir!"

"Well, people, I think I will try to go back to sleep. If the situation changes, call me. Ensign Malkovich, the bridge is yours. Good night."

"Good night, Captain," the youngster responded, a note of pride in his voice as he resumed his place in the command chair.

#

"Wake up, sleepyhead!" Mark said, nudging Lisa gently with one hand. When she didn't stir, he nudged her again.

"Wha… what time is it?" the sleepy voice asked, muffled by a pillow.

"Oh-six-hundred. I just came off duty."

"Then take off your clothes, climb in, and don't disturb me until 08:00."

"Can't do that," he said, admiring his wife's naked back. "We had some excitement mid-watch."

"Excitement?"

"That Broan Avenger is on our tail!"

That did it. Her orange-and-black-striped head snapped upright as she raised her head to an angle that threatened to give her a stiff neck.

"What?"

"The Broan warship left orbit a couple of hours ago. It is heading after us as quickly as it can move."

"Damn!"

"That's what I have been saying to myself every minute or so since we spotted him."

"What are we going to do?"

"Dunno. The Captain has called a strategy session for 09:00 hours. As our foremost authority on the Broa, you are invited."

That news was sufficient to levitate her to a sitting position, giving him a view that he still appreciated.

Half an hour later, they were in the mess compartment, eating breakfast. Around them hovered a buzz of urgent conversations. News traveled fast aboard ship, and no news moved faster than word that they were being stalked by a Broan warship.

"Is it true, Mr. Rykand?" Spacer Donnelly asked as he paused en route to a nearby table. His breakfast tray, momentarily forgotten, drooped to the point that Donnelly's bulb of coffee was threatening to slide off.

"It's true," Mark replied, speaking around a piece of toast that he had just bitten into. "Spotted him departing Pastol parking orbit at 04:10 this morning."

"We going to outrun him?"

"We're postponing turnover to make sure we beat him to the gate. After that... well, the captain has a strategy session this morning to answer that question."

In the twenty minutes it took him and Lisa to eat, he must have answered that same question a dozen times. Finally, they got out of the mess compartment and Mark accompanied his wife to the Alien Technologists' compartment, more to hide out until briefing time than because he had duties there.

Finally, 09:00 rolled around and both of them excused themselves as they left the scientists, all of whom were clustered around a monitor, intently watching the sensor display that showed their pursuer.

They made their way to the wardroom, where they found most members of Captain Harris's battle staff already assembled.

The captain began the session by recounting what they had observed. He explained that they had prolonged the acceleration portion of their voyage, and that they would be going to higher deceleration in a few hours. He finished with, "We'll beat them to the gate unless they continue accelerating — barely. What do we do then?"

"We jump through," the Exec said.

Mark shook his head. "Can't."

"Why not? Isn't that how you departed Klys'kra't?"

"It is. We jumped through a stargate to an uninhabited system and then went superlight. The system beyond Etnarii is Gasak, the Subsector capital. We try to go superlight there and we can guarantee an audience.

"Besides, that Avenger is going to be right behind us. Even if no one in Gasak spots us, our pursuer will know something is wrong when he doesn't find us on his scopes after he jumps through."

"Then we take him out with a superlight missile," the Chief Engineer said. "Ships explode all the time. He strained his engines during the chase and blew up."

Harris nodded. "That is a possibility. Downsides?"

"Destroying a Broan warship in plain sight of one of their worlds isn't advisable, Captain," Lisa said. "Our whole strategy involves keeping a low enough profile that no one will ever put serious effort into finding out who we are."

"What do we do, then?" Harris asked, gazing at each member of his staff in turn. The response was an uncomfortable silence.

Mark frowned. They had come so far and now they were threatened by the same sort of ship that had killed Jani at New Eden. The thought brought with it a flash of his kid sister's laughing, red-curl-enshrouded face. That, in turn, was followed by an errant thought. Uncontrolled by conscious will, his mouth opened and words tumbled out.

"It's simple, really, Captain. They don't explode. We do!"

#

"They are past time when they should have begun decelerating, shipmaster!"

Pas-Tek was seated at his command station in *Blood Oath*'s control room, watching the Vulcan ship on his displays.

There was no law that decreed a ship had to begin slowing at the precise midpoint of a voyage. It was, however, a development he had not planned on.

"Engineer!"

"Yes, Commander," came the disembodied reply.

"Our quarry has passed the midpoint and continues to flee. Can we do the same?"

"No, Commander. We are running one-twelfth above recommended power now. Any more and we are liable to damage the generators."

"It looks as though our target will reach the gate first. We are going to need our jump engines."

"We're working on repairs as quickly as we can, Master. The acceleration is impeding the recalibration."

"I don't care, Engineer," he replied, using the idiom of command. "I want my ship ready to jump when we reach the gate. I don't want him to get too far into Gasak before we overtake him."

"Yes, Commander."

Saton's station was at the foot of Pas-Tek's command throne. The sailing master turned his head awkwardly and said, "It is a shame that you do not have the codes to deactivate the gate, Master."

"While we are at it, why not wish for a planet destroyer?"

The planet destroyers were a class of large warship held in readiness to deal with planetary revolts. It had been generations since one had been used, but Those Who Rule had long memories.

However, Saton was correct. It would have been much easier if he had access to the disable code for this particular stargate. However, the gates were critical to the proper functioning of Civilization. Shutting down a gate for even a fraction of a cycle could disrupt an entire sector's economy. Chasing down one errant freighter did not seem a sufficient reason.

That thought provoked another. It was obvious that the Ruling Council wanted these miscreants badly, and much honor would fall to the officer who captured them. Yet, he was bothered by one aspect of his situation.

Those two images of the female alien haunted him. Why would the same individual show up on both Klys'kra't and Pastol, two systems many stargates apart? Were these criminals such a small gang that they had only the single ship? It seemed possible since both fugitive vessels were Type Seven freighters. If that was the case, however, what had they done so heinous as to warrant a Civilization-wide alert?

"Computer!"

"Yes, Master," the mechanical voice replied in his ear.

"Run the following data." He gave the reference for both the Klys'kra't and Pastol data files. "Is the female in both files the same individual?"

The computer reply was nearly instantaneous. "Yes. The two recordings are of one individual."

"They aren't clones?"

"Cloning is seldom without error. The medical data in the two files is identical in every important respect."

"Are any of the other records duplicates?"

"Male Number Three in Record One is identical with Male Number One in Record Two. The other four males represented in the data are distinct individuals."

Pas-Tek considered that information. He had not one match, but two. Curious, indeed. There was a saying among his people, "It is a small universe." However, it wasn't *that* small!

Perhaps there was more at stake here than a single shipload of thieves, after all.

#

Chapter Thirty Seven

"It's simple, really, Captain. They don't explode. We do!"

As Mark sat back, every face around the wardroom table was turned in his direction. As he scanned the faces, he had a sudden feeling of déjà vu. It was as though he had experienced this situation before. Suddenly, he remembered where and when.

On the retreat from Klys'kra't, the Gibraltar Earth plan had popped into his head as though it had been lying full formed somewhere in his subconscious, just waiting for the proper moment to show itself. It had been a moment very like this one.

"Care to explain that, Mr. Rykand?" Harris asked, his tone deceptively mild, a sign that the Captain's temper might be on a short leash this morning.

"I'm not sure I can... intelligibly, Captain."

"Try, Mister!"

"I was just thinking about our problem here... or rather, our double problem. That Avenger is coming up fast, and will be close to weapons' range when we reach the gate. At that distance, he won't need instruments to detect the gravity wave from our jump. He'll be able to feel it, or rather, *not* feel it. If we appear to go through the gate and the jolt doesn't come, he'll notice and begin wondering about this ship's propulsion capabilities."

"So we jump through the gate and take our chances in the Gasak System!" the chief engineer reiterated.

Mark shook his head. "Whatever we are going to do will be more likely to succeed here than there. In truth, there is only one way we can pull this off without raising that Broan captain's suspicions. We enter the gate, power up as though for a jump, and then explode, vaporizing ourselves and the gate in the process."

"Surely you aren't suggesting that we use the self destruct," Harris said.

"No, sir. The situation is far from the suicide stage. Perhaps I should say, 'We appear to explode, vaporizing ourselves and the gate.'"

From the looks he was getting, Mark realized that what was so shining clear to him was much less so to others. Only his wife's quizzical look indicated that she was half following his logic.

"Look, our stargate generator must maintain a precise balance of dozens of different parameters. What if the generator gets out of balance and we try to jump?"

"We blow up," the captain said.

"And what if we enter the gate, jump superlight, drop back to normal space, and let fly with an SM at the gate, all in the space of say a microsecond or two?"

Harris finally grinned. "Then we appear to blow up!"

"Yes, sir. Or at least, the gate blows up and anyone not watching too closely sees our ship disappear in the explosion."

"Won't our pursuer find it suspicious?" someone asked.

Mark shrugged. "Who cares? It presents him with a tragedy that has a mundane explanation rather than a mystery to be investigated further.

"Besides, the destruction of the stargate will trap the Avenger here in the Etnarii System for God knows how long. Its captain won't be able to report anything until someone notices that the Etnarii gate is down."

"They'll have their sensors focused on us," the Exec said. "Once they analyze the recordings, they will see that we disappeared an instant before the explosion."

"Then we obscure their view. Just as we enter the gate, we power up our jump generators. Their instruments will register that fact. Just as we reach critical power, we vent atmosphere and anything else we can think of to produce an opaque cloud. We momentarily cut off his view, then transition to superlight."

"Can we go superlight this close to the star?"

"This close? No," Mark responded. "But out where the gate is, we should be far enough from Etnarii's gravitational singularity to transition to superlight."

The captain thought about it for a moment, then nodded, "I like it. If we take out the gate, news of our presence doesn't get out for weeks or even months."

It took another two hours to flesh out Mark's idea. When they were through, they had a plan.

#

"The freighter is decelerating, Master."

"How long until they reach the gate?"

"One rotation."

"We will begin our own deceleration on schedule, Sailing Master."

"We could catch them if we continue accelerating," Saton reminded him.

"And fly past so fast that we would have a single opportunity for a shot? No, our mission is to capture these thieves and deliver them to the Council."

"We might disable them before they reach the gate."

"And we could as easily vaporize them with a misplaced bolt. No, we will capture them as intact as we can manage. If they beat us to Gasak, it will save us the trouble of transporting them there. We will hold to our flight plan."

"Command acknowledged, Master."

Pas-Tek watched passively as the weight on his chest continued at five-twelfths above what he was used to. The acceleration made it difficult to breathe, but was not yet debilitating.

The range fell more quickly now that their quarry was slowing its headlong flight for the gate. However, the gods of speed and distance were against them. The freighter would reach the gate before they closed to weapons range.

Let them think they have escaped, Pas-Tek thought with grim humor. They would soon discover their respite a brief one. *Blood Oath* would materialize in the Gasak gate before the Trojan ship could flee.

"Engineer!"

"Yes, Master."

"How are my jump engines?"

"The engines are calibrated and ready for use, Master."

"Very good. My compliments to your crew."

"I will tell them, Master."

#

"How are we doing, Astrogator?" Captain Harris asked 26 hours after turnover.

"Fifteen minutes, Captain," Mark replied, watching his displays carefully.

"And the Avenger?"

"Closing fast, sir. Even so, he's going to be late to the party."

"Thank God! Propulsion!"

"Yes, sir," the Chief Engineer responded from deep in the bowels of the ship.

"Everything ready on your end?"

"Ready, sir. I'm afraid there is going to be a jolt. Luckily, it will come and go so quickly that we probably won't be affected much. Still, I would have everyone strap down, just in case."

"Communicator, make the announcement."

"ALL HANDS. SECURE YOURSELVES FOR TRANSITION TO SUPERLIGHT! WARNING, IT MAY BE ROUGH. FOURTEEN MINUTES, AND COUNTING!"

Mark tightened his acceleration harness and keyed his communicator for the Alien Technology Section. Within seconds, Lisa's worried features were on one of his auxiliary screens.

"All secure there?"

"Secure."

"How are you holding up?"

"I'm okay."

"It won't be long now."

"I hope not," she said with a wan smile.

"I love you."

An indefinable emotion flashed across her features. Then she replied, "I love you, too."

"See you after we jump."

"I'll be waiting."

With that, he cut the connection and concentrated on his screens.

Ten minutes later, as the wedding-band shape of the stargate filled the main viewscreen, and continued to get larger by the second, Captain Harris ordered, "Astrogator. Activate the stargate jump generators. Bring them up slowly. Give him a good chance to see our field building."

"Aye aye, sir."

"Engineering. Prepare to vent plasma!"

Mark switched on the generators that, when in the embrace of a stargate's matching field, would send them to a distant system. He watched as the generator power bars grew apace, flashing from red to yellow to green.

"Generators online, Captain."

The next step involved considerable cross-talk between the ship's ersatz Broan computer and that of the stargate. The synchronization process took several seconds, and would end with a green READY TO JUMP message on Mark's screen.

Instead of the expected message, however, he found himself looking at a red, flashing HOLD warning.

"Captain, we aren't synchronizing. The gate just rejected our request to jump."

"What's the matter?" Harris demanded. "Something wrong with the gate?"

"Doesn't appear to be," Mark said, scanning his instruments.

"We need to look like we are about to jump, Astrogator," Harris said quietly. "And we need to look like it now!"

"Working on it, Captain," Mark replied as he resent the jump commands to the gate. Once again, he received a HOLD warning in response.

"Combat Systems! Where is that Avenger?"

"Coming on fast, Captain," Spacer Rodriguez, the offensive weapons systems tech, reported. "Two minutes to weapons range."

"Stand by to fire superlight missile on my command."

"Aye aye, sir."

"*Damn!*"

"Was that an official report, Astrogator?"

"Sorry, sir. I just figured out the problem."

"Don't keep us in suspense."

"There's nothing wrong with the gate, Captain. It is working perfectly."

"Then why can't we synchronize?"

"Because there is another ship coming through from the other side. What we are seeing is an anti-collision lockout!"

\#

"Master. The gate has been activated from Gasak!"

"Say again, Sailing Master."

"There is a ship in the gate in the Gasak System, readying to jump. The freighter cannot get a lock."

"Then we have them!"

\#

"Combat, where is that Avenger?"

"Just coming into weapons range now, Captain," Rodriguez reported. "He hasn't powered weapons yet."

"Then hold your fire until he does. At the first indication, take him out."

"Aye aye, sir."

"Astrogator, report!"

"The gate is powering up, sir. The jump field is almost at critical! I think…"

Before Mark could tell Harris what he thought, a shudder went through the ship, rattling every storage compartment door on the bridge.

"That was a big one!" someone exclaimed as the clatter caused by the gravity wave died away.

"And so is that!" Vivian Domedan responded, pointing to the viewscreen. Where before there had only been blackness at the center of the stargate, now there lay a massive spherical ship.

"Bulk hauler," Rodriguez reported. "Must be here for the annual harvest. She's starting to move out of the gate."

"Take us in!" Harris ordered.

New Hope was jolted again, this time by her own normal space engines. When he had been unable to gain a synchronization lock, Mark halted the ship a few kilometers short of their goal. Now that they were once again under power, *New Hope* responded like a race horse, sliding forward with ever increasing speed. Both the stargate and the newly arrived bulk hauler expanded alarmingly.

The bulk hauler dodged sideways to get out of the way of the suicidal fools rushing straight for them. *New Hope* slid past within naked-eye range. Entering the circle of the stargate, Mark brought the ship to a halt. They hovered for a dozen seconds while he checked his alignment.

He punched for synchronization. Power bars grew on his screen and flashing Broan script followed the lightning-like conversation between ship and gate. This time, almost to his surprise, the screen flashed READY TO JUMP.

Only when he exhaled loudly did Mark realize that he had been holding his breath. "Ready for jump, Captain," he reported.

"Engineering! Begin your toxic dump."

The starfield on the main viewscreen dimmed as glowing incandescent fog enshrouded the ship. Harris let the dump continue for five seconds until they could no longer see the glowing spark that was Etnarii. Hopefully, they were also obscured to the Avenger's sensors. As soon as the star disappeared, he gave the command.

"Superlight drive generators to power...NOW!"

#

Chapter Thirty Eight

"What's happening?" Pas-Tek demanded as his ship continued to slow in its headlong rush for the gate. A gravity wave strong enough to be felt without instruments had just passed through his ship, causing the usual clatter.

"A cargo carrier has appeared in the gate, Commander," his sailing master reported. "It is powering up to vacate the ring. The freighter is starting to move toward it... those fools are likely to collide with the larger ship if they aren't careful!"

As Pas-Tek watched, the freighter barely missed the big cargo ship and took its place within the stargate while the other craft moved visibly on the screen.

"They are powering generators, Commander," his sensor operator reported before issuing forth with an oath in his native tongue.

Such a breach of protocol would normally have brought punishment down on the head of the hapless crewman. As it was, Pas-Tek barely noticed. For the scene on the screen held his full attention.

Their hull camera was at full magnification. The small Type Seven freighter could be seen surrounded by the silvery ring of the gate. Suddenly, the outline of the toy ship softened as several plumes of vapor began issuing from vents all over its surface.

The vapor quickly built in thickness until they lost sight of the craft.

Then the universe exploded!

#

At Captain Harris's command, Mark Rykand tapped the 'execute' key. From that moment on, the ship's computer took over as it stepped through a preprogrammed series of maneuvers.

The first was a crash engagement of the stardrive generators. The jump engines were at full power when several high power switches shunted the coils that would have sent the ship to the Gasak System directly across the coils of the stardrive generator. The result was a short circuit that generated an overload in the stardrive, throwing *New Hope* out of normal space. To an outside observer, the ship simply disappeared, without producing a gravity wave.

Their superlight voyage was a short one. A mere 2.7 nanoseconds after breaking free of Einstein's barrier, they dropped back into normal space at the limit of missile range. The computer launched a superlight missile at the stargate and again crashed power to the stardrive. The next leg of the voyage was longer than the first, but still too quick for human senses to perceive.

All the human beings onboard detected was an indefinable sensation, as though someone had taken hold of their insides and twisted. The ship seemed to shudder for an instant. The shaking was accompanied by a sudden drop in illumination that lasted for about as long as it takes to blink. The overhead lights brightened momentarily, then failed completely.

The computer displays were the next to go as their protective circuits took them offline rather than subject them to the power spike. The bridge was plunged into murk. The only source of illumination was the multicolored glow emanating from various emergency status lights.

"Someone get power back!" the captain's voice ordered from out of the gloom.

Seconds later, the overhead lights illuminated. It took thirty seconds for the displays to return to life.

"Where are we, Astrogator?"

Mark commanded a hull camera to search for Etnarii. When it ceased slewing, a bright star sat at the center of the main viewscreen. At the stargate, Etnarii was shrunken, but still displayed a disk. No longer. The sun was now merely to the brightest of several stars in the field of view.

The computer immediately began searching for Pastol and the other planets. Within a few seconds, it had found three of them, enough to do a reverse parallax calculation.

"We seem to be one light-hour due galactic north of Etnarii, Captain. Right where we want to be."

"Thank God for that! Weapons, status!"

"I didn't see it go, sir," Rodriguez replied, "but we seem to be short one SM from our magazine."

"Congratulations, Mr. Rykand. Your plan seems to have worked, at least up to the point where we fired a missile at the stargate. Any indication that we hit it?"

"No, sir. Not at this distance."

"How long before the light from the flash reaches us here?"

"I make if fifty four minutes, Captain."

"All right. All sensors focus on the gate. In fifty-four minutes, we see if we hit what we were aiming for."

#

"What was that?" Pas-Tek demanded as every sensor on the side of the ship closest to the gate ceased transmitting.

"The freighter, Master. It exploded!"

"Suicide?" Pas-Tek demanded. Suddenly, all of his visions of future advancement faded, to be replaced by the thought that he would be carrying messages to the hinterlands for the rest of his life. He would forever be known as the ship commander who let his quarry take the easy way out.

"Malfunction, I would think. They were leaking something just before they blew."

"Sensors!"

"Yes, Master."

"Get me a view of the gate."

"I cannot, Master. All of the aft cameras are burned out and we can't rotate the ship while we are decelerating."

"Stand by," Saton answered. "We will be through with engines in a few heartbeats."

Almost before the sailing master's sentence was complete, the weight lifted from Pas-Tek's chest and he rebounded into the restraining straps. He wasted no time feeling relieved.

"Sensors. Rotate the ship. Get me a working camera!"

"Acknowledged, Master."

There followed several disquieting sensations as the ship spun about its axis until the bow once again faced forward. The main viewscreen lit. Of the freighter and the stargate, there was no sign.

An expanding fireball occupied space where the gate had been. The incandescent cloud was already large enough to overflow the edges of the viewscreen. At Pas-Tek's command, the sensor operator reduced the magnification until they could see the whole cloud. It roiled with turbulence, a beautiful white, translucent flower against the blackness of space. The size of the flower could be judged by the size of the small, off-center black dot

"Focus on the cargo vessel!" Pas-Tek ordered.

The view expanded once more until the large sphere was centered in the viewscreen. Even from this distance, the cargo vessel appeared misshapen, almost molten.

As he gazed at the horrific sight on screen, the implications slowly seeped into his consciousness. Not only was the Type Seven freighter destroyed, but so was the gate. At the edge of the cloud, one small sector of the ring could be seen spinning lazily away from the origin of the explosion. The rest of the ring seemed to be missing altogether.

With the stargate destroyed, he and his ship were stranded. There was no way for him to send a message to Those Who Rule to tell them what had happened. Nor were there any other gates in the Etnarii System. Stargate technology was the sole province of the Race. No other species could be trusted with the knowledge.

That meant that the replacement gate would have to be procured from one of his species' home worlds. It would be delivered to Etnarii via single-ended star jump. After that would come the careful maneuvering into position, followed by a delicate calibration process that could take a demi-cycle or more to complete. Only when the new gate was linked to the one in the Gasak System would his ship be free of this backwater system.

None of these time consuming positioning and calibration steps could take place until someone in Gasak noticed that the link between that system and Etnarii was down. Considering the amount of ship traffic that normally plied the route, he had no idea how long it would be before Those Who Rule realized his dilemma.

Until they did, he was trapped.

#

"You may begin your countdown, Mr. Rykand."

"One minute to go, sir.... Fifty seconds...."

The bridge crew of *New Hope* had just spent the longest hour of their lives hovering at the edge of the system, waiting to see whether or not they had fooled their enemy.

The Avenger had nearly caught them. At the time of their departure, the Broan ship had been close enough to record the whole event in excruciating detail. Broan scientists would study that recording in future months and how they viewed it was important.

The impression that everyone hoped the recording would leave was that *New Hope* had exploded while attempting to jump.

That perception would present the Broa with a minor mystery, but one that was reassuringly mundane.

However, that whole scenario depended on them hitting the gate with a superlight missile. They had just taken the fastest snap shot in history, in the midst of wild transients in *New Hope*'s entire electrical system. If the missile malfunctioned, or just plain missed, the Avenger would have full recordings of a ship that disappeared through a stargate without producing a gravity wave.

Once the Broa accepted what their instruments were telling them, they would have no option other than to recognize that somewhere among the stars there existed a race of aliens who they did not control.

"Thirty seconds," Mark announced.

Around him, the duty crew sat motionless, watching the main viewscreen. No one spoke and most did not breath. "Twenty seconds... Ten seconds...

"Five, Four, Three, Two, One!"

For the span of two heartbeats, nothing happened. The bright star at the center of the viewscreen remained unaffected. Then, suddenly, a third of the screen to the right of the star, another star appeared. This one popped into existence and brightened until it was as bright as Etnarii. It remained at maximum for a dozen seconds, then slowly dimmed, never quite dropping back to invisibility.

"Focus on that and magnify!" Captain Harris ordered.

The screen shifted and expanded. At maximum magnification, the new star showed as a tiny flower blossoming against the blackness of space. At first it was violet-white in color. Slowly, it shaded down to blue-white, then to green, and yellow.

"My God, I would call that a hit!" the Captain exclaimed. "Congratulations, Mr. Rodriguez, on your aim."

"Thank you, sir."

"Any sign of the Avenger?" someone asked.

"Too small to see at this distance," Vivian Domedan answered.

"Then what is that speck?"

Within the gradually fading nebula that had once been the local stargate was a bright white point. It looked solid.

"That must be the bulk hauler," Simon Rodriguez said from his weapons station. "It was close enough to have been caught in the blast."

"Do we have recordings of all of this?"

"We do, Captain," Vivian Domedan replied.

"Then there is nothing more to see here. Astrogator, set your course for Brinks Base. Transition to superlight on my command."

"Yes, sir!"

Mark keyed for the program that would put them on a path for the system that would be home for the next several years. Nor were they the only ones. Having seen the gate explode, *Chicago* and her consorts would already be en route to Brinks Base.

"Ready for superlight, Captain."

"Execute."

The star-studded blackness of the viewscreen turned suddenly to the absolute black of superlight as the stardrive generator thrummed in the bulkheads around them. Within seconds, they left the Etnarii System behind and were on their way home. In the captain's safe was the original record cube containing the Pastol planetary database. In the hold were several hundred liters of *vasa* juice.

All in all, it had been a successful mission.

#

Chapter Thirty Nine

If there is anywhere in the universe that can truthfully be called the Armpit of Creation, that place would have to be Sutton. Brinks' moon was an airless, lifeless ball of rock and stone, bereft of weather save the cosmic wind, covered with a fine coating of brown dust the consistency of talcum powder. The dust coated the suits of those foolhardy enough to venture out onto the surface, and drifted into Brinks Base despite the entire facility being hermetically sealed and below ground.

The moon's stark surface was alternately baked and frozen as it circled its primary every twenty days. During half the orbit, Hideout cooked it in its harsh rays; while at night, the surface temperature dropped to sub-arctic conditions while in stygian darkness, or else lit softly by reflected light from the blue-white world that was its parent.

This day-night-twilight cycle had gone on for an eternity before man arrived, and would go on long after humans departed. The only interruptions came when Hideout flared, causing it to grow solar prominences that reached to the inner planets. During these 'storms,' bright auroras flickered across the whole of Brinks' darkened hemisphere as charged particles trapped in the planet's magnetic field surged to and fro above its atmosphere. Even Sutton, with its miniscule magnetic field, saw dim glows dance in the sky when the moon was being bombarded by particularly powerful solar flares.

Sutton was a slagheap, a junkyard, a collecting place for the detritus of a dead system. Debris rained down onto the barren moon in the form of ionized particles, fine dust, and an occasional rock large enough to blast a crater out of the already pummeled surface. To this sky junk was added the clutter of the human occupation. It was a world only a mother could love.

"Isn't it beautiful?" Lisa asked as *New Hope*'s landing boat dropped toward the surface. In the distance, through the windscreen, could be seen the red beacon that marked the location of Brinks Base.

"Home never looked so good," Mark agreed.

The two of them were strapped into their customary places on the boat's front acceleration bench. Spacer Jorgenson shared their perch, causing Lisa to be squeezed between the broad shoulders of two large men. It was not an altogether unpleasant experience. A dozen other members of *New Hope*'s crew were packed like sardines behind them, until the atmosphere smelled of stale sweat and halitosis.

The truth was that the beat-up old moon *did* look good. To spacers who had just spent a month in enemy vacuum, the gray-brown panorama below might have seemed a Christmas painting. To nerves rubbed raw by the long chase and near battle with the Broan Avenger, this ball of hardscrabble dirt was the most welcome sight in the whole universe.

"Stand by for landing," the pilot said over his shoulder as he lined up the red flashing beacon on his instrument display. Their weight changed subtly as reaction jets hissed. In response, a fine layer of dust engulfed the boat and brought a dusty curtain down on the universe around them.

There was sudden brightening as they dropped into a floodlit underground hanger. A few seconds later, a bump told them that they had touched down. Gravity stabilized at Sutton's anemic pull as both lift and drive engines were shut down. Jorgenson loosened their common safety belt as the turbines whined down into inaudibility. Lisa turned and hugged Mark.

"Oh, darling. It's good to be home again!"

#

Dan Landon met them at the airlock leading out of the hanger and into the base. "Welcome home, Adventurers. I take it from your preliminary report that all went well."

"Yes, sir," Mark replied.

"Did you bring it?"

"I did," he said, fishing into a pocket of his jumpsuit and retrieving the record cube containing the original copy of the Pastol planetary database.

The Admiral took it with reverence. There were probably a hundred copies onboard *New Hope,* many of which had already been hand-carried down by others. Still, this was the original, the quarry they had been sent after, the jewel of great value after which they had sought for five long years.

"Any trouble?" Landon asked.

"You mean, other than the fact that we had to blow up a stargate to escape?" Lisa asked. "No, no trouble."

"I read Captain Harris's report of the action. That was quick thinking, Mark. Do you think we fooled them?"

"Hard to say. Our exit was spectacular enough. You really don't understand how much energy a few grams of shrapnel moving at 0.9c packs until you see it hit something."

"The gate was completely destroyed?"

"We spotted one small chunk spinning away from the epicenter of the cloud. Not much they could determine from that except that the gate came apart with considerable violence. That bulk hauler we nearly collided with was also caught in the blast. We were too far away for our recordings to show much except that it appeared damaged."

"Well," Landon said, "They may not know what happened, but they aren't likely to ascribe it to either supernatural phenomena or an alien race they don't control. That means we are probably out of the woods... this time."

"How many more times are we going to be able to say that, Admiral?"

Landon shrugged. "They'll discover what we are doing sooner or later. Let's make it as later as we can, shall we?"

"Aye aye, sir," Mark replied with a smile. If it were up to him, the Broa wouldn't find out what was going on until they had human warships in their sky. "When are the scientists going to be ready to review the database?"

"They're already hard at it. *Chicago* got back yesterday. They downloaded what you transmitted to them. We received a couple of copies of this," he said, gesturing with the original record cube, "a few hours ago. The astronomers are already pulling out data on the stargate network. It is, I'm led to believe, quite extensive."

"I hope they find something we can use," Lisa said.

Landon guffawed. "Don't worry about that! We're learning plenty. Haven't found the Broa home world or worlds, yet, but we've discovered a lot of useful information. In fact, you got back just in time. We were about to send out a couple of survey missions."

"Survey missions?" Mark asked, perplexed.

"Ask your wife. It was her brainchild."

Mark turned to Lisa, who seemed nonplussed. She was even blushing.

"What have you done now, my love?"

"It was just an idea I had while on the Gamma expedition. Watching all of that traffic through the system, I wondered if we might send some ships to join them. They wouldn't make contact with the locals, merely look around while en route from one gate to another before jumping to a new system. We could check out a dozen stars in one trip. It seemed good way to learn about the Broa quickly."

"It seemed that way to us, as well," Landon replied. "That's why I have authorized a couple of ships to give your idea a try. One Type Seven and another cargo craft. They were going to sneak back to Gamma and jump through the Nineveh and Tyre gates a day apart. We'll see what they discover. With the information you brought back, they won't have to jump blind. We can give them an idea of what to expect at each of their target stars."

"Can't we learn what we need to now from the Pastol database?"

The Admiral shrugged. "Maybe yes, maybe no. One thing we need to know is the location of their stars. Not where they are in the stargate network, but where they are actually located. The first thing our ships will do when they pop out of a stargate is a sky survey. We need to answer a question that has come up recently."

"What question?" Lisa asked.

"We need to figure out how close the Sovereignty comes to Sol."

"I thought we had decided that there are thousands of light years between Broan space and our own."

"We did. Now it's undecided. Ask your husband."

Now it was Lisa's turn to look quizzically at Mark, who said simply, "Gravity waves."

"What about them?"

"They aren't omni-directional like we thought. Not waves focused through gates. That means we can't rely on the fact that Earth has never seen one to estimate how far it is to the closest Broan world."

"I hadn't thought about that," she said.

"Neither had anyone else until Dr. Brainard mentioned it in passing the other day," the Admiral said with a grimace. "Scientists!"

"Sounds like you've been busy while we've been gone, sir."

"You don't know the half of it, Lieutenant. We're working on our master plan to steal a stargate. Now that we know where they are, we can pick out the best one to purloin.

"But enough work for one day," Landon continued smoothly. "You two need to get settled. Have you been assigned quarters yet?"

"No, sir."

"Check with central housing. I think you will find they are more efficient than when you left. Get cleaned up, rest a bit, and then make sure that you are ready by 18:00 hours."

"Ready, sir? For what?"

"For the party, man!"

"What party, Admiral?" Lisa asked.

The 'Welcome Home' party in your honor. It's going to be quite a shindig. I've even authorized the alcohol to be broken out, so long as no one has more than two drinks. Now go get settled. That's an order!"

"Yes, sir!" they both exclaimed in unison, then snapped off exaggerated salutes.

Mark grabbed their bags and threw them over his shoulder before grabbing his wife's hand. The two of them set off down the long passageway leading to the interior of the underground base. They were in a hurry to occupy their quarters.

There was something they needed to do before they dressed for the party.

#

"Was it worth it?" Lisa asked lazily. She and Mark were both sweating, out of breath, and entangled in the sheets. Beneath them lay a pad of what appeared to be packing material. The bright blue rectangle lay on bare rock in one corner of their one-room cave. This was what passed for a bed in Sutton's low gravity. If somewhat rudimentary, they could testify to the fact that it served one of a bed's primary functions.

Lisa lay with her head resting on Mark's shoulder, basking in the afterglow of their lovemaking. She was conscious of his hard body pressed against her soft one and of the pressure of his fingertips resting at the base of her spine.

"Well?" she asked when her question was greeted by silence.

"Sorry," he said with a start. "I must have drifted off for a second. Well, what?"

"Was it worth it?"

"Always!" Mark replied with a leer, moving his hand to a protuberance and squeezing.

"Not, that, silly. Do you think the expedition to Pastol was worth it?"

"Sure. Don't you?"

She shrugged half-heartedly, a gesture he felt more than saw as he nuzzled her hair.

"What's the matter? Got the post-action blues?"

"No, I've never been happier. It's just that I was thinking about the enormity of the task in front of us. Do you really think we can pull it off? Beat the Broa, that is?"

"What did your mother tell you about eating elephants?" he asked.

"…One bite at a time?" she laughed.

"Exactly. So what's bothering you?"

"We traveled 7000 light years… almost 8000 if you count up all of the side trips… visited two enemy suns, risked our lives, and all we have to show for it is a little bit of sparkly crystal. It doesn't seem enough."

"I would remind you that sparkly crystal has all of our enemy's secrets in it."

"There is that," she agreed. "Compared to what is in front of us, however, it seems such a small thing. How can one small planet hope to prevail against a million star empire?"

"By stealth, cunning, smarts, grit, bravery, and just a little bit of luck," he replied. When he saw that she was not convinced, he rolled onto his side and propped himself up on one elbow. "Look, my dear. We didn't ask for this. I could have lived my life drinking Gunter Perlman's beer and racing his solar yacht with him. In fact, I thought I liked being a ne'er-do-well playboy. I was good at it."

"Not to mention the perks."

"Perks?"

"Moira Sims!"

"Oh, her. Yeah, she was nice, but not as nice as someone else I could name."

"You'd better say that," she growled, digging him in the ribs.

"Truthfully, with the settlement from my parents' estate, I had everything... and nothing. Life didn't mean anything to me. Now, here I am a gazillion kilometers from home, sleeping on the modern-day equivalent of a horse blanket, in a room carved out of bare rock with wires hanging from the ceiling, and I'm happy. Do you know why?"

"Because of what we just did?"

"That goes without saying," he laughed. "I'm a man, after all. I love you more than anything, my nude love. However, what I was speaking of was the fact that Sar-Say gave meaning to my life."

"When he popped out of nothing in the New Eden System, he gave me the chance to make a difference, to be of service to my clan, nation, and race. Lotus eating is overrated. Give me something important to occupy my time."

"Don't forget the danger," Lisa said quietly. She had attempted a bantering tone, but it hadn't come out that way. She sounded like a little girl asking her father about the distant thunder.

"I can't say that I enjoy that," Mark said, enfolding her in his arms once more. "Hell, I almost wet my pants when that Avenger took out after us.

"Still, it looks like danger is going to be an unavoidable part of life from now on. We have no choice. We either win this fight or we die... all of us. It is something we just have to do. We can neither shirk our duty nor hide from it. Humanity is counting on us, and I don't plan to let them down."

Lisa was about to respond when he silenced her with a kiss. When it was over, he delivered a light slap to where it would do the most good, eliciting the expected squeal.

"Now, Wench, roll out of bed. We have a party to attend, and later, some Galactic Overlords to slay. To quote a wise man, "Whatever else the future brings, it ain't going to be dull!"

#

The End

Author's Biography

Michael McCollum was born in Phoenix, Arizona, in 1946, and is a graduate of Arizona State University, where he majored in aerospace propulsion and minored in nuclear engineering. He is employed at Honeywell in Tempe, Arizona, where he is Chief Engineer in the valve product line. In his career, Mr. McCollum has worked on the precursor to the Space Shuttle Main Engine, a nuclear valve to replace the one that failed at Three Mile Island, several guided missiles, Space Station Freedom, and virtually every aircraft in production today. He was involved in an effort to create a joint venture company with a major Russian aerospace engine manufacturer and traveled extensively to Russia in the last several years.

In addition to his engineering, Mr. McCollum is a successful professional writer in the field of science fiction. He is the author of a dozen pieces of short fiction and has appeared in magazines such as Analog Science Fiction/Science Fact, Amazing, and Isaac Asimov's Science Fiction Magazine. His novels (originally published by Ballantine-Del Rey) include *A Greater Infinity, Life Probe, Procyon's Promise, Antares Dawn, Antares Passage, The Clouds of Saturn, and The Sails of Tau Ceti,* His novel, *Thunderstrike!*, was optioned by a Hollywood production company for a possible movie. Several of these books have subsequently been translated into Japanese, German and Russian.

Mr. McCollum is the proprietor of Sci Fi - Arizona, one of the first author-owned-and-operated virtual bookstores on the INTERNET, which first published *Gibraltar Earth, Gibraltar Sun,* and *Antares Victory.* He also runs Third Millennium Publishing, an INTERNET site that provides web and publishing services to independent author/publishers.

Mr. McCollum is married to a lovely lady named Catherine, and has three children: Robert, Michael, and Elizabeth. Robert is a financial analyst for a computer company in Massachusetts. Michael is a student and recently completed a stint as a Military Police Specialist with the Arizona National Guard, which included a year in the lovely land between the Tigris and Euphrates Rivers. Elizabeth is a graduate student at Arizona Sate University.

Sci Fi - Arizona

A Virtual Science Fiction Bookstore and Writer's Workshop
Michael McCollum, Proprietor

WWW.SCIFI-AZ.COM

If you enjoy technologically sophisticated science fiction or have an interest in writing, you will probably find something to interest you at Sci Fi - Arizona. We have short stories and articles on writing– all for free! If you like what you find, we have full length, professionally written science fiction novels in both electronic form and as hard copy books, and at prices lower than you will find in your local bookstore.

Moreover, if you like space art, you can visit our Art Gallery, where we feature the works of Don Dixon, one of the best astronomical and science fiction artists at work today. Don is the Art Director of the Griffith Observatory. Pick up one or more of his spacescapes for computer wallpaper, or order a high quality print direct from the artist.

We have book length versions of both Writers' Workshop series, "The Art of Writing, Volumes I and II" and "The Art of Science Fiction, Volumes I and II" in both electronic and hard copy formats.

So if you are looking for a fondly remembered novel, or facing six hours strapped into an airplane seat with nothing to read, check out our offerings. We think you will like what you find.

NOVELS

1. Life Probe - ^{US}$4.50

The Makers searched for the secret to faster-than-light travel for 100,000 years. Their chosen instruments were the Life Probes, which they launched in every direction to seek out advanced civilizations among the stars. One such machine searching for intelligent life encounters 21st century Earth. It isn't sure that it has found any...

2. Procyon's Promise - ^{US}$4.50

Three hundred years after humanity made its deal with the Life Probe to search out the secret of faster-than-light travel, the descendants of the original expedition return to Earth in a starship. They find a world that has forgotten the ancient contract. No matter. The colonists have overcome far greater obstacles in their single-minded drive to redeem a promise made before any of them were born...

3. Antares Dawn - US$4.50

When the super giant star Antares exploded in 2512, the human colony on Alta found their pathway to the stars gone, isolating them from the rest of human space for more than a century. Then one day, a powerful warship materialized in the system without warning. Alarmed by the sudden appearance of such a behemoth, the commanders of the Altan Space Navy dispatched one of their most powerful ships to investigate. What ASNS Discovery finds when they finally catch the intruder is a battered hulk manned by a dead crew.

That is disturbing news for the Altans. For the dead battleship could easily have defeated the whole of the Altan navy. If it could find Alta, then so could whomever it was that beat it. Something must be done...

4. Antares Passage - US$4.50

After more than a century of isolation, the paths between stars are again open and the people of Alta in contact with their sister colony on Sandar. The opening of the foldlines has not been the unmixed blessing the Altans had supposed, however.

For the reestablishment of interstellar travel has brought with it news of the Ryall, an alien race whose goal is the extermination of humanity. If they are to avoid defeat at the hands of the aliens, Alta must seek out the military might of Earth. However, to reach Earth requires them to dive into the heart of a supernova.

5. Antares Victory – First Time in Print – US$7.00

After a century of warfare, humanity finally discovered the Achilles heel of the Ryall, their xenophobic reptilian foe. Spica – Alpha Virginis – is the key star system in enemy space. It is the hub through which all Ryall starships must pass, and if humanity can only capture and hold it, they will strangle the Ryall war machine and end their threat to humankind forever.

It all seemed so simple in the computer simulations: Advance by stealth, attack without warning, strike swiftly with overwhelming power. Unfortunately, conquering the Ryall proves the easy part. With the key to victory in hand, Richard and Bethany Drake discover that they must also conquer human nature if they are to bring down the alien foe ...

6. Thunderstrike! - US$6.00

The new comet found near Jupiter was an incredible treasure trove of water ice and rock. Immediately, the water-starved Luna Republic and the Sierra Corporation, a leader in asteroid mining, were squabbling over rights to the new resource. However, all thoughts of profit and fame were abandoned when a scientific expedition discovered that the comet's trajectory placed it on a collision course with Earth!

As scientists struggled to find a way to alter the comet's course, world leaders tried desperately to restrain mass panic, and two lovers quarreled over the direction the comet was to take, all Earth waited to see if humanity had any future at all...

7. The Clouds of Saturn - US$4.50

When the sun flared out of control and boiled Earth's oceans, humanity took refuge in a place that few would have predicted. In the greatest migration in history, the entire human race took up residence among the towering clouds and deep clear-air canyons of Saturn's upper atmosphere. Having survived the traitor star, they returned to the all-too-human tradition of internecine strife. The new city-states of Saturn began to resemble those of ancient Greece, with one group of cities taking on the role of militaristic Sparta...

8. The Sails of Tau Ceti – US$4.50

Starhopper was humanity's first interstellar probe. It was designed to search for intelligent life beyond the solar system. Before it could be launched, however, intelligent life found Earth. The discovery of an alien light sail inbound at the edge of the solar system generated considerable excitement in scientific circles. With the interstellar probe nearing completion, it gave scientists the opportunity to launch an expedition to meet the aliens while they were still in space. The second surprise came when *Starhopper's* crew boarded the alien craft. They found beings that, despite their alien physiques, were surprisingly compatible with humans. That two species so similar could have evolved a mere twelve light years from one another seemed too coincidental to be true.

One human being soon discovered that coincidence had nothing to do with it...

9. Gibraltar Earth – First Time in Print — $6.00

It is the 24th Century and humanity is just gaining a toehold out among the stars. Stellar Survey Starship *Magellan* is exploring the New Eden system when they encounter two alien spacecraft. When the encounter is over, the score is one human scout ship and one alien aggressor destroyed. In exploring the wreck of the second alien ship, spacers discover a survivor with a fantastic story.

The alien comes from a million-star Galactic Empire ruled over by a mysterious race known as the Broa. These overlords are the masters of this region of the galaxy and they allow no competitors. This news presents Earth's rulers with a problem. As yet, the Broa are ignorant of humanity's existence. Does the human race retreat to its one small world, quaking in fear that the Broa will eventually discover Earth? Or do they take a more aggressive approach?

Whatever they do, they must do it quickly! Time is running out for the human race...

10. Gibraltar Sun – First Time in Print — $7.00

The expedition to the Crab Nebula has returned to Earth and the news is not good. Out among the stars, a million systems have fallen under Broan domination, the fate awaiting Earth should the Broa ever learn of its existence. The problem would seem to allow but three responses: submit meekly to slavery, fight and risk extermination, or hide and pray the Broa remain ignorant of humankind for at least a few more generations. Are the hairless apes of Sol III finally faced with a problem for which there is no acceptable solution?

While politicians argue, Mark Rykand and Lisa Arden risk everything to spy on the all-powerful enemy that is beginning to wonder at the appearance of mysterious bipeds in their midst...

11. Gridlock and Other Stories - US$4.50

Where would you visit if you invented a time machine, but could not steer it? What if you went out for a six-pack of beer and never came back? If you think nuclear power is dangerous, you should try black holes as an energy source — or even scarier, solar energy! Visit the many worlds of Michael McCollum. I guarantee that you will be surprised!

Non-Fiction Books

12. The Art of Writing, Volume I - US$10.00

Have you missed any of the articles in the Art of Writing Series? No problem. The first sixteen articles (October, 1996-December, 1997) have been collected into a book-length work of more than 72,000 words. Now you can learn about character, conflict, plot, pacing, dialogue, and the business of writing, all in one document.

13. The Art of Writing, Volume II - US$10.00

This collection covers the Art of Writing articles published during 1998. The book is 62,000 words in length and builds on the foundation of knowledge provided by Volume I of this popular series.

14. The Art of Science Fiction, Volume I - US$10.00

Have you missed any of the articles in the Art of Science Fiction Series? No problem. The first sixteen articles (October, 1996-December, 1997) have been collected into a book-length work of more than 70,000 words. Learn about science fiction techniques and technologies, including starships, time machines, and rocket propulsion. Tour the Solar System and learn astronomy from the science fiction writer's viewpoint. We don't care where the stars appear in the terrestrial sky. We want to know their true positions in space. If you are planning to write an interstellar romance, brushing up on your astronomy may be just what you need.

15. The Art of Science Fiction, Volume II - US$10.00

This collection covers the *Art of Science Fiction* articles published during 1998. The book is 67,000 words in length and builds on the foundation of knowledge provided by Volume I of this popular series.

16. The Astrogator's Handbook – Expanded Edition and Deluxe Editions

The Astrogator's Handbook has been very popular on Sci Fi – Arizona. The handbook has star maps that show science fiction writers where the stars are located in space rather than where they are located in Earth's sky. Because of the popularity, we are expanding the handbook to show nine times as much space and more than ten times as many stars. The expanded handbook includes the positions of 3500 stars as viewed from Polaris on 63 maps. This handbook is a useful resource for every science fiction writer and will appeal to anyone with an interest in astronomy.